Endorsements
for *And Then There's Life*

"Vivid descriptions transport the reader to another time, another place, moving at a pace that keeps the reader's attention piqued. The characters' responses to their circumstances unveil the prescription for a life of meaning and purpose... an excellent read!"

Verna Peters

"What a simple, profound, touching ending to an engaging story!"

Doris Wig, B. Ed

"Romance! Adventure! Drama! You will enjoy being part of it all as you are encouraged in your walk with the Lord."

Sheila Wiebe, B. Ed.

"An inspiring read that demonstrates the value of faith in facing life's challenges."

Joyce Sawatzky

AND THEN

THERE'S
Life

THE MINITONAS DIARIES
——— BOOK TWO ———

SANDRA V. KONECHNY

ISBN: 978-1-4866-2431-7
eBook ISBN: 978-1-4866-2432-4

Word Alive Press
119 De Baets Street Winnipeg, MB R2J 3R9
www.wordalivepress.ca

WORD ALIVE
—P R E S S—

Cataloguing in Publication information can be obtained from Library and Archives Canada.

Dedicated to my sons
and sons-in-law:

Jason, Creighton, Don, and Clayton

Foreword

I NEVER INTENDED to write a series. I had one idea, which had rattled around in my head for years. My plan was to write it out, not just think about it, reasoning that this would be the way to get it off my chest.

I used a setting I was familiar with as a young girl. Of course, any number of characters would have to be created along the way. I discovered for myself what I've heard other authors admit to: fictional characters have a certain reality to them that isn't much different from the flesh-and-blood people we're familiar with.

Besides that, in writing *Rock Bottom* I set up a few mysteries along the way to make the story interesting. But when I'd reached book length, most of them weren't solved. So between having "real" characters to contend with, as well as a few outstanding mysteries to resolve, I figured that I had to keep going.

These characters have messy, imperfect lives, just like the people we know, along with what makes them loveable and admirable. If we're paying attention, their lives resonate with our own experiences and we can learn from them. And that would be the point…

Acknowledgements

SPECIAL GRATITUDE IS extended to my beta readers, consisting of a few family members and friends. In their feedback, they always asked for more to the story, which is what inspired me to keep writing. The encouragement means a great deal to me.

I must also thank my good husband, Michael, who when asked if I should pursue publishing said, without batting an eyelash, "Go for it!"

My gratitude goes out to my parents, Edward and Ruth Tiede, who instilled in me a love for God and the Bible since I was born to them. (Dad lives with Jesus now, but it is still appropriate to give credit where it is due.)

I would like to express my deepest gratitude to the editor and staff at Word Alive Press for their commitment and expertise in refining the manuscript and for ensuring the message is clear to reach the heart of the reader.

My deepest gratitude, however, is reserved for Jesus. We wrote the story together. Every time I got stuck, I'd pray, *What happens next? Where does it go from here?* Soon insight would come. If the reader comes away with a blessing, a wise thought, or a word of help—thank Jesus, the Saviour. Such as it is, I cast this meagre "crown" at Jesus's feet. To Him be the glory forever and ever.

Prologue

IN 1938, JOHN and Elizabeth Bauman began their married life on a mixed farm just a few miles directly north of Minitonas, Manitoba. They raised a family of three sons and a daughter according to their Christian heritage and beliefs.

In her teen years, their daughter Ella Rose determined that the Christian faith was too restrictive and old-fashioned. As soon as she graduated from high school, she and a few friends relocated to Winnipeg to train for careers and live modern lives free from traditional and moral restraints. For more than nine years, Ellie and her friends lived the amoral hippie lifestyle introduced in the 1960s.

In March 1980, a life-changing event occurred when Ellie and her lover Paul became pregnant. After getting an abortion, Ellie was thrown into a freefall of depression.

When her elderly mother died suddenly at home of a massive stroke, the combined tragedy was more than Ellie could cope with. She put in for a sabbatical at the hospital and, with her eldest brother's permission, moved back onto the family farm on the morning of June 10, 1980, to process her grief and return to practising the faith she knew while growing up.

Their closest neighbours were the Fischers, whose farm was almost directly across the road. However, they were hardly friends. The Fischer farm was originally homesteaded by Rudolf and Huldah in the 1920s. They had two children, a daughter and a son. After Rudolf died in 1945, his wife moved in with her daughter in Toronto, who had earlier eloped with a young man from Minitonas, leaving the farm entirely to her son Frederick.

From his youth, Freddie was inclined to wild living with questionable friends. He also had a thirst for alcohol and a penchant for brawling. Despite that, he took a wife and sired three children—two daughters and a son he never accepted as his. He became increasingly abusive and kept his family under tight control.

The last straw for his son, Hugh, came in mid-October shortly before he turned sixteen. On the day of his sixteenth birthday, he fled to Winnipeg to escape his father's cruelty. He fell in with the family of the truck driver who gave him transportation to the city. After hearing his story, the family took him in and encouraged him to finish his high school education and, after that, train as a mechanic.

In the fall of 1977, Hugh's parents died in a single-vehicle accident. With his parents out of the picture, he became captivated by the idea of returning to the farm to make a new start for himself. He arrived home on June 9, 1980, intent on dealing with his past and making a new life for himself.

When Ellie and Hugh met that first week, Ellie was intrigued by his project to destroy the old farm buildings, now entirely derelict, and rebuild. They got to know each other by working together, uncovering the truth of Hugh's past in the process. Meanwhile, Ellie became reacquainted with her Lord and Saviour, Jesus Christ, and shared her renewed faith with Hugh. There was a lot of resistance at first, but in time he relented and gladly embraced Jesus as his Lord and Saviour, too.

The drama came to a head one day at the Swan River rodeo, when Hugh saw something that triggered the worst of his memories—an especially cruel beating by his father. Ellie, too, was forced to confront her painful past. Together, through mutual encouragement, they faced the root of their troubles and realized that the Lord Himself had brought them together, first as friends and then as potential life partners...

One

October 1, 1980

HUGH AWOKE IN a panic. His immediate sensations were of being confined like a straightjacket. Also, of heat. He felt sweaty from the top of his head to the bottom of his feet. All around him was the darkness of night, yet he peered into the shadows to discern if he had an intruder. Everything seemed normal. He could even hear the refrigerator humming.

Purposefully slowing his breathing to a calm rate, he looked down his bed to see himself cocooned in his bedsheet and blanket. He realized then that he had rolled over and over in his bed, wrapping himself in the linens. Slowly, he reversed the movements and landed on the floor beside his bed in the process. The short fall didn't feel good, but at least he was free.

Rising clumsily, he reached for the light switch, the resultant brightness blinding him for a few seconds. The alarm clock read 4:13 a.m.

Sitting on the edge of the bed, he strove to understand why he had been so restless as to bind himself in the covers.

He had dreamt. But the subject of his dream seemed to be beyond recall. The feelings it produced, however, were still with him. Anger and fear, primarily.

Hugh tried to shake it off. The bed was completely dishevelled, so he set about straightening the top sheet and comforter while trying to recall the subject of his dream. Soon Ellie came to mind and he wondered if the dream had included something about her. He thought so, but what?

The bed, now remade, was ready for use, but he was too awake to fall immediately back asleep. A glass of milk seemed like a good idea.

Hugh left the bedroom and made for the fridge. As he guzzled the milk, it came to him. Pa, Freddie Fischer, had invaded his dream, shouting obscenities at him for getting involved with the Baumans—specifically, for his plan to marry Ellie. In the dream, Hugh had told him to go fly a kite. There had been fisticuffs, but Hugh had awakened before it was clear which one of them prevailed.

Hugh marvelled that he still occasionally experienced these unwelcome nightmares. Having figured out the problem, he climbed back into his bed.

"You're lying, Pa... or whatever's masquerading as you," he murmured. "Not gonna fall for it. You're not allowed to influence me anymore. Go away."

∼

It was time to get up.

Ellie spent more time reliving and revelling in the magical date of the night before than she meant to, culminating in Hugh's formal marriage proposal. Twice now she had removed the silver band to read the inscription from the Song of Songs: *"My beloved is mine and I am his..."*[1]

It was now 8:30 a.m., way past her normal rising time of 6:30 for a light breakfast and some soul work. Suspecting Hugh would likely show up soon, she quickly dressed in a pair of slacks and light knit pullover.

True to her instincts, Hugh drove up the lane just as she was filling up the coffee maker with water. Ellie met him at the door and greeted him with a kiss, which he hungrily accepted.

[1] Song of Songs 2:16, RSV.

"Have you had breakfast?" asked Ellie while placing two slices of bread in the toaster.

"Yeah, I fed myself. I don't mind another coffee, though." He pulled out a kitchen chair and took a seat. "You usually have your breakfast a lot earlier, don't you?"

Hugh glanced at the clock on the wall. It read 9:05.

"I might have lolled in bed dreamily for longer than I should have the morning after being romanced beyond anything I could have imagined," said Ellie sentimentally.

The telephone rang. Ellie jumped up to get it and Hugh listened to her side of the conversation.

"Yes, this is she... Of course... This afternoon would be perfect... I'll see you at three o'clock... Goodbye, and thanks for calling."

Hugh eyed her with raised eyebrows.

"Guess what!" said Ellie, beaming. "That was the hospital in Swan River. I put in an application a couple of weeks ago and now a part-time position has come up. I have an interview this afternoon."

"Feeling ready to get back into the workforce, are you?"

She squared her shoulders. "I am. A part-time position would be perfect. I could still help out at your place on off days."

"If you run away with me today, you can officially call my place your place," said Hugh huskily, pulling her close and kissing the top of her head.

"No way! Deprive me of my dream wedding, you will not. But I'm not gonna lie... I look forward to feathering that little nest."

Hugh suddenly grew serious. "I've also been thinking about going back to work in a garage somewhere. Partly because my funds are getting low, and partly because I'm not ready to start a new business without knowing more about the need, if there is one, for another mechanic around here."

"Sounds wise to me," said Ellie. "Opening a business is a big deal. You need to research it extensively. And you need the proper facility, which you don't yet have. Perhaps next spring, after you've built your-self a new shop."

~

The first item on their to-do list was to see Leland Wirt, pastor of the First Baptist Church. When they announced their engagement, he congratulated them warmly and asked to hear the story of how it had come about.

At this, Ellie and Hugh quickly exchanged glances. Ellie recognized the subtly troubled look on Hugh's face and understood it at once. She shared the same sentiment. They each had painful experiences they weren't ready to go public with. Between themselves, though, these were among the very reasons they felt God had brought them together.

Ellie took the bull by the horns. "Since we both returned to the area, we got reacquainted as neighbours. Hugh had big goals to rejuvenate his place and I offered to help. We've been working together every week, getting to know one another, and… well, love happened. We believe God's purpose included bringing us together as a couple."

Pastor Leland nodded and looked over to Hugh, as if to hear his side of the story.

"What she said," said Hugh, relieved.

"We came to talk about setting a wedding date," Ellie remarked, changing the subject. "We're thinking of January 1. Would you be available to officiate?"

"Are you sure you want that date?" The pastor had a twinkle in his eyes. "Typically there won't be any restaurants open to celebrate subsequent anniversaries…"

Ellie looked over at Hugh. "Would that be an issue?"

"If it's not an issue for you, it's not for me."

"We like the idea of starting our life together on the first of the year," she said. "It fits with our reasons for coming back to Minitonas. Besides, our guests won't have to worry about taking time off for work or school."

Hugh nodded his agreement.

"Very well then," said Pastor Leland. "I would be happy to officiate your wedding on one condition. It's my policy that every couple I marry complete a pre-marriage counselling course. It's proven to be very helpful. Couples can discuss the major issues affecting their marriage in depth *before* they tie the knot. It reduces the number of nasty or unexpected surprises that often show up when two people actually begin living together."

"I'm all in for that," agreed Hugh hastily. "I didn't come from a happy, loving home like Ellie did. I admit, I have a lot to learn about having a wife, and being someone's husband. I look forward to it."

Before they left, they also agreed to have their engagement announced in the next church bulletin.

~

"Congratulations!" squealed Sarah when Ellie and Hugh told them the news.

The young couple had come over directly after leaving Pastor Leland, a mere two blocks away. They'd managed to catch Rob, Ellie's eldest brother, just before leaving to attend to some mechanical repairs at the farm.

Sarah, Rob's wife, immediately sought Ellie's hand to see the ring.

"I specifically said 'no diamonds,'" clarified Ellie at once. "But you might like to read the inscription on the inside."

She pulled off her silver band and handed it to Sarah.

"That's so precious," said Sarah after reading the engraving. She passed it along to Rob.

"So when is the big day?" asked Rob, passing the ring back to Ellie.

"New Year's Day," Ellie replied. "It falls on a Thursday this year. An unusual day for a wedding, but we like the symbolism."

Rob offered a wry smile. "I shouldn't be surprised. You seldom like to do things the same way normal people do."

"Phffffff." Ellie made a face. "If it's all right with you, I'd like to ask Charlotte to be my junior bridesmaid, and Beanie to be my flower girl."

Sarah nodded. "I'm sure they'll be thrilled to have a part in your wedding day."

To Rob, Hugh said, "I'd like to ask you to be my best man, and Trevor to be my groomsman."

"No doubt he'll be thrilled to be asked." The corners of Rob's mouth lifted. "But as for myself, I doubt you can afford my services."

Hugh chuckled. "What's your price this time? Another cup of coffee?"

"Whatever it is, you'll have to charge double," Ellie broke in. "I also want you to walk me down the aisle and give me away... in lieu of Dad."

"Two high-profile jobs! And it probably won't end there," Rob said in mock annoyance. "Next you'll want my vehicle for a wedding car, and want me to pick up wedding flowers and transport the bridal party around, and God only knows what else before this thing is done..."

Ellie pursed her lips. "As long as you're going to charge us, you should know that I expect premium service. Nothing shoddy, or else you'll be fired."

Hugh wasn't sure what to think. He thought he knew the Baumans fairly well, but he couldn't quite tell whether they were kidding each other. It sounded very serious.

Sarah noticed the confused look on Hugh's face and came to his rescue. "Stop it, you two. Hugh thinks you're being earnest. You've got him worried."

"That's what you think," said Rob in his most solemn tone of voice. "I'm deadly serious."

Ellie was unfazed. "And I'm a monkey's aunt." She turned to Sarah. "I intend to ask Hugh's two sisters to be my bridesmaids. Since Mom's gone, would you be willing to help me with the planning?"

Sarah smiled happily. "Of course I will. We all miss her terribly. I can easily imagine how excited she would have been to hear your news. She was often impatient in recent years over the fact that a wedding wasn't yet in the works. She wanted so much to put together a very grand day for her only daughter."

The room suddenly became sober over the felt loss of Elizabeth Bauman in the spring.

"Of course, it's bound to take an awful lot of time and work to put on a wedding that meets with Bauman standards," Sarah continued with all seriousness. "I'll have to add my fees to Rob's…"

But unlike Rob, who could string someone along indefinitely, Sarah couldn't hold it. The corners of her mouth twitched and Hugh realized it was all a game.

"Okay, you guys!" he said, laughing. "You had me going there. I hope I know what I'm getting myself into, hooking up with this family."

~

Because Ellie had a midafternoon interview at the hospital in Swan River, she decided to make a stop on the way to see her beloved aunt and uncle in the Bowsman area. She wanted to personally introduce them to Hugh and share her great tidings.

When the couple drove onto the farmyard, they found Ruth cleaning up her flowerbeds alongside the house. Ruth didn't recognize Hugh's silver and red truck at first as he pulled up and parked. She gazed at him with solemn curiosity when he jumped out.

He stepped aside so Ellie could slide out behind him.

"Hi, Aunty Ruth!" Ellie's smile was almost as wide as her face. "I've brought someone I want you to meet."

She ran to her aunt and hugged her while Hugh trailed behind. Ruth dropped her giant garden shears and squeezed her niece in return.

"I'm guessing you're going to introduce me to an answer to prayer, am I right?" asked Ruth, breaking into a warm, inviting smile.

"That's one way of putting it." Ellie reached for Hugh's hand. "Hugh, this is my Aunt Ruth, my mother's younger sister. Aunt Ruth, this is Hugh Fischer—my neighbour, friend, then best friend, and now my husband-to-be."

"Oh, how wonderful for you both." Ruth clapped her hands, then lowered her head to Ellie's and whispered conspiratorially, "He fits the bill for tall, dark, and handsome. Does he have a good heart, too?"

"He so does, Aunty," replied Ellie dreamily. "Wait until I tell you how he proposed to me… Besides that, he's skilled in mechanics and carpentry… and he's given his life over to Jesus. I don't think it gets much better than that."

Ruth looked directly at Hugh. "Does he know what a prize he has in choosing you?"

"Yes, ma'am, I believe I do," he answered.

Ruth clapped her hands again. "Congratulations! When is the big day?"

"January 1," said Ellie and Hugh at the same time.

"New Year's! Well, why not? I can hardly wait." Ruth looked towards the house. "It must be nearly lunchtime. I have a pot of borscht simmering on the stove, and I baked buns this morning. Come inside. Let me feed you before you carry on with the rest of your day."

Ruth Wagner's borscht was an end-of-season soup that included every vegetable she had grown that summer, and a handful of barley joked to have come from Uncle Herb's pockets following the field harvest. The result was a rich red colour. The blended flavours, perfectly seasoned, were lip-smackin' good. One bowl wasn't enough. They each had two helpings of soup and fresh buns.

While they ate, Ellie asked her aunt if she would be willing to bake a three-tiered cake for their wedding.

"Why, I would love to do that for you! It would be an honour," crowed Ruth. "Would fruit cake be all right?"

"It would be perfect, as long as you leave out the nuts."

"Understood," agreed Ruth, nodding. "It'll be fun browsing through recipes."

It was nearly two o'clock when they rolled into Swan River, the largest town in the region. And they still had enough time to share their good news with Hugh's only aunt, Gertie Johnson, before making their way to the hospital.

As they pulled up to the house on Sixth Avenue North, Gertie was just stepping outside cloaked in a fall jacket and carrying her purse. She broke out in a wide grin upon seeing her visitors.

"Looks like we came at a bad time," said Hugh, getting out of the truck.

"I was going to run a small errand uptown and thought a walk would do me good," said Gertie. "But it can wait. It's so nice of you to come by."

The woman turned around and led the couple into the house. They went into the kitchen where Gertie immediately put the kettle on to boil water.

"Ellie has an interview at the hospital in less than an hour, so we can't stay long," said Hugh. "We just wanted you to be among the first to know our good news."

Gertie smiled. "I'm sure I can guess."

"Go ahead then. Guess."

It was a foregone conclusion. "You two are planning to get married, aren't you?"

"Yeah, you guessed right. The date was set this morning for January 1."

"I'm not at all surprised, and I doubt your Uncle Ed will be either. I saw that coming a mile away." Gertie gave her nephew a hug. "Congratulations! You do seem well suited to each other, as far as I can tell. So much better match than your parents ever were…"

"Would you like to be part of the wedding?" asked Ellie tentatively.

Gertie seemed genuinely surprised. "Really? Do you mean it? What could I do?"

"I... uhh..." Ellie suddenly felt doubtful about making her request. "We were thinking you might like to begin the ceremony by lighting the tapers in the candelabras."

"Oh my, I would love to. In fact, it may be the only family wedding I'll ever have any part in." She sounded immediately sad.

Hugh tried to cheer her up. "David may someday..."

Gertie cut him off with a trace of bitterness. "I spoke with David only two days ago. I pleaded with him to come home this Christmas. It's been four years since he was here last. I wanted him to meet his newfound cousins, if seeing his parents weren't enough of a draw. He firmly declined, once again. He said he and his girlfriend just moved in together and they've already made plans to spend the holidays with her family in Toronto. I don't know what we did to lose our son. It's like he wishes we didn't exist..."

Gertie's voice cracked and a single tear slid down her cheek.

It was a potent moment, and uncomfortable. Neither Hugh nor Ellie knew what to say. Clearly she was deeply distraught over her relationship, or lack of one, with her one and only offspring.

"I'm very sorry your son doesn't honour his parents," Ellie ventured at last. "I wish there was something we could do."

Gertie forced a smile. "Well, it's all up to him, isn't it? What's that old proverb? You can lead a horse to water, but you can't make it drink. I just wish I understood. But let's not rain on your parade! I'm so happy for you..."

While Ellie attended to her interview, Hugh dropped by the various service stations in Swan River, seeking to learn if any of them needed a mechanic. No such luck, but a couple took his name to keep on file should their staff needs change.

Hope wasn't lost, though. He would look into farm and auto dealerships next.

The interview went well, and Ellie managed to get her foot in the door with a part-time position in post-surgery. She was guaranteed two twelve-hour shifts per week, but sometimes there'd be more. There would be night shifts, too, but Ellie came away thankful.

Her sabbatical from real life needed to wind down now that the immediate future was clear. She wouldn't be returning to Winnipeg, and soon she would have her own home—and a husband, too. Happiness reigned.

Two

NOW THAT THE nights were getting cool, Hugh planned to take his few things into the newly built cottage. He asked Ellie to help move the bigger items, like the fridge, stove, and Hoosier cabinet. Ellie immediately balked at this.

"Why not?" asked Hugh, surprised. "What's wrong?"

She proceeded cautiously. "Well... I was hoping we could purchase new appliances. White ones. The older pieces worked well for the summer cabin lifestyle, but I'm not excited about making them a permanent part of our life together."

"Why would we buy a new fridge and stove when these here work just fine?"

"So the front room doesn't look like the top of a deluxe pizza."

"What are you talking about? What's that got to do with pizza?"

"It's just that... well, it would mean a mishmash of colours that wouldn't look good together." Ellie's facial expression held the odd combination of apology and determination.

Hugh frowned, as though he were encountering a whole new side of the woman he loved. "It would only be temporary, until they break down or until we build a bigger family home once the kids start to arrive."

"I know what *temporary* means. It usually lasts years. Often many years. But you know that aesthetics is important to me—and being clean, neat, and tidy. I get grumpy when my environment isn't harmonious. So yes, I'll help you move those appliances into the house, but I'd like *temporary* to have a deadline. Say, December 31."

Hugh sucked in his breath, plainly disappointed with being given an ultimatum.

"I don't think I can spare the cost of a new kitchen," he said heavily. "I'd have to dip into the farm account, or my inheritance money. I really don't want to do that. Those funds are allocated for other expenses."

"I have a savings account I've hardly touched. I'm happy to contribute. Besides, we'll need other furnishings, too. Like a bedroom suite. We'll be getting a new sofa, paid for by the proceeds of the yard sale. And remember that lovely lamp I bought from the thrift store? I refinished a table to go with it. The steamer trunk will serve nicely as a coffee table. For the kitchen, I don't mind reusing the little table and chairs in the cabin, although I'd like to repaint the chairs in navy. So you see, quite a lot is already to hand."

"And what about the cost of this dream wedding of yours? Where's the money going to come from for that?"

Ellie hesitated. He'd made a good point. Money wasn't unlimited, and neither was her savings account. If her parents were alive, they would have paid for their daughter's wedding, having fully expected to do so. They would have wanted her to have a grand day.

"I don't know yet, but it may be that my parents set aside some money for that eventuality. Sarah seemed to allude to it yesterday. And don't forget that we'll also receive wedding gifts. I'm sure we'll be given plenty of new practical things, and even some cash."

Hugh nodded, but he felt the pull of a familiar fear. At the moment, the reality was that his bank account was low—and he didn't yet have a source of steady income. When he'd lived on this farm as a kid, they'd had precious little money. He didn't want to live in poverty again.

"Please don't worry, Hugh," she encouraged. "We're going to be all right. It's all going to be okay. Everything is going to work out. You'll see."

Together they went back to Hugh's place and brought over everything they could carry from the summer cabin. To Ellie, what had looked cute in the cabin now looked like a dog's breakfast in the new house. She tried to point that out to Hugh, but he couldn't see it.

"That's because all your taste is in your mouth," said Ellie drily.

⌒

After they'd finished moving in Hugh's few possessions, he left to continue job hunting in Swan River. Meanwhile, Ellie drove her car into Minitonas to check in with her friend, Cynthia Clifford. They'd gone to high school together. Whereas Ellie had gone to Winnipeg to train as a nurse after graduation, Cynthia had married her high school sweetheart and pursued a cottage business as a seamstress, specializing in formal and bridal wear. She was also a brilliant designer and creator of upholstered furniture.

That summer, Ellie had rescued an antique sofa and chair from the derelict farmhouse on Hugh's property. He'd been bent on destroying it, but she had taken it to Cynthia for restoration.

"I had a feeling you'd be by soon," said Cynthia inviting Ellie inside. "I just finished sewing for a bridal party last week and I've only started on your project. I think it's going to be awesome."

"I can hardly wait to see it."

They went into Cynthia's garage, which had been insulated and outfitted as a workshop. The sofa and chair sat in the centre of the space, completely stripped of their old stuffing and fabric. The springs were repaired and the exposed carved wood along the arms had already been refinished in a deep, rich brown.

Ellie beamed. "Wow! It already looks wonderful."

"Brent took care of the woodwork," said Cynthia. "Just wait till you see the plaid."

She walked over to a long shelf and retrieved a rather large box. Next, she lifted out a heavy bolt of pure wool tartan that had been woven in Scotland by special order. Cynthia carefully laid it on the deck of the sofa frame, stretching a length of it across the back. The plaid was predominantly dark green and navy with strips of black running through it, accented with slender red lines. Narrow white lines formed squares that also ran the length and width of the fabric. The effect was classic and beautiful.

Ellie felt thrilled. "It's going to be out of this world."

"I think so, too," agreed Cynthia. "But it will take at least two weeks, if not more, to get it done. There's all the padding and filling to get right. And of course the plaid lines have to match. It won't be a walk in the park."

"That's just fine. The house is ready to receive it, but you don't need to feel pressured…" She trailed off. "I have something else to ask you about, though."

"Shoot!"

"I just got engaged to be married and the wedding is set for January 1. I'm hoping you'll be free to sew a wedding dress for me, as well as for my bridal party." Ellie crossed her fingers. "After the upholstery project is complete, of course."

Cynthia laughed. "Congratulations. Is the lucky guy anyone I know?"

"You might… if you knew Hugh Fischer back in the day. He moved away when he was in the tenth grade and came back this June."

"Nope. I don't recall. But the only project I have lined up is a mother-of-the-bride outfit for a woman who won't need it until next spring. I'm sure I can do your wedding outfits by the end of December. Have you thought about what you want for styles and colours?"

"Only since I was about twelve!"

The women returned to Cynthia's kitchen, where she produced a notebook and recorded in detail all of Ellie's ideas, supplementing a few of her own and making sketches.

⁓

Her business with Cynthia concluded, Ellie went to the post office to empty the mailbox before continuing on to the community store to see about some navy spray paint and a few grocery items. While putting her purchases in the car afterward, she happened to look to her right and down the street. An old man was sitting on the sidewalk up against the wall of the hotel. Ellie immediately guessed who it might be without seeing his face and had a bad feeling about it.

She hurriedly approached the figure and confirmed that it was Tipper—or rather, Lenny Wallen—just as she'd suspected. An old associate of Hugh's father, he wore the same soiled clothing in which she had last seen him in the summer, but this time he also had on a warm jacket.

As she came near, Ellie saw that he was swatting at invisible objects and talking to them.

"Get away from me… go away… lea' me alone… scram… I don't want to go with you… go away…"

Ellie smelled the foul odour he emitted. It was more than the unwashed pong she remembered from before; something very disgusting was added to the stink and it was beginning to turn her stomach.

The sight of him up close was ghastly. Tipper had always been thin, but now he looked emaciated. Immediately Ellie realized she was looking at someone who was dying.

He didn't seem to notice her.

"Hi, Mr. Wallen, do you remember me?" She crouched down next to him. "I'm Ellie, remember? Hugh's friend. Do you remember Hugh, Freddie Fischer's boy?"

Mentioning Freddie's name got his attention and he peered at her, trying to place her. But the spark of recognition quickly vanished and he went back to muttering and swatting the air.

"Stop poking me… go away… let me be…"

As pathetic as the situation was, Ellie's heart went out to the old man. He was a human being, after all. A lifetime of bad choices had brought him to this place, yet she felt she should reach out.

"I'll be right back, Tipper," she said. The terrible odour he emitted was giving her a headache, but she felt she must endure it and help. "I'm going to get some soup for you."

Ellie ran across the street to the café and ordered chicken noodle soup to go.

She'd only been gone a few minutes, but when she returned he somehow appeared even worse off than before.

"Here, Lenny," coaxed Ellie. "Have a little something to eat."

She placed the filled spoon on his lips. As soon as Tipper perceived what she was trying to do, he gagged and turned his head away. Ellie tried again, but he steadfastly refused to open his mouth.

Then his eyes seemed brighter as he tried to focus on her.

"They don't like you," he said darkly.

"Who? Who doesn't like me?"

"The aliens."

"Aliens? What aliens? Where?"

He sounded so very tired. "There's a bunch of them here, trying to make me go with them."

"I can't see them. Tell me, what do they look like?" asked Ellie, an idea forming in her mind.

"Black... lizards..." He seemed to be agitated, as if trying to fend off blows. "They... they..."

"Tipper, call out to Jesus. Do it! They have to leave if you call out to Jesus to save you."

Suddenly Tipper sat upright, as if he'd gotten a second wind. He stared at Ellie with dark, bright eyes that emanated unabashed hate.

"He's ours," said a voice Ellie didn't recognize. "He's coming with us *now*."

Tipper's body shuddered and then slumped over.

Ellie knew what death looked like, and this was it. Leonard Wallen was no more.

Realizing there was nothing more to be done, she slowly got up, went into the hotel, and approached the front desk.

"You need to call the police," she said dully. "A man just died on the sidewalk in front of your hotel."

Ellie waited until the police arrived, which was about fifteen minutes. They recognized Tipper right away as a frequent vagrant. The two officers donned special overalls, masks, and gloves as they handled Tipper and placed him in the body bag.

She gave them her statement, recounting all she knew about where he had lived, his proper name, and that he had been friends with Freddie Fischer. The officers raised their eyes at this but didn't divulge what it meant to them.

After they left, Ellie drove home with a splitting headache and nauseous stomach. The awful smell emanating from Tipper seemed to be stamped on her brain. She hadn't even touched him, yet the powerful stench had clung to her and followed her home.

Driving past Hugh's place, she noticed that his truck wasn't there. That was very disappointing. She wanted to unload the events of the last hour on him, since he was the only other person who had known Tipper and would understand her story.

When she got home, she took off all her clothes and threw them in the washing machine. Next, she jumped in the shower and soaped down her entire body. She shampooed her hair twice. Even freshly cleaned, Ellie believed she could smell the repulsive odour.

After fixing herself a cup of weak tea, she went to the living room to sit in the armchair, the sweet spot from where she could usually find her centre again. She needed to focus on Jesus by imagining Him seated at the end of the couch, as she usually did.

"Jesus, I need help." Tears spilled over onto her cheeks. "Tipper is gone, and it was so very obvious that he didn't leave this world to be with You."

She brushed away the tears, but they kept coming.

"Lord, what's the matter with me? Why am I crying? I hardly knew the guy!"

In response to her own question, she picked up her smallest journal, the one reserved for daily assignments, and opened it to a new page. *Name things worth crying about*, she wrote across the top of a fresh page. Slowly she began to write out her thoughtful responses:

- being always alone
- being unloved
- being rejected and abandoned
- not going to live with Jesus in eternity upon passing away

An insight came to her: apart from faith in Jesus, her list fairly described the human condition. On the other hand, faith in Jesus was the answer to every one of the sorrows she had so far listed. Trusting in Him, one could live without being enslaved to things. In Him, one was never alone; He was always there. In Him, one was always loved. The Bible said so—often! In Him, one was accepted and made whole. In Him, one found peace and joy in spite of circumstances.

The recent shower, hot tea, and big comfy chair all conspired to make Ellie sleepy. Instead of fighting it, she set down her journal and crossed the room to the couch where she lay down and fell asleep.

⁓

Hugh returned to the farm midafternoon feeling somewhat discouraged. He'd had no success securing a job in Swan River. Although he hadn't exhausted every possibility in the other nearby towns, he felt the prospects unlikely.

At any rate, he wanted to talk things out with Ellie. She'd have some ideas he hadn't thought of. She usually did.

The October air was cool and crisp, yet also refreshing under a bright sun. He breathed deeply as he walked the few hundred yards to her place. Since their engagement, he now felt free to let himself in without knocking. The house was eerily quiet, until he noticed Ellie asleep on the couch.

He stared at her sleeping form for a minute, thinking what a beautiful sight she was. He debated whether to wake her, then decided against it. Instead, he sat in her favourite chair to wait.

Immediately he felt the comfort she often claimed. If it was possible for a chair to love someone, this one did. It felt like sitting in a hug, the way it came up around anyone who sat in it.

Ellie's small journal lay open in the upside-down position next to the chair. Hugh picked it up, curious about what she had been writing. He read her list about things worth crying about, which only increased his curiosity. Was it possible she had been feeling alone, unloved, and rejected despite their engagement?

At last she stirred and opened her eyes. She started upon seeing a man in the armchair across the room, but then smiled.

"Oh good," she said, sitting up. "I wanted you."

"And shazam! Here I am, at your service."

Hugh's smile faded when she recounted the whole incident about Tipper.

"That's rough, babe," he said soberly when she concluded her story. "I'm sorry you had to see that."

She felt her tears welling up again. "What I'm sorry about is that I couldn't offer him more. It was too little, too late. I feel so responsible."

"Is that why you wrote this?" asked Hugh, picking up her journal.

Ellie nodded. "I came home crying over someone who was little more than a stranger to me, but the scene is inscribed indelibly on my mind. I'm sure I'll never forget it... nor the terrible stench of death. I don't know how he was alive at all, because he smelled like he'd been dead for days."

"If you... if we... made mistakes concerning Tipper, all we can do now is confess them and leave them with Jesus, isn't that right?"

"Yes," she agreed. "But seeing how he died has reminded me of how very important it is to share the truth about Jesus while people have a chance to respond. I think maybe that's why the Lord caused me to notice him."

They sat quietly together, each occupied with their own thoughts.

At last Hugh spoke up. "Thanks for caring about me enough to keep after me to accept Jesus as the answer. I resisted what you said, but you didn't give up. The more I learn about what the Bible says, the more grateful I feel."

Ellie expressed her "You're welcome" with a kiss.

"You know Ell-berta, it crosses my mind that it would be a good idea to do what you call soul work together," said Hugh pensively. "You're ahead in this area, and I'd like to catch up.

"I like what I see in Rob and, for that matter, in you too. And I know it's because you guys have made habits out of reading something in the Bible regularly."

Hugh paused then and rubbed his chin with his hand.

"I'm pretty sure that explains the confidence and grounding you have for meeting the whammies that keep showing up."

Ellie looked at Hugh with amazement.

Hugh suddenly appeared doubtful. "The look on your face makes me think you don't like the idea."

"No. Not at all," breathed Ellie with wide eyes. "I think it's a great idea. I'm just stunned that you're the one proposing we do this. It suggests a rather rare display of fine leadership in a man. I'm all in for this."

Three

HUGH STILL HADN'T told his sisters about his engagement or forth-coming wedding. Wanting to do this in person, he called them each to plan for a visit. Diane was open to having him come on Friday, while Margo opted for Sunday afternoon.

Friday, after lunch Ellie and Hugh jumped into her car to make the milk run to Yorkton, Saskatchewan. The drive was uneventful but lovely. The fields were bare and most deciduous trees were a brilliant yellow, expressing their last hurrah of the season. It had been years since Ellie had been on this stretch of road and the outing refreshed her spirits.

They used the time to learn more about each other. Ellie liked spicy food; Hugh, not so much. Ellie's favourite colour was blue; Hugh's was red. Ellie's favourite season was spring; Hugh favoured fall, when it wasn't so hot. Hugh liked high drama and action movies; Ellie liked romantic chick flicks. They were very happy to discover they were of the same mind when it came to politics, the philosophy of money, and work ethics.

Sometimes they didn't talk at all, opting to drive along quiet-ly immersed in their own thoughts. Ellie especially enjoyed the fact that they could be companionable without talking all the time. She'd once seen a poster that said, "A real friend is one with whom you can be silent," and agreed with the sentiment. Small, ordinary moments like this confirmed that she and Hugh would do well when they lived together.

When they arrived in Yorkton, it didn't take long to find Hugh's sister. Diane lived in one of the older, established neighbourhoods in a small and unimposing bungalow. The boulevard was lined with mature trees. Up the street, a couple of kids were throwing a frisbee. Somewhere a dog barked. In the other direction, a woman pushed a stroller along the sidewalk.

Hugh and Ellie approached the house with anticipation and rang the doorbell.

"You found us!" said Diane, stepping aside so they could enter.

"You gave excellent directions." Hugh gave her a hug, then gestured to Ellie beside him. "Do you remember this girl?"

Diane studied Ellie. "She does seem vaguely familiar..."

"This is Ellie Bauman."

"Right! We rode on the same school bus. We used to be neighbours, if I remember correctly." Diane turned to Ellie, looking a bit nonplussed. "I thought you left the valley for good."

"Ten years ago, I'm sure I thought I was going to be a city girl for the rest of my life." said Ellie. "But life has a habit of changing without giving notice, so I came back. You look well."

"Uhhh, thanks."

A little girl peeked around a corner.

"Come here, sweetie," Diane said. "Amanda, come say hello to your uncle Hugh... and his friend..."

Hugh made a motion to hold her, but the little girl was shy and leaned into her mother instead.

"How old is she?" Ellie smiled her friendliest.

"She's three."

"She must take after her daddy," Hugh remarked. "I don't recall any blonds among us."

"She does." Diane led the way into the living room, taking the armchair while Hugh and Ellie seated themselves on the couch.

Amanda stayed close to her mother, crawling on her lap after she was comfortably seated, staring at the strangers and not knowing quite what to make of them.

Ellie took note of Diane's decorating style. The rooms were painted in what was often referred to as carpenter's beige. The sofa was of dark brown frieze, the kind of fabric that stood up to everything a household could throw at it and outlived most owners. Besides the matching armchair, she noted the autumn-coloured floral print on the upholstered rocker. A television sat on a low stand in the corner across from the couch and faux wood coffee table. The room also featured a pair of two-tiered end tables with tall ceramic lamps. A large painting hung on the wall over the couch featuring a mountainous landscape on black velvet inside a simple brown frame.

"So what's your big news?" asked Diane, getting down to brass tacks. "What's so important that you had to make a special trip to talk about it?"

"I'm getting married January 1. I wanted you to hear about it directly from me."

"That's nice. To whom?"

Hugh looked at her uncomprehendingly. "To Ellie, of course. That's why she's with me."

"You two are going to get hitched? Sheesh! That seems awfully fast. How long have you been dating?"

Ellie shifted uncomfortably. Clearly she wasn't too excited for them.

"We've been working together since mid-June," Hugh said, sounding defensive. "She's the best thing that ever happened to me. I feel like I'm the luckiest man alive."

His sister followed his words with furrowed brows.

"I don't get it, Diane," he said. "I thought you'd be jumpin' up and down happy for me. What's your beef?"

"I just remember Pa telling us to stay away from the Baumans." Diane avoided making eye contact with Ellie. "He said they were uppity people or something. And here you are, marrying one of them. I can't imagine our parents would be too happy."

"Yep. I heard Pa say that, too, because he was jealous as a body can be with their good fortunes." Hugh's tone was beginning to get heated. "Which, by the way, came to them through hard, steady work, not wasting their earnings on an alcoholic's diet. Ever since I returned to the farm, Ellie and her brother have been nothing but good to me. Helping me out before I ask. Encouraging me in the quest to get ahead. Wanting me to do better than just get by." He shook his head in frustration. "I'm shocked that you would believe Pa would say anything truthful about the Baumans."

Hugh was ticked and hurt. His instinct was to get up and leave—to return home and be done with all this family criticism—but Ellie squeezed his hand. He relaxed a bit and sat still, willing to hear Diane out.

"You make a point," Diane conceded. "Pa said bad stuff about everyone. Jealousy was probably the root of it, because he handled money pretty badly."

"That's putting it mildly," huffed Hugh.

"But why did you run away? Why did you leave Mom and us high and dry?"

"You're kidding, right?"

"No. You left like a sneak, without saying goodbye, and nobody knew where you went. Mom cried and cried. Pa was madder than a hornet. Margo and I felt like we'd been abandoned."

He lowered his head. "I wrote to Margo, and I got letters from her... and a couple from you, too, at first. So don't try and tell me you knew nothing about my whereabouts. And don't try to tell me you didn't know why I ran away."

Diane was quiet for a moment. Ellie also kept quiet. This discussion didn't concern her, yet she felt that Diane had a right to express her pain and disappointment. She certainly had a right to ask the hard questions. Ellie hoped that Hugh understood he wasn't the only one in the household who had grown up in pain. He would do well to acknowledge her hurt and help her get through it.

But she refrained from saying so aloud.

"Margo said Pa beat you bad," said Diane haltingly. "But we didn't see it, or at least not much. Mom sent us to our room."

"Yeah. Well, the last time it happened, I thought I was gonna die. I wasn't stickin' around to give him another chance to finish me off." Hugh felt some of his former bitterness rising up again. "The fifteen-year anniversary is almost here. Not a day I like to remember…"

"But, Hugh, I had a brother, and then all of a sudden I didn't. You left us… me… so completely that you might as well have been dead. I did get the occasional tidbit of news about you through Margo, but you never contacted me. I thought you were mad at me, and I couldn't think why."

"I wasn't mad at you. Ever. I was only making sure Pa never got wind of my whereabouts. I felt sure that if he knew where I was, he would come after me. Not sending letters home was my way of protecting you all from Pa grilling you for information. I was sure he hated me, and I hated him, too. It burned for years, like a slow roast."

They all sat in silence for about a minute. Little Amanda seemed to sense the gravity of the discussion and sat quietly on her mother's lap, staring at the two strangers on the couch, her thumb in her mouth.

"Look, I'm sorry. I really am. But I was in survival mode." Hugh felt weary of the subject. "Maybe I didn't handle family matters very well, but you could have reached out if you wanted to keep in touch so bad. Margo had the addresses and phone numbers."

Diane sighed sheepishly. "You have me there. I shouldn't blame you when I'm just as guilty. I'm sorry I took you to task."

"It's all good. Just… can we be friends now? Can you be happy for Ellie and me?"

"Yes. I can," said Diane, suddenly cheerful. "Congratulations. I hope you'll be very happy together."

"Thank you." Hugh exhaled, then looked over at Ellie. "I think you can make your pitch now."

"I'm looking forward to having a sister," Ellie said, attempting to lighten the mood. "In our family, I was the only girl after three older boys. That's a recipe for the makings of a tomboy! And about our wedding... well, I was wondering, would you honour us by being one of my bridesmaids?"

Diane's eyes flared in surprise. "Seriously? Why me? Wouldn't you rather ask one of your girlfriends?"

"I'd rather it be family. My brother Rob and nephew Trevor will be standing up for Hugh. I'd like you and Margo to stand up for me."

"That's sounds really nice. What did Margo say?"

"We haven't talked with her yet. We'll see her on Sunday."

"Hmmm. Actually, it sounds like it might be fun. So yes, I accept your invitation. It's nice of you to ask."

By this time, it was four o'clock in the afternoon and they were startled by the sounds of a waking baby. Amanda's eyes went wide with delight as she clambered down from her mother's lap and disappeared down the hallway.

"That will be Sean, waking from his nap," said Diane, rising to fetch her one-year-old. A few moments later, she brought out a plump little man with blue eyes and dark hair like his mother's.

"I'll bet those are classic Fischer genetics," said Ellie.

"That could be." Diane nodded. "He'll be hungry. I'll feed him in the kitchen."

They all rose and followed Diane into her kitchen where she put little man Sean in the highchair. Hugh and Ellie took seats at the kitchen table. Amanda stayed close to her mother. Both children stared curiously at the strangers in the room.

"What does your husband do for a living?" asked Hugh.

"He paints houses. He and a buddy went into partnership and started the company a few years back. Mostly residential. It's a living."

Hugh peered out the window. "What time does he usually get home? I've yet to meet him."

"Around five. And Bill is curious to meet you, too," said Diane.

It was quickly agreed that Hugh and Ellie would stay for supper, although Diane had to admit that she wasn't much of a cook.

"Why don't I give you the night off?" Hugh said. "I'll pick up a couple of pizzas."

"That's a great idea, but you're my guest. I'll send Bill for them."

"Nah. It was my idea. I should pay."

"That's all right. Bill can cover it."

Sensing this might go on a while, Ellie stepped in. "Thanks so much for sharing your home and pizza with us. When you come our way, we'll share our home and meals with you, too."

Hugh got the hint and immediately backed off.

Bill came home right on time, stripped himself of his paint-splattered coveralls, and then got back in his work van to "bring home the bacon," as he joked. Hugh went with him.

"Looks like we have a few minutes for girl talk," said Ellie once they were alone.

"Did you want to talk weddings? I don't have a lot of ideas, if that's what you're looking for."

"Actually, I'm mostly interested in getting to know my new sister. Tell me about the things that matter to you. About your wedding, about being a mom, about what flies your kite."

Diane looked nonplussed again. "Okay. Well, I can tell you about my wedding. It was six years ago and I was twenty. I did have a white dress, but the wedding itself was very small. The guests were mostly Bill's family and relatives. Margo was the only one invited from my side of the family. She was my bridesmaid, and I was hers.

"Not your parents?" asked Ellie, surprised.

"It would have been nice to have Mother there, but I couldn't trust my father not to do something embarrassing," said Diane without hesitation.

"I know quite a lot about how it was for you growing up, at least through Hugh's eyes. I'm so sorry."

"It's history. Water under the bridge. I try not to think about it. Compared to that, I'm doing well. I have food, clothing, a roof over my head, a couple of great kids, and a husband who doesn't beat me. I figure that means I have a good life."

Ellie listened in awe. For an introductory visit, she was somewhat surprised that Diane had been willing to share what she would have thought was intensely personal and delicate information.

"I'm happy that you're happy," said Ellie, trying to be positive.

"I'm only as happy as far as those things can make a person happy." When Diane spoke, she was completely straightforward. "You asked what flies my kite. That would have to be my kids. They make me laugh, melt my heart, and are the reason I get up and clean the house and stuff."

They fell into silence for a moment and Ellie had to fight her instinct to fill it.

"Your turn," Diane said. "Tell me about yourself."

Ellie did a little gulp and tried to think of a quick answer. "About my wedding, I've been imagining the day since I was a girl. I only intend to do it once, so I hope it will be as pretty as possible. We haven't put together a guest list yet, but I doubt it will be as small as the one you just described. My parents won't be there either. My dad died of a heart attack about a year and a half ago, and my mother passed away in April. I guess that's something we have in common. We're both parentless."

"Were you close to them?"

"Not at the time of their passing. I used to be close to my mother, but I didn't maintain that relationship after I moved to Winnipeg. It's one of my greatest regrets."

Diane's face softened but didn't comment.

"I'm not yet a mom, but I hope Hugh and I will have a few kids." Ellie smiled jokingly. "Or maybe a dozen."

Diane's eyes opened as wide as saucers.

"Just kidding!" Ellie laughed. "I love the sound of children giggling. I love cuddling with them. I have nieces and nephews who are as important to me as the children I hope to have."

"Nice. And what flies *your* kite?"

"Well, I like soft instrumental music... a good belly laugh... hugs and kisses, of course... flowers... eating by candlelight... watching a fire burn in a fireplace. I also like to jump rocks when the rivers are low... good novels... drawing... romantic movies... fluffy blankets... interior decorating... and I'm sure there's lots more, but that's all I can think of this minute..."

Ellie trailed off, feeling a little breathless.

"Wow! There's a lot on your list I haven't even tried," said Diane. "I guess I should get out more. Do more stuff. But what about the question you haven't answered yet?"

At first, Ellie didn't know what she meant.

"You know," Diane prompted. "What matters to you?"

"Quite a few things. Hugh matters to me, of course. My family, my friends, my work as a nurse... they all matter more than stuff. But at the top of the list, and this might sound weird to you, but what matters most to me is my relationship with God. He is very real to me. Without Him, nothing makes sense, and nothing else in my life works right."

Right then, the men returned in Bill's van. Their pizza supper had arrived.

"You're right," Diane said, bringing the conversation to a close. "That's weird. I don't believe in God or Jesus or any kind of religion. I put them in the same category as Santa Claus or the Easter bunny. It's just made-up hogwash..."

Before Ellie could say anything in response, the men came in. Bill set the two pizza boxes on the kitchen table and then raced into the living room to turn on the television.

"The football game is about to start," he called loudly. "Let's eat in here."

Diane sighed and shook her head. But she just picked up the boxes and took them into the front room where Bill was already comfortably seated on the sofa with his feet resting on the coffee table.

Hugh and Ellie followed close behind.

Bill was different than Ellie had imagined. Of average height, he might have been slim if it weren't for the belly that hung over his belt. His hair was dirty blond and a bald spot was showing. His cheeks and chin displayed a day's growth of stubble. In contrast to Hugh, who spoke in a deep bass tone, Bill was a confirmed tenor.

But he was also friendly and invited Hugh and Ellie to sit down and make themselves at home. Keeping one eye on the game, he asked questions about their livelihoods and listened to their answers, managing to keep the discussion going while keeping abreast of the game, too.

At one point, Ellie returned to the kitchen with Diane to bring back a tray of beverages.

"As you can probably tell," Diane remarked as they got the drinks ready, "what flies Bill's kite is sports. Baseball in summer, football in fall, hockey in winter, and also curling. That's his first love. I'm only his mistress. So there. Now you've met Bill and Diane Taylor and family. What you see is what you get!"

⁓

The drive home from Diane and Bill's place made for lively discussion.

"I hadn't thought much about how my sisters felt about my sudden departure," admitted Hugh reflectively. "I should have realized the impact it had on them. I was only thinking of my own safety at the time."

"Your parents were broken people passing along their brokenness because that's all they knew." Ellie sighed. "Brokenness was passed on to them as well. That's what dysfunction is…"

"Pastor Leland would call it 'the problem of sin.'"

"True. It's like that drawing I made for you. I suppose it's still tacked up in your cabin?"

"I never threw it out." A few minutes of silence passed before he continued. "The more I observe how people live, the more I under-stand what the Bible means when it talks about the lost. Given where I come from, I'm more thankful with each passing day that I belong to Jesus."

"I'm glad to hear that, love, because if you hadn't come round to making that commitment, it would never have worked out between us."

"I get it."

"While you guys were out getting pizza, Diane and I got to talking. I asked her to tell me about herself. After listening to everything she had to say, it amounted to a life of disappointment and boredom. The novelty of marriage wore off long ago, and her daily routine holds little joy. She looks for the meaning of life in her children while Bill seems to stave off emptiness by immersing himself in sports year-round."

Hugh got very quiet for a few minutes.

"Ellie, how are we going to prevent ourselves from falling into the same disillusionment?" he asked. "I want to feel as much love for you fifty years from now as I do today."

"Honey, I believe that depth of love is the by-product of maintaining a close relationship with Jesus individually and as a couple as well as being each other's priority every day."

"Is that how Rob and Sarah do it? I love watching them together."

Ellie suddenly looked thoughtful. "I'm sure it is."

Four

AFTER CHURCH ON Sunday, they enjoyed a hastily eaten lunch at Ellie's place before striking out on the road again, this time heading east and south to the small city of Dauphin. They took Hugh's truck.

"I haven't recovered yet from folding myself up like an accordion to get into your little car," he teased.

The drive would take a little less than two hours, if they kept to the speed limit, so they had lots more time to get to learn more personal things about each other.

"I'm curious about something, Hugh-man," said Ellie. "I'd like to hear about your dating life. You've never really talked about it."

Hugh paused, showing reluctance. "There's not a lot to tell. There haven't been many girls in my life. I was shy and suffered from what's popularly called poor self-esteem."

"Still, I'd like to know more about your experiences."

Hugh inhaled, and then exhaled with a sigh. "There were only three girls I spent any time with. The first was my lab partner in twelfth grade chemistry. Her name was Bonnie. Because we had to work together, I got over some of my shyness. We got along pretty well. One day towards the end of the school year, while walking to the lab, we passed an open door to the janitor's supply room. All of a sudden, she yanked me in there with her and planted a big kiss square on my mouth. I was so shocked that I didn't know what to do. But it did the job of waking me up, if you know what I mean. I don't know about her, but that was my first kiss, and it was a doozy."

Ellie giggled. "That's so cute."

"Well, after that I asked her to be my grad date, and she said yes. But later she told me I first had to meet her dad or she wouldn't be allowed to be my date. That made me pretty nervous. By appointment, I showed up at her house. Her folks seemed nice and all, but her dad wanted to know about my parents and where I lived and far too much personal stuff. Stuff I refused to talk about with anyone. I think they got the impression I was some kind of juvenile delinquent because I wouldn't divulge much about my past and had only recently come to live in Winnipeg. The following Monday, Bonnie told me that her dad refused to let her be my grad date. In the end, we both went as singles. I didn't stay for the dance or the afterparties. The Turners were shocked that night when I was home by ten. I just wasn't in the mood to hack it up."

"Aww, Hughie, that's too bad. Do you feel you've missed a rite of passage somehow?"

"Nah. I don't think all the hoopla around graduation is all it's cracked up to be. For what it's worth, I never saw Bonnie again after that."

Ellie sat back, taking it all in. "Okay. Who was the next girl?"

"Someone I don't much like remembering," he said unhappily.

"She broke your heart, did she?"

"In a way…" He slowed down to drive through the village of Cowan at posted speeds. "After high school, I took courses in auto mechanics at the Manitoba Institute of Trades and Technology. There were no girls in my class and I didn't run into many in my travels anyway. Sometimes, at the end of a school day, I went to the pub with some guys. We had beers, but I didn't fit in much with that crowd. The talk was mostly about sports or women. You wouldn't have liked it, and I couldn't exactly relate, not being well versed in either topic."

"I know a thing or two about how men think."

"After graduating from college, I got a job at a service station as an onsite mechanic. This girl, Roberta, got hired to work as the cashier. For some reason, she took a shine to me and it wasn't long before she asked me out."

Ellie raised her eyebrow. "Was she pretty?"

"In a heavily made-up sort of way. She wore all the latest fads, too, and her clothing was skintight. Anyway, it turned out she was mostly after one thing. It got to the point that we always ended our evenings together at her place. I guess you know what I'm talking about…"

"I know the drill," admitted Ellie. "I was part of that culture myself for a while."

"We only dated for a couple of months. Maybe less. The day she broke up with me was weird. I came into the station close to quitting time, as I usually did, expecting to be told what we were going to do that evening. You know, like going to a movie or something. But she was acting all kinds of funny, plus she wouldn't look me in the face. Then a bright yellow, souped-up sportscar with extra-wide tires pulled up and stopped in front of the station. Roberta grabbed her purse and said, 'Look, there's no easy way to say this, but it's over between you and me. I found someone else.' Then she got in that fancy yellow sportscar and they took off. I was stunned. I never saw it coming. And that was the first time I felt dirty from all the things we'd been doing together."

"I know that feeling, too," said Ellie with empathy.

"I was pretty angry after that. I felt like I'd been taken advantage of. I was seriously off girls for quite a while. I didn't think they were trustworthy. I thought all girls were more or less the same as Roberta. Fickle as all get out."

"Some girls are fickle, but not all. Just like not all men are troublesome or one-track-minded." She broke into a smile. "Just most of them."

Hugh elbowed her ribs.

"Where does the third girl fit in?" asked Ellie.

"Some time after Roberta, I went to work at a different garage. I also moved into a small bachelor's suite on the eighth floor of an apartment block close to downtown. It wasn't fancy, but it had what I needed. I often rode the elevator with the same girl in the morning and again coming home from work. Finally she broke the ice… because I was too shy to start a conversation. She said, 'If we're going to keep meeting like this, we should introduce ourselves. My name is Marilyn.' Then I told her my name."

"What did this girl look like?"

"She was about your height, maybe taller. Short blond hair. Nice looking, but not as beautiful as you." He winked at her.

Now it was her turn to elbow him in the ribs. "I see somewhere along the line you've learned how to inveigle a woman."

Hugh chuckled. "Seriously, I do think you are especially beautiful."

"I know you do. And to me you're the most handsome man I've ever met. I suspect it's one of God's ways of helping people find each other as mates. A man and a woman become drawn to each other while others are left to wonder whether they have poor vision or something. Sometimes there's just no explaining how coupling comes about."

Ellie's eyes sparkled. "Tell me more about Marilyn. Was she another Roberta?"

"Oh no. Marilyn was a very nice and decent girl," said Hugh. "Mostly we just talked in the hallway, or maybe on a walk down the street for ice cream. It was like this for a few weeks before I got the idea to take it to the next level. We stepped off the elevator one day and I pulled her close and kissed her on the mouth. She didn't pull away and I thought I must have done it well."

Suddenly, pain and doubt crept into his voice.

"But the next morning, after riding the elevator down she stopped me in the foyer and told me that although she thought I was a nice guy, we should stop seeing each other. She didn't say why. So once again, I thought all girls were fickle and not to be trusted. They took your time, your money, your favours, and then left you high and dry."

Ellie felt a surge of sympathy. If they hadn't been driving, she probably would have granted him a consoling hug.

"From my perspective as a girl, I bet that Marilyn was considering you as a potential mate," she said. "It was all positive… until the test of a kiss. Something about your kiss didn't work for her. Maybe it had about as much excitement to it as kissing her brother. If so, then she did the right thing by breaking it off as soon as possible. Better that than stringing you along. If you know it's not going to work, the sooner the better."

"I suppose you're right," said Hugh. "But at the time it just felt like more undeserved rejection. I didn't want any more of that, so I closed my heart off to all girls and concentrated on making money. My parents had already died and I was beginning to turn over the idea of coming back to the farm anyway. You know the rest of the story."

She looked out the window at the passing fields. "I believe we both came back at the same time as part of God's plan. And just for the record, in case your insecure heart needs some reassurance, I think your kisses are wonderful and delicious."

"Good to know."

A moment later, he slammed on the brakes, pulled over onto the shoulder of the highway, and put the truck in park. He turned to Ellie who sat next to him in the middle of the seat. Wrapping his arms around her, he leaned in and gave her a long, passionate kiss.

She broke away breathlessly. "Stop, Hugh. You have to stop. We should be saving those kisses for our wedding night. They're too arousing."

Hugh was panting, too, and couldn't seem to speak for a moment. "I love you, Ellie, and it's starting to hurt to keep it under wraps." His voice sounded hoarse.

"I promise to make it worth the wait," she replied.

It took a minute or two to get their feelings settled down again. Then they got back on the road.

⌒

The address Margo had given Hugh was a new one. She and her husband had just recently moved into a new neighbourhood of lately built upscale houses. The house Ellie and Hugh drove up to was rather large.

Margo had been watching for them and met them at the door as they came up the walk. She greeted her brother with a brief hug and a wide smile, all the while staring at Ellie, trying to place her.

"Your friend looks familiar," said Margo, "but I can't pull up a name."

"I'll give you a minute to figure it out," said Hugh as they stepped inside.

Ellie wasn't prepared for what she saw inside. Crisp white walls surrounded an open concept space filled with white leather furniture along with chrome and glass coffee and side tables. The lamps were also made of chrome and had white shades. As for the floors, it was a lightly stained hardwood covered in part by a shag area rug in the sunken living room. The fireplace was built into the main interior wall and served as a natural room divider. Built-in shelves and cupboards adorned the room, as well as a late-model television and some other electronics Ellie couldn't identify.

Margo's outfit complemented her decorating style. She wore a loose white shirt open to her cleavage, bloused, and belted in stylish stone-washed jeans. Golden hoop earrings hung from her ears and a colourful scarf, fashionably arranged, was wrapped around her neck. Shag-cut, mid-length, blond-streaked hair framed Margo's face. Her makeup was impeccable.

Ellie had dressed suitably for the occasion, too, coming in cuffed navy slacks with a loosely fitting blue and grey pullover knit sweater. Although she had taken special care to look nice, Margo's appearance made her feel a bit frowzy.

"This is nothing like your old place," observed Hugh, unsure where to begin.

"Do you like it?" asked Margo.

"I don't know. I kind of feel like I shouldn't touch anything!"

"It's lovely!" put in Ellie quickly. "Like something right out of an interior decorating magazine. It looks like someplace a celebrity would live in."

"Thank you," purred Margo, pleased. "Let me show you around."

She showed them the galley kitchen with all the latest built-ins and modern appliances. The dining area was similarly outfitted with contemporary stylings. The large tabletop was made of extra-thick wood, thickly glazed with a satin sheen and had chrome legs. Eight matching wooden chairs completed the set. A bowl made of pottery and filled with red apples graced the centre of the table. The mirror on the wall, also chrome-framed, dominated the wall.

Beyond the kitchen was another sitting area with yet another television. The sofa here was covered in black leather. Margo's husband was stretched out on it watching a football game, although he immediately sat up to greet them.

"Larry, you remember my brother Hugh, right?" reminded Margo brightly.

Larry extended his arm for a handshake. "Hey, Hugh, good to see you. How's it going?" He acknowledged Ellie with a nod.

"It's all good," replied Hugh. "How about you?"

Larry sat down again. He turned down the volume but kept the TV on while the other three took seats nearby.

"We sure are having nice fall weather, don't you think?" said Larry.

Ellie noticed that he had avoided Hugh's question.

Margo stepped in quickly and wore a forced smile. "We're doing well. But never mind us. Tell us about your big news, Hugh. You said you wanted to make a big announcement. What is it?"

Hugh looked at Ellie, then back at Margo. With a big grin, he said, "I'm engaged to be married. The big day is January 1, and I know Ellie has a special request of you."

"Ellie!" Margo snapped her fingers in sudden recognition. "You're Ellie Bauman, aren't you? I knew you looked familiar. And you're going to marry my brother? Wow!" She turned to Hugh. "That's quite a step up for you, bro. Way to go. Congratulations."

It could have been an awkward moment, as if the tacky comment reflected on a misalignment of status or social class, but Ellie changed the subject at once. "I'd like you to be one of my bridesmaids."

"Me?" Margo asked. "Really? Why? We hardly know each other."

"We want the wedding party to be made up of family. Diane has already said yes. I hope you will, too."

"January 1, you said?" Margo paused, as if thinking very hard. "Well, that should work. It's not a workday. I don't know if you've been told, but I was promoted to manager at the clothing shop where I work."

Larry snorted and held his head braced in one hand.

"Yes, you mentioned it when we were with Aunt Gertie and Uncle Ed in July," Hugh said.

"Right. I guess I did."

"How nice for you," said Ellie. "That sounds like a lot of responsibility."

"It is. And it's an important position."

Hugh noticed Larry's eyerolling. He started shaking his head, too, which made Hugh feel a bit uncomfortable. The room felt tense, and the tension seemed to be growing thicker by the minute between Margo and her husband.

He tried to divert the conversation onto a new topic. "So why'd you move into this new house? Your last one looked pretty nice to me."

"Yeah, how come the new house, Margo?" Larry echoed, just short of a sneer. "I haven't figured that one out yet myself."

Margo sent him a withering look. "I've explained it a thousand times, but you seem to be braindead or you'd understand. But for the sake of our guests, who I'm sure will understand the first time, I'll repeat it." She turned to face Hugh and Ellie deliberately. "I decided to invest my inheritance in property. Besides, I was ready for a change...

something new and different. I got a nice raise and saw it as a good opportunity to make some upgrades."

Larry stared stonily at the TV and made no further comment.

Though the house talk was becoming increasingly ill at ease, Ellie pressed on. "Is this furniture you brought from your previous home?" She panned the room with her arm. "What did you do with your old furniture? Were the old pieces similar to what you have now?"

"Oh no," said Margo quickly. "They were very traditional. That's why I got tired of them."

"What did you do with them?"

"The pieces are stowed in the garage, if you'd like to see them."

"I would."

Margo got up and led Ellie to a door off the kitchen. The garage was crowded with classically styled furnishings that appeared to be in excellent condition. Some of the brand names were recognizably high-end. Ellie privately thought they were much more inviting than the cold-looking pieces that filled the house now.

"Our first house is going to be pretty little," said Ellie. "I have a few pieces to contribute, but we do need a bedroom suite and I like the style of this one. I'd also be interested in the entertainment cabinet. If the price is right, I'll happily take them off your hands. That is, if Hugh likes them."

"Why do you need to ask Hugh? The house is a woman's prerogative."

"I want Hugh to have an opinion," insisted Ellie.

She returned to the kitchen. After catching his eye, she motioned for Hugh to come hither with her index finger.

He came directly.

"What do you think of this?" Ellie pointed out the bedroom suite and cabinet, all finished in dark walnut.

"They look all right," he said. "Why?"

"Margo is selling all this stuff. I wondered if we could use this opportunity to outfit our future home affordably."

"If you like it, go for it," said Hugh and shrugged.

With that, he returned to join Larry watching the football game.

Margo and Ellie discussed prices for a few minutes. After learning what the original prices were, Ellie offered her half that amount. The offer came to $1,450.

She was about to write out the cheque when she noticed a picture tucked in between the sofa and its matching armchair. She paused to pull it out and found herself gazing at a pastoral scene set amidst craggy hills and a flowing stream. In the foreground was a flock of sheep with black faces and legs surrounding a plaid-caped shepherd who carried a lamb around his neck.

Immediately Ellie thought of Scotland and how well this would go with the reupholstered sofa set Cynthia was working on. The imagery also reminded her of Jesus and His declaration about being the Good Shepherd.

"How much for the picture?" asked Ellie.

"Oh, that? It's just a cheap thing I bought on impulse a few years ago. You can just have it." Margo sounded indifferent.

"Thank you so very much. I actually love it and will accept it as a wedding gift."

Margo was visibly relieved. "Then your wedding gift it is."

Ellie went back to her chequebook and began to fill in the date.

"Say, do you have a bit of cash on you?" asked Margo with a measure of embarrassment.

"Not a lot. Maybe about fifty dollars."

"I'm out of cash and I'd like to give you guys a bite of supper before you go back to Minitonas. But we'll need to go pick up some groceries. Do you mind giving me the fifty dollars and making out the cheque for fourteen hundred…?"

As soon as the women had left for the grocery store, Larry relaxed and began to open up to Hugh.

"I guess you can see things aren't so well between Margo and me," he began.

"It is rather obvious," said Hugh. "I suppose it has something to do with this new house."

"Our relationship's been going downhill for the last couple of years, but this house and all the expensive furniture has been the last straw for me. I haven't told her yet, but I'm seriously thinking of leaving."

This was starting to make Hugh feel uneasy. "Man, you don't have to tell me this stuff."

"You're her brother," Larry insisted. "You should know. She's never content with what we've got. She always wants more. Bigger, better, newer. That promotion did come with a small raise, but you'd think she was the CEO of a major corporation. She supervises three clerks and is making a dollar more. Not enough to live on if she were on her own, but she'd have you thinking she was in the upper class now."

"I don't know what to say, Larry."

"Never mind. Just hear me out. When she came home with her inheritance cheque in July, I was hopeful we could pay off our credit card debt and start a retirement savings account. But no. The bank took the whole amount for the down-payment and she maxed out the credit card special ordering furniture from all over the country. She makes payments and then promptly maxes it out again on clothes. She could turn her closet into its own shop! But she just keeps buying. 'I have to look up-to-date for the sake of our customers...'" Larry imitated her high-pitched voice. "The bottom line is, we're strapped. We're house poor with no wiggle room. Thank God Ellie's buying some of that old furniture. At least we'll be able to buy some groceries for a few weeks! But you wait. Margo will probably spend some of it on more things we don't need. I've had it. I don't want to be angry all the time, feeling like I have nothing going for me..."

Hugh leaned forward and asked, "If it wasn't for the money problems, would you two still be tight? I mean, as far as the marriage goes?"

Larry didn't answer right away. "I might not be as near to the thought of leaving her as I am now, but it's a good question. She's not easy to live with, you know. More and more she sounds like your old man. Bossy. Thinks she's the only one who's ever right about anything. She puts her job above everything, including me. I'm ready to have a family, but she doesn't want kids. Says they'll ruin her figure and be more work and responsibility than she wants. Honestly, I'm so fed up. I don't even want to have sex with her anymore."

"I don't need to know this," said Hugh quickly. "What about marriage counselling? Couldn't you talk with a financial advisor?"

"I don't think I care enough anymore to see a counsellor. I'd rather just start over with someone else. But I won't rock the boat until after your wedding…" He put up a hand. "Please don't say anything to anyone. Let me handle it when I'm ready."

They heard the garage door opening and knew the ladies had returned. Hugh was glad. He didn't want to hear any more intimate details concerning his sister's private life.

He felt bad for Larry, though. If he was in that man's shoes, he'd probably be just as frantic, unhappy, and disillusioned. But he didn't know what to say to his brother-in-law, or how to help.

Worse, Larry had made him question himself. Was marriage worth it? Once the honeymoon period was over, it didn't look like so much fun. Unhappy. Monotonous. What was the point if it all came down to that?

But the mood improved substantially after the women came in and started preparing dinner. Margo's relief at having some cash in hand was palpable.

They enjoyed a casual supper of homemade hamburgers, which Ellie cooked. Margo claimed she hardly ever cooked anything from scratch and didn't know how. Working full-time meant she almost only ever heated up prepared food packages.

After supper, Hugh backed up his truck to the garage so they could load the furniture. He packed it with blankets and cardboard to avoid scratching.

After mutual thank-yous and goodbyes, Hugh and Ellie found themselves back on the highway headed for home. They'd gotten through the visit amicably enough, but both were relieved to be away from all the tension seething beneath the surface.

Five

THE DRIVE HOME was a lot different than the trip out. Before, Hugh had been chatty and affectionate, amiably sharing his former experiences. Now he was pensive, not at all attuned to what Ellie was talking about. He seemed withdrawn.

"Yoohoo, Hugh-manuel," called Ellie, waving a hand in front of Hugh's eyes. "This is earth calling to Hugh-misphere in outer space, come in please."

Hugh blinked. "What? Sorry. I was thinking about something else. What were you saying?"

"I was trying to discuss my concerns about Margo and Larry, but I don't think you heard a word I said."

"You're right. I wasn't listening. I was thinking about my own worries."

"Care to share?"

"Larry asked me not to."

She seemed a bit surprised. "Well, I'll tell you how I read them. Those two are on the cusp of divorce. I'd bet dollars to donuts that Larry is thinking about walking away."

"Was it that obvious to you? I mean, you guessed right. He is thinking about it. He told me so but asked me not to say anything."

"It doesn't take a rocket scientist to see that they're in over their heads financially. And they aren't on the same page in other areas of life either."

Hugh looked at her warily. "Are you suggesting we get involved?"

"No. It's none of our business. Unless they specifically ask for our input."

"Are you hoping they will?"

"Not really. Who am I to think I could counsel someone else's marriage problems? However, I might view it as an opportunity to talk about Jesus."

They drove along in silence for a few minutes.

"You see the pattern, don't you?" Ellie said. "Both of your sisters are still responding to their upbringing under your parents."

"You're probably right. But I'm not bothered by it so much. All three of us had to grow up and figure out life for ourselves."

"What's bugging you then? Clearly something is bothering you."

Hugh let out a huge sigh. "All of a sudden, I'm afraid of marriage. Both of my sisters are locked in obviously unsatisfying relationships. The guys aren't googly-eyed over their women, either, and I'm afraid it will happen to us, too. The thought terrifies me. That I could wake up one morning and think I don't want to live with you anymore. The normal progression of marriage seems to be that we'll get tired of each other. One day you'll be totally bored and disappointed with me, like Diane seems to be with Bill. Or what if we start moving in different directions? Will one of us want a family while the other wants a career? What's the point if the love that brings a couple together doesn't last?"

Hugh's outburst stunned Ellie into silence.

"I hardly think either one of us is like your sisters or their spouses," she finally said. "I believe our marriage will be a good, strong, loving, stable union. A lot closer to the example Rob and Sarah have set, not to mention my parents before them. It's because of our faith and commitment to live by biblical principles."

"I'm not so sure. You once told me that I would be what I grew up with. Like, if I grew up with criticism, I would be critical, etc. I know what I grew up with, and if that's what you have to look forward to, then you don't want to be with me."

"You forget one essential point."

"What would that be?"

She spoke emphatically. "*God*. Your sisters are living out their brokenness, same as you were when I first met you. But God came into your life the evening of July 19, 1980 and has made all the difference. You now have what it takes to overcome the brokenness you inherited through your family. You're already very different from the man I first met back in June. You just need to believe it, Hugh."

"I don't know. That sounds like wishful thinking." Hugh sounded clearly doubtful.

They drove the last half-hour without talking, listening absent-mindedly to the country music on the radio.

After they pulled into Hugh's yard, Ellie helped to unload the furniture, relieved that none of it had gotten damaged on the two-hour trip. They placed the entertainment unit in the cottage's living room and stowed the rest in the bedroom on either side of Hugh's single bed. There was no point in setting it up until a queen-sized mattress was purchased to complete it.

Besides, Hugh was rather emphatic that he would not sleep in a larger bed until he was ready to share it with his wife.

Ellie studied him as she folded up the blankets and placed them in a box. Every time Hugh glanced at her, she saw the fear in his eyes. She reasoned it was something he had to work out for himself; she'd said all she could say to reassure him.

When the tidying was done, she picked up the shepherd and sheep painting, along with her handbag, and walked to the door. She rested her hand on the doorknob and turned her face to him.

"Don't come to me until you get this figured out," she said.

Then she opened the door and went out into the darkness.

As soon as Ellie had closed the door behind her, Hugh's heart lurched in his chest. Had he just initiated a breakup with the only girl he'd ever truly cared about? It took a few minutes to calm his inner self and realize that he was misreading the situation. She'd only said he had to figure things out for himself before they could talk again. And she was right. His thoughts and feelings were all in a turmoil.

The hour wasn't exactly late, but all the recent travel had exhausted him. Sleep, he believed, would go a long way towards revitalizing him, and hopefully get rid of all the angst and terror he'd picked up over the weekend.

Except sleep didn't come. He spent the entire night tossing and turning, reliving the marital horrors he'd witnessed.

In the meanwhile, Ellie was a combination of cross and anxious. The recent uncertainty had only surfaced as a result of visiting Hugh's sisters and seeing their lives up close for the first time. They didn't have wonderful, happy marriages. But surely Hugh understood that the problem was their own brokenness, playing out in a broken world. They didn't have what he and she had, what they needed to deal with their despairing situations effectively.

But whatever had passed between Hugh and Larry had been heavy enough to plant serious doubts. Hugh seemed very worried that the wonderful love they felt for each other now would wane into boredom, even dissatisfaction. Ellie didn't believe it would ever come to that.

On the other hand, the future didn't come with guarantees. She got that, too.

Upon returning home, she hurriedly undressed and dropped into the big armchair clad in her nightclothes and chenille housecoat. There, she sat thinking for a long time. She imagined Jesus sitting in the corner of the couch as she often did, waiting for her to speak about what was on her heart.

"You know everything, Lord. I don't have to spell it out to You," she finally said. "What I ask is that You meet Hugh in his time of doubt and give him the reassurance he needs. Perhaps You're allowing this as a time of testing, the way You tested Job. Please see to it that he comes through intact. Give him the help he needs. Increase his faith. And by the way, what should I do in the meantime?"

Despite listening earnestly for what seemed like a long time, it didn't yield any great insights. So she finished her prayer.

"I take it that I should do nothing except wait it out."

On that note, Ellie went straight to bed.

⁓

On Monday morning, she got up refreshed and resumed her routine of reading the Bible and journaling. She took her time with it and wasn't surprised when Hugh didn't show up to join her.

Later she went into Swan River early and made arrangements to have the sheep painting reframed to suit the décor of the little house. She then began her first shift at the Swan River hospital at 7:00 p.m. It was a good evening. She enjoyed being a nurse again and had a good time with her coworkers.

On Tuesday, she slept a good part of the day and afterwards caught up on her soul work. She hoped Hugh would come by, but when he didn't she began to read a novel to distract her from thinking and pining after him too much.

It mostly worked, but not entirely.

~

Hugh had a hard time deciding what to do with himself. He'd already been to all the businesses that hired mechanics. There seemed little point in hitting the streets again unless he tried for a different kind of job altogether and he wasn't ready to change course yet.

The lateness of the morning suggested that Ellie would have completed her time of soul work. Suddenly he missed her painfully. Reading the Bible was something he had specifically asked to do together, and here he was baling on her.

His own Bible lay on top of his dresser. Hugh picked it up and tried to read the next chapter where they had left off. It wasn't the same. He had trouble focusing. The printed words seemed flat and meaningless.

Soon the Bible was closed and returned to the top of his dresser.

Donning a jean jacket, he coddiwompled around the yard. The barn, he noticed, had a more pronounced sag than when he'd first arrived in June. Ellie loved that old barn and wished for it to be preserved as a grand symbol of bygone days. But Hugh wasn't in the least interested. That ancient barn was one of the few places where he'd fled to hide from his cruel father. Yes, the Fischers could be cruel. They were inclined to be controlling, he remembered Larry saying.

He was a Fischer...

The walkabout took him into the bush behind the new house where so many outdated, broken, and useless bits and pieces of trash had been thrown away over the past many years. It was an embarrassing mess, and even dangerous. Twice he tripped, nearly falling over.

Enough is enough, he told himself. *It's time to clean this place up*.

The old grain truck fired up immediately, thanks to the repairs and maintenance service he'd given it during the summer. He backed it to the edge of the bush and immediately began throwing metal trash into the box. Rolls of rusted, brittle barbed wire, old syrup pails, tin cans, paint pails, dairy milk and cream cans, barrels, broken tools, and parts of motors were all heaved into the back of the truck. Burnables and glass got pitched into a pit behind the big shed to be burnt and buried later.

Even here, Ellie's voice seemed to ring in his ears. "Check all containers before you throw them away. Could be hidden treasure inside..."

And throughout all this hard work, Hugh tried to come to terms with the subject of marriage, specifically the one he had proposed himself.

The conclusions he drew towards the end of the week weren't much different than his assessment after visiting his sisters: marriages began on a sweet and exciting note but faded over time into boredom or downright unhappiness.

He couldn't see how it could be worth the trouble. The decline appeared to be inevitable, even if some people did seem to make it work. Like Rob and Sarah, for example. He couldn't think of any other couple that seemed to enjoy each other like they did. Even the Turners seemed to have a ho-hum quality to their lives when he thought about it.

By all appearances, most couples seemed to be locked in relationships that were miserable at worst and monotonous at best... far from the glow and warm fuzzies they'd had at the beginning of their union.

And from what he'd seen in his own family, he concluded the Fischers certainly weren't good candidates for marriage.

~

Wednesday found Ellie antsy. After trying to focus on more soul work, which was increasingly difficult, she gave up.

"Jesus, I need to talk to You with skin on."

The closest she could come to that was to talk with someone wise in the Lord. She thought of her beloved Aunt Ruth but decided she wasn't the right one today. Sarah came to mind, but Ellie decided against it after further consideration.

Who else?

Darcey. Of course.

She put in a call to her friend.

Darcey met Ellie at the door when she arrived and they went directly into Darcey's neat-as-a-pin kitchen where the water in the kettle was already boiled to fix a cup of tea. Without asking, Darcey began to concoct a fruity beverage that included cinnamon and cloves. Sweetened with honey, it was one of the most delicious, comforting tisanes Ellie had ever tasted.

As soon as Darcey sat down to join her, Ellie began to sob.

"I take it there's been a lover's quarrel," said Darcey in her practical and unemotionally observant way.

"Not exactly, but you're warm."

She told Darcey about their visits to Hugh's sisters; how different the girls were and yet how obviously troubled were their marriages. She finished the story by recounting their confrontation in the little house, and her telling him not to talk to her until he'd sorted himself out. Now she hadn't seen or heard from him since and was beginning to worry.

"You told him right," said Darcey. "Marriage is a pee-or-get-off-the-pot kind of commitment. One of the hardest things we women sometimes have to do is let people stew in their own juices. Seriously. We always want to fix everyone! You know, kiss it and make it all better. Doesn't work for everything."

"I understand and agree with you." Ellie sniffled. "But I didn't think it would take him three days to smell the coffee and come around."

"I suspect most guys go through this second-guessing thing. My Tony did, too, but in our case it was the morning after our wedding night."

Ellie's eyes went wide.

"Oh yeah! That was a shocker for me, I'll tell you," said Darcey. "I thought it meant I was a complete disappointment to him. Turned out it wasn't about me at all. It was just that he'd suddenly realized what a big responsibility he'd taken on and it scared him a little. He worried he wouldn't make a good husband and father, or provide well enough. He got over it, but it was a tough couple of days at first."

"So you think this is normal?"

"Yes, I do."

"And you think I should…"

"Leave him alone to think it through for himself. Your marriage won't go well if you have to twist his arm into doing it."

"What if he doesn't come around?" Ellie asked. "What if he talks himself out of it?"

"I suppose it's a risk, but I greatly doubt it. I've got a bead on your man, Ellie. He'll come around, even if it's later instead of sooner. That guy is crazy about you. My guess is seeing his sisters has reminded him of how much baggage he inherited from his dysfunctional family. It's more than he realized. Keep praying and wait patiently for the Lord." Darcey patted Ellie's arm. "Also, keep busy while you wait. You won't be as tempted to interfere with the process."

Hugh stuck with the task of clearing out the trash for three more days. It ended up filling the big old truck box three times and he was paid per ton when he offloaded it at the scrap metal yard. Besides covering the gas, it provided a bit of extra pocket money, a help when no other source of income was yet in sight.

By the end of Thursday, the job was mostly done. Occasionally he stumbled on a glass jar he had missed, or a strip of metal partly buried in the ground, but the great bulk of it had been removed. He had thought of Ellie many times during the process, including how pleased she would be. The tidied bush was really quite attractive. The rock pile actually seemed like a nice feature now.

Even so, he hadn't found any money. If his pa really had hidden his moonshine cash, he'd done it brilliantly. Hugh couldn't think of any more plausible area in which to look for it.

On Friday morning, Hugh took the final load of scrap metal to the recycling yard. Upon returning, he nearly drove the few yards further to look in on Ellie. To say that he missed her would be the understatement of understatements.

But her last words continued to ring in his ears: *"Don't come to me until you get this figured out."*

He believed he had reached a right but unhappy conclusion. He would let Ellie go. He'd gone from harbouring a negative expectation of marriage to believing he, as a product of Fred and Alice Fischer, would turn out to be a bad mate. Ellie deserved so much better than the likes of him. For all her talk about God changing lives, he didn't believe he had what it took to be a good husband and father.

And yet, as he thought these things, he felt sorely troubled. His decision brought no peace. By the time he had put the big farm truck away, he felt he was going to be physically sick.

It was lunchtime and he couldn't eat. He lay on his bed hoping to catch a nap, but the lack of diversion just brought more intense turbulence to his thoughts and feelings.

Suddenly he remembered that they were supposed to be attending their first premarital counselling session with Pastor Leland that afternoon. That was in a half-hour's time!

Hugh leapt to his feet and quickly showered. In fifteen minutes, he left the house, turned towards Minitonas, and raced to make it on time to the appointment—without Ellie. His intention was to explain to the pastor that they wouldn't be getting married after all, and why.

⌒

After receiving comfort and encouragement from Darcey, Ellie managed to get through the rest of Wednesday, Thursday, and Friday morning without fretting too much. She carried on with her morning routine, worked another shift at the hospital, sprayed more layers of navy paint on the three chairs she'd brought to the shop, and carried out other small chores.

However, her state of mind began to break down Friday afternoon. Whatever Hugh had to work through, she nevertheless believed he would come to get her for their first premarital counselling session. In anticipation, she showered and dressed.

The minutes ticked by and Hugh didn't show. The time of the appointment passed and Ellie began to feel the stirrings of panic. At a quarter past the hour, she pursed her lips and called his house.

No answer.

What could it mean?

At half past the hour, she slumped into her sweet spot—the great comfy armchair.

I'm sure there's a good explanation, she told herself, but the cold fear in her heart grew colder by the minute.

"Talk to me, Jesus," she cried, tears spilling over onto her cheeks. "Something must be terribly wrong. Help Hugh overcome his fears and wrong thinking and come back to me. Help *me* understand and be patient. Help me overcome my fears, because I am afraid. Something isn't right here. *Please* help."

Despite her desperate prayer, Ellie sobbed for a good long while. Her chest felt pinched at its core.

Suppertime came, but she couldn't eat. Her stomach felt so tight that she was sure she couldn't swallow so much as a cup of weak tea.

Hugh didn't show in the evening, either, which produced a fresh round of sobs. There was still no answer on the phone at his house.

About 8:00 p.m., Ellie changed into loungewear, having arrived at a conclusion. It was obvious now that Hugh was breaking up with her. Sorting out his fears of relationship and marriage had come to this.

She would have to face this new reality bravely. Removing the silver band on her left hand, she again read the inscription. After sighing deeply, she placed it in her jewellery box. Immediately her hand felt naked.

Get used to it, she told herself.

There was no place to go except back to the living room, but instead of collapsing back into the armchair she sat on the couch, in the same spot where Hugh usually parked himself.

"Lord, I need comfort," she prayed. "Lots of it."

It always helped the soul when soft instrumental music played in the background. She got up and put on a stack of records, turning the volume down low.

To distract herself from her sorrow, Ellie decided to play a childhood game. She picked up her Bible and brought it to the sofa. Holding the book loosely by its spine, she allowed it to fall open and then put her finger on the page. The first couple of times yielded no meaningful verses.

However, on the third try Ellie gasped at how appropriately the selected passage fit with her pain and anxiety. Her finger had landed on Isaiah 50:10: *"All of you that honor the Lord and obey the words of his servant, the path you walk may be dark indeed, but trust in the Lord, rely on your God."*[2]

"That's me, Jesus," croaked Ellie. "I'm the one who honours You, who wants to obey You in everything, but I feel like I'm drowning in darkness. Increase my faith to trust You implicitly."

A wee measure of peace returned, like a tiny light at the end of a long tunnel.

~

It was after nine and the last six hours spent with Pastor Leland had been some of the most liberating of Hugh's life. He could hardly wait to tell Ellie about it, and to be with her. The terrible week-long battle for his mind and soul was over; the fixation on wrong conclusions, broken.

He needed to restore himself with Ellie and quickly. He was pretty sure his avoidance had hurt her deeply enough that she'd want to be done with him. Another minute could not be wasted.

---

[2] GNT.

Hugh raced up the road to Bauman Farms, parked in front of the house, and cut the motor. Slightly worried he might be rejected at the door if he knocked first, he slipped in quietly and tiptoed towards the living room.

He stopped at the entrance. Ellie was sitting in her sweet spot, sipping from a mug with one of her journals open on her lap. She seemed to be at peace, but her countenance looked sad. Her face was blotchy, her eyes puffed, and her nose a bright pink. Instead of writing, she was reading one of her entries. To Hugh, she had never appeared more vulnerable, or more beautiful, and he wanted very much to hold her tight.

Ellie must have felt his gaze because she looked up and saw him there, standing still in the entrance. Without a reaction, she sighed and looked back down at her journal.

A few seconds later, though, she looked up at him again, this time with a puzzled expression.

"It's really me," said Hugh barely above a whisper.

Ellie gasped. "You scared me! I thought you were a figment."

He shifted his weight, uncertain whether it was all right to rush in and collect her in his arms as he ached to do.

"I'm so sorry I took so long to get my act together," he stammered, choked with emotion. He looked into Ellie's tear-filled eyes. "I almost gave up on us, but some timely help from a wise man saved the day for me... for us. I've been a fool, and a jerk, and I'm sincerely sorry. Will you take me back, Ellie?"

Ellie was too full of emotions to speak right away—and when she did, she didn't answer with a yes.

"When you didn't come for me this afternoon, I was sure that meant you wanted to break up," she said. "I even took off the ring you gave me."

"If you'll just give me another chance..."

"Yes. Yes, of course I will. I was rereading what I wrote in my journal not so long ago, back when I realized... when we both realized we were meant to be together. You were of the same mind. I don't know how in the world you got knocked off-course so quickly and thoroughly."

"The short answer is, I was bedevilled," said Hugh ruefully. "Can I come to you now?"

Ellie nodded and rose from her seat. Then Hugh gathered her into his arms for a long hold.

A few moments later, Ellie pulled away. "I'm ready to hear all about it."

They sat on the couch, each turned towards the other so Ellie could catch every word and gesture as Hugh recounted the multiple layers of turmoil he had strained under all week. He told her about his appointment with Pastor Leland, who had asked all sorts of pertinent questions. Before Hugh had known it, he'd shared the whole story of his family history, his personal pain, and that of his sisters, admitting to his fears about marriage and husbanding as well as his insecurities. And when he was done, the pastor had taken his Bible to show him, verse by verse, the antidote to all the lies that had been whispered into Hugh's mind.

"He showed me the strategies by which I'd been deceived... by the same devil that wreaked havoc with my grandparents, parents, and now us siblings, too," Hugh breathed. "He also showed me that as a believer in Jesus Christ I can resist him, that I can live as a new creation, cut free from all the sin that has formerly enslaved me. He showed me John 8:36, which says, *'So if the Son makes you free, you will be free indeed.'*[3] I don't have to worry about turning into another Frederick Fischer. God's Spirit living within me will make me into a new person over time, as I trust Him."

Hugh fell into silence, fully relieved of the scepticisms Ellie had previously heard in him.

"Pastor also said that every marriage lived out God's way is guaranteed to be successful and happy," he continued after a few moments. "Actually, a lot of what he told me was very similar to what you said when I expressed my doubts."

---

[3] RSV.

"I'm too nice a girl to rub it in your face," teased Ellie, getting up.

She left the room and returned with the silver band back on her finger. It was getting late, but both seemed to need a little canoodling before saying good night.

Six

"PUT ON SOME good walking shoes," said Hugh the next morning after they had concluded their soul work. "I've got something to show you."

They walked back to his place, holding hands and enjoying the fall sunshine and refreshing crisp air. Ellie wanted to know what he intended to show her, but he promised she would know soon enough, that the surprise was worth waiting for.

Once they turned towards the bush, Ellie quickly figured out what it was. The changes were immediately visible—and impressive.

"Wow! What a difference this makes," she praised. "Bravo, Hugh-mungous! What made you do it?"

"I went at it while trying to work out all those doubts that were eating at me. The effort put a little extra cash in my pocket, too. I took all the metal to the recycling yard. I also saved some unbroken glass jars in case you're interested."

He showed her the small collection that he'd neatly piled up next to a stump near the edge of the bush.

"Hmmm! There are some interesting shapes there. Thank you for thinking of me."

Ellie pointed to a heap of a dozen or more discarded rubber tires. "What are you going to do with that?"

"Destined for the nuisance grounds. Unless… are you going to tell me you have a use for them?" Hugh suddenly felt apprehensive.

Ellie laughed. "No, dearest. I have no creative ideas for how to reuse old tires, though I'm sure there are those who do."

They wandered around the yard enjoying the freedom to walk about without tripping or stumbling. On an impulse, Ellie made a dash for it and ran up the rock pile. She stood on top, looking down on Hugh.

"Be careful not to turn your ankle," warned Hugh.

"I'm the queen of the castle!"

"But I'm the king wherever…"

Ellie found herself suddenly gazing westward. "What's that over there?"

"I don't know what you're looking at."

"Maybe you can't see it at ground level. Come up here."

Hugh inhaled deeply but backed up a few feet. Then he took off running up the rock pile to stand on top with Ellie. She pointed to a rather dark spot approximately five hundred feet away to the west.

"It just looks like a thicket to me," said Hugh.

"Let's check it out."

Getting down off the pile of boulders was trickier than running up. The stones were loose and inclined to move unstably.

As they got close to the so-called thicket, they realized that the dark spot was actually some kind of solid object. Not until they got up close did they realize it was an abandoned vehicle. Hugh brushed away the shrubbery and saplings that had grown up around it and then let out a low whistle.

"I think we just found something super cool," said Hugh, a little awed.

"No kidding. This is a really old relic. I bet forty years or more. Can you determine the make and model?"

"Not yet. And I'm not familiar with vintage vehicles, generally speaking." Hugh continued to walk around the vehicle, quickly realizing that it was a half-ton truck. He brushed away the growth hemming it in. "It's actually in pretty good shape. No broken windows. It's rusted, but not all the way through the metal."

Ellie looked more closely. "The remaining paint shows black fenders and running board, with a green body. I bet it was very handsome when new."

"Plymouth," announced Hugh, running his hand over the tailgate. "It's impressed in the metal."

He went around to the driver's side and tried to open the door. It wouldn't budge.

"I'll try the passenger side," said Ellie.

The door creaked and complained, but it did open. She slid inside and then scooched over to the centre of the bench because Hugh was right behind her.

"This is amazing," said Hugh. "I had no idea these old relics were back here. My granddad must have used them and my pa shoved them back here when they weren't worth running anymore. I've never explored these parts of the bush in all my years out here as a kid. Never bothered to go any further than the pond."

Ellie pointed straight ahead. "Look, there's something else over there."

They left the half-ton and made their way over to what turned out to be an early model tractor with steel wheels front and back. The hood label read "McCormick Deering 10 20," although it was badly rusted.

Hugh closely examined the tractor. "The weather has all but ruined it. But such as it is, all the parts seem intact." His voice rose in excitement. "Enough to do an autopsy, if you get my drift."

Ellie turned to stare at him. She hadn't heard him speak in enthusiastic tones like this before. He was touching the machine here and there like a boy who had just opened a birthday present and discovered his favourite, wish-come-true toy.

She also saw something else. "Look behind you," said Ellie.

Approximately thirty feet away sat another abandoned vehicle, parked close to an ancient Manitoba maple. The tree was clearly half-dead and some of its large branches had broken off and fallen onto the rusting vintage car, causing considerable damage to the roof especially. Despite that, it piqued Hugh's interest.

"This one says 'Studebaker.' I think it's salvageable." He looked up into Ellie's face and found her staring at him with a funny look on her face. "What?"

"I think I'm looking at a man falling in love," said Ellie with something like disbelief. "Is it possible I might be losing my man to another sweetheart, that I'll merely be his mistress?"

"Nah, never." It sounded unconvincing. "The better explanation is that I've woken to the value and pleasure of old things, kind of like you are to old furniture and antiques. I think these old automobiles must have belonged to my granddad. I swear they weren't around the yard when I was a kid."

"I've never seen that adoring look in your eyes for me. You're in love with these old-timers. Admit it!"

Ellie reached out to poke Hugh in the ribs, but he skillfully evaded her. She tried again, and again he dodged her.

"You're not even denying it!"

Hugh chuckled and scooted to the left. Ellie ran after him and a short game of tag ensued. She pursued him amongst and around the trees and discarded vehicles.

At last, he caught her.

"I'm tired out," said Hugh panting, holding her at arm's length so she couldn't poke or tickle him. "Let's not compare apples to oranges, okay? You are the love of my life. But what just happened is the discovery of a new hobby I intend to have. I'm a mechanic and love what I do. I intend to get these vehicles out of here somehow and do my best to restore them. They'll make beautiful collector items. Kind of like you took the old sofa set from the previous house and are having it restored. Fair?"

"Fair." Ellie had stopped struggling to poke him. "I hope you realize you just locked onto an expensive hobby, though. Lots of guys are interested in vintage vehicles, but they can't afford to restore them as they would like to."

"I promise you I'll be responsible. I won't be selfish with money or spend the grocery budget on parts. Besides, I have most of the skills needed to tear these beasts apart and rebuild them. Lots of the expense goes to paying others. I want to do as much as I can myself. Capiche?"

"Capiche." Ellie nodded and smiled. "Truthfully, I think these are cool finds. I'm happy you'll have a hobby that fits with your interests and skills."

"Thank you," said Hugh relieved, and grateful for her support. "I love you."

"Love you, too." She kissed his cheek.

"Let's sit in the Plymouth again before we go back."

When they reached the old pickup, Hugh entered first, sliding across the seat to the driver's position. He immediately began testing the steering wheel and clutch for freedom of movement.

"Hey!" he cried happily. "The key is still in the ignition. Bonus!"

Ellie slid in, too, but stayed on the passenger end of the bench. Suddenly curious, she pulled down the cover of the glove compartment. There sat a tin box. It was primarily yellow with an image of a tall ship in full sail embossed on the top.

"Whoa. What's this?" She lifted out the box for Hugh to see. Instantly, they each got the same hunch at the same time. "Do you suppose…"

"I do," finished Hugh. "But let's check it out at home."

Seven

HUGH CARRIED THE small tin box into the house and set it on the table. There was only the black captain's chair on which to sit.

"Let's get the other chairs from the shop so we both can sit when you open it," Ellie suggested.

Hugh looked at her, puzzled. "I would have thought you couldn't wait to see the contents."

"I'm very curious. And also a bit nervous. I think I need a minute to prepare myself for a major disclosure. That's all."

"I think you're being weird. It's just a tin box, but…"

They climbed into Hugh's truck and drove to the Baumans' shop. They set the three newly painted navy chairs in the back of the truck. Then Ellie decided the other pieces destined for the new little house may as well go, too. They added the tall side table Ellie had refinished, along with the lamp found at the thrift shop. She also talked Hugh into bringing back the steamer trunk from her room.

"How many times have I handled this trunk now?" asked Hugh, annoyed.

"I don't know. Three, maybe four. Why does it matter?"

"Well, this will be the last time."

"Someday we're going to get it opened up. I bet we'll find wonderful, fascinating curiosities and you'll be so glad you didn't automatically destroy them."

Hugh just grunted.

It only took a few minutes for them to bring the pieces into the house. Ellie found the place already somewhat crowded, even without the impending sofa and chair. She sighed and reminded herself that though the space would be tight, it would also be beautiful and cozy.

Hugh sat down and placed his hands on the yellow tin, about to open it.

"Wait!" halted Ellie. "How about I make us some coffee first?"

"What? Seriously? I don't understand why you keep stalling, Ella-buster."

"I just sense this is a major discovery. It could turn out to be really wonderful, or heartbreakingly bad. I need a minute to prepare myself. A cuppa java will help."

She pulled out Hugh's percolator and got a half-pot brewing while Hugh drummed his fingers on the table. The truth was, he was also a mite nervous as to the contents of the box. Mostly he was afraid of being disappointed. In the past, anything to do with his pa had disheartened him, to say the least.

Within a few minutes, Ellie set a pair of mugs filled with black coffee on the table, then sat down. She took a deep breath, rubbed her hands together, and exhaled. "Okay. I'm ready."

The snug lid yielded to Hugh's pressure. When he pried it up, what he saw caused him to let out a low-whistled breath.

"What do you know?" he said, astounded. "Tipper told the truth. We found us some pot o' gold!"

Inside were two thick rolls of paper money secured with elastic bands. Below were a few loose bills, mostly in denominations of twenty dollars. Hugh lifted out the cash and found a small spiral notebook underneath, alongside a couple of ballpoint pens.

Ellie watched as Hugh quietly counted the loose bills first. While he took apart one of the elastic bound rolls and began to count the rolled-up notes, Ellie picked up the notebook and began to flip the pages. They appeared to record the names of Freddie's customers. The used pages took up approximately half of the notebook—and if the dates were anything to go by, Fred Fischer had started selling moonshine in 1965. His accounting had been ultra simple. At the top of each page was printed the name of the customer. Below was a date, presumably when the customer placed an order. Underneath the date was another number, such as 20, 12, or 6, or the word *ALL*. Ellie surmised that it reflected the quantity ordered. Below that was another date, usually weeks later, with a checkmark. This must represent the day the transaction had been completed.

Ellie continued to flip through the notebook, curious whether she would recognize any of the names. She noted Tipper LW, Chiclets RA, Monster BS, Hoss IK, Butch DD, and deduced these were the nicknames of Freddie's cronies. The letters probably represented the initials of their given names; in Tipper's case, his name was Leonard Wallen—a fit for LW.

Quite a few other names were listed in the book's pages, most of which were meaningless to Ellie, but two of them she recognized. She let out a small gasp.

"What did you find?" asked Hugh, still organizing the ten, twenty, and fifty-dollar bills.

"I'm sure this is Fred's customer list. Tipper is in here, and so are some other names. Members of the band they rode with, I suppose." She hesitated. "But I'm troubled by these two..."

"Why?"

"They're the names of men who attend the First Baptist Church in Minitonas. One of them is Otto Hoffman, who happens to sit on the elder board. His wife Agnes was one of my mother's good friends. The other is Al Weber. I only know him as someone who sang in the choir. Since I came home, I've seen him serving as one of the ushers."

"And you're wondering why good Christian men would be doing illegal business with my pa."

"Exactly. Also, why would they be buying up alcohol? From these records, I surmise they each bought twenty-four bottles. Are they closet drunks? Do their wives know? How could they not? Booze stinks, not to mention the other highly noticeable side effects of drinking..."

She trailed off, deep in thought, before continuing. "And Baptists frown on using alcohol. If you press them, they admit that the Bible doesn't go so far as to forbid it, but they'll point out the many warnings regarding drunkenness. A good Baptist will tell you that the best way to avoid alcohol-related trouble is to steer clear of it altogether."

She looked up.

"This can't be good," she murmured.

Hugh seemed much more sanguine about the situation. "Are you at all curious about the total amount of cash stashed in this tin?"

"Of course I am."

"The rolls contain one thousand dollars each, and the loose bills come to $440. That's $2,440. It'll beef up the fund to build my shop nicely."

"Excuse me!" said Ellie rather sharply.

"Now what?"

Ellie averted her eyes away from the table.

"Right," said Hugh with a sigh. "My bride wants a proper kitchen."

~

Sunday was Thanksgiving and the FBC church was decked out in attractively arranged garden produce that included potatoes, pumpkins, squash, carrots, beets, onions, and sheaves of wheat. Together with the jars of home-canned goods, they created a festive ambience.

Pastor Leland delivered a stirring message on the importance of being a thankful people, even if a person finds themself in unwelcome circumstances. After all, the Bible doesn't say one has to be thankful *for* everything; rather, we are to be thankful *in* the midst of all circumstances.

The message was followed by a churchwide potluck dinner. The church ladies roasted turkeys, boiled potatoes for mashing, and made bread stuffing in the church kitchen. Rows of tables were set up in the large basement with long strips of newsprint in lieu of tablecloths. Dry, colourful fall leaves were sprinkled down the centre of each table.

Happy chatter filled the air as people loaded their plates from the huge, delicious buffet.

Before going to lunch, Hugh sought out some of his new FBC friends to talk about the discoveries of the three old relics in the backwoods of his property. The guys showed keen interest and in turn cited the names and years of some of their own relics, compliments of their forebearers. They had in common a desire to restore the old vehicles into showpieces and quickly agreed on a loose pact to help each other by sharing their skills and brawn. "If you scratch my back, I'll scratch yours…"

In the meantime, Ellie sought out Darcey, her go-to person anytime she wanted information or a recommendation. The woman seemed to know something about everything.

It wasn't hard to spot her taller-than-average friend.

"How's it going, girlfriend?" greeted Ellie. She reached out to hold baby Abigail so Darcey could retie the belt on one of her little girls' dresses.

"Thanks," said Darcey. "I'm doing great for a mama who averages about four hours sleep per night. Abby's teething and fusses a lot. I'm sorely tempted to buy a bottle of cherry brandy and feed it to her undiluted just to knock her out for a while. But there's probably a rule somewhere that states it's unlawful to give infants alcohol. And we all know what an upstanding pillar of the community I am! I wouldn't actually do it, of course. Just wishing… in fact, I wouldn't have come out today at all except for the lunch. I don't have to cook! I know very well I'm blathering on and on, by the way, and that's because I'm jolly tired. That's how I am. Thanks for asking. How about you?"

Ellie giggled at her friend's whinge but also sympathized with her.

"If I didn't have to work tonight, I'd take your girls off your hands for a few hours this afternoon so you could get in a nap," said Ellie. "But I have a question. Do you know anyone who builds kitchen cabinets?"

Darcey raised her eyebrows. "You've seen my kitchen cabinets, haven't you?"

Ellie nodded.

"My Tony built them, off my measurements and wish list," said Darcey. "He builds well. Not too slow. He's fussy and takes pride in his work."

"Can we afford Tony's rates?"

"He'll be cheaper to work with than a professional. If you give him the job, I'm sure you won't be disappointed. And it'll be the answer to my prayer for extra spending money this Christmas."

"Then let's see what he has to say," said Ellie.

By the time Hugh and Ellie had gotten their meal and joined Rob, Sarah, and the kids, the family was finished eating and ready to leave. They hung around long enough for Sarah to remind Ellie that they should get together soon and make wedding plans, to which Ellie agreed. Rob also piped up; he wanted to meet with her to attend to some family business.

Family business? Ellie wondered. *What's that about?*

Rob had sounded abrupt. She hoped she wasn't in trouble with him.

Before they could leave, however, Tony Unger caught Ellie at the church's front doors.

"I hear you want a kitchen built," he said.

Ellie smiled. "Wow! News sure travels fast."

"No grass grows under your feet, does it." Hugh smirked wryly as he shook his head.

"What did you have in mind?" Tony asked.

"Would you like to come by the house at Hugh's farm?" suggested Ellie. "We can talk about it there."

Within the hour, Tony had taken all the measurements and Ellie produced a quick sketch of what she wanted. For the cabinet doors, they agreed on a Shaker style using weathered barnwood siding.

Hugh had mixed feelings about this. It meant more hard labour on his part. He would have to carefully remove the barn boards so they wouldn't split, and Tony suggested there was bound to be a lot of waste in choosing the best parts of the old wood. Hugh was sick of demolishing old buildings by hand, and he really tired of having to salvage the wood.

On the other hand, it reduced the amount of cash outlay. In light of their future building and vehicle restoration projects, he was happy for a way to save a few dollars.

Although reluctant, Hugh agreed to supply Tony with a stack of barnwood. He had time on his hands for such work. Upon seeing Ellie's hopeful face, he really did want to please her.

Eight

ELLIE'S MEETING WITH Rob and Sarah couldn't happen sooner than Tuesday because of her hospital shifts. Sarah sweetened the pot by inviting her and Hugh to stay for dinner. That way, they'd have lots of time to discuss the upcoming wedding.

They arrived late in the afternoon on Tuesday, after Ellie had caught up on much-needed sleep and Hugh dropped off a large stack of barnwood at the Unger residence. While at the Ungers', Darcey had shown Ellie more refined drawings of the kitchen cabinets, based on Ellie's quick sketch, complete with measurements and other custom details.

"I find that with men, you have to spell everything out," said Darcey. "They seldom have the imagination to come up with the little details, the ones that make the difference between something that's efficient and something that's frustrating, between attractive and downright ugly."

"That might be because they don't use a kitchen themselves," Ellie replied. "At least, not much."

"Point taken. But honestly, I totally get why God said, *'It is not good for the man to live alone.'*"[4]

Ellie chuckled. "We're not so good by ourselves, either. I think the conclusion is: two halves make a whole."

---

[4] Genesis 2:18, GNT.

"Of course. Be that as it may, you'll soon discover that they need training in common sense. A few months ago, for example, I left the house early to go to an appointment. I left Tony in charge of the girls and told him to give them breakfast when they got up. I thought that was self-explanatory. When I got home, their hands and faces were covered in chocolate! He had given them a piece of the oatmeal chocolate chip snacking cake I'd made the day before. What did he think he was doing? His answer? He knew the cake was made with many breakfast staples—oatmeal, eggs, milk, and flour... so why not cake for breakfast?"

Ellie let out a peal of laughter. "I get your point, girlfriend, but I follow his logic, too. I confess I've eaten oatmeal cookies and called it breakfast."

"Then there was the time I left him with the baby so I could have a couple of hours to myself shopping. I came home and found Abigail's diaper was so wet, her back teeth must have been floating. Had her diaper been any wetter, she'd have had to tread water! I said, 'Tony, love, why didn't you change her diaper?' Without a word of a lie, he looked me straight in the face and said, 'The box says each one is good for thirty pounds.'"

Ellie laughed outright, but Darcey maintained a straight face.

"A couple of weeks ago, I sent Tony to the grocery store to pick up a few things for me. I itemized what I needed so the list wouldn't be confusing..."

Darcey sighed before continuing while Ellie waited for the other shoe to drop.

"He came home an hour later. It took three trips to unload the van. Altogether he brought in one jug of milk, two bottles of vanilla, three packages of sugar, four cartons of eggs, and five sacks of flour! My point is, you can't assume a man knows what you want or expect."

Ellie went into another paroxysm of laughter. She wasn't sure the generalization held true in all cases, but before she could comment Tony and Hugh came into the house. Darcey promptly ended her little lesson on the idiosyncrasies of men.

~

When the kids got home from school at Rob and Sarah's, they immediately descended on Hugh and Ellie. Hugh and Trevor went into the living room where Rob was reading the latest copy of *The Western Producer*. Ellie and the girls veered into the kitchen.

"Is it really true, Aunty Ellie, that Beanie and I get to be in your wedding?" asked Charlotte excitedly.

"It wouldn't be my dream wedding without you," Ellie assured her.

"What kind of fancy dresses will we get to wear?"

"Don't know yet. Maybe you have a suggestion?"

Charlotte cooed. "Something that looks as elegant as a princess!"

Sarah let out a little chuckle from where she was peeling potatoes at the kitchen sink. It drew Ellie's attention.

"You've changed your hair," said Ellie to her sister-in-law. "The style looks good on you. Makes you look younger, somehow. Not that you looked old before. Just sayin'."

Sarah's hair had just that morning been cut and styled into an inverted bob. Although she was almost forty, Ellie felt she could pass for years younger. Her dark brown eyes complemented her brown hair that had yet to show any grey. She was a little heavier set than she'd been on her wedding day, but she still maintained a shapely figure. Her personal style was conservative, made up of clothing that fit without being too revealing. She favoured solid colours over prints.

Kind of like my own preferences, Ellie mused.

"I'd like to think I'm not completely old-fashioned," said Sarah. "Girls, set the table please. As soon as the potatoes are cooked, we can gather round and eat."

"What colour are you thinking for bridesmaids?" asked Charlotte.

Ellie pursed her lips in thought. "Well, since it is a winter wedding, I'm trying out the idea of a really pale blue... like icy blue."

"That sounds super pretty, Aunt Ellie."

Sarah turned away from the sink. "What other details have you thought out? What do you want me to look after?"

"I've spoken to everyone in the wedding party. And I've even asked Aunt Ruth if she'd be willing to make a three-tiered wedding cake. She agreed to that rather exuberantly! That's all so far."

"Well, I've made a list of all the things we need to discuss." Sarah began mashing the potatoes. "We have to make decisions regarding the meal, invitations, flowers, table decorations, favours for the guests, tuxedos, and wedding photos, among a few other things."

Ellie felt very thankful for the help. "Sarah, I'm so glad you're taking on these details. I wouldn't know where to begin. I so appreciate you."

"It's not my first rodeo! Besides, I enjoy the opportunity to put my experience to good use."

Supper was, as usual, a joyful affair anytime Hugh and Ellie were invited to join with the family. Charlotte and Beanie flanked Hugh, occasionally glancing up at him with adoring looks. Ellie found it amusing that Hugh seemed totally oblivious to the crush his soon-to-be-nieces had on him.

Trevor took his seat next to Ellie. His fun came from trying to direct Ellie's attention away from the table and play tricks on her. First he liberally sprinkled salt on her mashed potatoes. Next, after diverting her attention, he slipped his uneaten olives onto her plate. Another time he exchanged his empty water glass for her full one. She didn't seem to notice anything amiss, although the others around the table struggled not to laugh.

Only when he added a spoonful of sugar to her water glass did she finally catch him in the act. Everyone was relieved the game had been found out so they could share a big laugh over it.

After supper, Sarah brought out her wedding prep list and showed it to Ellie. They seated themselves across from each other at the kitchen table.

"I've dreamt about my wedding day since I was about Charlotte's age," Ellie said. "How amazing my bridal gown would be, the beautiful flowers I would carry, how my groom would look... tall, dark, and handsome. How pretty the church would be. I never thought about the invitations or the banquet or who would take the pictures or what music we'd play. If this is fun for you, Sarah, then you're welcome to it. I'd prefer to attend to the details I care about most."

"Are you sure? Do you mean it?" asked Sarah, very much surprised.

"I'm sure my mom would have taken the bull by the horns and worked it all out without even consulting me…"

She then realized with a shock that her dear mom and dad were indeed out of the picture. Her chest felt a weight as heavy as stone, and her face scrunched up to give way to a fresh wave of grief. Without any forewarning, she missed her parents dreadfully and hated that they wouldn't be there to see their only daughter take one of the most life-changing, monumental steps of her existence—or meet the surprising man who had captured her heart.

"It's all right, little sister," said Sarah softly. "Cry it out if you need to. I got a little misty-eyed myself putting together this to-do list. I kept wondering how Elizabeth would do it. What would she like to see for her daughter's wedding?"

"The other thing we have to talk about is the budget." Ellie blew her nose into a facial tissue, composing herself. "I have some savings, but I had hoped to use most of that towards furnishing our home. What does the average wedding cost these days?"

Sarah seemed surprised. "Hasn't Rob talked with you about this?"
Ellie shook her head.

"Robert, could you come in here please?" called Sarah.

Seconds later, Rob came into the kitchen with Hugh following behind.

"Ready for me, are you?" Rob seated himself across from Ellie.

"Apparently you haven't told Ellie about the wedding funds your mother set aside," said Sarah.

"Ah. No, I haven't. I meant to do it all at the same time." Rob got up, left the room, and returned with an envelope in hand. He took his seat again. "We can now settle our mother's estate. The taxes and other details had to be finalized, and it's all complete now. As executor for her will, the cheque in this envelope represents your fourth. I sent our brothers' their portions by registered mail this morning."

Rob handed Ellie a sealed envelope.

"The other thing is, not long after Dad passed away, Mom set aside some money in a trust fund for you when you would marry," he continued. "She set aside five thousand dollars for wedding expenses, and another five thousand as a wedding gift so you could outfit your new home as needed. That's the amount they gave each of their sons. I put that cheque in the envelope, too."

Rob's face took on a soft, mellow expression.

"Maybe she had a premonition about dying before your wedding day. Or maybe she thought you were taking so long to find a husband that she couldn't assume she'd be around. Whatever the reason, it was thoughtful and wise of her to make a contingency plan and set aside money to cover the costs, as parents traditionally do."

Ellie's eyes began to water again.

"Mom is deeply missed tonight, Rob," said Sarah. "It's a sensitive point this evening, the folks not being here for Ellie's big day."

"May I open the envelope?" asked Ellie tentatively.

Rob nodded. "Be my guest."

Ellie tore it open from the end and pulled out a pair of cheques. The one on top included the proceeds for two wedding funds, totalling $10,000. The second one caused her mouth to fall open. She showed it to Hugh, whose eyes grew wide.

"That's pretty generous, brother. Thank you," said Ellie. "And I know exactly where I want to invest this little windfall."

"It's no thanks to me, sis," Rob replied. "Our parents did well with their farm and lived an economical lifestyle. On top of that, they went home to be with the Lord without first having to move to a seniors care home, which can be costly."

"By rights, I should tithe this money, correct?" Ellie held up her inheritance. "What about the wedding expense fund and wedding gift? Mother would have tithed the money before setting it aside, wouldn't she?"

"Absolutely. It's from our parents, and how they handled money, that I learned the secret to living a financially blessed life. I'm still not at their level of generosity, but my faith is growing steadily in that department, too. If it was me, I would tithe the money I received as income. In your case, that includes the inheritance and the wedding gift. The wedding expense fund? That represents spending dollars on Mom and Dad's behalf. That's how I see it."

Hugh looked a bit confused by all this talk of tithes. "So what exactly is a tithe?"

"Ten percent," answered Rob, Sarah, and Ellie simultaneously. They exchanged looks and smiled.

"Ten percent of what?" asked Hugh, still puzzled.

"Ten percent of the whole of your income." Seeing Hugh still did not understand, Rob paused. "You don't know what I'm talking about, do you? Here, I'll show you from scripture."

He rose and retrieved his Bible from the living room. Turning to Leviticus 27:30, he showed Hugh the passage which first laid out the principle of tithing.

"Since it was given as an item of law, it becomes a point of obedience. It's not a suggestion. Let me show you how obedience leads to a promise." Rob turned to Malachi 3:10 and read: "'*Bring the full tithes into the storehouse, that there may be food in my house; and thereby put me to the test, says the Lord of hosts, if I will not open the windows of heaven for you and pour down for you an overflowing blessing.*'[5]

"In the New Testament, Jesus affirms what Malachi recorded: '*Give, and it will be given to you; good measure, pressed down, shaken together, running over, will be put into your lap. For the measure you give will be the measure you get back.*'"[6]

Hugh looked troubled. It was dawning on him that ten percent of the money Ellie had just received and intended to give up wasn't a mere few hundred dollars, but thousands. By extension, he did a

---

[5] RSV.
[6] Luke 6:38, RSV.

quick calculation of the money that had come into his hands since he had returned to his family farm, including what he'd found in the tin his pa had squirrelled away from selling moonshine. In his case, ten percent came close to $8,000. That represented a great fortune.

Rob saw the troubled look on Hugh's face and at once understood. He also understood that his soon-to-be brother-in-law was a rookie to the faith and needed time to process God's ways, which were counter to the ways by which the rest of the world operated.

Realizing that Hugh needed encouragement, Rob thought of another verse that might help. He turned to 2 Corinthians 9:6–8.

"I can see this is a lot for you to swallow, so let me encourage you with this next passage: *'The point is this: he who sows sparingly will also reap sparingly, and he who sows bountifully will also reap bountifully. Each one must do as he has made up his mind, not reluctantly or under compulsion, for God loves a cheerful giver. And God is able to provide you with every blessing in abundance, so that you may always have enough of everything and may provide in abundance for every good work.'*[7]

"You see, because of Jesus, we don't give a portion back to God on account of being forced to by the law, which by the way is how the world operates. The world's system imposes taxes without asking, and it is considerably more than ten percent. We're invited to give back to Jesus according to our level of love for Him, according to the amount of faith we have in Him. I'm a witness that since Sarah and I started tithing, after we got married, we have *never* been short to cover the bills, never gone without having our real needs met, even in years when the crops were poor. We enjoy many blessings, just like the Word promises."

Hugh took this all in. "So, if I understand you right, if I return ten percent of my income to the Lord, He's going to give it all back with interest?"

"I don't want you to think of it in terms of cause and effect. It's not about 'If you do this, I will do that,'" said Rob. "With God, it's always

---

[7] 2 Corinthians 9:6–8, RSV.

about *relationship.* We're His children. And when His children obey Him, He delights to bless His child for their loving obedience."

Rob suddenly snapped his fingers, thinking of the perfect example to illustrate his point.

"The other day, I asked Trevor to sweep out the garage after school. When I came home for supper, I saw that he had not only swept out the garage but reorganized the shelves and thrown out everything that was broken. That he not only obeyed me but went the extra mile blessed my socks off. He doesn't know it yet..." Rob looked over his shoulder to make sure Trevor wasn't listening. "...but I'm going to return his act of obedience with a big blessing by taking him to Winnipeg one of these weekends to watch an NHL hockey game, just father and son."

Hugh nodded with understanding.

But even though he believed every word Rob said, it was still a humongous pill to swallow. He needed time to process this. It seemed to him an expensive proposition.

When he glanced at Ellie, she only responded with a slight nod, as if to say, *"Rob's right, and we will do likewise."*

The discussion ended when Sarah got up and proposed to make another pot of coffee. With that, the men returned to the living room and turned on the television to watch a sports program.

Going back to the discussion of wedding plans, Sarah and Ellie agreed to keep to Elizabeth Bauman's budget of $5,000, which seemed very doable.

"I suspect Hugh's sisters, whom I've asked to be my bridesmaids, are short on cash. So I'd like to pay for their gowns," said Ellie. "I've retained Cynthia Clifford to sew the gowns, including my dress. She does beautiful work."

"Great! Something we can at least partially cross off the list."

"Instead of renting tuxes, I'd also like to buy the groom and the groomsmen their suits. Hugh doesn't own a suit. I'd like to use this opportunity to expand his wardrobe."

"Sounds good to me," agreed Sarah. "I'll happily sew my daughters' junior bridesmaids gowns, too. I'm no slouch behind the sewing machine."

"Perfect!"

"It seems to me that if you pursue the clothing and decorations, which is where you shine, I can plan out the music, banquet, favours, invitations, and perhaps the photographer. What do you think?"

Ellie sighed with relief. "That sounds very fair. By the way, I'd like the tone of our wedding ceremony to be regal, full of pomp and circumstance. But the reception should be a great amount of fun."

After agreeing to check in with each other periodically, they joined the men in the living room.

Hugh took Ellie home around 10:00 p.m. and followed her into the house.

"I can tell you want to talk some more," said Ellie, pulling out a kitchen chair. "About money. Specifically, about tithing. Am I right?"

"Yeah. I did the calculations. Between the two of us, according to what we've been given, ten percent comes to a whopping $18,825! That's about what I spent on supplies to build my house! *Our* house."

"So? What's your point?"

"It's a lot, and we could use it for our other building projects."

"Look, you forget. We give back to God ten percent, but we get to keep and manage ninety percent! That's a great deal, partner. I already know that I want to dedicate the remaining ninety percent I've received towards us building a much larger family home. Your little house is a cute little nest for starters, but it's hardly big enough for the two of us, never mind for kids."

"And I don't know if I have enough money to build the kind of shop I want, never mind giving away $8,000 and know for sure that I'll be short."

"I want the blessed life, Hugh-bertina," she said. "I want to be obedient to the Lord and reap the benefits of being His child. I want what my parents had, and what Rob and Sarah have, not just for myself but for *us*."

She reached for her handbag, sitting in the middle of the table, and pulled out her chequebook.

"What are you going to do?" asked Hugh.

"I'm going to write out a cheque for my tithe."

In just a few minutes, she had made out three cheques. Some of the money went to FBC, because it was her home church. The other two were made out to Christian organizations Ellie was partial to—one that rehabilitated men and boys who had gone off the rails through drugs and alcohol abuse, and the other to an organization that supported women facing unplanned pregnancies. The total amount came to $10,950.

Hugh watched while she put them each in an envelope, wrote out the addresses, and licked the stamps. When she was done, she placed them in her purse, looked at Hugh, and smiled.

"All done! I look forward to the mystery of God's blessing on that act of obedience."

Hugh shook his head, impressed on the one hand, but highly reluctant on the other.

Back at his place, Hugh fetched his own chequebook from the top drawer of his dresser and set it on the table. He went through the calculations another time and found that his ten percent came to $7,875.

He recognized the tug of war in his mind: to give or not to give. It seemed ludicrous, no matter how he looked at it, to give away money for which he had a specific use.

In the end, he couldn't do it. He left the chequebook on the table and turned in to his bed.

He wanted very much to sleep, but all he got was tossing and turning. He tried to pray but felt his words bounced back to him off the ceiling.

After a few hours of this, it dawned on Hugh that the voice in his head sounded an awful lot like the voice that had caused him to doubt his commitment to Ellie, and it sounded an awful lot like the tones his father had used with him in bygone days. He remembered what Pastor Leland had shown him in the Bible: *"Your enemy, the Devil, roams around like a roaring lion, looking for someone to devour."*[8]

Midway through the night, Hugh got up, went back to the table, and wrote out a cheque to the First Baptist Church for $7,875.

"If you don't shut up, I'm going to write out a cheque for everything that's in the account!" said Hugh aloud to the dissenting voice inside his head.

After that, he went back to bed and promptly fell asleep.

~

After Hugh awoke in the morning, he stepped into his kitchen area while stretching his arms high and wide. He saw, with a start, the cheque he had written to FBC lying on the table. Immediately he had the mental image of his pa rolling over in his grave.

The voice in his head returned and told him it wasn't too late; he could rip up the cheque. No harm done. But then he remembered how easily and joyfully Ellie had given up an even greater amount. Her cheques were in sealed and stamped envelopes, ready to go out in today's mail.

On that note, he turned on his heel and brought back his wallet. He stuffed the cheque into the billfold, ate a hurried breakfast, and took off for Minitonas at five to nine.

His first stop was to the bank to rearrange some of his finances. Then he hurried over to FBC to meet with Pastor Leland. The pastor was much surprised by Hugh's early appearance.

---

[8] 1 Peter 5:8, GNT.

"I came to leave this with you," said Hugh, removing the cheque from his wallet. "I was afraid if I waited till Sunday I might talk myself out of it."

Pastor Leland raised his eyebrows. "That's very generous of you, Hugh. What's the story behind this?"

Hugh relayed everything he had learned through Rob and Ellie about tithing. Though the concept was still pretty foreign, he wanted to live a life of obedience to God and enjoy all of God's promises regarding sonship.

Pastor Leland listened carefully, smiling all the while.

"It appears to me you've passed a great test," he said once Hugh had finished speaking. "One that many longtime Christians are still hung up on. I believe God is very pleased with your act of obedience and that you will indeed be blessed for it." He paused. "I would like to add a word of clarification to what the Baumans told you."

"What would that be?" asked Hugh, puzzled.

"*Everything* you have belongs to the Lord. Not merely ten percent. Keep that in mind."

Nine

AFTER THE NOON hour, Hugh was back inside the old barn, hard at work carefully removing a few of the big posts and planks that had at one time made up the animals' stalls. Darcey Unger had called asking for more barn wood of the heavier and thicker sort for some reason. He couldn't imagine why Darcey wanted them, but she had been good to Ellie and himself. For that reason, he didn't begrudge her the request. Perhaps she was interested in a project for herself.

By midafternoon, an unfamiliar gold-coloured half-ton slowed down and turned into the driveway. Hugh heard it pull up and went outside to greet his visitor. A man about his own age stepped out and approached.

"Hello," said the man. "My name is Gerald Friesen and I've come to ask about some of the farm implements you have lined up there."

He pointed to the outdated farm equipment Hugh had parked in a row along the south end of the yard several weeks earlier.

The unexpected interest brought a smile to Hugh's face. "I'm Hugh Fischer. What can I show you?"

Hugh extended his hand for a handshake, which Gerald accepted.

"Actually, I've been eyeing that swather and baler for a few weeks now. Today I finally decided to look into it. My wife and I bought an acreage a few miles north of here this past summer. She wants to raise a flock of sheep. There's a fenced-in area for pasture and another area where I want to grow hay and bale it for winter feed. I figure I don't need big fancy equipment for just a few acres. Do the swather and baler run?"

"They do," Hugh answered. "Or at least they did. I drove them to where they're parked now. Let's go have a look."

He led Gerald to the swather first. They looked over the motor, wriggled the levers, and kicked the tires. Hugh then jumped up onto the machine and turned the key. It didn't take a lot of coaxing before the motor fired up, much to Hugh's relief and Gerald's delight.

After a few minutes of warming up the motor, Hugh demonstrated the workability of the controls and Gerald drove it around the yard. To test the baler, it had to be hitched to the tractor. It, too, passed the test of being operational.

"What are you asking for them?" asked Gerald, ready to talk business.

Hugh paused a moment. "Whatever they're worth to you. I'm renting out my land and won't be using any of the equipment. I just need them gone."

Gerald walked around the swather and baler again. "Would you take five hundred for the two?"

Hugh pursed his lips and didn't answer immediately, not wanting to appear too quick to accept.

"I suspect they're worth more, but I don't mind helping someone else get started," he finally said. "Do you need a tractor? I'd be willing to give this one up. I know for sure it runs well because I overhauled it this past summer."

"We have a small one, but it's not powerful enough to pull the baler. What would you be asking for the tractor?"

Hugh paused another moment, considering. He walked over to the front end of the tractor and lifted the cover. "Like I said, I took the motor apart in July, cleaned it up, and replaced a few parts. It runs like a charm. Take it for a drive if you like."

Gerald climbed aboard and drove a lap around the yard.

"Handles real well," he said when he pulled up next to Hugh. "I'm interested."

"I think it's easily worth three thousand," offered Hugh. "Tell you what. Give me three thousand for the tractor, five hundred for the swather and baler, and you can also have anything else that's of interest from that row of implements, no charge."

Gerald rubbed his chin. "You know, I think I'll take you up on that. You got yourself a deal!"

Both men shook hands and Gerald drove away after saying he'd come by the next day with the money.

Hugh returned to his task of pulling apart barnwood for Darcey with a heart so light and happy that he thought he might float.

～

The next morning, Ellie walked over to Hugh's farm carrying her Bible. They would carry out their time of soul work at his place today just to switch it up from always being at her place.

Hugh was expecting her, and at the time of her arrival he had the coffee percolating and was stirring up a mess of eggs, diced onion, and shredded cheese with a bit of seasoning he liked to call his secret ingredient. Strips of crispy bacon already lay on a plate lined with paper towel. He'd been cooking for himself long enough now to make a few dishes quite well. He considered himself a modern man who didn't expect that a woman had to do all the cooking all the time.

"Smells good in here," said Ellie upon entering the house.

"Good!" Hugh said, concentrating on his omelette. "I'm hoping to impress you."

Ellie quickly set the table and poured two mugs of hot coffee. At just the right moment, Hugh flipped the omelette into a perfect fold and slid it onto Ellie's plate.

"Whoa," she said. "I can eat maybe a third of this with one piece of toast. The rest is yours."

While they sorted out the portions, the telephone rang.

"Hullo," said Hugh. There followed a lengthy pause while his eyes grew wide. "My apologies, sir. I haven't been inside near the telephone much in the last couple of days... Yes, I'm still interested... I could meet with you this morning... Sure. I'm just having my breakfast, but I'll come right over after... Goodbye, sir."

"Obviously I couldn't help eavesdropping," Ellie said when he was off the phone. "That sounded like an invitation for a job interview."

Hugh looked thoughtful. "Yeah, it was. For my truck dealership in Swan River."

"It doesn't get more perfect than that, does it?" said Ellie. "But beware. Rob will razz you mercilessly if you really get on there. He's a confirmed guy for the competing dealership."

"It will go both ways!" Hugh chuckled.

They ate their breakfasts quickly. Hugh wanted to leave as soon as he gulped down the last of his coffee, but Ellie wouldn't let him.

"I see this development as an answer to prayer, honey," she said. "You told me you read Matthew while harvesting with Rob. Remember this line?" She opened her Bible to Matthew 6:33 and read. "*'Instead, be concerned above everything else with the Kingdom of God and with what he requires of you, and he will provide you with all these other things.'*[9] I want us to put God first before you go out that door. We want to know this opportunity is from Him. Capiche?"

Hugh sighed. "Capiche."

On the road, Hugh was glad he had taken the time with Ellie to prepare for the day with their new routine of soul work. His first inclination was usually to jump the gun and race away to make things happen.

He'd changed his clothes. Still casual, as becomes a mechanic, but he had a clean-cut appearance. First impressions were important, Ellie had reminded him.

---

[9] GNT.

At the dealership, he was ushered into the office of the general manager. Wayne Gilbert was a man of slightly shorter stature than Hugh, but he was easily twenty-five years older. The hair at his temples was decidedly grey and his waist included a paunch.

He welcomed Hugh with a warm handshake.

The first thing they did was review Hugh's application. Hugh produced his graduation papers and certificate of achievement. He also produced a letter of recommendation from his former boss in Winnipeg. While it wasn't flowery, it admitted that Hugh did good work on engines.

After that, Mr. Gilbert explained his situation. The wife of his head mechanic had received a promotion, but to act on it they had to move to the city. The only other mechanic in the garage was young and too inexperienced to take on the responsibilities of head mechanic.

"Do you think you can handle it?" asked Mr. Gilbert pointedly.

Part of Hugh wanted to declare confidently that he could, but instead he said, "Before I answer, how about you show me the garage and some examples of the work that goes on here?"

Mr. Gilbert seemed very pleased with this answer.

When he gave Hugh a tour of their facility, Hugh found it to have a similar setup to most other garages. However, some aspects of the job would be new to him.

Upon completion of the circuit, Mr. Gilbert led Hugh back into his office and asked his previous question again.

"I feel confident I can keep the repair division running in good order," Hugh said. "But I have to admit I have no training for the auto-body side of things."

"That wouldn't be part of your responsibilities. Someone else oversees the autobody."

With that, they began to discuss salary expectations. Hugh looked at the number Mr. Gilbert jotted on a pad of paper.

"That's fair, for a starting wage," Hugh said, nodding.

"Can you start Monday? That'll give you some time to train with our outgoing head mechanic."

"Good idea," agreed Hugh. "I have one caveat, though. I have plans to marry January 1. I'm sure I'll need some time off before and after."

"Congratulations! That shouldn't be a problem."

Hugh left the dealership feeling ecstatic. He could hardly wait to tell Ellie the good news.

Since he was already on the road, he stopped at the post office in Minitonas to clean out his mailbox. He happened to meet Rob Bauman there running the same errand.

After filling him in on all the details of scoring his dream job, Rob clapped him on the back.

"Congratulations! But did it have to be that particular dealership?"

"Yeah, Ellie warned me you have certain biases. That's okay. I won't hold it against you." Hugh smiled teasingly. "Some other good news turned up yesterday that you might find interesting."

"I'll bite."

"A guy came over and offered to buy the swather, baler, and tractor. We agreed on price and I told him he could have whatever else was useful to him."

"No kidding! Good for you. But why did you let your tractor go?" asked Rob. "You'll still have need of one living in the country."

"I want an all-purpose tractor with a front-end loader."

After this unexpected visit, Hugh hurried home to find Gerald Friesen already waiting with his truck and flatbed trailer, trying to figure out how he was going to go about transferring the newly acquired items to his own place. He greeted Hugh with a certified cheque, which Hugh accepted and promptly tucked in the breast pocket of his shirt.

Still in high spirits, he offered to help Gerald in any way he could. They managed to get a couple of the smaller implements onto the trailer, and then Hugh followed Gerald to his acreage driving the swather. They returned in Gerald's truck to take another load on the trailer, this time with Hugh following on the tractor and towing the baler. Gerald proceeded to relieve Hugh of all the old implements except the disc tillager and the combine.

~

Rob pondered Hugh's remark for wanting a tractor with a front-end loader for quite a while. He had been thinking of upgrading to a newer model, partly to keep pace with his expanding operation and partly to offset his tax bill.

A new thought came to him, and the only way to know if it was a win-win idea was to discuss the matter with the tractor salespeople in person.

The salesmen were always happy to see Rob, a repeat customer. They showed him the latest in tractors, including increased power capabilities, various new operational features, and added comfort.

As part of the discussion on price, Rob wanted to know the trade-in value for his current model with the front-end loader. The salesman cited a number and Rob went home to talk things over with Sarah.

Later, Rob tried to call Hugh. There was no answer, but he thought it likely that Hugh was just spending the evening with Ellie. Next he called the Bauman farmhouse, expecting Ellie to answer. Instead, it was Hugh who said hello after the third ring. He'd come there to pass some time in front of the television.

"Just the guy who's on my mind," said Rob. "I have a proposal. Mind if I come over and talk about it?"

"Come on down!"

Within half an hour, Rob was explaining his proposal for Hugh to buy his old front-end loader for the trade-in value. It would be considerably more expensive for Hugh to buy the same tractor off the lot.

Hugh instantly recognized the good deal and heartily agreed to it. They shook hands.

As Rob prepared to return home, Hugh waylaid him. "You know, I took you seriously when you spoke about tithing the other day and brought over a large cheque to Pastor Leland. It was the hardest thing

I've ever done, but I wanted to be obedient to the Word. I wanted to enjoy the blessings of sonship with God. As soon as I did it, I had a guy buy my old farm equipment, including the tractor. I also got hired for my dream job. Then you come along and offer me a great tractor for an amazing price. Do you think it's related, all the great stuff that's come my way since I gave my tithe? Or is it just a coincidence?"

Rob didn't have to think very long or very hard. "When you're a child of God, fully yielded to Him, everything is related. His involvement in our lives, the blessings, the tests, everything. You're catching on well, bro. Keep it up!"

Ten

MONDAY CAME. HUGH went to his first day of work full of enthusiasm. Ellie began her day falling back on her old routine by reading her Bible and journalling. In her smallest notebook, she recorded the blessings they had most recently enjoyed as a couple.

During this exercise, the telephone rang. It was Cynthia, calling to inform her that the reupholstery project was complete. Ecstatic, Ellie determined to go over as soon as possible.

After hanging up the receiver, she set aside her journaling, speedily pulled on some jeans and a sweatshirt and lit out in her car.

Cynthia was watching for her. Upon arrival, she led Ellie to the workshop to view the finished product, grinning from ear to ear.

"Are you ready for this?" asked Cynthia, poised to open the door.

"I am!"

Cynthia threw it open and Ellie entered. She walked over to the newly clad sofa and matching armchair with lips parted in delight. They were gorgeous! Regal! And they bore no resemblance to the pieces she had removed from the old farmhouse.

"I love it!" Ellie gasped. "And so will Hugh. He once said he didn't want his place looking feminine. Well, this is as non-girly as it gets. You did such a great job, Cynthia. I wish I had another project for you."

Cynthia suddenly looked worried. "Are you cancelling the wedding dress order?"

"Oh no. I just meant I would hire you in a heartbeat to cover more furniture."

"You might not say that when I show you the bill. It took more time than we thought to match the plaid and pound in all those antique-looking tacks around the woodwork."

She hesitantly handed Ellie the invoice.

Ellie just looked at the bill and smiled. "It's all good, Cynthia. It's within my allotted budget. And if you don't mind using your van to deliver it, I'll round it up even higher."

Cynthia exhaled with relief. "You're different than most customers. Everyone seems to expect things to be done for next to nothing. My time and skills have value, too. And I also have bills to pay."

The van had to be turned around and backed up to the garage. The two women then managed to load the pieces without too much difficulty. Soon they were off to Hugh's place.

Before they unloaded the furniture, Ellie had to quickly move the steamer trunk and a few other items Hugh had carelessly parked on the floor of the cottage. The women then carefully brought in the sofa and set it in place. Next came the armchair, set adjacent so the two were at right angles to each other. The tall end table remained in the corner between them with the navy lamp on top. To finish off the room, Ellie lugged the steamer trunk into its former place to serve as a coffee table.

Stepping back to get a long view, the room now felt somewhat crowded, but it was also beautiful and warmly welcoming.

"The wall behind the sofa needs a little something," noted Cynthia.

Ellie grinned. "I have just the thing!"

From the back seat of her car, she retrieved a large flat package and brought it into the cottage. Together they unpacked the reframed painting Ellie had brought back from Dauphin.

Fetching a tape measure, pencil, and a hammer, the two young women joined forces to hang the large picture carefully above the sofa at the ideal height. Afterward they stood back to admire their work.

"Stunning!" pronounced Cynthia. "A perfect theme for the plaid furniture."

"I think so, too."

"May I make one suggestion? I feel like the room is bottom heavy. The white walls are a good choice, helping to make the room feel spacious. But the darker details end midway up the walls. It's a current trend to install border wallpaper. Maybe you could find something classic to paper the walls along the ceiling."

"It's a good idea, but I think I have one to top it," said Ellie. "I've seen pictures of European doorways with words painted above them. What if I painted, in calligraphy, a wise, encouraging quote or two? That should tie the room together in a beautiful and interesting way, don't you think?"

Cynthia let out an excited breath. "It's a super idea! Gives me goosebumps thinking about it. And I have a time-saving way to help space the words."

"You're on!"

Cynthia turned her attention to the rest of the front room, lingering in the kitchen area.

"We've agreed to build a new kitchen," said Ellie, reading Cynthia's thoughts.

"I did wonder how far you were going to go with the antique approach."

"It's going to be a contemporary cupboard system, with shaker-style door fronts made with old barnwood. Which is to say, they'll be a weathered grey. I think it'll go well with the front room, but Hugh is insisting that we keep the green and gold appliances because they still work just fine. I'm afraid they'll be an eyesore."

"Oh, men!" huffed Cynthia flashing her eyes. "I will say that Brent is usually pretty good about such things, but sometimes he doesn't get it either. It can be quite frustrating." She hesitated for a moment. "Speaking of Brent… I'd like to ask you something."

"Ask away."

"He's been studying photography as a kind of hobby, hoping to one day do it professionally. So far he's focused on iconic buildings, interesting topics of nature, and still life forms. Now he wants to do an assignment on photographing people and I thought of you and Hugh. How about some engagement photos? If you like them, maybe you'd consider hiring Brent as your wedding photographer. Photography is becoming quite an artform, you know. It's so much more than those tired old studio poses. I would assist him, too, which would give me an opportunity to get involved... and get creative." She paused to gauge Ellie's reaction. "I'm pretty sure he wouldn't disappoint you. We'd do them for you as a wedding gift."

Ellie's mouth dropped in surprise. "Wow! What a generous offer. You know what? I think that's a great idea. I don't know Brent, but if you're involved, I'm confident the photographs will be amazing. We'd have to do it on a weekend, though, because of our jobs."

"Thanks so much, Ellie. We really appreciate this opportunity." Cynthia seemed visibly relieved. "Do you have the rest of the day free? We ought to go to the fabric store and zero in on some material for the wedding dresses."

"As a matter of fact, I do," said Ellie. "I'd love to go shopping with you."

They drove together in Ellie's car to Swan River. Cynthia was well-acquainted with the proprietress of the fabric store and wanted to see what they had on offer. Together with the owner, Francis, they went directly to the section devoted to specialty fabrics. Ellie pinpointed the pale blue chiffon she wanted, although none of the laces in stock were appealing. Francis agreed to source some heavier, textured materials.

Next, they looked for patterns. Ellie chose a simple yet lovely design for the young girls, as well as something Cynthia could use as a base for the bridesmaids.

While Francis and Cynthia discussed details, Ellie wandered over to the drapery section. She encountered a selection of plaids, a few of which seemed like they'd go well with the new furniture.

"What are you thinking?" asked Cynthia, joining Ellie by the bolts of plaid.

Ellie fingered a predominantly red plaid. "I'm wondering if this would look good in the front room."

Cynthia closed her eyes to picture the scene in her mind. "I think the two plaids will look well together, but I wonder if it'll be too much for the room. It may shrink the sense of spaciousness. Perhaps some of these sheers would serve the same purpose…"

Now it was Ellie's turn to shut her eyes and visualize the room more clearly.

Upon reflection, she concluded that Cynthia was right. She came away from the fabric store with her arms full of white roller shades as well as sheer white curtains to dress the windows at the cottage. She'd also picked out a lacey valance with a pattern depicting country sheep; it would go well over the kitchen window.

But having fallen in love with the red plaid, she bought a dozen meters with which to sew a duvet cover and matching shams for their bedroom. The whole house would have a tartan plaid theme, she determined as she left the fabric store in high spirits. She'd definitely been bit by the decorating bug.

The afternoon was still young when Ellie dropped Cynthia off at home and then sped to Hugh's place. Before going inside, though, she peered through the window to look in at the living room.

"I'm going to love coming home to this," she said aloud to herself.

Once inside, she set down her window treatment purchases and began to put the little house in order. Hugh had piled up his soiled clothing in a corner. She took a notion to wash his laundry, including the bedding, and fix a casserole which she intended to eat with him for supper. She wanted to be on hand to see his response to the new furniture.

She also rearranged the bedroom, busy little bee that she was. It was stuffed to the gills with the furniture suite they'd gotten from Margo. And then there was Hugh's single bed and the tall dresser he'd been given by his Aunt Gertie.

This is silly, she thought to herself. *The redundancy is ridiculous. I don't care what he says.*

Ellie decided to position the main dressers where they ought to go and empty out the old dresser Hugh had been using. As soon as they were set against the most accommodating wall, she transferred Hugh's remaining clean clothes. She then dragged the old dresser to the summer cabin piece by piece. When that was completed, she placed Hugh's single bed in the middle of the room, flanked by the recently purchased night tables. That left the head and footboards of the bedroom suite; those would wait until Ellie moved in.

She stepped back to admire her handiwork. The room was ever so much more spacious and the arrangement made sense.

Hugh would be returning from work soon. Ellie popped the casserole in the oven and set about remaking the bed. Aunt Gertie's summer gift of a blue bedspread was the final touch.

In the living room, she noted that the entertainment centre was bare save for the white push button telephone on top. Hugh's boombox sat where eventually a television would go. From the bedroom closet, Ellie retrieved the Royal Doulton ball figurine Hugh had gotten from his maternal grandmother, as well as the framed picture of the pond he had purchased at the FBC auction. She placed these accessories on top of the entertainment unit to cozy up the ambience.

Wanting everything to be as perfect as she could make it, Ellie stowed her window-related purchases in the small storage room.

At last all the tidying and organizing was done. The clock on the stove read 5:15 p.m. and she expected Hugh to arrive any minute. She turned off all the lights and locked the front door to avoid suspicion. Finding a hiding spot behind the bathroom door, she settled in to wait.

Five minutes later, Hugh raced into his yard and parked his truck beneath the carport. Ellie tingled with anticipation as she heard his boots on the boards of the front deck, followed by the sound of the key turning in the lock.

The door opened and the lights came on. Hugh stood stock still, trying to take in the changes, eyes wide with astonishment. Then he slowly smiled.

Removing his jacket and hanging it on one of the kitchen chairs, he gingerly sat in the armchair to test it out. Next he swung his legs to rest atop the steamer trunk.

That's when his nose informed him of supper warming in the oven. He quickly rose to see what it was. By this time, Ellie had opened the bathroom door and stood in the open doorway, all smiles.

Hugh startled when he noticed her but then broke out in a sunny grin.

"I see that you like it," said Ellie happily.

"It's great, Ellie, it really is." He gestured to the new living room furniture. "Doesn't look anything like the heap of junk it was when you took it away. I recognize the woodwork, but otherwise it's altogether different."

"Does it bother you that it's the same set you grew up with?"

"Nope. It doesn't remind me of my past at all. The plaid is great, too, not all flowery and such." Hugh's attention turned to the oven. "It smells like you made a tasty supper for us."

"I did. But first look at what else I did."

Taking his hand, Ellie led him to see the bedroom. When Hugh stepped in and saw it for the first time, he squeezed her shoulders.

"Looks really good in here, Ellie. Where did you put my dresser?"

"It's back in the summer cabin. And your clothes are washed, folded, and put away. It's in the new highboy."

Hugh frowned. "I wanted to wait until we used the set together," he said.

"Oh, stop being silly. There isn't room to keep it all in here, even temporarily. This way a person can actually get around the room!"

"Fine," he conceded. "You know, if this is a taste of the kind of wifely-ness I'm going to come home to as of January, I sure like it. You could still talk me into eloping tonight and forget the whole wedding hoopla."

"Phffff. Not a chance!"

Eleven

MIDMORNING THE NEXT day, Ellie went back to Hugh's place to follow up on a new idea. She had decided the previous night that it might be cool to use a slender stick as a curtain rod, particularly if one end featured a bit of branch or twigs. The property had lots of scrub brush to look through, as well as mature deciduous trees.

Armed with a handsaw, tape measure, calliper, and clippers, Ellie set out to explore the bush. She found numerous saplings in the area where the refuse had recently been removed, but none had the size or general shape Ellie was looking for. She broadened her search area to cover the pond, where a stand of willows stood. Nothing there pleased her either.

She kept looking, however, judiciously examining every branch that looked like it had possibilities. She wandered here, there, and over yonder until she realized she was right back to where they had found the old half-ton truck left to rust in the backwoods. She briefly admired it again, happy that it represented a new hobby for Hugh. She had a vision of him carefully dismantling the vehicle, repairing, replacing parts, and reconstructing it.

She was coming around the front when she heard the sound of an animal behind her. An instant process of elimination ruled out every likely possibility except cat. Granted, this was not the sound of a regular household cat.

Ellie stood frozen in place, then very slowly inched around to the passenger side of the vehicle. She turned in a casual manner to face the direction from which the animal had made the sound—and when she got to the door, opened it quickly and hopped inside, slamming it shut after herself.

Immediately a big cat dropped out of a tree and leapt onto the hood of the car in two bounds. Although Ellie had never seen the likes of this animal in person, she had seen enough pictures to know what it was and to regard the creature with respectful fear. The tawny fur coat, white muzzle, blue eyes, and black fur behind the ears identified it as a cougar. It had probably wandered down from the nearby Duck Mountain Provincial Park. Plenty of wildlife came from that direction, including bobcat and lynx. It was rare to see a cougar, though. Their nomadic and elusive ways made it hard to establish their territory.

The cat looked at Ellie through the front windshield, swishing its tail in a steady rhythm. It lifted its paw and tapped the glass, perhaps thinking it could reach in and touch Ellie. She automatically pressed herself back into the cold bench, hoping the glass was strong enough to withstand the animal's pressure.

When the animal realized the window was a barrier, it sat back on the hood and continued to fix its eyes on Ellie.

"Oh God," she prayed fearfully. "Please keep this cat from getting through to me. And please present me with a way of escape. I'm feeling very trapped right now..."

She slowly leaned forward, trying to get a better view. The cat leaned forward, too, as if it was curious, or perhaps it was just trying to sniff her. It seemed young to Ellie, not full grown. Perhaps it had just recently been released by its mother. It could have come up from the East Favel River. It wasn't far away.

At any rate, a personal encounter with a cougar couldn't be taken lightly, and she didn't know enough about the animal's ways to risk getting out of the car and attempt to frighten it away long enough to run back to safety. The house wasn't terribly far away, but it would be too far with a hungry predator on her tail. She couldn't hope to outrun it.

All Ellie had for defence was the small handsaw she had brought along—and she would certainly do her best to use it should the cat break through the window.

Ellie wanted to check the time, but she was too afraid to take her eyes off the cat to look at her wristwatch. Instead, she continued to pray... for her safety and a means of escape. Maybe God would send a meal for the cougar by way of a rabbit or fox, something, or anything...just not her.

All of a sudden, the cat got up, jumped off the truck, and disappeared into the underbrush. Ellie let out a huge sigh of relief. Was this the means of escape she had prayed for?

The time on her watch read nearly noon. She guessed that her encounter with the cougar had taken up a half-hour, perhaps longer. But she still wasn't confident about leaving the safety of the truck. Was the animal merely hiding, waiting for her to come out? She decided to wait a little longer, to see if it returned.

Ellie let out a shiver, and a new concern entered the picture. She was becoming cold. The air was close to freezing, which was comfortable enough if one were dressed for it. But here she was, sitting motionless on vinyl seating wearing only a fall jacket.

And yet it was still too soon to leave the truck. She determined to wait an hour. That would give the animal enough time to travel a long way.

To pass the time productively, Ellie tried to think of more ideas they could use in preparation for their upcoming wedding. She had told Sarah that she wanted a majestic ceremony, with pomp and circumstance and poignant formality. As for music, it occurred to her that the church had an organ. She visualized the bridal party making their entrance to a full-throated rendition of "Ode to Joy." And as for her own entrance, perhaps something with electrifying trumpets to announce her arrival. She imagined the thrilling strains of the organ playing a traditional bridal march as she walked up the aisle to meet her husband... a man who would be overcome by her ravishing beauty and the great solemnity of the occasion...

"Ella Rose Bauman, get a grip!" she said to herself. "Your name is Vanity. At twenty-eight, you should think more maturely. Stop mooning like a twelve-year old girl."

Her thoughts moved on to the reception. Sarah had already suggested the Minitonas town hall, which was at least as roomy as the church basement. There would also be fewer restrictions on the kind of music and activities they might want to include. She wanted to play a series of famous love songs in the background while they ate.

She crossed her arms and tucked her hands into her armpits to warm them. Not having a paper and pen to keep track of her ideas, she spoke aloud, hoping it would help with recall later.

"We could do 'We've Only Just Begun,' by the Carpenters. Then there's 'You Are My Sunshine.' That a good oldie many will know. And 'There is Love,' by Peter Paul & Mary." Her teeth began to chatter. "Let's see. How about 'Love Will Keep Us Together,' by the Captain and Tennille, or 'Dedicated to the One I Love,' by the Mamas and Papas. Hugh likes Kenny Rogers, so we'll have to include 'You Decorated My Life.' And he must have many other love songs. Think, think, think…"

But that was all she could come up with while she blew warm breath into her hands.

Suddenly, the cougar leapt on to the hood of the truck again. Startled, Ellie screamed. The cat hissed in reply. It sniffed the windshield for a moment in curiosity, then hopped onto the roof of the cab. Ellie could hear its movements as it turned a couple of times before jumping down into the rear box of the truck. Now it looked at Ellie face to face through the rear window, sniffing… raising a paw to the pane as if to touch her face…

"Go away," said Ellie in her sternest tone of voice. "Go back home. You're not welcome here in the valley. Someone will shoot you dead for sure. Forget about me! I'd make a terrible meal. Shoo! Shoo!"

The cat let out its characteristic sound again, something between a growl and a meow, and Ellie retreated from the window. She picked up her handsaw, just in case.

Then, as suddenly as it had reappeared, the cougar paced around the box a couple of times and jumped out, wandering away in a southerly direction.

Ellie exhaled with relief and relaxed her posture. Her watch now indicated that it was midafternoon. This discouraged her for several reasons. She was trapped and virtually helpless, growing colder by the minute, and the day was being wasted away to no one's benefit. To make matters worse, she was beginning to feel hungry and thirsty. And a new concern emerged: her bladder was full. How in the world was she going to safely relieve herself?

For the time being, she remained as still as she could.

As the afternoon waned, Ellie lost interest in thinking about her wedding. Uppermost in her mind now was how to keep herself warm while she waited for help to come and find her. The cat, she believed, was stalking her. It had only left the scene as a diversion tactic, hoping she would leave the shelter of the cab and expose herself so she could be attacked.

Her only hope was to wait for someone to notice she was missing and send out a search party. She couldn't imagine but that it would take several hours yet before she could anticipate rescue. Hugh would likely be the first to grow concerned, but that might not happen until after he had come home, eaten supper, and showered.

And what if it took days for someone to find her? Nobody would even know where to begin to look.

All these dismal thoughts depressed Ellie to the point of tears. She cried out a new set of prayers for herself, her rescuers, and even that stupid cat.

~

Hugh arrived home between five and five-thirty as per his new routine, hoping that perhaps his fiancée had fixed him another great supper like she had the day before.

He also wondered if she had done more to feather the nest. He'd never taken an interest in interior decorating before, but he was beginning to catch on. A room's design could have major effects on one's sensibilities. His childhood home had been comfortable enough on the one hand, but it's increasing shabbiness had also contributed to the depression of everyone who lived there.

The Turners, on the other hand, had kept a nice house filled with fashionable furnishings. Still, there had been no wow factor.

Diane's house had been very casual, of the sort that no one would bother to remember. Entirely unremarkable.

What about Margo's house? Pristine and cold. "Don't touch," it seemed to scream. There was nothing warm or comfortable about that place at all.

His mind turned to Aunt Gertie's house. It was eclectic, with an assortment of different styles collected under one roof. The only thing they had in common was that she liked them.

As for the Bauman farmhouse, it was typical of the older people who had once lived there, comfy albeit outdated. Ellie hadn't changed it at all since moving in.

But the way Ellie was adorning the little house for them to start their married life together befitted Hugh's taste as well as hers. And he hadn't even known he preferred one style over another. He just knew that when he came home, it felt good to be there.

To his disappointment, Ellie wasn't waiting for him. He quickly showered, changed, and gulped down leftovers from the night before. To save a couple of minutes, he drove across the road eager to plant a kiss on Ellie's mouth.

Reassured at seeing her car parked outside, he bounded up the steps and let himself in.

The house was strangely dark and quiet. His first thought was that she might be working a hospital shift that he'd forgotten about. But a look on the calendar indicated that she wasn't scheduled to be at work that day.

Beginning to feel uneasy, Hugh called Darcey. Ellie wasn't there either, and Darcey didn't have any idea where she could be.

Hanging up the phone, he thought of all the people Ellie might be with, dismissing them one by one according to the mysterious detail of her car being parked out front.

"Hello," answered Rob curtly when Hugh called.

He bypassed the normal pleasantries. "Yeah, I'm looking for Ellie. Her car is here, but she isn't."

"She's not here either. Have you checked our shop? She might be refinishing some furniture. You know how she gets these big fat ideas—"

"No, I don't think so. I have a bad feeling about this. I'm going to start looking for her, but I don't know where to begin."

There was a pause on the other end of the line. "Well then, I guess I'd better come, too. We'll form a search party. Be there shortly."

Hugh hung up the phone.

To be able to say he had covered all the bases, he checked the shop, the garage, and the machine shed before going back to his place across the road. He had just gotten there when Rob and Trevor showed up.

Ellie had reached her limit as far as holding her bladder. She figured she was so full of retained water that her back teeth would soon be floating. No amount of twitching or changing positions could help anymore.

"God, please distract that cat long enough for me to have a much-needed pee," she pleaded.

She lifted the handle of the passenger door and ever so slowly eased it open, taking every precaution not to make a squeak. Hefting the handsaw, she eased herself out of the cab, gingerly crouched on the ground, and completed her business.

Oh, the wonderful feeling that went with being emptied! Quickly she got back into the cab and slammed the door shut.

It didn't take long for the cougar to return and investigate the noise. It stopped by the passenger door, sniffed the ground, and then rose on its hind legs to paw the window.

"Shoo! Get outta here!" commanded Ellie, flashing the handsaw across the window.

The cat went down on all fours and then bounded back onto the hood, peering at Ellie through the windshield and padding the glass with one of its paws.

"Shoo... Go home! Forget about me."

The cat jumped onto the roof of the cab, and then into the box behind. Ellie launched more desperate prayers. "Oh Lord, please don't let it break the glass. Please bring me rescuers!"

She checked her watch again. The time was just after five. Hopefully Hugh would be home soon and figure out she was in trouble.

Meanwhile, she hugged herself and rocked in an effort to retain some warmth. The chill had permeated her body and she could see her breath as she exhaled.

"When was the last time you saw her?" asked Rob when he got out of his truck. Trevor got out on the passenger's side and joined his dad to stand with Hugh.

"Last night," answered Hugh. "I'm sure she's out somewhere because she took her fall jean jacket, the one with the fleece lining. And she's got her walking boots."

"Uh-huh." Rob removed his cap and scratched his scalp. "So what did you two talk about last night? Did she say anything about what she wanted to be doing today?"

"Not that I can recall." He buried his face in his hands, trying to concentrate. "She set up the new furniture. She bought curtains for the windows. In the evening, she asked me to hold them up to see if I liked them…"

"Did you?" asked Rob, a little grin playing at the corners of his mouth.

"Did I what?"

"Like the curtains?"

"Sure. I don't know. What do I know about curtains, for crying out loud?"

Rob smiled cryptically. "So did you hang up curtains last night?"

"No, because she didn't buy a curtain rod. That's it!" cried Hugh. "She said she didn't buy rods because she had an idea to use slender tree branches. She probably went searching for them today and got lost or something."

"It's hard for me to believe she got lost. She knows the area pretty well, and there are lots of ways to figure out where you are. But I agree. Combing the bush would be a good place to start."

All three men equipped themselves with their best flashlights and tramped through the bush. They began searching the area just off the road and behind the new house, spreading out. They cleared that vicinity quickly until they passed the former trash grounds, where the trees and shrubbery grew more thickly. Moments later, Hugh veered towards the pond, to make sure she hadn't fallen in and drowned. They searched that area in growing darkness before resuming their hunt heading west.

Darkness covered the woods, the trees and shrubs taking on an eerie quality that made Ellie uneasy. She strained to see specks of light out of the east from where she expected her help would come.

At last she saw something, like fireflies in the distance.

"Yes!" she shouted. "Keep coming! You'll find me."

Suddenly the lights veered off to the south and Ellie realized they must be checking the pond. She couldn't blame them, but she felt more forlorn than before when the lights disappeared and didn't come back.

"Don't panic," Ellie instructed herself. "They'll be back when they don't find me there. Please God, get them moving in this direction again..."

The minutes dragged on like hours, but at last she saw the specks of light return. A search party of three, counted Ellie.

She waited until she thought it was possible for them to hear her. Then she rolled down the window and yelled at the top of her lungs. "Help!"

$\sim$

"Hey, I heard something!" said Trevor, turning in the direction the call seemed to have come from. "Shhhh. Listen!"

The call came again. It definitely sounded like someone was crying out for help.

Trevor felt certain now. "It's her. It's Aunt Ellie, I'm sure of it!"

"Then I know where she is," said Hugh. "Come with me."

The three of them loped together with Hugh in the lead. As soon as his flashlight lit up the old Plymouth, Ellie came flying out of the cab and rushed into Hugh's arms, relief flooding both of their faces.

But only for a second.

"Hurry," she insisted. "Everybody, get in the truck right away. There's danger lurking!"

Hugh entered the cab first with Ellie right behind. She sat on his lap, sort of, to make room for Trevor and Rob, who had to squeeze close in order to shut the door.

"You don't look worse for wear," said Rob, looking Ellie over. "What happened here?"

"I've been trapped all day by a cougar!" lamented Ellie. She told the story of the day's events.

Although relieved to have been rescued by her loved ones, at the end of her tale tears of great relief slipped from her eyes.

"It's okay, babe," said Hugh huskily. "You're safe now. We'll get you home."

"What do we do now?" Trevor peered outside. "I kind of wish I could see it. I've never seen a wild critter like that up close before."

Ellie sighed. "Well, I have, and the experience was scary. I can admit it was beautiful, but I'd rather look upon it from behind the bars of a zoo."

As if on cue, the cougar hopped up onto the hood. Rob immediately adjusted his flashlight so that it illuminated without shining in the cat's face.

"Cool!" said Trevor, awed.

"Looks like a young one, or else a smallish female," observed Rob. "Not disregarding the danger these animals present, but we are kind of privileged to be seeing one. It's not common. Pretty little thing, isn't she?"

The cougar paced back and forth across the hood. It wasn't clear whether it was pacing out of curiosity or scheming.

After a minute or two of observing the animal, Rob declared, "Okay, this is what we're going to do. I'm going to get out and try to scare the cat away. When it runs off, we'll form a pack and walk quickly, without running, back to Hugh's house. Keep flashing your lights in all directions to keep the cat from getting close if it takes a mind to. Everybody got it?"

"Oh Rob, do be careful," whimpered Ellie.

Rob sent her a dirty look and couldn't resist teasing her. "Here kitty, kitty, kitty," he said, getting ready to get out.

But he took the handsaw with him, just in case.

The cat stopped and crouched, ready for anything as soon as Rob got out. He suddenly yelled at the top of his lungs and lunged towards the cat. The cougar couldn't get away fast enough.

"Okay, let's go!"

Before long, they had all reached Hugh's house, feeling relieved yet thrilled by their adventure. Except Ellie, of course. She suddenly felt ravenous and couldn't seem to get warm quickly enough. She was tired of all the talk of cougars and adventures in the wild.

Rob called the authorities to report the encounter. He was told conservation officers would come the next morning with dogs to capture the animal. It would need to be removed from the valley altogether.

Even so, Ellie decided to give up her quest for a natural branch curtain rod. She'd lost interest and was perfectly happy to buy a black rod with decorative finials—and no amount of cajoling would convince her otherwise.

Twelve

COMPARED TO THE unexpected adventure in the backwoods, the next few days were filled with predictable and unexciting activities. Ellie's routine included going into Swan River to do some shopping, sitting at the library for a couple of hours, making phone calls, working two nightshifts, and consequently day-sleeping.

Hugh came to the end of his first full week on the job. He was still being shown the ropes and had so far enjoyed getting to know his new coworkers. Of special interest to him was the autobody guy who looked after the collision unit. Occasionally Hugh was able to watch him at his work, looking on as he prepared a vehicle for painting and then actually spraypainted it. Hugh had every intention of restoring the old vehicles on his property, and these were skills he'd need to add to his personal repertoire.

On Sunday morning, Hugh went to church alone as Ellie was sleeping following a nightshift. He sat with Ladd Moore, a friend he had first met at the FBC picnic earlier that summer. Ladd was approximately five years younger than Hugh and still living with his parents as he worked with his dad on the family farm. Next to Ladd was his younger brother Jeremy, whom Hugh surmised to be about twenty years old. Hugh didn't know a lot about the Moore boys, but he did know this: they were somewhat obsessed with old cars and trucks.

While sitting in the pews waiting for the service to begin, the brothers told Hugh about their current project. They'd dragged their granddad's first car, a 1938 classic sedan they had discovered abandoned in the woods, to their shop and begun to take apart the motor. They were pretty excited about it and invited Hugh to come over for lunch after church so he could see it for himself, as well as the other vehicles around the place.

It was the first time Hugh had been to the Moore Farm, and he wasn't prepared for what he saw. He thought his own property had been a junkyard mess, and it had been, but the Moores had it many times worse. He had never seen so much clutter in one place. It looked like a scrapyard. All that was missing was a large, colourful billboard proclaiming it to be a place to buy obsolete auto parts and anything else of yesteryear vintage: *If you can't find it here, you won't find it anywhere...*

The farmhouse was an old two-storey building with weathered grey clapboard siding. The back end of the house had an obvious addition since it was covered separately with faux brick made of asphalt-like linoleum. The peaked roof finished short on one side and long on the other, giving it the appearance of a house style called saltbox. While the immediate grounds surrounding the house appeared to be spared the clutter which dominated the other side of the driveway, it nevertheless showed a lack of interest in keeping the grass cut—or attempting any other beautifying efforts.

The three younger men followed the parents into the house towards the appetizing smell of food roasting in the oven. Mrs. Moore, as tall as her short husband and plump, shooed the men away to wait in the living room while she prepared the kitchen table for their meal.

The interior bore some similarities to the exterior. While it seemed clean enough, the rooms were disorganized. Numerous house plants dotted the main floor rooms growing out of clay pots, a cracked teapot, and even a syrup pail. Stacks of periodicals and newspapers topped every flat surface. A couple of drinking glasses hadn't yet been returned to the kitchen for washing. A large tabby cat lay curled up in one of the club chairs. Jeremy picked up the cat and tossed it to the side.

"Have a seat," invited Jeremy. "It won't be long until Mam calls us to the table."

Heavyset and balding, Mr. Moore sported a thick moustache. He still wore his striped suit and tie when he joined the young bucks in the front room.

"The boys tell me you're new to these parts." His voice had a high tenor quality. "What do you do for a living?"

"I've been in the neighbourhood since June," answered Hugh respectfully. "I'm a licenced mechanic for a car and truck dealership in Swan River."

The man frowned slightly, glancing towards his sons. "Oh, I thought you had a farm."

"I've inherited our family's half-section, but the land is rented out."

"He found an old-timer in the back bush," spoke up Ladd. "An old Plymouth half-ton, right?"

Hugh nodded. "More than one. There's also an old Studebaker and a really old tractor back there."

Mr. Moore show mild interest, but Jeremy lit up like a lightbulb.

"What year is it, do you know? Does it run? What are your plans for it?" asked Jeremy with considerable excitement.

"I don't know. I'm sure the motor is seized up, but I plan to bring it to the yard and eventually restore the thing. I know Pa didn't drive it, so I assume my grandfather used it."

"Cool." Jeremy seemed especially eager. "Can we come and see it?"

"Sure. When were you thinkin'?"

Just then, Mrs. Moore called them all to come to the table. Lunch was a thick and tasty oven stew served with homemade buns baked the day before.

There was more talk about restoring old cars, and at one point Mr. Moore added his opinion.

"The cars they made years ago were built to last," the man declared. "Vehicles today don't give you the milage out of the parts and motors we got back then."

"All depends how you look at it, Pop," responded Ladd stoutly. "Today's vehicles travel longer and farther than what you drove when you were a young chap. It's just that old-timers have a *style* about them. New cars today don't have the same pizazz like some of them oldies have."

"That's why I want to paint the '38 Chev something bright," put in Jeremy. "To show off its pizazz!"

"Nah. It stays black. Black like a mafia car." Ladd was getting ready to argue. "We just need to find some white-walled tires for it."

"Good luck," Hugh said. "I don't think they're available in every size."

The conversation would likely have gotten lively at that point, but Mrs. Moore intervened. "You boys are always and forever talking about fixing cars like nothing else matters. How about fixing the vacuum cleaner or figuring out why my treadle sewing machine doesn't work like it's supposed to?"

"Awww, Mam, there ain't no fun in that," said Jeremy. "Pass the stew. Hugh still looks hungry."

"No thanks. I've had plenty. It's very tasty, ma'am."

"Well, you make sure you get enough to eat. I don't want it said I never fed you," kidded Mrs. Moore.

Soon she served dessert: a moist chocolate cake slathered with a soft creamy chocolate frosting. It topped off the meal perfectly.

After thanking Mrs. Moore for the delicious meal, Hugh followed Ladd and Jeremy on a tour of their private collection of mostly dysfunctional vehicles. He couldn't get over how many cars, trucks, tractors, and implements were lined up like a used car lot.

"Did you own all these machines?" he asked.

"Nah," replied Ladd. "Pop likes to go to auctions and buy them up for a song."

"What's your point of keeping them around?"

"Because we can strip them for parts when needed. Sometimes we have to modify them..."

"We always have to modify them," corrected Jeremy.

Ladd nodded. "To make them useful for whatever motor we're trying to get running again."

Both Ladd and Jeremy had taken courses in auto mechanics and small engines in Winnipeg. They were knowledgeable in how engines worked and adept at recreating new parts from old. Hugh was impressed when they showed him some of their ingenuity.

At last they came upon their prized old relic, the 1938 sedan. Had Ellie been there, Hugh knew exactly what she would have said: "It's so cute!" Naturally it was quite badly rusted, but for all that it looked like a promising project.

The excitement of the Moore boys became contagious. Hugh invited them to follow him home and have a look at his own relics, which they were keen to do.

~

The brothers pulled up alongside Hugh in front of the dilapidated shed. The first vehicle he showed them was the grain truck from the 40s sheltered there. Jeremy wanted to hear the motor run, so Hugh fired it up. To their ears, they said it purred like a kitten, though one had to wonder what species of kitten they were thinking of.

Then Hugh took the guys for a walk into his back woods. October would soon be over and the air was especially chilly due to a north wind.

Ladd shivered and rubbed his hands together. "It smells like it's going to snow."

"I hope not," said Hugh. "I'm not ready for a long winter."

"Winter schminter," quipped Jeremy. "It don't matter as long as there's a warm, roomy shop in which to work on motors."

When the Plymouth half-ton came into view, Ladd let out an enthusiastic wolf whistle. Jeremy grinned from ear to ear and caressed the front bumper.

"It looks to be in great shape for having been out here for who knows how long," said Ladd.

"Can you open up the hood?" asked Jeremy.

Hugh shrugged. "Let's give it a try."

Just as curious, he released the latch and raised the hood even as the hinges squealed and grated. Immediately all three guys had their heads together touching wires, hoses, spark plugs, and dipstick.

"You know, I don't think it would take too much to get this motor running again," said Ladd.

Jeremy nodded. "I think you're right. Will you keep it the same colours?"

"Don't know yet," Hugh smiled, very much enjoying the camaraderie. "Come on. I have more to show you."

The boys found the McCormick Deering 10 20 tractor politely interesting, but they didn't gush over it. The nearby Studebaker was another matter.

"Whoa! She's a beauty!" Jeremy could hardly contain himself. "It's too bad the roof is damaged."

"Fixable, though," said Ladd. "Everything is fixable if you have the money to do it."

"I'm thinking I should pull these old-timers out and bring them back to the yard where I can cover them with tarp for the winter," Hugh remarked. "Then they'll be handy to look at while I'm trying to come up with a strategy for restoring them."

"Good idea. We'll help you," said Ladd.

On the walk back to Hugh's house, the three of them noted the trees that would have to be cut down to create a broad enough path to tow Hugh's tractor through. They were still discussing this when they arrived at the house and saw Ellie walking up the driveway.

"Hi guys!" she greeted cheerily. "What have you been up to?"

Hugh let the Moore brothers jabber on about the cool vintage vehicles they had just seen and how they planned to help Hugh get them home before winter set in.

"That's real nice of you," said Ellie. "How are you thinking of doing it?"

All three escorted her to the bush and pointed out the path they intended to create.

Ellie wrinkled her brow. "How is this a good idea? Surely it's simpler to tow them south to the edge of the field, which is a lot closer. Not to mention you wouldn't have to cut down nearly so many trees."

"Well…" Hugh was beginning to realize the superiority of her practical recommendation. "Because it would just make too much sense."

⁓

After the Moores left, Ellie told Hugh that she had invited Rob and the family over to the farmhouse for a homemade pizza supper.

"I thought it would be great simply to be together and perhaps discuss more wedding ideas with Sarah," she explained.

The pizzas were assembled and ready to go into the oven when the Rob Bauman crew arrived. It had been quite a while since any of them had paid a visit to "Grandma's place." The kids ran into the house in high spirits.

Beanie wore a pointed birthday hat on top of her head. When Hugh asked her about it, she explained that she had been to a birthday party that afternoon and had lots of fun. She'd come home with a yummy goodie bag and offered some of her candy to Hugh.

Hugh withdrew a piece of short-twist wrapped bubble gum. "Can I have this?" he asked, holding it up.

The Bean nodded vigorously.

"So what did your friend get for birthday presents?" asked Ellie.

"Lots of stuff."

"Like what?"

"Umm… storybooks, paper dolls, a board game, some modelling clay, and a pretty pink T-shirt." Beanie turned to Hugh. "What kind of presents did you get for your birthday?"

The unexpected question seemed to put Hugh on the spot. "Me? I'm too old to have birthdays and birthday presents. Those are just for kids."

"Well, when you were little then," pressed Beanie. "What did you get for your birthday?"

"That was so long ago, I don't even remember," said Hugh, dodging the subject. "My favourite toy when I was little was a tiny red pickup truck. It's lost now."

The answer satisfied Beanie and she let the matter go.

However, Ellie became thoughtful.

On Wednesday, October 29, they had a plan: as soon as Hugh got home from work, he should shower and be ready to get picked up ASAP. Ellie was going to take him out for a juicy hamburger with fries in celebration of his birthday.

Looking forward to Ellie's treat and going out on the town with his girl, Hugh left the dealership on the dot of quitting time and raced home. He anticipated lots of fun being on a date like a couple of teenagers.

As they ate, Ellie watched the clock carefully, as the next part of the plan involved going to see a movie together during the early show. *Private Benjamin* had just come to the Swan River cinema and it looked like they could enjoy a few laughs.

Shortly after eight, the movie ended and they got back in her car to head home.

"We can hang out at my place this evening," said Hugh with a wink. "I've got a comfy couch on which we can snuggle."

"Tempting as that is, I have a birthday cake in the fridge for you at my place."

Minutes later, she turned into the driveway and parked in her customary spot.

"Go on ahead of me," she urged. "Turn on the lights. I'll just be a minute."

Hugh bounded up the steps and entered the small landing. As soon as he cast on the kitchen light, a loud chorus of "Surprise!" startled the bejeebies out of him. This was quickly followed by a discordant rendition of Happy Birthday. There was standing room only in the kitchen and living room.

Hugh was stunned. Only the birthday song had made him realize that he was the centre of attention.

The guests parted so he and Ellie could enter the kitchen, but shortly after Hugh was sent into the living room to begin visiting with his friends while the women stayed behind to set out bowls of popcorn, cheesy snacks, potato chips, and assorted soda pop.

When Ellie had called upon their friends and a few relatives to come for the surprise birthday party, she had stipulated that gifts were unnecessary. However, the coffee table in the living room was covered with several colourfully wrapped parcels.

Once the nibblers were set out, Hugh was urged to open his gifts. Beanie, who had wound her way through the gathering, sat on the floor nearby. She reached into the pile and pulled out a small package attached to a homemade card. She passed it to Hugh with a proud smile on her expectant face.

"You must have drawn this," said Hugh, holding up the card. It was the seven-year-old's drawing of his red and silver half-ton. The writing was scrawled in her beginner penmanship:

HAPPY BIRTHDAY UNCLE HUGH
from Mommy, Daddy, Trevor, Charlotte and me

Beanie nodded proudly.

"This is awesome," said Hugh, referring to her drawing. "I'm going to tape it to my fridge where I can see it all the time."

He opened the small parcel to reveal a Swiss army knife. A chorus of ooohs and aaahs emerged from the guests. Hugh was tickled with it, too.

After that, the gift-opening progressed a lot more quickly. The Moore brothers had come up with a large pinup poster featuring a gleaming red and black 1949 vintage truck.

"Well, if that isn't the sexiest thing you ever saw!" quipped Aunt Gertie, who then blushed when her remark produced a series of snickers.

Brent and Cynthia Clifford gave him a Rubik's Cube.

Aunt Ruth and Uncle Herb brought him a large square tin filled with two layers of butter tarts. Immediately a cry went up for him to share, but Hugh adamantly refused, stating that not even Ellie would get to have one. He reclosed the lid and tucked it under the couch to humorously make his point.

The Ungers' gift to him was a cartoon character necktie and black T-shirt imprinted with white text that read *Limited 1949 Edition*. This produced more giggles.

A bigger box revealed a plug-in electric kettle from his Aunt Gertie and Uncle Ed.

"I know it's a boring gift," piped up Aunt Gertie apologetically, "but I couldn't think what a thirty-two-year-old man might possibly enjoy."

"It's great," Hugh assured her. "I'll be able to make myself other hot drinks besides coffee. Thank you."

"Thirty-two!" exclaimed Ladd, as if shocked. "What does it feel like to be over the hill, man?"

"I'm sure in a few short years, you can tell us."

Uncle Herb rolled his eyes. "Aach. At thirty-two, you're practically still a baby."

"I wish I was thirty-two again," murmured Aunt Gertie.

Uncle Ed nodded. "I was in my prime at that age!"

The last gift on the coffee table was large, flat, and heavy, suggesting a book. The card revealed that it was from Ellie.

With Hugh's permission, Beanie peeled off the wrapping paper, revealing a picture book, the kind typically left on coffee tables to serve as conversation starters. In this case, Ellie had struck gold. The book was titled *A Visual History of Cars*, beginning with the early models of the 1920s right up to the present day. Some three hundred pages showed cars by every brand, year of release, and story.

Jeremy Moore put out his hands to look through the book after Hugh's first glance. Green with envy, he pretty much forgot about the rest of the party for a while, combing through the pages with a serious case of tunnel vision until Ladd poked him in the ribs.

The time came for Hugh to blow out thirty-two candles on a tall angel food cake covered with white boiled frosting and colourful sprinkles. He managed it in one fell swoop, earning him a few handclaps and some teasing about being full of hot air.

Ellie served cake with ice cream and strawberries while a lot of good-old-fashioned visit went on. She loved the sounds of people enjoying each other.

Rob and his family left first, citing the school night; the kids needed to get to bed. After that, the others left couple by couple, each wishing Hugh their heartiest best wishes. The Moore brothers were the last to leave. As a joke, Jeremy tried to say goodbye with the book tucked under his arm.

"I don't think so," said Hugh, reaching for the book.

Jeremy sighed wistfully. "Aww, shucks. I hoped you wouldn't notice."

It had been a wonderful evening filled with joy, laughter, and comradery. After the Moores left, Hugh and Ellie sank into the sofa, tired from a full, and busy day.

Hugh pulled her close. "Thanks, honey. This is the first time someone has thrown me a party. Though I'm still feeling weird about it."

"Why weird?"

"I guess it's just that I feel like such a late bloomer. My first birthday party at age thirty-two? It's embarrassing."

"I hoped to change the flavour of your birthdays going forward."

"I think you probably have," said Hugh. "Fifteen years ago today, I ran away from home, bitter and angry. My birthdays were reminders of that fact and little more. Marcie Turner made me birthday cakes, but there weren't any parties to go with them. Tonight showed me that I actually have friends who want to hang out with me... with us. And presents! Look at all these great gifts. Wow! I feel as giddy as a little kid with this haul."

Hugh reached under the sofa and brought out the square tin filled with butter tarts. He offered one to Ellie, but just as she was about to take one he quickly pulled the box out of reach.

"Sorry," he teased. "Not sharing after all."

He recovered the tin and set it on the table with all the other things.

"What made you do it, Ell? It would have been a great birthday with just the two of us eating out and going to the movie."

"Well," began Ellie slowly, fitting herself into the hollow under his arm, "when Beanie asked you about your birthdays as a kid, I realized you never had what most kids probably take for granted: being celebrated at least once a year and reminded of how precious they are. I wanted you to have at least one birthday where you were celebrated just for being you."

Thirteen

IT TOOK QUITE a lot of time, but at last Ellie determined that she'd found enough quotations to print on banners across the wall of the front room. If anything, she'd found far too many. Twelve pages, in fact. Because she liked them all, it wasn't easy to pare them down to just a few.

She showed the options to Hugh and asked him to check off his favourites.

"They're all good," said Hugh after reviewing them. "I suppose I like the Bible verses best, because they're the most encouraging. If I'm going to be reminded of something every day, it should have the effect of building me up before I head out the door and reassuring me when I come back inside."

That reasoning made good sense to Ellie.

The perimeter of the room came to approximately forty-two feet. She didn't know how much length to ascribe to each quote and therefore chose a couple of extra, in case she had more space than she thought.

As promised, Cynthia helped by creating the banners on her home computer.

"Where did you get these quotes?" Cynthia asked while typing them in. "They sound like they're from the Bible, or some kind of prayer book."

"Right on! I wondered if the average person would know that. These are a few of my favourite Bible verses. They encourage me, and Lord knows some days I'm in sore need of it."

"I think that's what makes you different from nearly everyone else I know."

"I'm different? What are you seeing?" asked Ellie, surprised. "Suddenly I feel like you've discovered a wart on my nose or something."

"Nothing like that. It seems to me that most people believe in God, and so do I. Yet God, religion, the Bible... it's all sort of relegated to Sundays, or emergencies. For you, though, it seems more like a life-style. Am I close?"

Ellie smiled. "You are, actually. The word 'lifestyle' is close, but 'personal relationship' would be closer. It's become important to me since returning home in June. Even though I was brought up in hard-core Christianity, I mostly shelved the idea of living biblically when I moved away from home after graduation."

"Well, I do believe people can be too religious," put in Cynthia wryly. "Life should be balanced, I think."

"I know what you're saying, but my views have changed a bit. While I truly believe in God, I don't actually believe in religion."

Cynthia frowned. "What's the difference?"

"I believe God is real and personable, even as He is a Spirit who created humankind for the purpose of interacting with them. I get that from reading the Bible, by the way. But it's not an automatic thing—having a relationship with God, I mean."

"Why not? I thought God loved everyone. And when we die, we'll all go to heaven where He is."

"He does love everyone, personally so, but it's not automatic that everyone goes to live with God in heaven upon their death. And there's a good explanation for that."

"I'm listening," said Cynthia wrinkling up her forehead doubtfully.

Ellie wasn't sure if Cynthia was intrigued or piqued. But seeing as she seemed to be indicating interest, Ellie decided to give her the same history lesson she had given Hugh a few months earlier.

"The reason is because of what happened at the beginning of time on the earth," Ellie began. "Are you familiar with the story of Adam and Eve and the Garden of Eden?"

"Of course."

"Well, what happened there was a really big deal. A game-changer."

"You mean the story about the serpent tricking Eve and Adam into eating the forbidden fruit? I've never been able to make sense of that. It seems petty of God to kick His first two humans out of the garden just for eating an apple."

"The Bible doesn't say it was an apple," said Ellie quickly. "That's a made-up notion. That original garden had two unique trees in the centre: the Tree of the Knowledge of Good and Evil and the Tree of Life. At the beginning of time, we're told, Adam and Eve lived in easy companionship with God. They enjoyed each other's company in an unspoiled environment."

"Unspoiled as in perfect?"

"It's hard to imagine a world without crime, or death, or evil playing out in some way, isn't it?"

Both women nodded.

"God made one rule," continued Ellie. "It was *not* to eat of the Tree of the Knowledge of Good and Evil. Because if they did, it would result in their death. They could help themselves to the fruit of everything else."

She reached for a blank sheet of paper. Similar to what she had done for Hugh, she drew two stick people on one side of the page, as well as markings to represent light and glory on the opposite side.

Cynthia watched over her shoulder. "Why would God put something in their environment that would wreck the relationship? Don't good parents remove items of temptation so the children won't be harmed?"

"I don't think these trees were planted in the garden to tempt Adam and Eve. I think they represented something uniquely personal relating to God Himself. In this case, I believe this one rule represented a twofold test: a test of obedience, and a test of choice."

"Obedience I get, but choice?"

"The choice to obey linked with the choice to love God and be in relationship with Him," said Ellie. "If the trees hadn't been there, Adam and Eve would have been like preprogrammed robots, like the talking dolls we buy for kids. You know, the ones with the string on the back? Pull the string and the doll will say 'I love you' or 'I'm hungry' or giggle or something. Even kids know that the doll isn't talking for real. They lose interest in that feature. So, God risked giving humans free will, the power of choice, in order to allow the prospect of relationship to be sincere and reciprocal."

"That makes it sound like God didn't know how things would turn out." Cynthia sounded doubtful. "Isn't God supposed to know everything, even before it happens?"

"Oh, He did. Let me illustrate this for you further." Ellie returned to her drawing. "Imagine that this sheet of paper represents the freshly created earth, an environment in which humanity had seamless access to God in the Garden of Eden... a kind of heaven on Earth. Then Satan came along, as the serpent, and tricked Eve into disobeying God's one and only rule. Adam participated, too. That choice cut off the source of power Adam and Eve were connected to. Like snipping electrical wires, like cutting the umbilical cord between mother and baby, suddenly they were disconnected from their Creator and Father God. And their flawless nature immediately became sin-stained and broken."

She drew a chasm between the earth side of the page and the heavenly side.

"Now what? Was this situation salvageable?" resumed Ellie. "God said that it was and made a promise to repair the damage. In the meantime, however, humans could give birth to more humans... but they were born with the same sin-stained, broken nature as their parents. In other words, because of this chasm, everyone is born separated from God. And we also have a limited lifespan. Every human eventually dies and disintegrates back into dust. Eating the forbidden fruit therefore made two deaths very real, just like God said: there was the immediate spiritual death, with them being disconnected from God, and then there was the eventual physical death after a brief lifespan. Humanity struggled along for some four thousand years of difficult and painful history. Then God sent His Son, Jesus, to pay the death penalty for all sin so humans could have a legitimate way to close the chasm and reconnect with God."

Here, Ellie drew the shape of a cross spanning the chasm. It functioned as a bridge between the two sides of the paper.

"And that, in a nutshell, is the gospel of Jesus Christ," said Ellie. "That's why people don't automatically go to be with God when they die. They have to personally choose to accept Jesus's payment for their sin before they can have that privilege. In other words, they must get over the chasm by crossing the way of the cross. That's the only thing that can bridge the chasm. Otherwise, the default human condition stands: sinfulness and separation from God."

"So then Easter…" began Cynthia thoughtfully.

"Easter is the anniversary of the event when perfect, sinless Jesus shed His blood and died on behalf of sinful humans. That includes you and me, Cynthia. That death was critically important because it paid the debt for sin… all sin for all time. But the resurrection, when Jesus defied the power of death and returned to life, is the great clincher. It means that humanity has also been restored to eternal life, following a brief life on the earth. Believers get to live with God in His realm forever. Am I making any sense?"

Cynthia nodded contemplatively. "I'm with you so far."

"Because Jesus effectively and successfully paid the penalty for sin through His death on the cross, humans can once again have easy access to God through their prayers, through His Spirit once again residing internally, and through a subsequent day-to-day personal relationship, much like Adam and Eve originally enjoyed."

A bit of wonder crept into Cynthia's voice. "I never realized the concept was so simple. So… the reason you can claim to have a personal relationship with God is because…"

"Is because I have personally accepted, by faith, Jesus's payment for my sins. As a result, His Spirit lives within me and we go through life together dealing with whatever comes my way."

"Why did you say 'by faith'? What does that even mean?"

"By convinced belief. By believing in Jesus and in what He accomplished. Reconnecting with God can't be done with a physical 'thing.' I can't buy a special kind of battery or power source and voila! I've re-established a link with the Master of the Universe."

Cynthia shook her head. "I wonder why the minister in the church our family went to never described the significance of Jesus like that."

"I can't answer or explain that," she replied. "What the Bible says is pretty clear. It's a straightforward read. But I hope you realize you have the privilege to make a choice regarding having a personal relationship with God."

"Well, if what you're telling me is true, then it's a no-brainer. Of course I want to accept Jesus's payment for my sin. Where do I have to go to do this? What do I have to do?"

Ellie's eyes went wide with surprise. "Are you serious? Most people want to take some time to think about it."

"Really? What's there to think about? If I had cancer and someone offered me the cure, I wouldn't hesitate. Isn't this the same kind of thing?"

"It is to me. But a lot of people don't see that they're broken. They think this life we live, with all its problems, is normal. In a way, I guess it is, the default human condition. But normal, as God originally created it, is what Adam and Eve had before they disobeyed and brought sin into the world."

"Let me play devil's advocate for a minute," said Cynthia. "What's the proof that I'm a sinner? After all, I haven't done anything bad. I haven't committed any crimes. I've been respectful to my parents and teachers and customers. I'm nice to people. I contribute to Christmas hampers and help with fundraisers for good causes. Maybe I'm not broken like you say."

Ellie canted her head. "You forget, though: you were born on this side of the chasm, cut off from God. We're born disconnected from the power to do good. And even if you're trained to be a basically nice person by this world's standards, your good works don't measure up to God's holy standards. There's a scripture that calls our good deeds 'filthy.'[10] How's that for a reality check? Like my mother sometimes said, 'Put that in your pipe and smoke it.'"

"Did you just tell me that my volunteer work and good deeds are worthless?" asked Cynthia darkly.

"No, I didn't. Good deeds and acts of kindness help us get each other through the troubles that show up in life, but they are woefully insufficient towards making us good enough to live with a pure and holy God."

"I've never heard anyone put it like that before," said Cynthia. "But I follow the logic. I'm getting the picture."

The girls paused to pick up the banner as pages came out of printer. They placed them into neat stacks.

"Keep talking," urged Cynthia. "I'm fascinated by this."

"Okay. Well, there's another reason people reject God. They have the right idea that He is holy and good, and that He wants His family of believers to live good clean lives. However, they would rather stay addicted to their sinful pleasures than give them up and live by God's standards," said Ellie. "I fell for this argument when I was a teenager and young adult. I thought that belonging to Jesus meant I couldn't have fun. I got burnt bad before I realized something: that which the world called fun was actually trying to kill me..."

"That sounds like a story I'd like to hear about."

"Maybe another day I'll tell you the long version. I'm still sensitive about it." Ellie let out a long breath. "Too many people think that all talk of God and the Bible is about 'religion,' something separate from our day-to-day reality. I'm thinking of those people who think that belief in God is just a crutch, that having faith means you're weak or naïve. To them, religion is all twaddle. You know, there is no God or

---

[10] Isaiah 64:6, GNT.

He's dead or He's not interested in our puny lives… like it's all made up so people can comfort themselves in their hardships."

"But if you've explained it to me right, then the measures that God and Jesus took to make a bridge over the chasm isn't about religion," Cynthia said. "It simply reflects the nature and reality of the world we live in, isn't that right? It's like a law of the universe, along the same lines as the laws of gravity or the laws of physics."

Ellie felt totally shocked. "Wow! You are the most quickly perceptive woman I've ever met. It takes some people years to figure this out, if they ever do. So many people claiming to be Christians think that accepting Jesus into their life is about adopting the routine of going to church and practicing a list of dos and don'ts. There is some validity to all that, but it has to be borne out of a relationship with God. We go to church to learn more about the God we're in fellowship with, and we do some things and not others as part of our loving response to Him. Otherwise a person is just going through the motions, doing stuff hoping to please God. They miss out on what should be a natural relationship with the God who lovingly created us for companionship with Himself."

"Right. I get it." Cynthia leaned in closer. "You still haven't told me how to begin."

"You address the Lord Jesus directly," said Ellie. "I'll model a prayer for you and then you can repeat something similar in your own words. 'Lord Jesus, I recognize and agree that I am a sinful person separated from You. I confess my sins as proof that I'm cut off from You and ask You to cleanse me with the shed blood of Jesus, who died in my place. I ask You to come and take up residence in my heart and life, and to help me to live for and be like Jesus in all that I say and do. I ask this in His name, amen.'"

Cynthia repeated Ellie's prayer almost word for word without any hesitation. When she finished, she smiled and looked up.

"I'm having a feeling," Cynthia said softly.

"A feeling? Tell me about it."

"It's a feeling like…." Cynthia paused trying to come up with accurate words. "…like I've finally come home after being away for a long time and been terribly homesick. Does that make any sense?"

"It so very does, my sweet sister," said Ellie with a catch in her throat. She reached out and hugged Cynthia. "It's another way of confirming you've been reborn into the family of God. You are His child, a daughter of the King of Kings and Lord of Lords, with all the benefits and responsibilities that come with it."

Cynthia was glowing. "Then I suppose this fulfills my childhood dream of being a princess for real…"

⌒〜

As soon as Ellie's chosen quotes were printed, she got ready to return to Hugh's house and begin mapping out the border. Cynthia offered to come along and help since she couldn't work on sewing Ellie's wedding outfits yet. The fabric they had ordered hadn't arrived. Ellie was thrilled to have her along.

At Hugh's place, they tried different combinations of quotes, but none made the border come out perfectly within the forty-two-foot space. Ellie's favourite layout still had approximately twelve inches left over.

"I need an idea, Lord," prayed Ellie aloud.

Cynthia was puzzled only for a second before understanding what Ellie was up to. She smiled and added, "I second that."

Insight came.

"Got it!" cried Ellie. "And it's perfect!"

Having worked out the spacing issue, the two young women taped up the quotes near the ceiling and began the time-consuming task of transferring the letters to the wall using carbon paper.

By four o'clock, Ellie had the place tidied up again, ready to begin the calligraphy paintwork the next day.

On the way back to Minitonas, Ellie turned to her friend. "Do you have a Bible?"

"Yeah. Somewhere," Cynthia replied.

"Dig it out and begin to read. Try to read a portion every day and spend some time talking with God directly, too. I call it soul work. And it's got so that whenever I miss a day for some reason or other, I seriously miss having that one-on-one time with the Lord. It's changed me, and for the good."

"Will do, girlfriend. I'm truly curious about what's in the Bible. Looking forward to it."

Fourteen

MIDMORNING THE NEXT day, Ellie had to shove the furnishings away from the walls in the front room to make space for the stepladder so she could paint the border. She had some plain paper on which to practice her strokes before applying them to the wall, as well as a plastic ice cream pail lid to mix her colours. The plan was to make the lettering look vintage. She gently swirled a glob of navy paint with a smaller glob of dark green, and a dot of gold. After a few practices, she was ready to go for broke.

With a steady hand, Ellie painted the first letter, a capital T. Success!

When the first word was completed, she got down to view it from across the room. From the front door, the word was easily legible. With a happy sigh of relief, she got back onto the stepladder and carried on.

Ellie had gotten around to the second wall when she heard the familiar sounds of a vehicle driving onto the property. A quick glance through the front window informed her that it wasn't anyone she knew.

She hesitated, not wanting to abandon her project. The water-based paint she mixed dried quickly. But soon enough she heard the lumbering treads of someone coming up the steps, followed by a knock on the door.

"Come in!"

The door opened, letting in a stocky man that straightaway reminded her of her Uncle Herb who farmed in the Bowsman area. Long grey-haired sideburns bristled under the edges of his red cap, common headwear amongst the farmers of the Swan Valley. His hands were also among the largest Ellie had ever seen. They reminded her of baseball gloves.

He gazed around the room, crowded with furniture, and looked for the owner of the voice who had invited him in.

"Oh, there you are," he said loudly upon spying Ellie on the step-ladder. "You must be the new Mrs. Fischer."

"Nearly so. And who might you be?"

"Otto Hoffman."

"The Otto Hoffman who's on the FBC elder board?" asked Ellie, astonished. "And whose wife is Agnes, a good friend of my mother's?"

Otto seemed suddenly wary. "Who wants to know?"

"Ella Rose Bauman, daughter of John and Elizabeth Bauman."

He visibly relaxed. "I knew your parents well."

"What can I do for you, Mr. Hoffman?"

"I've come to bring the younger Mr. Fischer the remainder of what I owe for renting his land this past season."

With a sigh, she plunged her small paintbrush into the glass of water, kept on the shelf of her stepladder, and came over to receive the cheque. Immediately she judged that the amount didn't seem right.

"Did you rent both quarters or just one?" asked Ellie.

He seemed to get wary again. "Both quarters."

"At three hundred and twenty acres, times the going rate of at least $35 an acre..." She trailed off, doing the calculations in her head.

"I rented the land from Miss Margo at the agreed price of $25 an acre," said Otto, plainly perturbed over being challenged.

"That would have been three years ago following the accidental death of Fred and Alice."

"That's correct."

"And the rate hasn't been increased since? I mean, the land is worth more and grain sells for more today, too. Rent is supposed to keep pace with those increases."

"Well, Miss Margo didn't ask for more and no person in their right mind goes up to the owner and makes a point of *offering* more."

"You're right," agreed Ellie. "The average Joe would work out the best deal possible for himself even if it meant taking advantage of an orphaned young woman who didn't know beans about the business of grain farming. But a man of integrity might be generous enough to explain things to a naïve woman and work out a win-win proposition."

Otto pursed his lips and glared at her. "When I first rented this place, the land was a mess," he snapped. "You wouldn't believe the thistles and other noxious weeds that had been allowed to overrun the place."

"But you got a reduced rate and took care of those problems, right?"

"That I did," said Otto, smiling smugly while crossing his arms.

"That's very good of you, Mr. Hoffman. You were a good steward of the land. I can't fault you for that."

Aiming to offer a modicum of hospitality in the midst of the upside-down room, Ellie invited him to pull out one of the kitchen chairs and sit down. She asked him to wait a moment, then left the room.

Otto sat on the chair, bouncing one knee and nervously wondering what the Bauman woman was keeping him waiting for. She soon returned carrying the file folder Margo had passed along to Hugh earlier in July. She rifled through the different pockets until she found what she was looking for.

"I have here a copy of the receipt for the deposit you gave Margo in spring for $2,000," she said. "This cheque is for $4,250. A total of $6,250. Divide that by $25 and you're paying rent on... a mere two hundred fifty acres on two quarters?" Ellie looked up, feeling affronted. "How do you figure? I realize there's some bush on the home quarter, but I can't see there being seventy acres of it."

"I admit we guesstimated the farmable acres," said Otto, clearly ill at ease. "But another thing: the East Favel River runs along the back of the property and clips the corner. There's not three hundred twenty acres of farmable land here."

"You're probably right, although I'll be surprised if there's very much less than three hundred. But you know what? I concede that you made this agreement with Margo. Since she accepted your guesstimate, we'll just have to do the same. But this ends our rental relationship. If I have anything to say about it, and I believe I will, we'll rent our land to our nearest neighbour who treats both people and the land with integrity."

Otto scowled, not liking her inference. He shook his head but didn't say anything more. His little gravy train had reached the end of the rail, and he knew it. There was nothing else to do but get away from the woman who knew how to think and do arithmetic before she figured out more things that could get him into trouble.

He meant to stand up and take his leave, but Ellie spoke again. "Actually, Mr. Hoffman, I'd really like to talk with you about something else."

"What would that be?" grunted Otto.

Though the furniture was pushed into the middle of the room, Ellie managed to take a seat on the arm of the sofa before continuing. "Even though we Baumans were neighbours of the Fischers for so many years, I never met Hugh's father in all that time. I was wondering, can you tell me anything about him?"

"Not a thing. Never knew the man." Otto made another effort to rise to a standing position.

"Well, now I've caught you in a lie." She looked straight into Otto's wide-set eyes. "Not so long ago, Hugh and I found a little booklet that belonged to Freddie Fischer. There were lots of names written in it. Yours was one of them."

"That don't mean anything."

"Oh, I'm sure it does. This past summer, we discovered that Hugh's dad ran a moonshine operation, and we're one hundred percent sure this little booklet with its list of many names represents his customers. Since your name is in there, that's proof to me that you knew him."

Otto frowned. "What are you inferring, young lady?"

"Why don't you tell me? You know, we found some bottles filled with the hooch he made. Hugh tried a mouthful. It just about flattened him out!"

The man chortled. "Oh yeah, Fred cooked up some powerful brew."

Suddenly he froze and glanced up at Ellie. She had a "Gotcha!" look on her face.

"I didn't know the man well," insisted Otto. "It wasn't like we were friends or anything. We didn't travel in the same circles at all."

"Given what I have so far learned about him, that's a relief. The notebook listed the nicknames of the regular buddies he hung out with. Names like Chiclets, Monster, Tipper…"

"I heard Tipper is dead now."

"He is. I witnessed his death personally. He died on the sidewalk outside the hotel in Minitonas."

"One more piece of riffraff off the streets, and the world is better off for it." His self-righteousness rose like steam from his breath.

Ellie ignored the remark. "What I'm getting at is this: I'm curious what Freddie Fischer's nickname was."

"He was known on the streets as Sly," said Otto. "It fit him, too."

"Paint me a picture."

"Your husband looks just like him, though maybe a tad taller."

"So I've heard. A handsome man then."

He crossed his arms, resting them on his chest. "His good looks made him popular with the ladies, at least the ones in the bar. He was what you call a womanizer. Maybe you should watch out for that in his boy. Apples don't fall far from the tree, you know."

"Did you ever meet his wife, Hugh's mother?"

"Nope. I told you. We weren't friends." Now Otto sounded annoyed. "Why don't you ask his boy? He'll know better than anyone what they were like."

"Hugh ran away from home when he turned sixteen, so I know about the early years. I'm curious about the dozen years that came after he left. Did Hugh's leaving shake Freddie up into becoming a better husband and father?"

"If reputation and rumour are any indication, then no. He probably didn't care much."

"What about their deaths? Apparently the case remains a mystery, other than that they careened off the edge of the highway by the bridge. The truck they were driving rolled over a couple of times before landing on its roof in the river."

"That's what it said in the newspaper. I don't know nothin' more than what the paper reported, and that's a fact."

Ellie believed him. He didn't exhibit the shifty, telltale signs of someone lying or hiding something. Still, the attitude of this farmer sitting in the kitchen, his arms smugly folded across his chest, rankled her.

"I guess I won't learn more about my new family from you," conceded Ellie. "But what I can't get my head around is the First Baptist Church in Minitonas having a sot as a member of the elder board."

"Watch your tongue, young lady. I am no sot." He glowered at her. "I just have the odd nip now and then. There's no sin in that."

"I don't know what else it can mean, with you having put in such a large order for moonshine with Freddie Fischer, albeit a few years ago. I'm guessing you're a secret drinker. Maybe a secret alcoholic. Does Mrs. Hoffman know? How can she not? And I wonder, does that mean you don't treat her well? Alcoholics are seldom kind to their families..."

The longer Ellie spoke, the redder became Otto Hoffman's jowls. His eyes narrowed into steely slits and he uncrossed his arms, leaning forward on the chair. It looked like he wanted to speak, but Ellie wouldn't let him get a word in edgewise.

"I wonder if drinking is your only secret," she kept on going dryly. "Maybe you also secretly gamble. Since you're not above cheating people out of money that should be coming to them, maybe you cheat on your taxes, too…"

She was poking the bear and she knew it, but somehow she couldn't seem to stop herself. Her mouth was like a runaway train in need of a steep hill to slow her down.

"Now listen here, Ms. Bauman, you don't know nothin' about me—"

"You said you knew my parents well. Did my dad know your secrets? Given his strict view of morals, I can't imagine he would have turned a blind eye. What does our pastor know? I think maybe nothing—yet. You've managed to pull the wool over his eyes and the other elders, right?"

Suddenly, the realization came to him. His closet sins had been found out. Proof could be brought forward. It would create a scandal in the church and in the community.

Otto was so angry that upon standing up he trembled all over like a bowl of jelly. His mitt-sized hands clenched and unclenched. He looked very much like he was about to take a step towards Ellie and wring her slender neck.

"You should mind your own business, woman!" An idea suddenly came to him and he continued in a slightly quieter voice. "If you say anything about this to anyone, you'll be guilty of gossip."

"Since when does telling the truth pass for gossip?"

"What do you want?"

"I want you to give up your sins, Mr. Hoffman. Be an honest, genuine Christian. Be worthy of the role you play in your position with the church!"

"I've had just about enough of this." Otto turned on his heel and marched out the door, not bothering to shut it behind him.

"And don't bring shame to the name of the Lord Jesus," called out Ellie after him.

She wasn't sure Otto heard that last part, since he slammed the door of his truck just as she concluded her words. He started the truck, revved the motor, and spun out of the driveway, kicking up dirt and gravel as he fled.

While the exchange was happening, Ellie had felt as cool as a cucumber, but after Mr. Hoffman left she began to shake all over.

"What have I done? What got into me?" wailed Ellie. "Good heavens, I'm not usually rude like that. Where did that come from? I suppose I'll have to go to him and apologize. But... for what... exactly?"

It took a few minutes for Ellie to settle down. The paints she had stirred on the ice cream pail lid had dried. She busied herself with cleaning off the dried paint and mixed a fresh palette so she could resume her calligraphy.

By and by she calmed down and was able to finish her project just as Hugh rolled into the yard at the end of his day's work. He walked into the house and stood still just as Ellie came out of the bathroom from cleaning her painting equipment.

"Whoa! Is it all right for me to be in here?" he asked, noting that the only available space in which to move was around the edge of the room.

"Yes. I've just finished." Ellie looked to him in anticipation. "Tell me what you think."

Hugh read the border aloud: "'*Trust in the Lord with all your heart, and do not rely on your own insight. In all your ways acknowledge him, and he will make straight your paths.*'[11] '*Do for others just what you want them to do for you.*'[12] '*Three things I pray; to see thee more clearly, to love thee more dearly, to follow thee more nearly, day by day.*'[13] '70x7' It's very cool, Ellie. I like it a lot. But what do those numbers at the end mean?"

"It's from a story where one of Jesus's disciples asks Him how many times he should forgive a man. The disciple suggests that it could be as many as seven times. But Jesus corrects his thinking by telling him to forgive seventy times seven times. In other words, forgiveness should be unlimited. I thought that was the perfect way to fill in my leftover space."

---

[11] Proverbs 3:5–6, RSV.
[12] Luke 6:31, GNT.
[13] Richard of Chichester, "Day by day, dear Lord..."

Together they moved the furniture back into their places, allowing the room to resume its cozy ambience. Only the kitchen corner remained out of sync with the rest of the space. Ellie had to bite her lip to stop herself from complaining about it.

Hugh opened the refrigerator to see what they could throw together for supper. There weren't enough leftovers to satisfy both appetites.

"I'm tired and I don't feel like cooking," said Ellie. "Let's have supper at the café tonight. Then I want to go over to Darcey's for a while. I need a counsellor."

"Oh? Sounds like something happened today. Do I want to know what it was?"

"At least part of it, you do. The farmer who rented your half section came by this morning and paid what he owes."

She showed Hugh the cheque and then told him about the full discussion she'd had with Otto Hoffman over the farmable acres and rate of rent.

"I'm glad it was you and not me," Hugh remarked. "I doubt I would have caught on to the discrepancies. I think you handled the situation well. Likely better than I would have. You rightly honoured Margo's agreement, even if it was a poor one."

"Well, I kept him back to talk about other matters, and I don't think I handled that so well…"

"Tell me about it over supper. I'm starving."

They ordered the soup and sandwich special at the café, and while waiting for their order to arrive Ellie told Hugh about the second part of her encounter with Mr. Hoffman.

He listened attentively while she recalled the exchange regarding Otto's connections with his pa over orders of moonshine. Her tale took on a rueful tone when she admitted to challenging him on his drinking as it related to his role with the First Baptist Church and more.

When she'd concluded her story, Hugh leaned back on his bench and laughed.

"I don't think it's a laughing matter," said Ellie, frowning. "I feel bad for calling him out like I did, but I'm not sure what I should do about it."

"It sounds like the guy had it coming and you delivered." Hugh tried to be serious, but then broke out into another chuckle. "You have it in you to speak plainly, all right. Have you forgotten the time you took me to task because I didn't want to forgive my father?"

"That was different."

"Not a lot. I was pretty mad at you for a while, but I came around eventually. When someone is right, they're right. Nobody *ever* likes to have their wrongdoing pointed out to them."

"But I feel like I should apologize. It's just that I'm not sure what I'd apologize *for*."

"I think you should let it go and let the chips fall where they may," said Hugh, not in the least perturbed. "You're a force to be reckoned with, babe. You've got more nerve than I do, for sure, and I like that about you... at least when we're on the same side."

He winked at her, then paid the tab.

When they arrived at Darcey and Tony's house, Darcey led them straight to the garage, thinking they had come to check on the progress regarding the kitchen cabinets. Tony was busy sorting through the barnwood, looking for the best parts to create the shaker-style door fronts. He had already constructed the basic units, having set them aside in the order they would eventually be installed.

Immediately Ellie could visualize how it would fit into their little house. The sight cheered her up substantially.

But not long afterwards, her heartache returned. She left Hugh and Tony to catch up and sought out Darcey, who was in the middle of putting her three daughters to bed. Once she was available to chat, Ellie described her meeting with Otto Hoffman. Much to Ellie's surprise, Darcey's response was somewhat like Hugh's.

"First, I should tell you that while I know what faces go with those names, I don't know much about the Hoffmans," said Darcey. "Beyond that, it doesn't sound like you actually accused him of bad behaviour. You just suggested it, and he didn't actually deny it, did he?"

"No. He did say that if I repeated it to the church community, I'd be guilty of gossip, which by the way I have no intention of doing," said Ellie, still feeling glum.

"Hmm, I think you inadvertently stumbled upon the man's secret sin and called him out. Jesus did that, too. Remember, He told the woman caught in adultery, *'Go, but do not sin again.'*[14] And He told the lame guy by the pool of Bethesda to *'stop sinning or something worse may happen.'*[15] There's a place for calling a spade a spade, girlfriend. And there's a reason why we also say, 'If the shoe fits, wear it.'"

"Then why do I feel so awful about it? Why do I feel like I should apologize?"

"That's easy. You're a Christian woman who's been taught that we're supposed to be nice and sweet about everything all the time. And that if we question someone's behaviour, we're immediately accused of being out of line for judging. I think that's piffle! When people claim to be Christian, it's the responsible thing to do, and an act of love, to call out sinful behaviour. It's not about being self-righteous… it's about getting the erring person back on a right track" Darcey spoke with absolute certitude. "I think you feel bad because you spoke the truth bluntly. And because Mr. Hoffman is a peer of your dad. It's not usually appropriate for young people to call out their elders. But who else knows about his skeleton in the cupboard? Seems like no one. On the other hand, we're supposed to stand up for what is right."

Ellie's countenance still looked unhappy.

Darcey continued. "Look, I wasn't there to witness the exchange of words for myself, so I don't know for sure. Maybe you need to work on your manner of speaking. Like not resorting to yelling, for example. Did you yell at him?"

Ellie shook her head dismally.

---

[14] John 8:11, GNT.
[15] John 5:14, GNT.

"On the other hand, I also know there's a time and place for giving someone's arse a good swift kick. Sometimes that's the only way to get through to a body. Look, if I'm wrong, the Lord will convict you and give you no peace until you make things right by apologizing."

"He will, won't He," agreed Ellie submissively.

She smiled. "Now, I think the cure for all contrite feelings is some special, fruity, sweet-spiced tea. Given how bad you feel, you might need a quart of it."

Fifteen

THE FOLLOWING TWO and a half weeks unfolded in a normally busy way. When Ellie wasn't working shifts at the hospital, she sewed the tartan yard goods she had purchased into a duvet cover and shams for the bedroom. Then, when the furniture store in Swan River staged a pre-Christmas sale, she scored a good buy on a queen-sized mattress and pair of handsome lamps. She and Sarah worked on wedding invitations and brainstormed ways to decorate both the church and reception hall. They consulted a florist, too, and ordered bouquets and boutonnieres.

And as for the men, they found the time to shop for suits, shirts, ties, and shoes. Hugh and Ellie also fit in two premarital counselling sessions with Pastor Leland and his wife. They found them to be surprisingly valuable.

One Saturday, the Cliffords made good on their promise to take engagement photos of Hugh and Ellie. They went around to different outdoor settings around the neighbourhood. Cynthia wanted to use the old swayback barn as one of the backdrops, but Hugh wouldn't hear of it. He was willing to use other old buildings, but none at his own place.

Ellie had to take Cynthia aside to explain that it had to do with bad memories.

They took a few photos by the pond where Hugh had proposed, though it looked rather forlorn with the trees and shrubs bare of all leaves. Other photos were taken by bridges, beside the East Favel River in Minitonas, while leaning on an old wooden fence, and even by Hugh's pickup; it was, after all, still his pride and joy.

Brent had the photos developed *tout suite*, and Ellie was so pleased by the results that she had a hard time selecting just one for the invitations. Two others she framed, setting one on her bedside table and the other on top of the entertainment unit at Hugh's house.

Needless to say, Brent got the job of being the official photographer for the wedding.

On another Saturday, the Moore brothers came over. With the assistance of Hugh's tractor, they joined forces to drag the three vintage vehicles out of the bush and bring them onto the main yard. They parked them along the south side of the farmyard, near to the old combine and disc tillager which still sat out front, unwanted by anyone. The brothers also helped Hugh reposition the summer cabin next to the carport beside the little house so it could serve as a storage room.

Meanwhile, Hugh was settling into his role as chief mechanic at the dealership. He found his role to be satisfying, for the most part. Occasionally he had to deal with a disgruntled customer, but he worked on himself to take those occurrences in stride instead of getting impatient as he would have done in the past.

Whenever he could spare a minute, he went over to the autobody division to learn what he could about the skills he would need to restore the Plymouth. One day, an elderly man brought in a very old and quaint bicycle that had once belonged to his wife. He wanted it repainted in pink for his granddaughter—and he wanted it in time for Christmas. Ralph, the autobody guy, said it wouldn't be a problem; he would fit it in between jobs.

That gave Hugh an idea. He discussed it with Ralph, who promised to help him out.

～

The weather felt increasingly wintry. Occasionally snow fell, but then it melted the following day. But the third week of November finally brought a heavier snowfall that heralded the onset of winter, despite the solstice still being a month away. The denizens of the Swan Valley woke to a thick blanket of snow deep enough to warrant winter boots, not to mention winter tires on their vehicles.

When Trevor came home from school, Sarah asked him to shovel snow off the steps and sidewalk by their house. After dropping off his homework and wolfing down a pair of chocolate chip cookies with milk, he went back outside to do as his mother asked. He had just about reached the end of the walk when a souped-up sedan from 1964 pulled up, newly painted in metallic green.

Three of his hockey teammates were in the car. Driving was Brock, the youngest in a family of four boys and the first among these friends to get his driver's license. In the passenger seat was Lonny, a dashing hunk of a teenager with the eyes of every girl in eleventh grade following every move he made. The guy in the back seat was pimply faced Ken. The acne made him a little self-conscious, but he also happened to be one of the best players on their team.

"Hey Trev!" called Lonny as he rolled down his window. "Come for a ride with us."

Trevor scraped the last bit of snow away and set the shovel aside. He glanced at his watch, and then at the house. In a split second, he decided he had a few minutes to spare to cruise around town with his buddies for a bit. He got into the back seat with Ken.

"Nice wheels," said Trevor, truly admiring the car outside and in. Besides the fancy paint job, the car sported broad mag wheels. The interior was whistle-clean and the upholstery appeared new.

Brock turned up the radio so the bass pounded out a throbbing beat a person could feel in their bones.

"Yeah!" Brock had to shout to be heard over the music. "It belongs to my brother Larry. He said I could take it for a spin around town. He just got it back from the autobody on Monday. It was his rebuild project last year."

"It's way cool." Trevor ran his hand over the smooth vinyl and cloth upholstery.

They drove past a couple of girls walking along the street and knew immediately they were Susan and Helen, also from their grade. Lonny rolled down his window and wolf-whistled. The girls looked at each other and smiled shyly, although they seemed thrilled with the attention they were getting.

Brock stopped the car and the girls approached Lonny's open window.

"Wanna come for a ride with us?" asked Lonny in his smoothest voice.

"I don't know," said Susan. "Where're you going?"

"Nowhere in particular. Just cruising around town."

Helen peered in the window. "Doesn't look like there's any room."

"We can fit one in the front and the other in the back, no problem."

"I suppose... if there's room..." conceded Susan.

Lonny and Ken jumped out of their seats and the two girls climbed in between the boys in both the front and back seats. The party spirit kicked in and they all began to yuk it up, teasing each other and making smart-assed remarks.

Lonny pulled out a package of cigarettes from the inside of his jacket, withdrew one, and lit it up like a practiced smoker.

"Hey, when did you start that up?" asked Trevor, surprised.

"Not long ago. Why?"

"I thought you wanted to play professional hockey. Smoking won't help you get there."

Lonny released a long stream of smoke. "I'll be fine."

"Who are you?" cut in Brock, turning around to look Trevor in the face. "His mother?"

With a thunderous noise and a great shaking, all the lights and sounds around them suddenly went out.

~

Trevor's hearing returned first to the sound of his own moaning. He tasted blood and then tried to open his eyes. At first everything was a blur, but as his senses gradually resumed he became aware of other sounds, including a person struggling to get off his chest. It was Helen attempting to right herself into a sitting position and having to deal with Ken on her left, who had somehow gotten partially trapped beneath her. When she was upright, she looked at Trevor and they exchanged stunned looks.

"You're bleeding," she said.

"What?" asked Trevor stupidly. The world churned chaotically; his vision of her doubled and then narrowed back to normal again.

"Your nose. You've got a nosebleed." She began to cry as the pain of her own bangs and bruises began to register.

Time seemed suspended, but it was probably not more than a minute or two before people in nearby houses poured outside to investigate the sounds of the crash and then run to help the victims.

They were at the intersection of Third Avenue and Highway 366 in Minitonas, having T-boned a blue and white pickup. The driver of the truck had only realized at the last second that the car wasn't going to stop, and at that point there had been no way to avoid the collision.

Trevor couldn't get his bearings. The confusion seemed to last an eternity, although in reality it was only a couple of minutes before men were pulling at the doors, trying to assess life from death, hurt bad from minor injury.

"Hullo!" said a man knocking on the passenger window next to Trevor. "Are you all right in there?"

Trevor looked at him, hardly comprehending what was going on.

The man opened the rear door. "Do you think you can walk? Can you come out?"

He helped Trevor turn sideways and set his feet on the ground. The boy stood and took a few steps. His legs seemed to work. No broken bones.

A woman approached and draped a blanket over his shoulders. She led him away from the car so the others could be helped out.

"What happened?" asked Trevor, still dazed.

"There's been an accident," replied the woman kindly. "And judging by the wreck, you're lucky to be alive."

One by one, the young people were helped out of the car. They stood with the adults who had come to help them, except for Brock.

"I can't feel my legs," Brock said to the man enquiring of him. He began to shake violently as the shock took over.

"We need another blanket here!" called the man at Brock's side.

The driver of the pickup had fared worst. The side where he'd been sitting was totally smashed in. The men trying to help saw that he was out cold; they decided not to move him until the ambulance arrived to assess his condition.

The police and ambulance sped up with flashing lights and sirens blaring. They identified the man behind the wheel of the pickup as none other than Robert Bauman.

A bystander immediately took responsibility to inform Sarah of the crash. Their house wasn't far away, and he ran all the way.

"There's been an accident," he said to Sarah when she opened the door. "Rob's truck was hit. Looks like he's hurt bad."

"Oh my gosh! Where is he?"

"Just two blocks away. You should come quickly."

Sarah turned to Charlotte. "Daddy's been in an accident. I have to go. Turn off the stove and look after your sister. I don't know when I'll be back."

She arrived on the scene along with her neighbour just as the paramedics were carrying Rob on a stretcher into the ambulance. She saw her husband's bloodied head and face and ran up to the attendant.

"He's not dead, is he?"

"Are you his wife?"

"I am."

"We have a pulse, but it's weak. He's lost a lot of blood. We'll do our best to keep him alive," said the attendant brusquely. It was an emergency situation and he couldn't take the time to say anything more.

Sarah's neighbour pointed across the road. "Isn't that Trevor over there?"

"Oh Lord! Yes, it is." Sarah was wide-eyed with confusion at seeing her son standing with a cluster of young people, draped in a blanket. A police officer was speaking with them.

She left the scene of the ambulance to approach Trevor.

"Trevor, what are you doing here? Were you in the accident, too? Are you hurt?"

The realization of the severity of the accident was beginning to register and she fought the urge to panic. Two of the most beloved people in her life were involved.

"Mom!" cried Trevor, throwing himself into her arms. "I'm okay. At least I think I am. I just got thrown around a bit and got a nosebleed. But I'm getting a terrible headache. I just want to go home."

Sarah held him while listening to the police officer. He had taken everyone's name and contact information and then urged them all to get to the hospital for an emergency checkup to ensure they hadn't sustained hidden injuries.

The ambulance sped away bearing Rob and Brock, the sirens shrieking all the way into Swan River.

Sarah hurried Trevor home. Charlotte and Beanie looked on in frightened astonishment while their mother wiped the dried blood from Trevor's face.

"Charlotte, I have to run into Swan River to get Trevor checked out… and to see what they're doing with Dad. Please tidy the kitchen after you eat, and look after Bernadette. I would greatly appreciate that. I probably won't be back until late."

She had a very controlled tone of voice, one that none of her children had ever heard from her before.

"What about Dad?" asked Trevor hurriedly. "Where is he?"

While Sarah rushed as fast as she dared to Swan River Valley Hospital, she told Trevor what scant information she had regarding the accident.

"I'm told a car with teenagers rammed into your dad's truck," said Sarah coolly. "And now I find out that you were in that car. I'm sure you have a good explanation…"

"It was nothin', Mom. Brock was just showing off his brother's new rebuilt car. They invited me to come for a ride to see how cool it was." He cradled his severely aching head in both hands.

"Well, that ride just about cost me my husband and my son," cried Sarah, near her breaking point.

Neither said another word for a few moments.

"Stop the car!" Trevor suddenly shouted.

Sarah pulled over and brought the station wagon to a halt. Trevor got out and lost his cookies almost immediately.

"You're still in shock," said Sarah, reaching across to take hold of Trevor's hand when he got back inside.

He groaned. "My head hurts so bad."

"We're almost there, honey," said Sarah, trying in vain not to worry.

The emergency room, having already received Brock and Rob, were expecting others involved in the crash to appear. Thus, when Sarah and Trevor arrived, he was registered without delay and assigned to a hospital gurney for examination.

As much as she wanted to be on hand for her son, Sarah was deeply anxious about Rob and his injuries. From the little she had seen, he appeared to be in critical condition and she desperately needed an update, not to mention a large measure of reassurance.

She excused herself from Trevor's side to make enquiries about her husband.

The emergency room had gotten very busy. More accident victims had arrived and the cubicles were full. The nurses were suddenly run off their feet.

Sarah took the initiative to peek into various rooms to find Rob and the medical team working on him. On the third try, she found him with what looked like two doctors and two nurses leaning over him. Hours earlier, Rob had still sported some tanned skin from the summer; now he looked as pale as death.

"How is he?" she asked in a voice tight with anxiety.

One of the doctors stepped forward and spoke firmly. "You should not be in here."

"Don't say that to me," snapped Sarah. "I'm his wife, and my children and I need to know."

"I'll speak with her," offered one of the nurses.

The nurse escorted Sarah outside the examination room and led her to a waiting area at the far end of the ward where there were no other people around.

"Your husband has sustained some serious injuries, Mrs. Bauman," the nurse began, "but I believe the doctors are optimistic about his recovery. Both the tibia and fibula bones in his left leg are broken, and also his right clavicle. No doubt that came as a result of being thrown around in the vehicle upon impact. His head has been severely lacerated, but luckily the tender spot at his temple was not struck. I believe the doctors are cautiously optimistic for a full recovery there as well. However, he is still being examined. It's possible further discoveries will change these initial estimations."

Sarah calmed down somewhat. "I understand. I appreciate you telling me what you know so far."

"I need to go back," said the nurse. "Will you wait here for further updates?"

"I'll be here or in the emergency department where my son is being examined. He was involved in the crash as well, though not as critically."

"I'm so sorry, Mrs. Bauman. Your husband is a healthy man with a good strong heartbeat. I believe his chances are very good."

"Thank you," said Sarah, faltering as the stress gave way to delayed emotion. "Please take care of him."

A tear slipped from her eye which she quickly brushed away. Crying could come later. Right now she needed to be strong for Trevor.

Trevor's examination revealed no broken bones. However, the doctor noted whiplash and a possible concussion. The staff meant to keep him overnight for observation and treat him for the crushing headache. At length, he dozed off with his mother holding his hand.

Sixteen

CHARLOTTE AND THE Bean tried to eat some of the supper their mother had prepared, but both found they had little appetite. Soon the food was put away in plastic containers. As Charlotte tidied the kitchen, being worried made her abrupt and irritable with Beanie, who couldn't handle the added stress and began to cry.

"Don't cry," instructed Charlotte, feeling annoyed. "It doesn't help."

That caused Beanie to cry all the harder. "I want Mommy!"

"We can't have Mommy right now!" But then, in a softer tone, she added, "Maybe we can have Aunty Ellie."

Beanie's sobs quieted down to a few sniffles.

Charlotte reached for the phone and dialled. Several rings later, she hung up in frustration.

"Not home. Maybe she's at Hugh's place."

She had to look up the number and soon found it handwritten on the cover of the phone book. She dialled it at once.

"Hairy's armpit!" answered Hugh cheerfully on the second ring.

Charlotte paused, nonplussed. "Sorry, I must have dialled the wrong number."

"Nah, I'm just messin' with ya." Hugh chuckled. "You got Hugh Fischer. What can I do for you?"

"I'm looking for Aunty Ellie," said Charlotte.

"Charlotte? Your aunt isn't here. She's working tonight."

"Oh…"

Hugh heard the faint sounds of stifled sobbing. "Is something wrong, honey?"

With the words tumbling out in a rush, Charlotte told Hugh everything she knew about her dad and Trevor being in an accident, including the fact that they were at the Swan River Valley hospital. She and Beanie wanted Ellie for comfort and reassurance.

"I'll be right over," promised Hugh.

Twenty minutes after hanging up, he drove into Rob Bauman's yard in Minitonas, his hair still wet from the hasty shower. Both girls rushed to embrace him.

"Tell me again everything you know," said Hugh after he removed his jacket.

The story was repeated, with Beanie describing what their mother had told them about Trevor's bloody face.

"Would you like to go to the hospital and see what else we can find out?"

"Yes, please!" they chorused.

In minutes, they were on the highway.

～

They found Trevor resting comfortably. The pain medication he was given for the headache was finally taking effect, allowing him to receive his sisters gladly.

"How are you doing, bud?" Hugh greeted gently.

"Your nose… your nose is red like Rudolf the red-nosed reindeer," said Beanie with child-like concern.

Trevor looked irritable. "That's because I bumped it good."

"Can you tell us what happened?" Hugh laid a hand on Trevor's arm, hoping to convey sympathy.

Trevor eyes glistened, but he fought to maintain control of his emotions. "My friends were driving around town and invited me to come along. Brock, the driver, was showing off his brother's newly minted souped-up car. We picked up a couple of girls from our class who were walking along and then suddenly, out of nowhere, we got in a crash."

Something about Trevor's explanation sounded off to Hugh—as though the details he had shared were carefully selected out of all that could have been said. But he didn't push it.

"That's tough, bud. On the bright side, at least you weren't killed. Doesn't look like you got hurt too bad either, thank goodness."

"Yeah, I'm all right. But the guy we crashed into turned out to be my dad, and Mom said he's hurt real bad."

Charlotte leaned closer to her brother. "Where is Mom, by the way?"

"She went to find out what's going on with Dad."

"We'll come back in a bit, Trev," said Hugh. "We'll look for your mom and see what we can find out."

They found Sarah in the waiting area, speaking with Brock's parents. They were trying to piece together everything they had learned about the accident.

Beanie rushed to her mother and threw her arms around her neck.

"How's Daddy?" asked Charlotte, taking a seat next to her mom.

"Oh my," said Sarah, surprised. "I wasn't expecting to see you here. Is Ellie with you?"

"Ellie's working tonight, so she's in the building." Hugh gave Sarah a hug. "I'm not sure if that means she knows about the accident or not. What can you tell us about Rob?"

Sarah repeated the details about Rob's injuries. The doctors were still at work setting the broken bones and dealing with the worrisome gash on his head.

After this, they decided to look up Ellie.

"Hi guys," greeted Ellie, surprised to see three Baumans plus Hugh approach the nurse's station on her ward.

"Daddy's been in a terrible accident," blurted Beanie.

"Trevor was in it, too," added Charlotte.

While the girls and Sarah filled Ellie in regarding the excitement of the last hour, Hugh excused himself to return to Trevor. He wanted to follow up on his hunch that the young man had more to say about the accident.

He found Trevor lying on his back, staring up at the ceiling. The boy looked back at him with the same underlying troubled expression Hugh had noted earlier.

"You're looking rather rough," said Hugh sympathetically. "Is it because you're sore?"

Trevor rolled over onto his side to face Hugh. "Where are my sisters?"

"They're with your mom. It's just you and me, bud. Do you feel like talking or...?"

"The accident was all my fault," said Trevor, hot tears escaping.

"Hmmm. Why do you think so?"

"Because if I hadn't challenged Lonny on his smoking, Brock wouldn't have turned around to tell me to back off."

"Whoa... wait a minute. Start at the beginning."

Trevor recited the conversation with Lonny and Brock word for word, including how Brock had looked him in the eye to mock him for being like a mother to Lonny.

Hugh sighed. "It's not your fault at all, Trevor. You were being a caring friend to warn Lonny about how smoking could impact his athletic goals. As for Brock, he broke a cardinal rule. A driver *never* takes his eyes off the road when the vehicle is in motion. Ever! If the cops come back to get your version of the story, tell them what you told me."

"I don't want to get my friend in trouble," pleaded Trevor. "His brother's car is wrecked. I can just imagine the hullaballoo over that alone."

"Do you think Brock and Lonny will blame you for the crash?"

"I don't know. Maybe…"

"It's not your fault. Stick to the truth, pal. Stick to the facts. They speak for themselves."

When Ellie, Sarah, and the girls came back in, nothing more was said about the accident. They just concentrated on loving Trevor and expressing their gratitude that he hadn't been hurt more seriously.

The medical team took an hour to set Rob's broken bones and clean and close the laceration on his head. When Sarah was finally allowed to see him, tears coursed down her face. Rob had always been the strong one in their family. The sight of him wan and helpless, swaddled in bandages, stitches in his scalp, and with his left leg raised in a cast was so inconsistent with the Rob she knew. She couldn't believe how quickly a split-second event could change the course of a life.

The doctor came to assure her that the broken bones had been set and only time and patience would heal them. The head injury was a greater cause for concern. Time would tell whether the gash represented the worst of it, or if there were other complications. In the meantime, they meant to keep him sedated and comfortable, watching for fever and other signs of distress.

For Sarah, real life was staring her in the face. What Rob would want was for her to be strong and practical. Also prayerful. She aimed to do her best.

The Bauman women and Hugh returned to Trevor's bedside, where Sarah passed along the doctor's report. She asked them to pray earnestly that no complications would arise.

Trevor turned away from them to face the wall.

Sarah noticed. "What is it, Trevor? It's not your fault your dad is hurt."

"Of course it is. I was in the car that hit him, even if I wasn't driving!"

She slumped in total weariness. "We'll sort that out later, son. For now, I believe, and I want you to believe, that none of this happened intentionally. So please forgive yourself, and forgive your friends." She patted him on the arm. "And rest tonight in peace."

Hugh marvelled at Sarah's strength and common sense, coming at a time when confusion still ruled the hour.

Trevor did seem to be calmer after that.

Sarah decided to stay the night at Rob's side. It was important for her to be the first person he saw when he woke up.

"Have you eaten?" asked Hugh. "Can I bring you some supper?"

Sarah shrugged. "I suppose I should eat something. Not that I have any appetite, mind you."

"I'll be back in a jiffy."

Hugh left on the spot, returning soon with a hamburger, fries, and a cup of coffee.

It was getting late and Sarah wanted the girls taken back home. She suggested a list of friends who would likely be willing to spend the night in the house so the girls wouldn't feel so vulnerable.

Even so, Hugh offered to look after them himself. Sarah sighed with relief.

～

That night, Hugh urged Charlotte and Beanie to get ready for bed. They shared a bedroom, although they slept in single beds.

Hugh stretched out on the couch, intending to spend the night. But it wasn't long before Beanie padded out to the living room dragging her favourite blanket.

"Uncle Hugh, I'm scared," she whimpered.

Hugh understood. It was upsetting to have one's world turned upside-down in all of a second, particularly when it involved the people one counted on for safety and security.

In fact, he was a little upset himself. Rob had become an important friend and mentor. If the unthinkable happened and he didn't pull through, Hugh thought he would grieve as deeply as the immediate family.

Beanie was feeling the great discomfort of uncertainty, and the fear of where things might go next. Hugh figured the best way to deal with that was to borrow a pillow and blanket from Trevor's room and sleep on the floor between the girls' beds. That seemed to do the trick.

But in the morning, he discovered that Beanie had, at some point in the night, brought her pillow and blanket down to the floor and slept next to him. On the other side of him, Charlotte had done the same thing.

What to do? The girls' trust in him was endearing, but now it felt like a slumber party... and he felt out of his element. He looked at his watch and noted that it was a little after seven o'clock in the morning.

He decided not to disturb the girls, since they'd gone to bed late. He just lay there wondering how Rob and Trevor had fared overnight, and about how he could be of further help to Sarah and the family.

Then, without any alert, Ellie appeared in the doorway. Her mouth dropped open at the sight of Hugh and her nieces lying in the centre of the floor, each with their pillows and blankets in a muddle.

Hugh smiled wryly at her. "Never in a thousand years... right?"

"Oh, it's just too cute for words! I wish I had a camera handy." On a more serious note, Ellie added, "Poor girls. It just shows how upset and insecure they feel. Thanks for standing in the gap for my family, Hugh-are-the-best."

"Am I now?" He stood up quickly, no longer caring if he woke the girls. He pulled Ellie close and kissed her forehead. "Tell me again what a great guy I am..."

"You are the most wonderful almost-uncle I know. I don't know of many men who would go the extra mile to make children feel so safe."

"You like that in a man, do you?" said Hugh huskily, kissing her nose.

"I very much do..."

She tipped her chin and Hugh's lips reached their target. They kissed sweetly.

"Eww! That's gross!" said a voice from the floor.

It was Beanie. She sat up and rubbed her eyes. Charlotte opened her eyes next and smiled at the sight of Ellie. Both girls, lugging their blankets, followed the couple into the kitchen.

"I have news," said Ellie brightly. "Your daddy woke up this morning and asked for something to eat. It looks like he is going to be A-okay."

"Yeah!" chorused both girls.

"And your brother passed the night without anything bad showing up," Ellie added. "Your mommy and Trevor should be back home with you about midmorning, I expect."

"I can't tell you how hard I prayed for Daddy and Trevor." Relief flooded Charlotte's face. "I pestered God without stopping until I fell asleep."

"How did you end up on the floor?" asked Hugh. "Did you fall out of bed or something?"

"No..." admitted Charlotte, suddenly shy. "I just wanted to be close to someone. If Mom had been home, I would have crawled into bed with her."

Hugh smiled. "Not a problem. It was a real surprise to find you there, that's all."

"I can't stay," said Ellie. "I need to go home before I fall asleep on my feet." She stood up, zipped her jacket, and got out her car keys. "See you later, alligators."

"In a while, crocodile," finished Beanie.

Seventeen

JUST LIKE ELLIE had said, Sarah and Trevor came home midmorning to the happy cheers of Charlotte and Beanie. The world looked like it might go back to being right-side-up after all.

Trevor immediately showered and closed himself in his room. Meanwhile, Sarah advised his sisters that their brother was still feeling sore from the accident and needed lots of rest and quiet before he would be his jolly old self again.

Having had next to no sleep, Sarah also showered and lay down on her bed for a long nap. The girls were given permission to look up their friends in the neighbourhood and spend time with them while their mother rested.

That evening, Sarah wanted to take her kids to see their dad, but Trevor refused to go. He claimed to have another headache and wanted to take it easy at home. His mother gave him the benefit of the doubt.

But the next day, he didn't want to go again. This time he explained that it still hurt to move.

On the third day, he tried another excuse, citing a stomachache.

This time, Sarah wasn't buying it.

"Your dad is asking for you," she said sharply. "I think you can put in a little effort to keep him company and bring him some cheer. You might not be a hundred percent, but you're a lot better off than he is."

That did it. Trevor turned on his heel and went to his room, slamming the door shut behind him.

Way to go, Sarah, she thought to herself. *I think you just poured salt on his wounds.*

She took a deep breath and knocked on the door to Trevor's room.

"I meant you no offence," she said. "And I'm serious. Your dad is asking for you and you need to come. Your obedience is required."

A moment later, Trevor opened the door and marched past his mother. "Fine! I don't know why you all can't just leave me alone."

The drive into Swan River was quiet and laced with tension. Trevor had taken the back seat in the station wagon, presumably to be as far away from his mother as possible. His sisters, usually chatty, didn't say a word, afraid they were going to start an argument with their brother without intending to.

Upon arrival, Trevor was the first one out of the car. He went ahead without waiting for his mother or sisters. He did stop for them, however, once he got to the foyer of the hospital, because he didn't know where to go next. Sarah ignored his cold shoulder and walked down the hall with her kids in tow.

Rob was being cared for in the post-surgical ward where Ellie worked, though she wasn't on shift this evening.

Beanie ran in first, calling "Hi Daddy!" as she pushed open the door.

Rob immediately laid down the newspaper he was reading. His face lit up like the morning sun.

"Hey! How's my little girl?" he said, beaming.

Beanie moved a chair as close to Rob's bed as she could. She then knelt on it so she could lean over to her daddy and give him a kiss, which he joyfully received.

Charlotte stepped up close on the other side and planted a kiss on his cheek. Sarah was next, placing a light kiss on his mouth.

When Trevor entered the room, he hung back near the window.

"Howdy, stranger," said Rob to Trevor. "Glad you came today. I've missed you. Missed you bigtime, buddy."

Trevor shrugged but didn't speak.

"You look like you'd like to be anywhere but here. What's bothering you, son? Is it that turban the doctor wrapped around my head?" Rob's voice grew gentle. "Does seeing me laid up like a trussed turkey trouble you?"

Trevor turned away to gaze out the window, though there was nothing to be seen; it was dark outside.

"Come on, Trev," Rob pleaded. "Talk to me."

Sarah broke in. "You know what? How about the girls and I go and get you a soda or something? What are you in the mood for?"

"A nice cold drink sounds perfect. Take your time. I'll be here when you get back."

After they left, the room fell silent.

"I take it I'm supposed to guess what the matter is," said Rob. "Okay. Let's see if I still have some wits. Maybe... you think I'm mad at you. I'm not mad at you, Trevor. Not even for a minute. And I'm awfully glad you weren't hurt worse than you were. Soon we'll both be healed up and be as good as new. We'll chalk it up to another life experience."

Trevor still didn't say anything. He maintained his stance in front of the window, his back to his dad.

"That's not it, hey?" said Rob, frowning. There was silence for another moment. "You know, being laid up like this has given me lots of time to think. Lots of time to try and figure things out. I was thinking about the accident. Just before it happened, I saw the car approaching the intersection. I saw that the driver had his head turned, looking behind him. I also saw there was a passenger, actually two, and they had their heads turned as well, either looking at the driver or maybe there was something, or someone, in the back seat. And another thing. I could feel the rock music throbbing all the way to my truck. My point is, there wasn't anyone paying attention to the road ahead. Not one. And then, *bam!* We collided. If you're thinking the accident was your fault, it wasn't. It's the fault of the three people in the front seat, particularly the driver. Not one of them was paying attention."

That stirred Trevor. He turned his head to look at his dad. "They weren't paying attention because they were looking at me!" he said bitterly.

"Okay. That's new information. I'd like to hear about it. Every little detail. In fact, start at the beginning. When they picked you up."

Trevor caved. At his father's insistence, he sat on the chair next to the bed and recounted everything from the time his mother had asked him to shovel the walk to the suddenness of the world seeming to be swallowed up in darkness.

"I heard every word you said, son, and I fail to see how the accident is your fault," said Rob in a kind voice.

"Because if I hadn't challenged Lonny for smoking, none of this would have happened!"

"Okay. I see your point, son. It sounds to me like it was just a conversation, though. By your argument, any kind of talk would have been a distraction. It's not your fault, son. No honest person would say so. And let me tell you something else. The cops have already spoken with me and I told them what I told you—that I heard the car before I saw it and nobody in the car was paying attention. The cop was kind enough to tell me that he'd already spoken with Brock, who admitted to taking his eyes off the road to talk to someone in the back seat. Brock doesn't blame you. He takes responsibility for the crash and he feels very bad about it. You would do well, Trevor, to give up your false burden and reach out to your friend. Let him know that you forgive him. Encourage him to feel like a worthwhile human being again."

"Do you know if he's still in the hospital?" asked Trevor, brightening a little.

"No. He's gone home. He's bruised up pretty good, but there aren't any broken bones. He came to see me before he left."

Trevor felt a little awed. "No kidding."

"Yeah. He came in here blubbering a heartfelt apology, and I forgave him for everything. I even thanked him for forcing me to slow down. I get to have a holiday on the healthcare system's dime." Rob had a twinkle in his eye.

"Da–a–ad!"

"Are you yourself again?" asked Rob. "Cuz if you are, come and give your old man a hug. Love will heal a body faster than any medication will, and that's a fact."

Trevor did his best to embrace his dad from the left side, because the right side was doctored up with bandages and slings.

"Thanks, Dad. Sorry I've been such a pill. I will look up Brock tomorrow, I promise." He felt about twenty pounds lighter.

"Good boy. Now what do you suppose is taking your mother so long? Is she concocting a soda from scratch, do you think?"

When Hugh and Ellie came to the hospital to pay Rob a visit, they saw Sarah's station wagon in the parking lot. Instead of just barging into the room, Ellie opened it a crack to peek through to ensure they weren't interrupting a private moment. She saw Sarah sitting close to Rob with an arm resting across his midriff. His good arm rested on Sarah's shoulder, his hand cupped around her neck. They seemed to be in earnest conversation.

"I hope we'll have what they have after twenty years of marriage," said Ellie.

"Don't you think we have that now?"

"I think…" Ellie trailed off, slowly and thoughtfully. "I think that love between two people is like a plant… a houseplant. If you nurture that plant over time with water, sunlight, and plant food, it will grow and never stop growing. It will thrive and be a thing of beauty for everyone to see. But if a plant doesn't get cared for properly, it will stay small and look a little pathetic. And of course, if it's neglected, it will simply wither and die. I see Rob and Sarah feeding and intentionally caring for their love. I think that explains why lots of couples are drawn to them. I hope time will show that we're like that, too, looking after each other in a way that makes love thrive and grow so we can say, on our twentieth anniversary, 'I love you more now than the day I married you.'"

Hugh nodded. "Do you think it comes easily or..." He was thinking of some couples he knew, such as his sisters, whose love plant didn't look so healthy.

"I think it comes with commitment, and making each other a priority," said Ellie. "That way, the challenging times bring a couple closer together instead of gradually driving them apart."

"I hope and pray I won't fail you."

Ellie squeezed his hand. "Nor I you."

"Hi, Aunt Ellie. You too, Hugh," said Charlotte trotting towards them.

She was followed by Trevor and Beanie. Beanie carried a takeout bag with some French fries to share with her daddy.

Charlotte looked puzzled. "Why are you out here and not in there?"

"We only just got here," replied Ellie. "I didn't want to barge in on your parents if they were needing a moment to themselves."

"Phfffff!" snorted Charlotte. "Not at their age! They're old, not young like you guys."

She pushed open the door and they all filed in. Ellie noted that Rob's colour had returned. He no longer seemed so pale.

"Geez, you look like a swami, all gussied up like that," teased Hugh. "I suppose you want me to bow down to you or something like that."

"Heck no," Rob said in mock seriousness. "You don't have to bow down to me. Just kiss my feet. That will do."

"Sure. That will be my honour... when hell freezes over!"

Ellie's heart swelled seeing the family's love and acceptance of Hugh, and seeing Hugh naturally showing his fondness for them. He was fitting in like a dirty shirt.

It wasn't long, though, before they could see Rob getting tired. They took their leave so he could rest.

The weather outside was cold. Hugh started his truck but didn't drive away immediately. He wanted the motor to warm up first.

But while they waited, he put his arms around Ellie, pulled her close, and gave her his very best kiss.

"Hugh Richard Fischer, sometimes you seem to think we're like a pair of giddy teenagers, grabbing every opportunity to kiss and make out." Ellie snuggled against him in the cold cab. "Although I must admit, that was an extra nice kiss."

"Oh no. It's not about being like teenagers making out. It's about looking after the love plant…"

Eighteen

ON THE LAST Thursday of November, Tony Unger hinged the final door front to the new set of kitchen cabinets. He called Hugh right after dinner to arrange delivery.

"I'd like to bring them over this evening," he said once Hugh picked up the phone.

"That's great. The thing is, Ell and I have premarital counselling class tonight. How about tomorrow?"

"Tomorrow evening works, or even Saturday, if you wish. But I need my garage back and I've already loaded the cabinets onto my truck. Shouldn't take long to offload if I come right away. You can still make it to your class."

Hugh sighed. "Okay, bring them. But I'd like to be around for the actual installation."

"Roger. I'll be on my way shortly."

Hugh then called Ellie, who came over straightaway. Together they emptied the Hoosier cabinet of all its contents into boxes and stowed them in the tiny storage and utility room between the sitting area and the bathroom.

Tony slowly rolled into the yard and backed up as close as he could to the front door. Before the cabinets could be brought into the house, Tony helped take out the old antique kitchen unit. While the men did this, Ellie got the table and chairs out of the way.

Bringing in the new cabinets was exciting. Even disjointed and scattered around, Ellie thought they had turned out beautifully. She stood back to gauge how the living room furnishings jived with the cupboards. The colours were not at all quarrelsome. She sighed with relief.

～

The next morning, Ellie went into Minitonas to see what she could find at the Community Store for kitchen sinks and faucets. Finding the necessities, she chose a double sink, straightforward faucet, and plumbing kit.

There was still the matter of a countertop, but she would need to go to Swan River for that. The building supply store had limited stock to choose from but there was no time to order anything especially decorous. At least not if she wanted the whole kitchen to be completed at the same time.

However, she came across a long enough one-piece coloured in brown splotches that reminded one of granite. It was attractive and neutral enough not to date too quickly.

This done, Ellie made arrangements for Hugh to bring it back with him after work.

～

The Ungers arrived shortly before 7:00 p.m. Ellie and Hugh greeted them at the front door.

"Wow! Love the border you painted around the ceiling," said Darcey as she pivoted to read the stream of words around the top of the room. "You're sure about the distance where you left off? Looks to me like a cabinet might could overlap..."

"I measured." Ellie smiled. "It should come out perfectly."

"You keep company with Ellie on the couch," directed Hugh firmly. "I'll help Tony put the units in the right order."

Darcey folded her arms across her chest. "Really? This I gotta see."

As luck would have it, the bottom cabinets were behind the upper cabinets, not handy to set in place. Tony picked up the corner upper cabinet—a bulky piece—while Hugh hoisted the largest upper cupboard. Neither of the men could see past the pieces in their arms. Tony and Hugh each took a step forward and crashed, mashing one set of Tony's fingers.

With a yowl, Tony turned and dropped the unit on top of a lower cabinet while Hugh apologized profusely and Darcey looked on disbelievingly.

"Somebody tell me where I should set this piece out of the way," Hugh said while Tony sucked on his fingers. "I can't hold on much longer."

Darcey quickly stepped forward to assist Hugh with holding it. But the result was taking three steps forward and then three steps back… twice. Meaning to be of help, Ellie stepped in to hold up one end. They moved sideways and bumped into Tony, who'd hoisted the former cabinet again and couldn't see them coming, mashing the fingers on his other hand. The cabinet was released with a yell, sliding down the front of his person and landing with a thump on both feet. Tony released another yowl.

"Stop this!" harangued Ellie. "We're not getting anywhere this way. Let me direct the traffic!"

It was the voice of reason, and it couldn't have shown up at a more welcome time. Standing on top of the trunk, Ellie told Darcey to back up three steps to the north and two steps to the west. But Darcey claimed she had no idea which way the cardinal directions were set and told her to try hours on the clock instead.

"Fine," exhaled Ellie. "Take three steps toward noon and then two steps to three o'clock."

That should have helped. But what was three o'clock to Darcey was nine o'clock to Hugh. An absurd tug-of-war ensued.

"Towards me!" corrected Ellie. "Now, set it down carefully."

They did, but now Darcey was trapped in the small hallway. Not for long, though; she hurdled over the cabinet like a practised athlete.

Hugh shook out his hands. "Just so you know, I moved toward midnight, not noon."

Ellie pursed her lips sardonically. "There's always a smart ass in every crowd."

Hugh aided Tony in setting the upper corner cabinet on top of the trunk without further mishap. Enough was now out of the way to dig out the lower cabinets with minor adjustments to the pieces hindering them.

The corner cabinet's placement was obvious, as was the double sink unit. After that, the two men had a puzzle to solve. They tried a couple of different arrangements, each time looking to Ellie for approval. And each time she shook her head.

"Did you bring the diagram I sketched for you?" she asked amiably.

"Nope." Tony sounded untroubled. "It was wrinkled and dark from coffee stains. I threw it out last night. Thought I would remember the way of it."

"Well, I'm pretty sure I remember how it's supposed to go," Darcey said. "And since I'm the helpmate in this establishment, I'll do the helping and you..." She turned to Hugh. "...can sit here with your betrothed. After all, that's why you're paying us the big bucks."

With the men looking on arms crossed, Darcey reset the lower units. She looked at Ellie, beaming with self-satisfaction.

Ellie shook her head. "You're almost right. The fridge goes between the counter and the pantry."

"Oh," said Darcey, only slightly embarrassed.

It was amazing how efficiently everything fit when positioned in the proper order. Tony retrieved his power drill and box of bits, as well as a brown paper bag of screws, then got to work.

But before he could start drilling, Darcey stopped him. "Check to make sure the pieces are one hundred percent level before pinning them to the wall," she chided.

Tony looked across the span of the two units. "They look level to me!"

He positioned a screw and prepared to drill it in.

"Looks can be deceiving." Darcey reached for the forty-eight-inch aluminium level stationed by the front door and laid it across the two units.

"It's out one-sixteenth of an inch," Tony said. "I don't worry about discrepancies in cabinetry that are less than one-eighth. And even then, it all depends on the situation. I'm sure nothing's going to roll off the edge of that countertop."

"That's because you never spend any time in the kitchen," retorted Darcey. "You wouldn't personally know..."

Meaning to be helpful, she held the first screw in place while Tony attempted to line up his power drill. As soon as he applied the power, the screw bounced and fell to the floor.

"Way to go, Darc," grumbled Tony, shimmying backwards.

Darcey grovelled around on her knees. Unable to find it, she merely got out another screw and held it in place.

When the corner unit was firmly attached to the wall, Darcey followed Tony on her knees to the next unit. She found the missing screw with a yelp and lifted her left leg to pry it off her knee where it had left a perfect indentation in her jeans.

"You're screwed," said Tony with a straight face.

"Very funny." Darcey reached across the cabinet to hold the screw in place. Tony's drill only touched it; then it fell out of her hands. "Maybe I should do the screwing, Mr. Butterfingers."

Tony smirked. "Oh no, that's my job.

By this time, the smile on Hugh's face was fairly pasted on and Ellie was giggling.

Within fifteen minutes, they had secured two units, both to each other and to the wall. Next they turned to the sink cabinet. Darcey set the level across the unit and they found it listed to the south one-eighth of an inch.

Tony glanced at Hugh. "What have you got to make this perfectly level?"

"I doubt I have anything that thin..." Nevertheless, Hugh looked through the wastebasket in the bathroom. He came back with a little cardboard box that until that morning had safeguarded a tube of toothpaste. He handed it to Tony. "Will this do?"

Tony slit the narrow box in two and folded one section in half. He slipped it under the base of the cabinet.

Darcey reset the level. The unit was now one-thirty-second of an inch too high.

"I'm not one to split hairs," Hugh said.

"You're my kind of guy, a real brother." Tony then fastened the unit to the wall, followed by the corner cabinet, holding the screws himself.

The last unit to be installed was the bank of drawers. Having raised the south end of the sink unit by a smidge, the drawers cabinet no longer fit evenly to the preceding cabinet.

"Anything worth doing is worth doing well," said Darcey in a dry tone of voice. "Make it even."

To which Tony raised his eyes to the heavens, as if asking for divine guidance.

They used the second part of the toothpaste box on one side of the drawers, then went looking for something to slip under the other side. Neither the wastebasket nor Tony's box of tools turned up anything useful. Not to be outwitted, Darcey emptied her purse on the steamer trunk. A gazillion items spilled out, the kind that only a mother of little girls would carry around.

"That's a good idea!" said Tony at once. "We can use your credit card."

Darcey rolled her eyes. "Don't be an idiot."

Sifting through soothers, combs, pens, pieces of paper, crayons, tissue packets, bobby pins, elastic bands, barrettes, and little bags of cereal, Darcey held up a pack of gum with six sticks remaining. Tony shook his head and squeezed his mouth as if to ask, *Now who's the idiot?*

"It looks to be about the right thickness," Darcey said.

Muttering something unintelligible, Tony lifted the drawers unit while Darcey arranged a row of gum along the base. Then she set the level across the bank of drawers and sink cabinet.

"Eureka!" she cried out. "It's perfectly level."

Against his better judgement, Tony left the row of gum intact and fastened the unit in place.

"Got any more gum, Darc?" he murmured after a few moments. "Now that you've brought it out, I have a hankering to chew some."

"I could lend you one of Abigail's soothers. I'm sure she won't mind."

Now that the lower cabinets were installed, Tony turned his attention to putting in the countertop.

Hugh had gotten the building supply store to cut the countertop in half and at forty-five-degree angles so they would fit the corner. He and Tony brought the two halves into the house while Darcey looked on with a jaundiced eye.

"I hope the precut ends perfectly match the corner. If so, it will be a first. If not, it might take us the rest of the evening to trim it to fit."

It was the voice of experience speaking.

"You worry too much, Mrs. Unger," said Tony. "Why don't you and Ellie go away and bake a cake or something so us menfolk can do our work in peace."

But Darcey's prophecy proved true; the corner walls were not quite square with the countertop. Thus began a long series of sanding and checking and sanding and checking. They seemed to waffle from sanding too much and then not enough. This went on for many minutes, causing Darcey considerable stress. Every time they pulled out the counter piece to sand or rasp the cut, Darcey contorted herself into another twisted pose, looking on in fear or horror.

"What's the matter, Darcey?" Tony left the counter to place his hands on his hips. "You look like you're trying to turn yourself inside-out!"

"I can't help it. It's painful watching you make those fine adjustments by the seat of your pants."

"Where's your faith?"

However, in the end, Hugh and Tony were successful—to Darcey's immense relief.

It was ten o'clock—quittin' time.

Tony surveyed the work they had done with evident pride. Darcey admitted that she was tired... that watching Tony do his work had exhausted her.

"So satisfying to see a job done well," Tony murmured. "Even though it was literally put together with toothpaste and gum."

At 7:30 the next morning, Ellie arrived back at Hugh's place with still-warm raisin bran muffins and a thermos of hot, fresh coffee. She let herself in and found Hugh sprawled out on his bed on his stomach. Calling his name didn't rouse him, so she tried tickling his feet. His reaction was to nearly send her flying with a kick to the head.

However, he did wake up, wondered what time of night it was since the sun hadn't yet come up.

"I thought we could do breakfast and read another chapter in the Bible before the Ungers get here," said Ellie.

"Sure." Hugh closed his eyes. "Wake me when it's morning."

Ellie backed out of the bedroom and put on the radio, turning up the volume to full blast. Then she sat on the sofa, poured herself a cup of coffee, and began to peel the paper cup off the muffin.

A moment later, Hugh appeared in the doorway, dishevelled and wearing a lopsided grin.

"Good morning, sunshine!" greeted Ellie with exaggerated warmth.

"Good morning yourself."

Beaten, Hugh returned to the front room a moment later in jeans and a sweatshirt. By this time, Ellie had fetched the glass from the bathroom and poured some steaming java into it.

Hugh took his usual place on the sofa, propped his feet on the steamer trunk, and waited for Ellie to nestle under his right arm, her legs curled around her. She began to read aloud, but stopped after five minutes. Tony and Darcey had arrived.

The Ungers entered without knocking and smiled broadly at the couple's affectionate pose.

"Tony, remember when we used to do that?" recalled Darcey nostalgically.

"Do what?" Tony reached for his toolbelt.

"Snuggle together."

"Nope. You must be thinking of someone else." He winked at her.

"No, I'm not. Remember how we'd be driving along and we'd be sitting so close together? How come we don't do that anymore?"

Tony turned to look at her, his head canted. "Darcey… you realize I'm not the one who moved!"

The delicious aroma of coffee wafted throughout the space.

"Got any more of that starter fluid to share?" Tony asked, rubbing his hands together.

"I do," answered Ellie. "But I'm afraid I can't access any mugs. Everything's packed away at the bottom of the heap."

"I can remedy that." Turning to his box of tools, Tony pulled out a soup can full of nails. He emptied the contents into his jacket pocket, then handed the can to Ellie.

Ellie raised her eyebrows. "Seriously?"

"Sure. Why not? A little dirt doesn't hurt anyone. Keeps you healthy!"

Darcey and Ellie rolled their eyes in sync with each other, but nevertheless Ellie took the tin and went to the bathroom to rinse out the dust and dirt. After filling it halfway with coffee, Tony nursed it like a life-saving nectar.

"I'm about coffee'd out," Darcey said when Ellie offered her some. "I've been up with the baby since five."

"Who's looking after your little girls?" asked Ellie.

"Tony's mom. She lives two doors up the street."

"How convenient is that!"

"It's more than a convenience. It's all the way to a gift from God."

Tony noticed the picture book on the history of cars, lying on the steamer trunk. This launched a lively discussion of the various vintage cars they had known. Tony waxed on eloquently about the classics his grandfather had proudly driven. After retirement, they had ended up in the scrapheap where vehicles go to certain death at the end of their lives.

The ladies spoke of old things, too.

"I see that you really like antiques," noted Darcey. "That and the country style o' things."

"You're right, but I especially like pieces that remind me of someone in the family, like a grandparent or even a dear friend."

"I don't mind antiques, as long as they're simple. You know, not too ornate or too big or too dark or too… well, too much in some way or another. I dislike pieces that draw attention to themselves. It spoils the balance of a well-furnished room."

"What about dishes? I have a preference for the old patterns. In fact, my favourite set wasn't a set at all. The stack in my grandmother's cupboard consisted of the leftovers of a dozen broken sets over the years. A motley assembly of one-of-a-kind plates, soup bowls, and nappies. The best part was that I could choose my own favourite plate at each meal."

Darcey looked aghast. "Oh my! No, I'm a sets person. If one dish breaks, the whole set is spoiled. I get rid of it forthwith and start over."

In this way, the four of them passed the better part of an hour, until Darcey gave her husband a firm nudge.

"I've been watching those upper cabinets, lovey, willing them to hang themselves up, but they refuse to budge." She wore a grave expression. "We'll need to be forceful and hang them ourselves."

"Right." Tony closed the picture book and returned it to the steamer trunk. He gulped down the last of his coffee and returned the nails in his pocket to the soup can. "Boss's orders."

They began with the upper corner cabinet. Tony and Hugh hoisted it onto the counter. Only then did Tony realize he'd forgotten to bring his pail from home to use as a spacer. Hugh came up with an old metal pail from the machine shed but it was two inches too short to meet the required distance of eighteen inches. A couple of one-inch boards placed on the upside-down pail made up the missing distance. The men lifted the corner cabinet onto the spacer and found the distance was still inexact.

Tony turned to Hugh with raised eyebrows, searching to see if the quarter-inch misalignment was an issue for him.

"Close enough," Hugh quietly said.

Tony sighed with relief, winked surreptitiously, and clapped Hugh on the back.

Before Darcey could notice and make a fuss about it, he screwed the cabinet to the wall.

Using the rigged-up spacer, the next two cabinets went up quickly. There was some doubt, though, as to which of the shorter cabinets should go over the fridge and stove respectively.

"You know, Hugh and Tony combined are about as clever as a potato," Darcey remarked quietly to Ellie.

She didn't say it quietly enough.

"The next time I undertake a project of this nature," Tony said with exaggerated pleasantry, "I'm going to send you and the girls to Ottawa to visit your favourite aunt."

At last, the cabinets were in place. The avocado green fridge looked almost natural tucked in its niche between the counter and pantry cupboard. The harvest gold stove seemed less repellent adjacent to the weathered wood, complemented by the glints of natural beige that marbled the antique wood. And the upper cabinet didn't overlap Ellie's border.

Tony graciously assisted Hugh with installing the range hood along with the double sink and faucet. He had experience in such matters, whereas for Hugh it would have been the first time.

After Tony took away his tools and box of sundry supplies, Darcey and Ellie brought back the white table and black and navy chairs.

"Cute as a button!" observed Darcey with delight. "A proper kitchen, and just right for this little nest of yours."

"Since it's to be *your* kitchen, I guess the bill goes to you." Jokingly, Tony held out a handwritten invoice to Ellie.

Hugh intercepted it. "I'll take that."

He nodded without expression as he read the numbers. Ellie peered at the paper and then pulled him along to have a word behind closed doors. When they emerged, they had a cheque for Tony.

Surprised, Tony passed it along to Darcey, whose mouth dropped open wide enough to bite an apple.

"Why?" she asked Ellie with a furrowed brow. "Who pays more than is asked for?"

"Because you have blessed me… blessed us… in more ways than you'll ever know. And we want to bless you back." Ellie wrapped her tall friend in the best hug she could manage. "You can call the tip a freewill collection for The Unger Comedy Hour, if you like."

"I have no idea what you're talking about." Darcey kissed the cheque.

Nineteen

A WEEK LATER, Rob was allowed to return home from the hospital. The gash to his head was healing nicely and showed no sign of hidden trauma. The family was exceedingly glad to have their husband and beloved daddy under their roof again.

The weekend passed with everyone paying a lot of loving attention to Rob's needs. He spent the night flat on his back in his own bed, his broken leg raised on a stack of three thick pillows. During the day he was established in his favourite armchair with his legs resting on the coffee table. He was surrounded by his newspapers, country magazines, a Bible, a crossword puzzle book, the TV remote, some writing instruments, and a piece of plywood to use like a desk. Snacks and beverage were placed within arm's reach, as desired.

Monday, December 1, was a different story. The kids went back to school and Sarah began her Christmas baking. The most exciting program on television was a children's show. Feeling a little lonely, Rob hobbled on his crutches to the kitchen and set himself up by the table where he could watch Sarah at work. He also hoped to find a bowl or spoon to lick clean.

The first sweet meat Sarah intended to make required mashed potatoes. It was a favourite recipe passed along from her grandmother. She counted out the necessary tubers and began to peel them with a short paring knife.

Rob looked on thoughtfully. "There would be less waste if you used a vegetable peeler."

"Possibly. But I learned how to peel using a paring knife, and that's how I do it."

Later, when the potatoes were cooked, Sarah put them through an old-fashioned ricer to mash out the lumps. The leftovers would be set aside for a batch of potato donuts. She started working on the donut dough in a big bowl and finished with kneading it on a floured area of the kitchen table.

"I thought the big mixer I gave you a while back had a dough hook," observed Rob.

"It does. But I like to feel the dough with my hands. That's how I know when I've added enough flour. Not too much, nor too little."

A lot of dirty dishes and utensils piled up on the counter. Sarah filled one sink with soapy water and let a thin stream run from the tap in the second sink for rinsing.

Rob grunted. "Wouldn't it be better to fill the other sink with rinse water and just dip your pots and bowls and things?"

Sarah reached for a small towel and dried her hands. She walked over to the telephone stationed at the end of the counter and dialled.

"Hello, Maggie. It's Sarah. Is Henry available to come to the phone?"

There was a brief pause.

"Hello, Henry. Say, can you come over and have a cup of coffee with Rob? He's bored and in need of stimulating conversation." Another pause. "That would be great. We'll see you in a few minutes."

Sarah hung up the phone, smiled broadly at Rob, and then resumed doing the dishes.

"I take it you don't appreciate my help in the kitchen," said Rob, smirking.

"What gives me away?"

While working in her kitchen that afternoon, Darcey came up with the idea of throwing Ellie a wedding shower—only she was going to need some help. She dialled a number and waited for her neighbour to pick up.

"So what do you think?" she asked Cynthia after explaining the proposal.

"That sounds like fun. What did you have in mind?"

"I'm thinking it should be a surprise party, but it needs to be unique and creative in some way. Got any ideas?"

After discussing all the possibilities, they landed on the idea of everyone just showing up at Ellie's place. They would lead a caravan of guests one evening when she was sure to be home.

The tasks were divvied up, with Cynthia handling the food and games while Darcey handled the secretive invitations and miscellaneous matters.

When Darcey finally got a hold of Hugh, he was immediately on board, though she had to explain to him what a wedding shower was. They chose a date in mid-December, for which Hugh would be responsible to keep open, no matter what.

⁓

The next morning, Ellie kept busy catching up on household chores. After lunch she went into Minitonas to spend the afternoon with Rob and Sarah. The plan was to make one hundred fifty favours with mint-flavoured candies to be put with each place setting at the wedding banquet.

Sarah undertook the task of cutting the powder-blue sheer fabric into squares. Ellie then determined the length of ribbon needed to tie the little bundles together. Rob's job was to count out a half-dozen peppermint candies for each bundle.

Ellie watched as Rob positioned himself at the kitchen table and expertly hoisted his cast leg onto an adjacent chair. He reached for the large package of mints and emptied them into a bowl Sarah had provided.

"I just realized you will have to walk me down the aisle using crutches," said Ellie thoughtfully.

Sarah nodded. "We've been thinking a bit about that, too."

"Doc says my leg won't be fully healed until the latter part of January," said Rob. "I think it will spoil things if I hobble on crutches beside you. I'd rather not do it."

"But... you have to!" gasped Ellie. "It's important to me that you stand in for Dad and give me away on his behalf!"

"Don't get your shirt all knotted up," he said. "We think we have a good alternative."

"We thought we would both sit at the front where your parents would have sat," Sarah explained. "After the bridesmaids, you could walk in yourself but then stop at the pew where we'll be sitting. When the pastor asks who gives this bride away to be married, Rob could stand up and say his part right beside you."

Ellie sighed with reluctance. "I guess that would work, given the circumstances."

Having come to the end of cutting up the ribbon, Ellie began filling the squares of fabric one at a time. Rob had counted out the candy into tiny containers and set them in a precisely straight row.

"That's very Dad-like of you," said Ellie with a snicker.

Rob frowned. "What is?"

"Placing all those containers in such a straight row. I've never met another man who liked things to be so perfectly ordered."

"Are you suggesting this was a fault of Dad's? I also like a place for everything and everything in its place. That way I can always find what I'm looking for. Dad also liked things clean, and so do I. And like mother used to say, cleanliness is next to godliness."

Ellie reached for another square of fabric. "Point taken. In Dad's case, I saw this as the expression of an extraordinarily straight-laced man."

Rob stopped his counting and studied Ellie for a few seconds.

"What?" asked Ellie, feeling his eyes upon her.

"Dad was only extraordinarily strict about things that mattered. After that, he was as generous and loving as you could want a Christian man and father to be."

"He would have been a much more enjoyable dad had he relaxed about a whole lot of stuff."

Rob could hardly believe this. "After all these years, you're still in a mode of rebellion against him?"

"I am not! I'm just saying that despite him being a generally good man, he was over the top in some ways. It was like we had to be perfect."

"Correction: he was very much aware of the natural inclinations of humankind, very aware of the temptations that seduced people to travel the broad road that leads to destruction, especially young people." When he spoke, echoing the scripture their father had often quoted, he looked pointedly at Ellie. "He also took his job as a parent seriously with regards to training up a child in the way he should go, so he won't depart from it when he's older."[16]

Ellie's eyes flashed in annoyance. "I don't disagree, generally speaking. I just wish he'd been a lot nicer and more understanding as he went about laying down the law."

"I didn't find him to be a heavy-handed parent. Don't recall that your brothers did either. If you did, I suggest it points to something else," he said, casually counting out more candies.

"Exactly what are you trying to say?"

"As I recall, you weren't exactly an easy teenager to raise."

"Even if I wasn't—and that would be a matter of viewpoint, I might add—Dad may have gotten through to me if he hadn't been so ridiculously strict. If it wasn't for Mom acting as mediator, who knows? I might have run away like Hugh did."

Rob rolled his eyes. "You're comparing our dad to the likes of Fred Fischer? Wow. That's rich."

"That's not what I meant at all."

---

[16] Proverbs 22:6.

"Then say what you mean, and mean what you say."

At that point Sarah decided to intervene. "Well, I wasn't going to enter into this discussion, but it sounds like you both need some help," she said. "In the first place, Robert John Bauman, I know exactly what Ellie means. Your dad was a wonderful man in many ways, but he did have a my-way-or-the-highway attitude sometimes. Maybe you didn't notice it because you're a man and it seems to me that most men think it's their right to control everyone in their family."

"Thank you, Sarah," said Ellie with sincere appreciation.

Rob gave his wife the side eye. "I believe that's called leadership, milady."

"That's the same mistaken idea that gave rise to the feminist movement," Sarah continued. "You're not like that, thank goodness, because you understand that God created males and females as equal partners. But a couple of your attitudes could use a tune-up now and then."

"Whoa there," Rob said, surprised at his wife's outburst. "I'm on your side!"

Sarah then turned to Ellie. "On the other hand, you *were* a difficult teenager. They were seriously worried about losing you to a world of 'sinful pleasures,' as your dad articulated it. Your mother often confided her worries to me. Just so you know, I stood up for you. I tried to explain what teenage girls like you would need to not feel out of step with your classmates. They worried that if they gave you an inch, you would take the whole proverbial mile. And they might have been right about that."

Ellie slumped in her chair; her face stricken.

"I think the hardest part for you is that you can't understand them properly because you aren't yet a parent yourself," Sarah added.

"I'll add an amen to that," said Rob.

"You can speak when I'm finished." Sarah gave him a deprecating look. "So far, our three haven't given us serious concerns. Trevor seems to be okay. He loves sports and his involvement keeps him away from a lot of potential trouble. He also loves and respects his dad, which motivates him to stay on the straight and narrow. But I'm starting to worry a little about Charlotte. She's a teenager and expressing a desire to be worldly like other girls at school. I watch and listen every day for clues that she may be enticed to follow the wrong kind of crowd. If it happens, I guarantee that you'll see and hear about my own super strict attitude. It might look a lot like what you heard from your folks, Ellie, and I won't apologize for it. Keeping my kids out of trouble, away from anything that could destroy them or entice them away from the truth and a relationship with Christ, is my greatest responsibility right now."

Sarah's voice was cracking with emotion.

"I'm prepared to interview the boys who want to keep company with my daughters with a long list of dos and don'ts while I keep a shotgun laying across my lap," added Rob. "Your old-fashioned daddy didn't go that far, but I might!"

"I get it," insisted Ellie. "I figured out that they were only trying to protect me from the evils of this world. They meant well. I was tempted to stray, just as they feared, but I'm over it. Living for Jesus, being in the centre of His will, is the most important thing for me now."

"That's now," said Sarah. "But what about ten, twelve years ago? How important was it for you to live biblically then? You could hardly wait to get away from your parents and Minitonas."

"What was your life like in Winnipeg?" asked Rob.

"You know what it was," replied Ellie quickly. "I went through four years of nurses training before getting a job at St. Boniface Hospital."

Rob nodded. "But I meant personally… socially. Did you keep the faith? Our parents suspected you didn't. Although when you did manage to sometimes find your way home, you went along with all the family traditions, as you knew they expected."

"I confess that I took a break from the Christianity I learned under Mom and Dad and the First Baptist Church," Ellie admitted. "Without listing the specifics, because I don't want to, I had a taste of many worldly pleasures, the kind our parents wanted to prevent me from having. I learned for myself that they were right, and that's probably the only way I was going to learn... by experience, and not through a lecture."

Before Rob could make further comment, Sarah cut him off.

"Understood," she said. "You must have dated. Wasn't there anyone special in your life in the past ten years? Surely Hugh isn't your first sweetheart."

"I did go out with different guys, but there was only one fellow I loved enough to consider marrying. He was an intern at my hospital. He hurt me really bad, and then it was over. Mom died suddenly soon after that and the rest is history..." A single tear escaped Ellie's eye.

"Well, we're awfully glad to have you back with us," Sarah said warmly. "Aren't we, Rob?"

"Yeah, I'm glad you're back, too." Rob smiled. "Glad, because I think this is where you belong. Your purpose is here. And I think you're the right kind of woman for that tall, skinny guy next door you're so fond of."

"Do you think Mom and Dad would have approved?" asked Ellie.

Rob gave that question a few moments of consideration. "Probably not at first. But after getting to know him and seeing him come to faith in Christ, they would have come around."

"C'mon, you guys," chided Sarah. "Work a little faster. You've only put fifteen candy favours together in the last half-hour. I want them all done this afternoon."

"I'm thinking maybe I should warn Hugh about marrying a beautiful woman." The corners of Rob's mouth turned up in a grin. "She may turn out to be a slave driver..."

"Let's put up the Christmas tree," said Ellie one evening after supper at her place. "My mom and dad had an artificial one and there's a big box of ornaments somewhere down in the basement."

"Sure, but not an artificial one," urged Hugh. "One of the cool things I experienced with the Turners is going out into the bush to cut your own tree. They made it a family outing, like a winter picnic with thermoses of hot chocolate, coffee, and thick sub sandwiches. Let's go get us a tree this weekend from somewhere in the forest."

"That actually sounds like fun."

On Sunday afternoon, they dressed extra warm and headed for the hills. There was a certain area in the region designated for Christmas tree searches—and when they got to it, a number of other families were pursuing the same quest.

"We'll look for a tall spruce with a nicely formed top," said Hugh. "I'll cut up the bottom trunk for firewood. Some evening, when the weather is nice, we'll have family and friends over for a bonfire."

Ellie smiled. "What a good idea!"

"I know it always surprises you when that happens, but I'm good for a few every year," joked Hugh.

He bent down and picked up some snow, then threw it in Ellie's face. She gasped with surprise and cold. Hugh chuckled and ran away, putting a few feet between them.

"I hope you have eyes on the back of your head, because I'll get you back when you're least expecting it," vowed Ellie.

They trudged through the forest until they found a promising option. There were actually two trees near each other with beautifully balanced tops. After a brief discussion, Hugh cut them both, intending to give the second one to Rob's family. They dragged them out of the forest and set them in the back of the truck.

But the wonderful idea of bringing home the rest of the wood for a bonfire had to be abandoned; the logs were too heavy and the truck too far away.

"That's too bad," lamented Ellie, sidling up to Hugh as he lifted the tailgate of his truck. "I already had a party planned out."

"Actually, it wouldn't have wor—"

Hugh's face was struck with snow. As if it was the most ordinary occurrence, he calmly wiped off the snow and continued his sentence.

"It wouldn't have worked, because the wood is green."

An hour later, Rob and his whole family expressed profuse delight to have been given a real Christmas tree. Hugh went so far as to trim the stem to fit the stand and set it up in the designated spot Sarah had quickly prepared in their living room. By then the kids had dragged out the boxes of lights and ornaments.

"Thanks for thinking of us," said Rob as Hugh and Ellie prepared to leave.

"Think nothing of it," he replied. "I would have done it even if you weren't a lame duck."

~

While Hugh set up the tree and strung the lights at her place, Ellie brought out her mother's collection of ornaments. Some of them went back thirty-five years, if not more, to a time when the Bauman kids had made ornaments at school to take home. Several were made from spruce and pinecones. Others were cutouts from past Christmas cards. A few were made of hand-painted plaster of Paris. She lifted out one that she had painted—a red poinsettia.

"I think I was in Grade Five when I did this in art class," said Ellie nostalgically.

Hugh stopped to see what she was looking at. "I remember doing something similar. I painted a gingerbread house."

"What were your Christmases like?"

Ellie braced herself for more sad stories, but Hugh paused for a moment before answering.

"Actually, Ma made an effort to put together nice Christmases for us," he said. "She brought in a tree from somewhere in our bush and we decorated it with strings of popcorn, paper chains, and sugar cookies. And there were the ones we made at school and brought home. She fashioned a star for the top out of tinfoil. It looked pretty good. When we got up on Christmas day, the tree had store-bought candy canes on it and there was a package under it for each of us."

"Neat, Hugh." She sighed with relief. "I was half-expecting you to tell me that your household wasn't allowed to have Christmas."

"Our Christmases weren't like yours. There were no religious elements to it. And our gifts were practical, like an item of clothing or maybe new mitts and a toque Ma knitted. The treats were the candy canes. And she usually put together a special meal of some sort, though it wasn't like the spreads I've seen at Sarah's or Gertie's. Still, it was better than the average day. We enjoyed it."

"Your dad...?"

"Pa was fairly reasonable on Christmas morning, but he usually brought out the bottle sometime in the afternoon. I'm sure I don't have to tell you any more about that."

"Shoot. And just when I thought I was going to hear about a good memory."

Hugh's face brightened. "I had good Christmases with the Turners. Not all my stories are sad."

"I have to admit something, too," she said. "The Christmases when I didn't come home were full of meaningless traditions. I guess what I'm trying to say is... not all my stories are good ones."

"It is what it is."

Twenty

ELLIE WAS ALMOST always scheduled to work on Saturdays, either daytime or the night shift, meaning that Hugh could pursue his personal interests. This mid-December Saturday, though, he had arranged to go back to the dealership to spend the day in the auto-body shop with Ralph. He brought with him the green fridge and gold-coloured stove to be repainted white. Normally they were both off on Saturdays, but Ralph had come in to complete a customer's specialty job. Since he was there anyway, he agreed to help Hugh with his project.

Hugh found Ralph's instructions and demonstrations easy to follow. He prepped the fridge and stove, carefully cleaning the parts and preparing them to receive paint. Then Ralph showed him the technique for spraying in thin coats so the paint wouldn't run, not to mention look smoother with each layer. Hugh's first attempt was very good, and Ralph said so.

At four o'clock, Hugh left the dealership to meet Ellie for an early supper. One of the nurses had recommended a small restaurant. The place wasn't outfitted with fancy décor, but the food was commended as very good.

Hugh arrived first. The waitress seated him at a table for two near the rear of the restaurant. Behind him, a larger table of men drank mugs of coffee, their empty plates in front of them. Hugh was only dimly aware of them as they weren't of interest while he looked through the menu.

Knowing Ellie would be pressed for time, he ordered two plates of the daily special to be delivered upon her arrival. He then drummed the table with his fingers, thinking about how surprised and pleased Ellie would be when she discovered the white appliances at his house. He just hoped he could keep her from finding out about them before he returned them to their places. All he needed to do now was spray a final coat of white paint.

"Yeah, well... it's not the same, like it was when Freddie Fischer was around to keep everyone in their place..."

Hugh froze, his wrist still in the upward swing. He would very much have liked to turn around and look at the party of men who were discussing his pa, but he dared not. Everyone noted how much he resembled his father. Suddenly, he did not want to draw any attention to himself.

"Do you ever ride out to old man Fischer's place?"

"Once in a while," said another voice Hugh thought sounded familiar.

He guessed it belonged to Chiclets, the companion who had dropped by the Fischers' farm with Tipper earlier that summer.

"Lots of changes going on there," continued the second voice. "His boy's come back. Tearing down the place. Cleaning stuff up. Built himself a little house, looks like."

A third voice chimed in. "Are ya worried he's going to find... well, you know?"

"No sign of it so far. I think Sly covered his tracks good. Not to worry. Anyways, the one who was there when it happened is gone now. Ain't no witnesses left who saw with their own eyes what went down."

"Ya mean Tipper, don't ya?" said a fourth man. "Poor old geezer. Heard he died in Minitonas in front of the hotel. Anybody know if it's true or not?"

"That's what the bartender in the hotel said," confirmed the first voice.

"It's just as well he's gone, ya know," replied Chiclets. "He was losin' his marbles. Did ya see him? He was talking to himself like he was seeing things. Ghosts or something. I was afraid he was going to spill the beans, ya know, and that would be something awkward for the rest of us."

"But why are ya worried?" asked the first voice. "I never heard of a search warrant or an investigation or anything."

"Shut yer trap," the third voice whispered hoarsely. "Talk about something else!"

Ellie walked through the door and Hugh jumped up to greet her at the entrance. He quickly and quietly relayed the predicament involving the company of men seated near their own table for two. Using her anonymity, he asked if she could casually look them over to see if she recognized anyone, such as Tipper's companion Chiclets. He would follow behind her, seeming indifferent.

Ellie understood at once and led as directed.

One of the men at the table looked up at her. He appeared to be at the upper end of middle age. A black toque covered most of his hair and his face displayed a couple of days' worth of stubble. A cigarette hung from his mouth. Ellie smiled nonchalantly and then sat down. Hugh quickly took his seat, his back again to the group.

A few moments later, the waitress delivered their dinner plates. She then turned to the group of men occupying the back corner and asked if they wanted more coffee. Immediately they all pushed their mugs in her direction. Sighing she fetched a fresh pot of java and poured another round.

The couple ate their supper with softly spoken small talk so they could hear if the conversation behind them was worth a game of eavesdropping, which it soon did.

"Whatever happened to Sly's copper kettles and stuff?"

"His boy discovered them and dropped them off at Tipper's place. He said he didn't want anything to do with his pa's former business operations."

There was a collective chuckle over this.

"And then I took 'em, because he owed me. He never had any cash to pay me back. The old bugger owed everybody."

Well, that confirmed it. The man was definitely Chiclets.

One of the men sniggered. "Yeah, but I bet he didn't owe you what they're worth."

"Are you planning to do some cookin'?"

"I would think about it serious if I knew how it was done."

"Do ya think Sly's boy knows the recipe?"

"No way. The kid's a pantywaist. Leastways compared to his old man. Doesn't seem to have his bent at all. Besides that, he weren't around when this business was going on."

"I thought the kid run off to the big city, or left the province even. Fred was glad and mad all at the same time. Scared the boy would sic the cops on him or somethin'. Why did he come back?"

"How would I know? To make somethin' outta the farm prob'ly. Only saw him the once. He was building a little bitty cabin outta old wood and had some woman workin' with him. Looks like his old man, but more clean-cut like. Wherever he run off to, he musta got an edjacation. Anyways, every time I drive by Fred's old place, I see he's got more buildings knocked down and more junk and stuff cleaned up. Pretty soon it ain't gonna look like Fred's place at all. Only the barn and the machine shed are still up, but I'll bet ya dollars to donuts he'll get rid of them, too. No love lost between Fred and his boy, though it makes no sense if ya ask me."

"Lots of times Fred made no sense, if ya ask me."

"Yeah. Never could rightly guess what Fred would take to and what or who he had no use for. He had his own way of figurin' and most of the time it had no rhyme nor reason."

"Can't say as I miss him exactly, but I admit things are a lot duller with him gone."

"Ya. Funny thing, that. Don't suppose we'll ever find out what happened there."

"Just goes to show ya never know which day is gonna be yer last."

"Good Lord, where did that come from? Next thing ya know you'll be preachin' on heaven and hell."

Chiclets pushed back his chair. "It's time to split, boys. There's other things I gotta do. Who's going to pay for coffee and pie today? I did it last time."

"I don't have enough for everyone."

"Me either."

"Fine then. Everyone pays for their own."

"Well, someone needs to spot me for my pie," said the third voice, on the edge of whining. "I don't have more than a dollar on me."

"You never have more than a dollar on you. Yer always freeloadin'. I don't know why we let you in on our company."

The four of them got up and filed past the table where Hugh and Ellie sat. Hugh kept his head down, but Ellie casually and nonchalantly looked into each face as they passed. She recognized Chiclets clearly, but he appeared not to have taken any notice of her at all.

"You were right," said Ellie when she was sure the men had left the restaurant. "The first guy was Chiclets, without his cowboy hat. I didn't recognize the other three, but they all seemed like birds of the same scruffy feather."

"Do you remember what kind of truck Chiclets drives? It sounded to me like he drives past our place monitoring the changes I'm making. We're making. That bothers me. I think I'll try to watch out for him."

"I believe it was a navy rattletrap of some sort. What I got out of their discussion is that they notice you're not of the same demeanour as your dad, which makes you an object of curiosity and apprehension. The big secret Tipper spoke of is apparently real. And it's not going to be a nice surprise, like finding hidden treasure. I very much fear that a crime was committed on your property. Maybe there's evidence of it hiding somewhere. Chiclets probably drives by to ensure that secret is still safely undiscovered."

"You're probably right," said Hugh. "But I don't trust the guy. I can well imagine him, or any of them, trespassing for the sake of stealing something. I think I'm going to reinstate a yard light and put locks on the sheds. That won't keep out thieves, but a broken lock will prove burglary if it happens. And maybe we should think about getting a dog."

"Don't you think you're overreacting? We have a great community and look out for each other."

"It's not our community I'm worried about. It's that motley band of ruffians. They have expressed undeniable interest in my... uh, *our* farm. It would be wise to look after our investment. Besides, I need to think about protecting you. Earlier they were talking about how much the farm has changed. They associate all the old buildings with my pa. It's possible they'll lose interest altogether when I get rid of the barn and old machine shed. In fact, that's what I'm going to do while the weather is fair. Knock it down and burn it. It has to go."

"You're really bent on purging the place of its history, aren't you?" Ellie sighed. "I suppose you're right, though. Those buildings have outlived their usefulness, and I do notice your personality is freer and more cheerful with every old something that's destroyed or carted away. Shoot, when the last of the old buildings are gone, you should be a riot to hang out with!"

Hugh looked down at his plate. "You're never going to understand the misery those old buildings represent to me. You didn't live it, but I did. Every time another one is gone, I feel pounds lighter. In a way, my memories get hazier, too, like those things happened in another world. Taking down the buildings helps me forget how things were."

"Do what you have to do, honey. I'm on your side."

Twenty-One

WHEN CYNTHIA TOLD Ellie that she needed to bring her bridesmaids in for a fitting as soon as possible, Ellie promised to get right on it. Cynthia had gone as far as she could and the wedding was only a couple weeks away.

The problem was partially due to Ellie. She wanted to be on hand when the girls came, to make a day of it: fitting, a luncheon, touring them around and the like. But Margo had insisted she would only come on a Sunday, since she was working long hours at the shop over Christmas and needed the overtime.

They ended up making special arrangements for Margo to visit on the afternoon of Sunday, December 14.

"This is a girls thing, and I don't know how long it will take," said Ellie to Hugh after church that day. "Plus, I want to treat Margo to dinner before she goes back to Dauphin. And I hope to bring her by your place to see the changes and our cute little starter home. I have no idea what time that might be, so you're free to entertain yourself however you want."

"I'll probably hang out with the Moore brothers. They've started taking apart their grandpa's old 1938 sedan. I'd like to see that old-time motor."

"Go for it. The house is clean, right?"

"Like always."

"I mean woman-clean… my kind of clean."

Hugh let out a long sigh. "Then I suppose I should make up the bed, wash a few dishes, and swish a broom around the floor."

"I figured," said Ellie.

~

"Dang!" said Hugh aloud to himself. He had not yet returned the repainted fridge and stove to his house, having originally planned to do it the following evening. A quick call to Ralph assured him that he could transfer the appliances if they were well-wrapped in blankets. His coworker agreed to meet him at the autobody shop and help him get his surprise ready.

Hugh grabbed some towels and blankets and sped towards Swan River. When he arrived, Ralph had the electrical bar reattached to the stove and the burners placed. Hugh got the oven door assembled while Ralph removed protective tape and reattached the refrigerator door.

Together they wrapped the appliances in blankets and towels, and cardboard on top of that, to prevent rubbing during the trip home. Ralph also offered to help with unloading and installation, which Hugh gratefully accepted.

All the way back to his place, Hugh fretted about whether he could get everything put back in place and tidied quickly enough before the women arrived. They borrowed a dolly from the autobody shop to help speed things along.

While Hugh set the stove in place, Ralph unpacked the fridge. Together they shimmied it all into place.

"Looks good," said Ralph as he prepared to leave afterward. "Nice little place you got here."

Hugh folded the towels. "Thanks, buddy. I owe you bigtime."

As soon as Ralph had gone, Hugh bustled around the little house, grateful that he had learned how to "woman-clean" while living with the Turners. He made up the bed from scratch and then got a load of light-coloured laundry going. Washing the dishes in the sink came next. This required soaking, because egg and other residue had hardened onto the plates. While they soaked, he swept the floor, surprised at how much dirt had piled up. Little scraps of paper and pocket miscellany dotted the surfaces here and there. Hugh gathered them up and threw them in a drawer. The bathroom got wiped down with a lick and a promise. At last, the dishes came clean.

All told, it took over an hour to get the place up to Ellie's standards. He had to admit, though, that the place looked good. He felt rather proud of himself.

Part of him wanted to stay and see the look on the girls' faces when they came into the little house. The other part wanted to be with the Moore brothers, dissecting an ancient motor. In which case, it was time to skedaddle. It probably wouldn't be long before Ellie and Margo swung by.

~

Margo's appointment was for 2:00 p.m. She drove up to Cynthia's house slightly early and was greeted by Ellie at the door. Margo was ushered into the sewing studio to find her gown hung on a dress form. Though incomplete, it was already lovely.

"Very nice," announced Margo in her practiced sales voice.

Without more preamble, she removed her slacks, slipped into her strappy high-heeled sandals, and removed her buttoned blouse. Just as quickly, Ellie helped Cynthia drape the gown over the woman's head. The pale blue fabric had a softening effect on Margo's skin and countenance. It was also too big.

"I think you should have given me a smaller size when we talked a few weeks ago," Cynthia remarked.

"I may have lost some weight. To be thin is to be beautiful in today's culture."

Cynthia and Ellie exchanged a concerned glance.

"Well, I daresay you've reached your goal," said Cynthia carefully. "If you drop any more weight, people may suspect you of some kind of wasting disease, or anorexia."

"Don't be silly. I'm perfectly fine."

Cynthia pinned in some tucks and then, after lending Margo her bathrobe, quickly resewed the darts where the dress needed to be taken in. In the meantime, the conversation remained light with talk of the cold weather, Christmas shopping madness, and the scourge of disrespectful truckers on the highway.

At one point, Margo shook visibly.

"Are you cold, Margo? Or maybe you're not feeling well?" Ellie asked.

"Oh no, I'm fine. Although a cup of coffee would be terrific."

"Sorry. No liquids allowed in the sewing room," said Cynthia. "But I've got what I need. You can get dressed now. Maybe Ellie can get you a coffee?"

"I can do better than that," promised Ellie. "I can treat you to a late lunch or early supper, whichever you want to call it, as thanks for taking the time to come out today."

Margo smiled like a Cheshire cat. "Seriously? That would be great. I didn't take time to eat before I set out."

The nurse in Ellie saw through Margo's bravado. She'd bet her last dollar that Margo was hungry… in fact, that she was quite possibly starving. Was she living on little more than coffee?

Acting on this hunch, Ellie quickly changed her plans. The hotel in Swan River had a nice restaurant. She would take Margo there for a proper meal instead of a greasy burger at the local café. The trick was to do it without embarrassing Margo.

"To thank you for being my bridesmaid, I'd like to treat you to a nice dinner," Ellie said as they walked out of Cynthia's house and approached the car.

"Oh, you don't have to…"

"I'd like to."

"Well, if you insist."

Ellie offered to use her own car for traveling, an invitation that seemed to fill Margo with relief. Thus Ellie surmised another issue; money for gas was tight.

As they drove to the restaurant, Ellie made a mental note to help in another way—to fill up Margo's car with gas before sending her back to Dauphin.

At the restaurant, Ellie suggested a steak, an offer which Margo accepted immediately. When the food came, Margo was so focused on eating that she could hardly hold up her end of the conversation. For Ellie, that was just as well; it seemed impossible to start a meaningful discussion. Margo deftly avoided all personal questions. Instead Ellie got updates on the latest fashion trends. Ellie pretended to be interested.

On the drive back to Minitonas, Margo definitely seemed more relaxed. The occasional tremors disappeared, as well as the subtle agitation. And she thanked Ellie for supper again and again.

The return trip was filled with small talk until they reached the turn-off to Minitonas. Ellie turned north instead of taking Margo back to her parked car.

"Where are we going now?" asked Margo, suddenly nervous.

"I want to show you our starter house. And I want you to see what became of the furniture I bought from you."

"I really ought to be getting back. It can be tricky driving at night in the winter."

"I won't keep you long."

A moment later, Ellie turned into the Fischer driveway, the early darkness filling the yard with shadows and obscurities. The moon, at first quarter, illuminated just enough for Margo to see that the house and smaller buildings were all gone. The barn, with its saddleback sway, still loomed large and spooky black, and the old machine shed stood like a dark void under the starry sky.

Margo exited the car and took a long look around the dimly lit yard. It was too dark for Ellie to read her face, but she thought she could feel Margo's discomfort.

"It looks a lot better without all those crappy buildings, even in the dark," said Margo in a tone Ellie recognized. It was similar to how Hugh sounded on occasion. "Good for Hugh. I hope it helps him get rid of his demons."

She turned on her heel and walked towards the front door, with Ellie right behind her.

"He says he feels pounds lighter every time he takes down another building," Ellie said. "The barn is destined for destruction next. Perhaps as soon as this weekend."

"Good riddance. That's all I can say."

Margo stepped aside at the front door so Ellie could enter first and switch on the lights.

"Wow!" exclaimed Margo. "I don't know what I was expecting, but this wasn't it."

"Does that mean you like it?"

Margo didn't answer at first because she was reading the words along the top of the walls. "Interesting... well, it's very handsome and cozy in here, but not my taste. I hope that doesn't offend you."

"Not at all. The world would be a very boring place if we all liked the same things."

"Some of this looks familiar. Besides the pieces I sold you, I mean," said Margo, taking a closer look. "Like that trunk you're using for a coffee table. Did you salvage that from the old house?"

"I did, although it's locked and we haven't yet been able to open it."

"I doubt there's anything of value inside, or even particularly interesting."

"I hope we'll know for sure someday," said Ellie. "Do you recognize anything else?"

"Hmmm. The lamp table in the corner? Was that in the house, too?"

"Yes. I refinished it myself. Looks great, doesn't it?"

"Sure. If you like that sort of thing. I'd say the couch has something familiar about it, but our old one was a wreck that should have been thrown away."

"I had it repaired and recovered in this beautiful tartan. Ordered it special from Scotland. I also rescued the table and chairs. My brother and I resized, repaired, and painted them so they could be useful and beautiful again."

Margo spoke without excitement. "Whatever floats your boat, I guess."

"Do you recognize the picture of the shepherd and his flock of sheep? I had it reframed to suit the rest of the room."

"No, I hadn't. It's very handsome in a yesteryear sort of way, I suppose."

"The kitchen was custom-built from some of the weathered barn-wood."

"And Hugh was okay with that?" asked Margo, wide-eyed.

"He came around to my way of thinking." Ellie suddenly turned around, stopped short, and gasped. "Oh my stars! He installed white appliances!"

"They look a little familiar to me, too. Are you sure they're new?"

"They do, don't they..." Ellie opened the refrigerator and the interior confirmed that it was the same old fridge but with a facelift. Likewise the stove. "Hugh didn't want to buy new appliances for a house that wasn't going to be permanent. But I'm so glad he took me seriously about the outdated colours. The room looks so much better with white appliances, just like I knew it would. The next time I see that man, I'm going to smother him in kisses!"

"I'm honestly surprised Hugh is willing to live with so many leftovers of the life he knew here."

As Margo scanned the room again, she took a peek into the bedroom and then the bathroom. She didn't pass comment on those areas.

"He says they're altered enough not to bother him anymore," said Ellie. "And I suppose he wants to please me, because I find dear old pieces homier and more comfortable than modern things. I also like their association with family."

"Unless they remind you of the Fischer family," said Margo dryly. "Not so sweet and nostalgic."

Ellie hesitated, knowing that the subject she was about to broach was a sensitive one. "You know, Hugh has told me about his experiences as a child. I'd like to hear about yours."

"Look, you've been really nice to me, so I'll tell you this once. After that, the subject is closed forever. I do *not* like going down memory lane. I'll bet Hugh doesn't either. Being in our family was hard, especially for him. Pa always picked on him. Guess he needed a scapegoat and Hugh was handy. For Diane and me, life was mostly a big bore. There were never any trips, never any shopping… we never visited friends or relatives. We never had any new experiences at all. It was like living in an open prison. We couldn't wait until we got away and began lives of our own."

"What about now? Is your life free and easy or is it still an open prison?" The question slipped out before Ellie had time to judge its appropriateness.

Immediately she regretted being so blunt.

Margo looked at her as though stung. With a touch of anger, she said, "We should go. I need to get back to Dauphin."

They got back into Ellie's car, but instead of going directly to Minitonas Ellie turned into her own driveway.

"What now?" asked Margo.

"I just want to get a few things together. You can come in, if you like, or wait in the car. I'll just be a couple of minutes."

Margo waited in the car.

Ellie ran down the basement to look for a small cardboard box and found one. Upstairs she filled the bottom with a couple of boxes of macaroni and cheese, canned meat, soups, and a jar of jam. Over those items she added a few apples, oranges, and a cucumber. Next came a loaf of bread, a few bran muffins, and some cookies she pulled from the freezer. Then she ran back to her car and placed the small hamper on the floor behind the driver's seat.

They didn't talk much on the short return trip to Minitonas. When they got to Margo's car, Ellie asked her to meet her at the gas station before leaving town. Margo nodded and a moment later they pulled up to the gas pump. Ellie asked the attendant to fill the tank.

As the gas flowed, Margo excused herself to use the washroom. Ellie used the moment to place the small box of groceries on the floor of the passenger side of the car where she was sure Margo would notice it eventually. She didn't want to embarrass the woman.

By the time the gas was paid for, Margo had returned.

"I'm not sure why you're being so nice to me, but I do appreciate it. Money is tight at the moment," began Margo. "And that was the best steak I've eaten in a long time. Thanks again. Your starter house is really cute, although if you ask me I think you and Hugh shouldn't get married at all. That way, if things sour, and it seems they usually do, it's a lot less complicated to part ways."

"Things between you and Larry aren't so good, I take it."

"Nope. They sure aren't," said Margo, sounding depressed. "I'd leave him in a heartbeat, and he'd probably say the same about me, but we're tied together because of *my* house. I need him to make it work or I'll lose everything."

"You know, if you need to talk…"

"It's way too late for that. Gotta go. Thanks for everything."

Margo drove off into the night.

It was thoroughly dark and the mercury was falling steadily towards its nighttime low as Ellie raced up the road. But the wintery chill was the farthest thing from her mind. She fervently hoped Hugh had returned home. If not, she intended to go looking for him at the Moores' farm. There was so much to tell him.

From afar, she noted the lights on in the little house. Relief flooded her from the top of her blond head to her boot-covered toes.

Bounding up the steps, she burst through the door and quickly shed her winter gear.

"I'm throwing together an omelette for myself," Hugh said with a mere glance her way. "Do you want one, too?"

"No. I couldn't eat another bite," said Ellie. "I... I just need you to hold me. I spent the most bizarre day with your sister and I'm not over it."

Hugh looked directly at her. "Oh. Right this second, or can I eat first?"

"Go ahead. Eat first." Ellie took a seat on the couch, then glanced at the white stove. "You should have seen my face when I saw the white appliances. I thought they were new! I'm thrilled with them, honey. Thank you for doing that for me. It's all come together to form a beautiful and coherent front room. I told Margo I was going to smother you with kisses because of your thoughtful surprise."

"I wish I could have been here, but I had to rush back to the auto-body shop. I almost stayed behind after the installation to wait for you girls, but I had a good time with Ladd and Jeremy. Smothered in kisses, eh? In a couple of minutes, you can get started on that..."

Shortly thereafter, he set his plate in the sink and joined Ellie on the couch in the snuggle pose they often arranged themselves in.

"Okay, tell me what's bothering you," he said.

Ellie recounted the details of the day, including Margo's unnaturally thin body at the dress fitting, her steak dinner, and then how oddly she had behaved upon visiting her old homestead as well as indifference towards their starter home.

"I felt so bad that I put together a bit of a hamper to send home with her so she had something to eat for the next few days. I filled her tank with gas, too. Just before she drove off, she admitted that her marriage was on the rocks. Apparently she has to stay in that bad relationship for the sake of *her* house. She advised us to cancel the wedding and just live together so parting ways will be easier when the bottom falls out."

They sat silently for several minutes.

"Aren't you going to say something?" Ellie faltered, as though she were on the verge of tears. "What do you think? I'm terribly worried about her and I don't know how to help."

"I think you've already helped more than you know," he began slowly. "There's nothing else either of us can do until she gets to the end of her rope, just like I had to. Meanwhile, she's a grown woman who gets to chart the course for her life, even if she fills it with serious mistakes. If she needs help, she'll ask for it. And I'll help her. But only on my terms. I'm not going to throw good money after bad. As sure as the sun is going to rise tomorrow, the only help she'll ask for is a pile of money so she can keep her sinking ship above the water line a minute longer, before the bank forecloses or Larry sells it from under her feet. Only God knows how it's going to end."

He took his arm away from Ellie, stretched out a cramp, and then interlaced his fingers, resting them on his chest.

"I would like to have been a fly on the wall when she talked Larry into taking out a mortgage for that big fancy house," he continued. "What was he thinking? And what kind of dishonest banker would go along with that scheme? She told you right, though. Unless she can sell the house for what she paid, or more, she stands to lose everything. That would be tragic, because our inheritance was a real sweet boost. I regret that my mom didn't live to receive it. It would have given her the freedom she needed. I wish she could have had that."

Hugh released a long sigh.

"Margo didn't exactly enjoy visiting the farm," said Ellie. "She was glad the old buildings are coming down. Her associations are different than yours, though."

"Really? What did she say?" asked Hugh with raised eyebrows.

"For you, all these old buildings represent the pain you experienced. For Margo, it represents the poverty. I'm sure that's what her big fancy house is about—an attempt to overcome the poverty-stricken life she endured as a child. She wants to put it far behind her."

"That sounds about right," agreed Hugh. "Too bad she didn't see the wisdom of taking things one step at a time. Ironically, she may soon be living impoverished again. But that's enough about Margo. Where's all them kisses you were going to smother me with?"

Twenty-Two

IT WAS THE middle of December and Christmas was in full swing. Almost every day on Ellie's calendar was filled with appointments or tasks to be completed. She spent numerous mornings with Cynthia, fitting her wedding gown. Christmas concerts at schools and churches had claimed several evenings. Then there were the sundry other tasks, like getting a marriage license, purchasing wedding bands, Christmas shopping, and marriage counselling. She'd mostly set aside the journaling part of her soul work, but she managed to maintain her regimen of reading a bit of scripture most days. She also discussed her concerns with Jesus in prayer while imagining Him seated on the couch across from her dad's armchair.

Today was designated as a shopping day with Aunt Gertie. The woman was excited to be the candlelighter for her nephew's upcoming wedding and wanted to be dressed especially nice. She wanted Ellie's input with choosing a suitable outfit.

Ellie rolled up to the Johnsons' house at 9:30 a.m. Gertie came to the door to let her in, dabbing her eyes with tissue.

"Oh no! What's happened, Mrs. Johnson?" cried Ellie, suddenly concerned.

The woman wiped her nose. "Please, it's Gertie. Or at least Aunt Gertie. You may as well practice the title. We're that close to it being the real thing now."

"Okay, Aunt Gertie. Please tell me why you're crying."

"Ohhh, it's just that ridiculous son of mine. I spoke with him a half-hour ago, imploring him again to come home for Christmas. All his long-lost cousins will be here and there'll be a real party, but he insists he can't make it." Her tears started all over again. "I just don't understand it. I even offered to pay for his flight to Winnipeg and rent him a car. He still won't come."

"That's too bad. I wish I knew how I could help. He really is being a little rat, isn't he? Neglecting his mother like this…" A seed of an idea came to Ellie. "Could I have his contact information? I doubt his name got on the wedding list. As a cousin, he should receive one. I may have to call him personally. Time is short."

"Yes of course, dear. That's very thoughtful of you. But don't get your hopes up. If he won't come home for Christmas, he most certainly won't show up for the wedding of a cousin he can't recall ever meeting."

But I'm going to have a turn at trying, thought Ellie.

The shopping trip turned out to be fun for both women. Ellie looked on as Gertie tried out as many as a dozen outfits the clerk thought might suit their purpose. In the end, they chose a burgundy crepe and lace dress that complemented Gertie's colouring and fit her like a glove.

Ellie would have liked to return home right after, but Gertie insisted on treating her to lunch first. Given the woman's loneliness, Ellie gave her the extra time. But the real beneficiary was Ellie. She learned what a lot of fun Gertie could be as she told story after story of her days as a young woman dreaming of her knight in shining armour—only to wind up with the likes of Ed Johnson!

"I have no regrets, though," she said. "He's been a good husband to me."

Upon leaving Swan River, Ellie went directly to Sarah's house to obtain an extra wedding invitation. On the spot, she filled out the name and address: Mr. David Johnson, Esq. in downtown Toronto. She then brought it to the post office before returning to Bauman Farms.

She wanted very much to put in a call to David's office and ream him out for his selfish behaviour, but at the last minute she thought it would be best to consult the Lord first. Simmering down, she then made some notes about how to approach the situation.

With a deep sigh, she took the plunge and dialled the Toronto firm where David was employed. It took several steps and explanations for her call to be forwarded.

"Hello. Is this David Johnson?" asked Ellie politely.

"It is, and with whom am I speaking?" David's voice rang with professionalism.

"My name is Ella Bauman, and I happen to be the fiancée of your cousin, Hugh Fischer."

"I see. What can I do for you, Ms. Bauman?"

"I have two reasons for calling. The first is to personally invite you to our wedding on January 1. We missed adding your name to the guest list, and I didn't want you to be offended. Besides, we'd really like for you to join our celebration."

There was a pause on David's end. "This sounds like the same wedding my mother referred to when we spoke earlier."

"I believe that's correct. I saw your mother this morning and she was crying on account of her son declining to come home for the holidays. I think Gertie must not understand that her son has truly legitimate reasons. If you'll be so kind as to explain them to me, I'll do my best to help Gertie understand."

There was another pause, but briefer. "That's magnanimous of you, Ms. Bauman. I appreciate that. The truth is I really do have a backlog of work piled high on my desk. Aside from that, I don't feel I'm out of touch with them. I call my parents about once a month."

"Uh-huh. Go on."

"I suppose I feel there's no pull for me to come to Swan River. It's pretty much a redneck community. I don't have any nostalgia for the place, not to mention it's halfway across the country! Getting there would be disproportionately expensive."

"I see."

"Besides that, my girlfriend has invited me to join her family for Christmas. As for the long-lost cousins, I don't recall ever meeting them. Making a special trip to meet strangers who probably won't ever be important to me? Well, it seems an exercise in futility."

Ellie asked, "Is that all?"

"Isn't that enough? Do you really need more?"

"Hmmm. I'm just wondering how I should go about helping Gertie understand your position here. After all, you've as much as said that the very people who gave you life and a loving home, who've invested great sums of money in your university education, and who yearn to have a close relationship with their only son, aren't worthy of your time, effort, and personal expense. Likewise you've prejudged that your relatives aren't worthy of making your acquaintance."

David sputtered, but Ellie interrupted his attempt to backtrack.

"I think you might be the most self-centred, arrogant, highfaluting, insufferably self-important, snooty, conceited, uppity, presumptuous, most supercilious jerk I've ever met, if only by phone. It's you who is not worthy of the fine, caring, generous woman who is your mother, or any of the other people who would have gladly and warmly accepted you as an important member of the larger clan. But apparently you don't treasure family. That would be your mistake and your loss. Goodbye, David!"

Ellie hung up the phone with a clang. There was dead air for about ten seconds. It felt more like several minutes.

"Oh my gosh!" she exclaimed to herself in wide-eyed horror. "What have I done?"

$\sim$

"Are you serious? Did you really call my cousin a self-centred, arrogant, highfaluting jerk?" asked Hugh with shocked amazement when they got together later that evening.

"Amongst other things," confessed Ellie. "I didn't mean to, I really didn't. Like I said, I asked David to share his reasons for not coming home for the holidays so I could help Gertie understand where he was coming from. His excuses just made me mad. It was like something came over me... and once I started, I couldn't stop. I tried to call him back to apologize, but all I got was an answering machine. I don't know what to do."

Ellie handed Hugh the paper on which she had taken notes of David's side of the discussion. Hugh maintained an expressionless face until he had read it all.

He broke out in a lopsided smile. "According to your notes, it would appear he had it coming."

"I believe he did have it coming," said Ellie with a rush. "But I don't want to be that girl... that shrew... who reams people out merely because they deserve it."

"Maybe it's one of those tough jobs, but somebody has to do it. It's the second time for you in just as many months, isn't it? Otto Hoffman doesn't look like he's the worse for wear from your tongue-lashing."

"It's not funny, Hugh-miliate."

"Okay, okay. I know why you feel bad. Maybe you could just mail him a note of apology, or something."

Ellie felt somewhat relieved at the suggestion. "That's a good idea. I don't know why I didn't think of it myself."

~

At home, Ellie sat at the kitchen table with a pad of paper to write out a draft of her apology. In her first effort, she wrote,

> I apologize for speaking so rudely to you, but your reasons are poor excuses...

Ellie stopped abruptly and crossed out all the words that came after *you*. She thought for a moment and began writing again.

...but I'm afraid you really deserved to be told the truth about your foolish reasons.

She shook her head and crossed out all the words after *you* again.

Her third, fourth, and fifth attempts were no better than her first two. She felt the need to apologize yet didn't want to compromise the message she believed he needed to hear.

At the end of the page, the only uncrossed words were the few she had begun with. They would have to be good enough.

From her box of stationary, she took out a blank card and wrote inside:

> I apologize for speaking rudely to you. Please forgive me, and have a Merry Christmas. All the best for 1981.
>
> Most sincerely,
> Ella Rose Bauman
> (your soon-to-be cousin-in-law)

Quickly she tucked the card in its corresponding envelope and addressed it to *Master David Johnson, Esq.* A licked stamp affixed to the top righthand corner represented to Ellie that it was as good as posted and on its way to Toronto.

~

On the morning of Tuesday, December 16, Ellie again found herself at Cynthia's for what they hoped would be the final fitting of the gown's bodice. The heavy, three-dimensional lace wasn't easy to work with and had to be just right; there would be no second chance in the event of a false snip of the scissors.

They were also waiting for Diane to arrive for her fitting. Margo's gown was complete and hung on a thick quilted hanger to the side. They both hoped Diane's size hadn't changed in the past few weeks, as Margo's had. Although at least Margo's size had decreased. Cynthia claimed it was easier to take things in than let things out.

Diane showed up just after 11:00 a.m., more or less on time. As she slowly walked up to the house, she looked around the neighbourhood. Ellie guessed the woman was trying to refamiliarize herself with the small town that had once been her stomping grounds. It was plain, however, that Diane was heavier than she had been at the top of October.

Before Diane entered, Ellie warned Cynthia that it might not be an easy fitting session.

"You told me you were size twelve," said Cynthia after draping the unfinished gown over Diane. She had pinned one of the side seams, but the fabric barely met on the other side.

Diane seemed somewhat embarrassed. "Ummm... well, that's what I was wearing when we talked in October. I'm closer to a size sixteen now."

It was decided that the best way to compensate for the change was to add an insert, otherwise the dress wouldn't flow as designed. It would be a lot more work than anticipated, but there was nothing else to be done.

"No point in crying over spilt milk," said Cynthia in feigned cheerfulness.

To give the seamstress time to cut and sew the necessary adjustments, Ellie offered Diane a tour of the town. It had been a few years since she had been this way. They also agreed to stop for lunch at the café.

"How does it make you feel, seeing where you used to go to school?" asked Ellie as they drove past both the high and elementary schools.

"Nothing, really," said Diane unemotionally. "I didn't mind school, but I was glad when it was done."

"That's probably what most everyone would say if we had a class reunion. I was glad to move on into the adult world of personal freedoms and getting a career."

Diane didn't pass comment but kept looking up and down the streets, noting how few businesses remained in the once bustling community.

Ellie picked up the mail at the post office and then parked in front of the café.

"They make good homemade soups here, and also buns," said Ellie by way of suggestion.

"I was thinking of a juicy hamburger with fries and a cola, if that's okay."

"Sure. Whatever you like."

When the waitress came to take their order, Diane ordered herself the deluxe burger with all the fixings, extra fries with gravy on the side, and a large cola. Ellie sighed. It was all too easy to see how this size twelve woman could have steadily inched her way to size sixteen and beyond.

Ellie ordered a small bowl of tomato soup with a side salad, no bun, and a glass of water.

"That's all you're going to have?" noted Diane.

"I can't afford to gain an ounce. My wedding dress is sewn to fit precisely. It can't be altered. Besides, I'm trying to stick to a healthy diet." She smiled. "The dress is going to be gorgeous. But I'm going to do like the royals in Britain and keep the details secret until I walk down the aisle."

Diane merely shrugged.

Trying to evoke a meaningful conversation, Ellie asked, "So what's new in your life?"

"Not much, although I've been trying out some new recipes. Billy complained about having the same meals over and over again. My mother-in-law is a very good cook and Bill wants cooking like his mother's."

"Do you enjoy crafting? You know, like counted cross-stitch? It's all the rage right now. Or maybe folk-art painting? That's pretty popular."

Diane listened politely until it was her turn to speak. "I don't think I have a creative bone in my body."

"Hobbies?"

Diane shook her head about that, too. "When I'm not busy, I just watch television or read romance novels."

Ellie remembered meeting Bill, recalling that his disposition and bearing was a far cry from romantic. She could well imagine Diane being disappointed enough to turn to cheap, sexy thrillers for a bit of left-handed excitement. Ellie felt sorry for Diane, but on the other hand the girl seemed void of any ambition or drive to develop herself.

After their lunch, Ellie brought Diane to the old Fischer farm to show her the changes Hugh had made.

"It looks better," said Diane simply. "I bet Hughie likes it better, too, without Pa's junk lying around everywhere."

"Yeah. Hugh tidied up the yard pretty quickly after coming back. And he can't seem to demolish the old buildings soon enough!"

Diane merely nodded.

Ellie unlocked the house and led Diane inside.

"Oh wow!" said Diane. "It's so nice in here."

This was the liveliest response Ellie had seen from Diane all day.

"Thanks. Does anything look familiar?" Ellie began tidying up the room, collecting the mugs and plates Hugh had left on the table and trunk. She set them in the sink.

"Yes. This trunk, for one. It looks like the one that was in our old house in the front room."

Ellie affirmed that it was one and the same. She also pointed out the other pieces she had salvaged and refinished.

"They look amazing," said Diane, somewhat awed. "It's too bad Mama couldn't see this."

"I'm sorry, too. I've heard about what it was like back in those days. I'd like to hear what it was like for you."

"Well... I suppose the worst part for me came after Margo graduated and left home almost right away. Margo and I were best friends, and when she left I was all alone. But I guess the good part about that was that Mama and I became close friends—at least until I graduated and left home myself."

"Tell me about your mother," encouraged Ellie. "I wish I could have known her."

"Mama... well, she tried to make the best of a bad situation. We were poor. She tried to give us kids nice things to wear and all, but there wasn't much with which to do it. She was usually sad and depressed. Never saw her smile much."

"You must miss her a lot. I miss my mother, too."

Diane spoke without emotion. "I'm not sure. Maybe I'm just used to her being gone now. I think of her occasionally. She might have enjoyed being a grandma. This may sound weird, but she might be happier dead than when she was alive. Pa wasn't easy, but I guess Hugh told you all about that."

Ellie glanced at the trunk in the middle of the room. "I'm wondering if you could help me with something. We haven't been able to open the trunk. Do you happen to know what's inside?"

"I saw it open once, but all I glimpsed was a bunch of old things that probably came from before Ma's time, because they were never set out. I know Mama kept her wedding dress in there, though. The day I saw the trunk open, she was crying into it. I didn't stick around to see anything else."

"Tell me... what was important to your mama?"

"I don't exactly know. We didn't talk about things like that," said Diane. "She once said to me that happiness is a moment here and there, but most of the time life is either boring or depressing and never seems to change. I think she was right. Life is a lot of the same old, same old. She said life was a cheat."

Ellie looked down at the floor. "To me, that's a very sad viewpoint, Diane. I would say that life is what you make of it."

"Unless you're prevented from making something of it."

"What prevents you from living differently?" She regretted the question right away. Once again she'd spoken without thinking.

Diane seemed surprised but not offended. She thought for a moment, and then shrugged.

"My life is better than it was when I lived in Minitonas," Diane said. "Billy doesn't beat me."

With that, they returned to Cynthia's for another fitting. This time the gown draped nicely over Diane's frame and everybody was happy. Once the hemline was measured, Diane was released to go on her way.

"Thanks for lunch, Ellie," she said on her way out. "I'll see you later."

"Later?" queried Ellie, puzzled.

Diane blushed. "I mean at Christmas."

"Right. Christmas. Next week at Aunt Gertie's," agreed Ellie. "See you then!"

After she left, Cynthia and Ellie turned to each other.

"Those sisters could not be more different from each other," Cynthia observed. "It's hard to believe they're from the same family."

"No kidding."

That same evening, Ellie expected to go on a date with Hugh to see a movie. She'd fixed a pizza for their supper and afterward hurried to clean up. Hugh seemed to move in slow motion while Ellie was chomping at the bit to go. Inexplicably, Hugh kept assuring her that they had lots of time, causing her to become increasingly annoyed. She just couldn't figure him out.

Five minutes before 7:00 p.m., a van pulled up outside. It turned out to be Darcey, who entered the house without knocking as though she owned the place. She greeted Ellie with a half-hearted "Hi," set a stack of three large food containers on the kitchen table, and went back out to her van.

"What's going on here?" asked Ellie, feeling completely dazed when Darcey re-entered the house. She was followed by Cynthia, who carried multiple packages. Next came Sarah, Charlotte, Beanie, and then a trail of FBC ladies. Bringing up the rear were Aunt Ruth, Aunt Gertie, and Diane.

"Do you mean to tell me you forgot?" asked Darcey in great earnest. "I told you to mark your calendar. How could you?"

Ellie was entirely flummoxed. "How could I what?"

"It's a surprise for you, Aunty Ellie," supplied Beanie, preempting Darcey from further stringing Ellie along.

Charlotte saw that Ellie still wasn't catching on. "A wedding shower surprise. A party for girls only."

"Aww! I suppose an all-girls party means our date is off." Hugh pretended to be hurt, then smiled and tweaked Ellie's nose between two fingers and a thumb. "Have fun, babe."

"Okay, you got me. You got me good."

Darcey immediately took charge and began setting up the kitchen chairs in the living room. Sarah retrieved card table chairs from the basement and set them up to accommodate the fifteen guests. That didn't include Beanie and Charlotte, who were told to flank Ellie on the arms of the great armchair where she was assigned to sit.

The room was soon crowded and one of the older ladies from FBC grumbled that the shower should have been held in the church basement. But with some amicable shuffling, they got all the ladies sitting high and low in a general circle.

Cynthia oversaw the games. For the first, she handed out small squares of paper and pencils. She then instructed each of them to place the paper atop her head and draw a wavy line, representing water. Next they had to draw a boat on the water, and after that a sail, followed by a stick man in the boat. Then they added a hat, and lastly a fishing rod with a line in the water and a fish on the end. There was a great deal of twittering and giggling, after which the papers were turned in to Cynthia with the artists' names signed.

Cynthia looked at the hilarious drawings in order to pick a winner: the one whose sketch most closely resembled a man in a boat.

Darcey then handed out recipe cards. Everyone was asked to give the bride their best tips for homemaking and a successful marriage. The room transitioned from sounding like a buzzing beehive to something close to dead silence in a matter of seconds.

Everyone scrawled down their advice on the cards, including Beanie and Charlotte.

After a few minutes, Darcey collected the recipe cards, intending to read them aloud later in the evening.

Next, Cynthia gave out the artistic award, gifting one of the elder ladies from FBC a pair of red, apple-shaped potholders she had sewn from scraps. The drawings were spread on a tray and passed around the room to be enjoyed by all.

Cynthia's next game required the women to pair up. Paper copies of a fictitious romance using Hugh and Ellie's names were given to the duos. The story was interrupted with numerous blanks. The women were instructed to fill in the blanks with soap brands to supply the missing words. Once again the roomful of women sounded like buzzing bees. There were several choruses of ooohs and aaahs, not to mention assorted chuckles, when a few minutes later Cynthia read the story, with the filled in answers, aloud.

For this game, Gertie and Diane won for having the most correct answers. They were given hemmed squares of pretty fabric intended to line baskets for serving bread and buns.

Before Ellie was given the go-ahead to open her gifts, Darcey read out the tips written on the recipe cards. There were some particularly good ones.

"*The couple that prays together stays together.*" Several heads nodded.

"*Put God first, husbands second, children third, and everyone else after that.*" There were more nods.

"*No lies and no secrets, period.*" A few of the women exchanged wary glances.

"*Blessed is the house that is clean enough to be healthy and dirty enough to be happy.*" This one produced a lot of nodding heads.

"*Pick your battles. You can compromise on some things, but not everything.*"

"*If you burn the dinner, throw in the towel and eat out!*"

"*Your wonderful husband is not perfect like Jesus. Have reasonable and realistic marriage expectations.*"

With this one, Ellie glanced over to Aunt Ruth. "I think I know where that one came one," she said. "I believe in your wisdom."

Ellie could guess the source of the next one, too: "*I think you should get a puppy.*"

Gales of laughter filled the room.

Beanie put up her hand as if she were at school. "I wrote that one," she said, grinning from ear to ear.

"Well, guess what?" Ellie briefly tickling her niece in the ribs. "Hugh and I actually brought the subject up not so long ago. So that might be something we actually do before long."

Charlotte and Beanie opened their mouths in delighted gasps and looked at each other with radiant smiles as if lightbulbs had just been switched on in their heads.

Darcey read on: "*Always kiss goodnight.*"

Beanie smiled. "Charlotte wrote that one," she tattled, causing Charlotte to blush and poke her little sister on the shoulder.

"It's a very good tip," Ellie assured them. "And I hope never to forget to do that."

There were a few more.

"*If you need your man to say yes to something, butter him up with his favourite meal first.*" Some of the ladies responded with agreement, but others claimed that this hadn't worked for them.

The next one produced a few laughs. "*Don't go to bed mad. Go to bed naked.*"

"I bet Darcey wrote that one," piped up one of the ladies.

"No I didn't," insisted Darcey. "But I wish I did. That's a great tip."

The advice kept flowing: "*Husbands need training, and it's a lot like training a pet.*" This produced a few snickers and an exchange of uneasy looks.

"*Submit to your husband like the Bible says, but don't be a doormat either.*"

"Occasionally, meet your husband at the door wearing nothing but saran wrap. (Take the kids to Grandma's first!)"

One of the elder FBC ladies turned to Darcey. "You must have written that one, right? That sure sounds like something you'd say."

Darcey chuckled. "I think I'll just keep you guessing."

"Don't stop going on dates just because you're married." A few of the women said amen to that one.

"If the wife ain't happy, ain't nobody happy." A few claps and nods came as response.

"Love needs maintenance. Be careful not to neglect each other."

That concluded the recipe cards. The evening's laughter put everyone in good spirits.

"Wow! This room is full of wise, experienced women," declared Darcey. "There's some good counsel here."

The time had come for Ellie to open her gifts. Beanie wanted to help, meaning of course that she wanted to open presents, too. Ellie didn't mind, and Beanie went at it by tearing off the pretty paper with abandon… to the consternation of some of the elder ladies who thought the paper should be carefully removed and saved for future use.

The gifts included tea towels, washcloths, baking pans, a recipe book, bathroom towels, a toaster, a waffle iron, and a supply of wooden spoons, ladle, and other kitchen utensils. One woman gave her a teapot-shaped wall clock. Ellie knew instantly she would never use it, but she graciously thanked the woman nonetheless.

Darcey's gift was a plate-rail shelf made by Tony from some of the leftover barnwood. Ellie was thrilled and many of the guests admired it as well.

Charlotte collected the bows and ribbons to create a party bonnet on a paper plate. This was set on Ellie's head after all the gifts had been opened. Photographs were taken.

But before Darcey dismissed the ladies to partake of the luncheon laid out on the kitchen table, she presented Ellie with one final surprise gift—a stack of assorted dinner plates, salad plates, and soup bowls.

Knowing that Ellie had always favoured her grandma's mismatched dishes, she had asked the guests to bring odd dishes from previous sets. Ellie beamed with pleasure. Most of the ladies, though, looked at her like she had a disfiguring growth on her face.

When it was all said and done, the shower had been a wonderful surprise. Ellie expressed her deep gratitude for everyone's thoughtfulness. She was blessed indeed.

"The only disappointment I have," said Ellie with a straight face, "is that the woman who suggested I meet my husband wearing only saran wrap didn't include it with her shower gift!"

Twenty-Three

ON THURSDAY, ELLIE was scheduled to work the night shift. When she got to the hospital, the ward was unusually busy. The nurses, including Ellie, theorized that the stress and pressure of the holiday season had contributed to people getting sick right at Christmas time, which only led to more stress and pressure. It was a vicious circle.

They were shortly to expect a new patient on their ward; a man who had spent the last thirty-six hours in critical care after a massive heart attack. Stabilized following the relatively new bypass procedure, he would be kept for observation. Ellie was assigned to resettle him in a designated room with other male convalescents.

The staff briefing was hardly concluded when the patient in question was delivered to the ward. Together, the nurses transferred him from the surgical gurney to the hospital bed, after which Ellie took over.

At least she intended to. Before checking the man's vitals, she looked at his chart to learn his name and nearly fell over. Surreptitiously looking up into the man's face, she recognized him immediately. He was the very same Otto Hoffman with whom she'd had words several weeks earlier.

She turned her back so he wouldn't see her face and took several deep breaths. The memory of their one and only meeting warmed her cheeks and caused her heart to race madly. She quickly prayed for the grace to nurse him kindly and professionally.

Otto had his eyes closed while she checked his pulse, took his temperature, and tucked in the hospital blanket. She went through a routine checklist of duties, and only when she took his hand and placed the forefinger into the oximeter finger clip did he open his eyes and peer directly into her face.

"You!" said Otto gruffly.

She looped the call button cord to the siderail of his bed. "Me."

But if he wanted to get into another tete-a-tete, his hopes were dashed. Just then, another nurse stuck her head in the doorway and asked Ellie to come and help with a different patient. Thankful for the escape, she hurried away to help her colleague.

This time, the patient in need was another woman Ellie knew: Mrs. Bradley from Minitonas. The elderly woman had fallen and broken her hip. It was now time for the nurses to wash her body, change her bedding, administer her medication, and get her settled for the night.

Every time they moved her limbs, she groaned.

"We're trying to be gentle," said Ellie. "Does it really hurt when we touch you?"

"Of course it does. I don't moan for the fun of it, you know." The woman peered at Ellie sternly. "Don't I know you from somewhere?"

"I believe we ran into each other at the grocery store in Minitonas last summer," Ellie replied in a friendly tone.

"Seems likely. Was there more to it than that? My memory isn't what it used to be."

"I don't think so."

As far as Ellie was concerned, there was no point in recalling the chewing out she had received from her for showing kindness to Tipper. The lady hadn't approved, after all.

"Is that Ellie Bauman I hear?" asked someone from across the room.

Ellie started at the voice. It was at once familiar and foreign.

"I'll be there in a minute," she called as she tidied up around Mrs. Bradley's bedside. She quickly disposed of the soiled linens and hospital gown into the laundry sack.

Then Ellie turned her attention to the voice that had addressed her from the other side of the room.

"Teresa!" exclaimed Ellie, astounded. "What a blast from the past! How come you're here?"

"I came home to do Christmas with the family," replied Teresa from her bed. "My brother took me out on the snowmobile and we hit a bump that sent us both flying. He's okay, but I landed on a good-sized rock and broke a few ribs. I'm doing lots better today, but don't make me laugh. Seriously."

Ellie took a seat in the bedside chair. "I can't visit for long, but bring me up to date. It's been a few years and you haven't changed much that I can see."

Teresa Westcot was a former high school friend, and one of the four girls who had shared an apartment when they moved to Winnipeg after graduation. She had also grown up a country girl on their family farm west of Minitonas.

"I'm doing okay, for the most part. Got myself a good office job. I assume you want to know that Patti is a teacher in Stonewall. Maureen took off to Calgary with some guy hoping to find a meaningful life there." Teresa rolled her brown eyes heavenward. "Haven't heard from her since. I thought you were still nursing at St. B. Why are you here?"

"I left in June. I needed a sabbatical and came home to do it. Both my folks have passed and I felt I should get back to my roots and reground myself."

Teresa gathered her long brown hair from behind her back and brought it around her neck to her chest. "I'm surprised. I can't imagine there's enough action going on around these parts to keep you from being thoroughly bored. I mean, is there even one good pub in the district?"

"I don't bother with pubs anymore. I'd rather visit with people over a meal or in a home. How long are you in town for?"

"I had intended on going back on Boxing Day. Hopefully this injury won't kibosh that plan."

"If you're still in the neighbourhood, I invite you to come to my wedding. I'm getting married on January 1."

"No!" exclaimed Teresa. "To whom? Anyone I know?"

"Did you know Hugh Fischer back in the day?"

"You're kidding! Nerdy, gangly, pimply-faced, greasy-haired Hugh Fischer?"

"He's none of those things today. If you saw him, he might remind you of Tom Selleck... without the moustache. He's a great guy. He's also recently returned to these parts to make a new start in life. I believe we make a good pair."

"Different strokes for different folks. I don't know what else to say," said Teresa. "I guess that means you won't be offended if I tell you I've shacked up with one of your exes."

Ellie waited for the other shoe to drop...

"Yeah, Curt and I are living together."

"Has he changed?" Ellie asked, feeling discomfited. "He used to be heavily into drugs. I'm glad I didn't spend a minute longer with him than I did. In fact, I regret every minute I did spend with him. He was not good news..."

"We're getting along okay. For now, at least. If he becomes a drag, I'll kick him out. There are more fish in the sea. That's what having a choice is all about."

Teresa looked away from Ellie, smoothing the wrinkles out of the light blanket covering her.

"I should get back to my duties," said Ellie, rising. "It's really good to see you again. And I mean it. If you're still in town January 1, you're invited to my wedding."

Ellie walked up to the door and stopped. Then she turned on her heel and walked back to the foot of her friend's bed.

"You're absolutely right, Teresa. Each one of us has a God-given right to our choices. Any kind of choice at all. What we can't choose is the consequences for those choices. If you choose to play with fire, you'll get burned. And that's a promise. If you choose to plant weeds, you won't get roses. You get what I'm sayin'? You reap what you sow."

Teresa was plainly annoyed. "Hold on there, sister. Apparently you've turned over a new leaf. And now you think you can lecture your friends? Your former friends, I should say."

"No, of course not," said Ellie, immediately contrite. She reached into her pocket and pulled out a small notepad, as well as the pen clipped to her uniform. "I'd like to have coffee with you before you head back. The café in Minitonas is pretty good. I'll tell you my story then. I'm not the same girl you knew in high school." She wrote out her contact information, then tore off the sheet and laid it on Teresa's hospital table. "I have to get back to work. But seriously, call me before you leave so we can have a proper visit."

After Ellie left the room, Teresa picked up the notepaper and stared at it for a minute. With one hand, she scrunched it up into a tiny little ball. Not seeing a wastebasket anywhere, she threw it into the tray under the table where she kept her personal hygiene items.

A moment later, a single tear slid down her cheek and dripped onto her hospital gown.

In the wee hours of the morning, Otto signalled for the attention of a nurse. Though one of the other nurses went to him, he rather emphatically insisted that he would make his request only to Ellie. Overall, the nurses weren't willing to play this game. Ellie had sighed and then explained that it likely reflected something of a personal nature and agreed to go to him.

"What is it, Mr. Hoffman?" she asked, aiming for a tone that was respectful and no-nonsense at the same time.

"I can't sleep," said Otto in a low voice.

"Are you in pain?"

"Not really."

"You were given a sleep aid earlier. You cannot have more. Perhaps you can try the old count-the-sheep tactic."

"I can't sleep because I need to talk to you, Ms. Bauman."

"Now isn't a good time, Mr. Hoffman. You have three roommates who are trying to get their rest."

"Will you be here tomorrow?"

"No."

"Then it has to be now."

"Why can't it wait?"

"Because I can't sleep. Because I may die any minute. Because I have things that need to be said before it's too late. Because."

"You do realize this room isn't private, don't you?" Ellie reminded him. "Whatever you want to say will most likely be overheard by others. Consider that."

Otto paused to think. "Help me out of bed and take me in one of them wheelchairs down to the sitting area. We can talk there."

"I'm sure the head nurse won't allow it."

"Then call the head nurse in here so I can make a gosh awful proper scene."

Reluctantly, Ellie went to speak with the head nurse and relay Otto's demand. She followed Ellie back to Otto's bedside, prepared to be tough. But Otto expected as much. Before she could get started, he threatened to wake up the entire wing if he couldn't have his one small request.

"You need to be careful about getting too excited, considering your condition," warned the head nurse gravely.

"I feel fine. If you deny me this one simple and reasonable wish, I'll raise Cain and become nothing less than your sworn nemesis. And that's a promise."

The head nurse stared at him with steely eyes. Otto stared back with a locked-in gaze.

She blinked first. In a much quieter tone, he promised in good faith to be as docile and cooperative as any lamb… if only he could have a few minutes in private to discuss something important to him.

Relenting, the nurses managed to transfer Otto Hoffman into a wheelchair and covered his legs with a blanket. Along with all the poles, tubes, and wires, they wheeled him to the end of the wide hall. Only when he was sure the head nurse was out of earshot did he turn to Ellie.

"I suppose you remember our last meeting in October," began Otto.

"Yes. I do."

"Well… I haven't been able to forget some of the things you said."

"Mr. Hoffman, I fear I spoke to you rudely and out of turn…

"I'm not looking for an apology, but I do want you to hear me out."

Otto began to rub his hands together, a gesture that made Ellie realize he was as nervous as she. She gave a little cough as if clearing her throat and waited for the castigation she was sure was forthcoming.

"I was shocked, angry, and scared that you figured me out so rightly. About my double life, I mean," he said. "After all, we didn't know each other. And when I asked what you wanted, I expected something along the lines of blackmail."

Ellie was stunned. "Blackmail!"

"Yeah. I thought you would press me for more money to rent the land. Otherwise you would snitch on me to the church folks and all."

"It never crossed my mind! Not once!"

"I know. Instead you told me that you wanted me to give up my sins, to be genuinely honest and worthy of my elder role at church. And you told me not to bring shame on the name of the Lord Jesus. The way it came outta you, I thought it was the Almighty Himself coming after me for sure."

"Perhaps I should call Pastor Leland," suggested Ellie. "He is much better qualified to hear your confessions."

"It started with you, so you'll hear the rest of the story. Leland is a good man and a good pastor, but I won't air my dirty laundry with him." Otto shook his head. "Anyway, what I wanted to tell you is that the Lord has been dealing with me. I've been convicted of a good many things and done some repenting. Been making things right between me and some of the people in my life, including my patient wife. Thought you should know you were used of the Lord."

"I'm glad for you and relieved for me," said Ellie, breathing easy again. "I thought you were going to chew me out for speaking so bluntly. I apologize for my rudeness."

"No, girlie. Got no call to do anything like that. And speaking the truth isn't necessarily being rude. I s'pose there are people who would call what you said to me as being bad-mannered. But I've been a hard and proud man. There. I admitted it. And the good Lord used you to get in my face because that's what it was going to take to make me reflect on my underhanded and ornery ways."

"I still wish He'd used someone else and not me." Ellie felt uneasy all over again.

"You were the only one that knew something about what I was secretly up to. You had Freddie Fischer's notebook. Who else could the Almighty have used? But never mind. Now I do feel tired. I expect sleep will come if you help me get back in that terrible hard bed…"

The head nurse assisted Ellie in returning Otto to his bed and got him resettled for the night. As promised, he obliged the staff in everything they asked of him, transitioning from severely cantankerous to model patient.

In the aftermath, Ellie became quiet and pensive. Her coworkers noticed but didn't bug her, sensing there was more to the situation with Otto than met the eye.

When at last her shift was over, she returned home as quickly as possible. Although tired, she went straight to her favourite armchair and wrote in her journal about the incidents with Otto, Teresa, and Mrs. Bradley. What were the odds of confronting three individuals in one night with whom she was so personally acquainted? But that's how it had happened.

In particular, the unexpected exchange between herself and Mr. Hoffman gave her pause. Though neither of her encounters with Otto had been easy or comfortable, she could follow the involvement of the Lord and offer Him praise that the church elder had repented of his backslidden ways.

Exhausted, she slept well into the afternoon.

Twenty-Four

ALL WEEK, HUGH had looked forward to Saturday. He had prepared for it with all due diligence. Shovels, pitchforks, chains, and other paraphernalia worth keeping from the derelict barn were restowed in the machine shed. He'd got his permit for a controlled burn.

The Moore brothers were asked to help and they gladly agreed. In fact, they were as excited as kids to be in on a major demolition. And when Rob and Trevor heard about Hugh's plan, they at least wanted to come and watch. Hugh understood. A fire was an awesome thing; whether large or as small as a candle flame, it could be mesmerizing.

It was snowing lightly, and a little breezy, when Ladd and Jeremy drove into Hugh's place around 8:30 in the morning. He had just finished his breakfast. Seeing the brothers exit their half-ton, he drained the last of his coffee and walked out to meet them. Already they were standing before the sagging structure, collars up around their ears as they discussed whether to simply light it as is or knock it down and crush it first.

"I'm thinking it should be brought down and compacted before it's lit," said Hugh. "I'm afraid of sparks flying and setting the machine shed on fire. It's gotta go someday, too, but I still need it in the meantime."

So the question became how to go about doing that. Hugh said he didn't want to pull it down in such a way that would cause the rubble to spread out. He preferred to bring the structure to its knees, so to speak, by pulling the corners down and inward with chains and a tractor. Jeremy suggested they use a chainsaw to cut points of resistance and create holes to pass the chains through. Hugh agreed it was a good idea.

Ladd and Jeremy went at it, each with their own chainsaw, and collapsed what was left of the interior partitions. Hugh then went to over to the machine shed to start his tractor.

Soon Trevor and Rob pulled into the yard. Hugh noticed their hardhats. That was a good idea! After he got his tractor started and idling, he went looking for his own hardhat.

He brought the tractor around to the far side of the barn and even drove inside the structure a few feet so the chains could reach the bucket and be attached. Wanting to be part of the action, Trevor helped secure the chains around the two front corners of the barn while Ladd attached the ends to the arms of the bucket.

Rob took it upon himself to supervise. As director of operations, he insisted that Ladd wear a hard hat and lent him his own. In these circumstances, maintained Rob, it was easy for things not to go as planned. It was simple wisdom to take every precaution.

As Hugh went round the front of the barn to check the chains for readiness, Ladd jumped on the tractor and inched it in reverse until the chains were taut.

One chain, incorrectly hooked, came undone. Hugh motioned for Ladd to inch forward again. He slipped into the barn and reset the chain and hook.

It suddenly occurred to Hugh that the only site on the farm that represented a modicum of relief and retreat to him was the loft of the old barn. In a moment, it would be brought down and destroyed forever.

Some nostalgic corner of his mind prompted him to take one last look.

He climbed up four steps until his head was high enough to catch a glimpse across the floor of the loft. There was nothing to see other than a scattering of old straw everywhere.

Down below, Ladd again inched in reverse. Feeling the tightness of the chain, he concluded that all was ready and pulled hard.

As anticipated, the front walls collapsed neatly to the ground. The centre of the roof sagged nearly to the loft floor, but the gable end remained largely intact.

Because Jeremy had cut the corner posts with his chainsaw, the chains pulled away from the beams easily. Exuberant, the men quickly got to work bringing down the other end of the barn in similar fashion.

~

Stupid! You stupid, stupid idiot! thought Hugh as he tumbled off the stairs to the main floor, landing on his stomach. Ladd had just pulled down the walls, causing them to collapse on top of him. He was fortunate that the collapsed wall didn't crush him. Mercifully, he was wedged between the barn floor and the width of the staircase stringer, which was about twelve inches wide.

But he couldn't move.

He didn't think he was hurt, but he was in a space as tight as a cucumber in a full jar of dill pickles. His hard hat, while still on his head, had pushed up his forehead so that his nose and face were planted in the dirt.

Drawing breath was difficult. He managed to twist his nose to the right just enough to allow him to breathe—that is, if he remained calm. He was pinched too tight to open his mouth and yell and sound the alarm. All that came out was a low growl, which he was pretty sure no one could hear, especially with the tractor running.

He hoped the guys soon realized he was missing.

Hugh heard the tractor moving to the south side of the barn and figured they were preparing to bring down the other end. He could also hear some talking but couldn't make out the words. He tried again to yell when there seemed a lull in their discussion, but all his efforts went unnoticed.

Lord, make them notice I'm missing, prayed Hugh. *Don't let them crush me to death. If I die, Ellie will kill me!*

~

Despite hobbling around the scene on crutches, it was Rob who dictated the logistics of the operation. Not many minutes later, Ladd was again on the tractor, inching in reverse. Through Rob's experience and knowledge of physics, they brought down the rear end of the barn and it came down almost as neatly.

When the dust settled, the guys whooped in celebration.

Ladd drove the tractor around to face the far end of the barn and quickly knocked down the gabled wall with the bucket of the tractor. When that was done, he returned to the front and similarly brought down the east gable until it lay in a flat heap.

Just as he finished, Ellie walked onto the scene.

"Hi guys! Wow! You sure work fast. Just looks like a stack of matchsticks now," she said, looking into all their faces by turn. "Where's Hugh?"

The four men looked around.

"Good question," said Rob. "Maybe he went into the house to use the john."

"I just came from there," said Ellie. "He's not in the house."

"I'll check the shed." Trevor was already running before he finished his sentence.

A moment later, the teenager returned shaking his head.

Rob took charge again. "Okay, who saw him last? And where?"

There was no immediate answer.

"Speak up, guys," said Ellie. "You're scaring me."

A few seconds later, Jeremy hesitantly said, "The last time I saw him was when we were getting ready to pull down the first wall. He went into the corner to reset a chain that had come loose."

He pointed in the direction where they'd been working.

"Did you see him come out?" asked Rob, business-like.

"No, sir, I didn't. But in all honesty, I wasn't watching."

"Anyone else?" asked Rob.

Trevor and Ladd mumbled that they hadn't been watching for him either. They had just gone about the job of pulling down the barn.

"You mean he might be trapped somewhere under all this… rubble?" asked Ellie in dismay.

Rob lowered a steadying hand onto her shoulder. "Nobody panic."

⁓

The pressure was getting painful. With every step the men took to bring down the barn, the debris pressed more heavily. Hugh had no room to expand his lungs, forcing him to breathe shallowly.

From his cocoon against the stringer, he could follow the movements of the tractor and determine the procedure they were employing to crush the old structure, yet he couldn't figure out why they hadn't noticed he was missing.

The tractor went silent and he heard voices again, including a voice that he thought belonged to Ellie.

Thank God! thought Hugh. *She'll get a search party going lickety-split. But hurry, honey. I'm strugglin'.*

⁓

"Ladd, get back on the tractor and bring it over here," ordered Rob. "Trevor, look in Hugh's shed for prybars and bring all you find. Jeremy, go to the other side of this heap and bring back some good-sized studs or beams or something. We may need them to prop up the larger pieces of debris."

"What should I do?" asked Ellie, wanting to be of help.

"Stay out of the way!" barked Rob. "And pray!"

Ladd brought the tractor around and under Rob's guidance slid the bucket just below the floor of the former loft. On Rob's cue, he hydraulically lifted the wooden corner. It broke off, revealing the opening where the staircase had led.

Rob motioned for Ladd to try again further down the structure. Slowly Ladd slid the edge of the bucket beneath the floor again and raised it. Beneath they could see the collapsed wall more or less intact. But there was still no sign of Hugh.

"He must be underneath," said Ellie as she clambered under the raised area. She began calling Hugh's name and listened intently for any sound that might indicate Hugh's location.

"Get out of there!" Rob shouted. "You don't even have a hardhat. What if the floor suddenly breaks off again?"

"I'll take my chances. Now be quiet so I can listen…" She concentrated on listening, her ear to the floor. Suddenly, she stiffened. "I heard something! Over there."

Ellie pointed to an area of debris about six feet from where the exterior wall had stood. She crawled towards the spot.

"Hugh, if you can hear me, make that noise again!" urged Ellie. Holding up her hand, she became perfectly still. "Here! He's under here! Hold on, we're coming for you, Hugh-bert."

"I've got the chainsaw," volunteered Jeremy. "I could cut him out."

"You could, if you could see him," replied Rob, annoyed. "You don't want to risk cutting him up. Come on, guys. Use the prybars to pull the boards apart and see what his situation is."

Trevor and Jeremy went to work with gusto and had soon removed enough boards to see Hugh's position along the stringer of the staircase. They quickly freed most of his body, except the beam that pinned down his hardhat. Jeremy revved up the chainsaw and with two swipes of the blade completely removed the offending wood.

Now freed, Hugh jumped up like a jack-in-the-box. He crawled out to safety beyond the fallen barn along with the others.

Rob cued Ladd to lower the former loft and retreat.

"Are you all right?" asked Ellie anxiously. "Do you think you have a broken bone? Are you hurt?"

"No. The only thing that is hurt is my pride. I dilly-dallied and that's how I got trapped." Hugh sounded sheepish. "It's all my fault and that's a fact. I'm sorry for all the trouble and worry I've caused you."

"Seeing that you don't seem much worse for wear, I think we should all take a coffee break and regroup before we set that thing on fire," said Rob, relieved and well aware that the situation could have turned out much differently.

He got no argument. The six of them began the short walk to the house.

On the way, Rob fell into step with Ellie. He caught her eye. "Hugh-bert? Where did that come from?"

"Private joke," said Ellie. "You wouldn't understand."

~

While the others waited for the coffee to brew, Hugh washed the grime from his face and brushed his teeth and mouth for what seemed like a long time, trying to rid himself of the taste of barn dirt.

Ellie then handed out mugs of steaming coffee and set out the sandwiches she had made. It was early for lunch, but once the fire was lit they would be obliged to tend it until it was reduced to ashes.

A half-hour later, Hugh was ready to carry on with the plan.

To ensure a fast burn, Trevor and Jeremy scrambled atop the broken heap, sprinkling gasoline. Hugh then had everyone stand back as he lit the pile with a torch from the middle.

The flames raced in every direction like wildfire. Had it been night, it might have appeared eerie. In the daylight, though, it simply looked like an oversized bonfire. There was just enough of a breeze to keep the fire roaring.

When most of the pile had burned to the ground, a series of mini-explosions split the air. They saw a large hole in the ground where something had fallen in. The guys looked to Hugh for an explanation, but he didn't know and shrugged, as puzzled as the others. He could only guess that his pa had dug some sort of secret cellar and stored some gas and oil in it.

He and Ellie exchanged a certain look. They both knew the possibilities didn't end there.

"I suppose that could be another of the secrets Tipper insisted this place was riddled with," Ellie said softly so the others wouldn't hear.

"Seems like," he agreed, nodding.

"I wonder what your pa kept in there."

"I don't even want to know. Whatever it is, I'm glad it's been destroyed. And now I have a good place to bury the ash."

By midafternoon, the bulk of the former barn had been consumed. Rob and Trevor returned home first, and shortly thereafter the Moore brothers left as well. Hugh used the tractor and bucket to scrape the remaining sticks and embers into a much smaller pile. By suppertime, the remaining coals no longer required his constant attention. He called it a day.

Later, after he had eaten and showered, Hugh went over to Ellie's place to hang out for the evening. He'd let himself in. She'd risen to greet him with a brief hug but then returned to her sweet spot and resumed writing in one of her journals.

Hugh stretched out on the couch like he often did, studying Ellie. The ambience felt so relaxing. Christmas music from her mother's record collection played softly in the background, something German that permeated the air with nostalgic Yuletide sentiment. The Christmas tree lights glowed in all the traditional colours, causing the shiny hanging balls to twinkle in the dim light.

She felt his gaze upon her and looked up. "What?"

"You tell me. It feels like you're mad at me."

"I'm recording the day's events in my journal. It was an interesting day." She continued to write without looking up.

"I know what you're doing," said Hugh evenly. "I want to know why you're angry."

Ellie put down her pen and clasped her hands together on her lap. "Maybe I'm still upset that I nearly became a widow today, and we haven't even tied the knot yet."

Hugh nodded, thinking earnestly about how he should respond to that.

"I'm sorry," he said at last. "What happened is that I reset the chain... and then I suddenly got an urge to see the loft one more time—just for a second, before it was physically erased forever."

"But why?" cried Ellie plaintively.

"Because the loft is where I went to find refuge when Pa had it in for me. It was my hiding place when it seemed like a good idea to keep outta sight. It represented my summer bedroom for a few years, too. I just had a sudden urge to take a last look. But I wasn't quick enough. Ladd was on the ball."

Her eyes glistened. "You know, sometimes I find your stories intriguing. Other times they're so painfully sad that I can hardly stand it."

"Aach. It's all water under the bridge. It's over. Been over for a long while." Hugh spoke lightly to forestall a depressing discussion. "The yard feels pretty empty with the barn gone. It'll take a bit of time to get used to the change. But emotionally it feels so good to be rid of it. Cheer up. All is well."

"How are you feeling? It's absolutely amazing you came out from under that demolition unscathed."

"Just a little achy from the tumble off the stairs," admitted Hugh. "I'm sure I'll sleep it off. I'm giving God the credit for sparing my life."

Ellie offered him a crooked grin. "Amen to that! Would you like a massage?"

"Sure... if Nurse Bauman would be so kind..."

On Sunday morning, Ellie walked hand in hand into the church with Hugh for the first time in many weeks. This was due to the fact that she had often been scheduled to work Saturday nights. It felt good to be in the house of the Lord and reconnect with friends.

One of the surprises was that Cynthia and Brent Clifford had started attending FBC, making it their new home church.

Ladd and Jeremy Moore also sought her out to teasingly complain that her presence meant they'd get no time with Hugh that afternoon. They had come to enjoy his input as they went about rebuilding a motor.

At last the service began with a familiar Christmas hymn. This was followed by a few announcements.

Pastor Leland then came to the stage and paused before speaking. "It is with great sadness that I announce the passing of our brother and elder, Otto Hoffman…"

Ellie gasped and listened intently while the pastor spoke. Hugh squeezed her hand, knowing her feelings would be in a turmoil with this unexpected development. She had told him about their private discussion at the hospital and knew it caused her to do a lot of pondering.

"He went into the hospital Tuesday after a heart attack," continued Pastor Leland. "The doctors performed bypass surgery, and he appeared to be mending. He was in good spirits when I visited with him last evening. However, around midnight another massive heart attack occurred and this time the doctors could not save him. That said, we believe what the scriptures say through the apostle Paul, when he said of believers that when we are absent from the body, we are present with the Lord.[17] Funeral arrangements haven't yet been made, but it has been suggested for next Sunday afternoon, December 28."

He went on to make other announcements, but Ellie had tuned out. It continued to astonish her that although she had played a bit part in the life of Otto Hoffman, it seemed it wasn't insignificant.

---

[17] 2 Corinthians 5:8.

Twenty-Five

"ELLIE, I THINK it's time you came by and we talked about icing your wedding cake," said Aunt Ruth via phone call. "Sooner is better than later. We want to avoid a last-minute, high-pressure job getting it done on time."

Midmorning on Monday, Ellie drove the snow-packed back roads to the Wagner farm. The bright sun's reflection off snow-covered fields caused her to squint so hard that she needed to slip on her sunglasses and pull down the visor.

About halfway there, in the distance, she saw a lone bull moose trotting across a field between clumps of bush. Ellie briefly wondered if Hugh or her brother had ever tried their hand at hunting game. She hadn't heard Rob speak of it, but they had grown up often having wild game for dinner.

Upon turning into the driveway, a large winter-white rabbit leapt across the road and a tiding of magpies scattered in every direction. Not many people had an appreciation for magpies, but Ellie couldn't deny that, for all their faults, they were among the most handsome of birds.

"A rabbit ran in front of me as I came onto your yard," said Ellie to her aunt as she removed her winter wear. "Are they going after your plants?"

"Goodness, I hadn't thought to check for that. I sure hope not," said Ruth with an undertone of warning. "If rabbits are chewing on my prize shrubs and perennials, I'll turn them into bunny stew first chance I get!"

"Aww, but they're so cute."

"Only when they aren't causing problems. Now, would you like tea or coffee to sip while we discuss wedding cakes?"

Ellie opted for tea.

On the kitchen table were a couple of cake decorating magazines and a book Ruth had borrowed from the library that was devoted exclusively to making and decorating wedding cakes. She picked up the book and began thumbing through it.

Ruth set a steaming mug before Ellie and another one for herself.

"This doesn't look like any tea I'm familiar with," said Ellie.

"It's a new recipe I got from my neighbour. Try it."

Obediently, Ellie took a tentative sip, and then a larger one. "Oh my. This is delicious! What is it exactly?"

"They call it Russian tea. Basically you make a big batch of strong regular tea and then add lemon, orange, and pineapple juices, along with sticks of cinnamon and a few whole cloves. You might add sugar if you think it's too tart. Let it steep for a while so the flavours meld. Then it's ready to serve."

"I'm pretty sure one cup won't be enough." Ellie passed the mug beneath her nose to inhale the sweet and spicy fragrance.

"I've marked some pictures I thought might interest you," said Ruth, getting down to business. She showed Ellie a half-dozen three-tiered wedding cakes that were quite similar in that they were heavily ornamented with roped fondant icing, intricate fondant roses with leaves, and a host of other elaborate details.

"They look like a lot of work," said Ellie. "I imagined something simpler."

"If I get started soon, I should be able to get it done in good time, even with Christmas. That's why we're having this meeting."

"Aunty, will you be hurt if I prefer something different?"

"Of course not." Ruth immediately closed the book, placed it in a tidy stack in the centre of the table, and looked expectantly at her niece.

"I'm thinking less is more. I think the tiers should be iced very smoothly, without any of the rope and roses work. Just plain. Then a garland of white and a few pale blue flowers can be laid in a descending spiral from the top and around to the bottom. If you have something to write on, I'll draw out my idea."

Ruth got up and returned with a pad of paper and a pencil. Ellie deftly drew the traditional three tiers, unadorned. Then she sketched a garland of flowers spiralling around the tiers from top to bottom.

"I see. It would be very pretty," agreed Ruth. "I know of someone who has bride and groom figurines to set on top. I'm sure she'd let me borrow it."

"No bride and groom figurines, Aunty. That's too yesterday for me. Sorry."

Ruth sighed. "Showing my age, am I?"

"Maybe just a little."

"And from where should I get these flowers?" asked Ruth, studying the drawing more closely.

"If you bring the cake to the Minitonas Hall on December 31, my family will be there to decorate. You'll have as many flowers as you need to choose from. And ribbon, too, if need be."

"Well, that sure makes my job a lot easier. Although if your mother were here, I'm sure we would have joined forces and put together a wedding cake that the editors of these magazines would want to put on their front covers!"

Ruth rose and topped off their mugs with more of the fruited tea.

Ellie smiled. "You and Mom always made a good team in the kitchen. I don't know if heaven has portals through which persons there can view earthly events, but if Mom could look in on my wedding I'd like to think she'd approve of everything. I just wish she could have met Hugh. I think she would have liked him."

"He seems like a fine man."

"Aunty, what do you think Mom would say to me about marriage, if she were here? What would she want me to know entering this stage of life?"

Ruth looked off somewhere beyond Ellie as if deep in thought. "I'll need a moment to think about it."

Just then, Ruth's husband Herb pulled up to the house in his pick-up. He stared at the navy blue car quizzically before coming inside.

"Kaffeeklatching with the local farmers, was he?"

"This morning was a little different," said Ruth. "The neighbour called for help to get his tractor started. Herb went to see what the trouble was. I'm sure his wife gave them both coffee and they solved the world's problems, or at least identified them, before coming home."

Ellie just smiled.

"So that's who belongs to that car," said Uncle Herb when he came into the house. He smiled from ear to ear at his niece. "Nice of you to look in on us old people. Are you ready for your big day?"

In the porch, he hung up his winter jacket and entered the kitchen rubbing his hands.

"All except for the last-minute stuff," answered Ellie cheerily.

"Good, good." He took a seat next to Ellie and addressed his wife. "Have you got something hot to drink, Mother?"

"Try some of this Russian tea." Ruth set a mug filled with the hot punch in front of Herb.

He took a sip, paused to think, then took another sip. "It's different," he said at length. "I prefer to stick to plain old ordinary tea, though."

Ruth wagged her head at him. "You're not one to try new things, that's for sure."

"So what are you ladies up to today?" asked Herb, quickly changing the subject.

"Actually, Uncle Herb, I just asked about what my mother might have said about marriage, since I'm about to take the plunge. Now that you're here, I'm wondering what you think my father would have wanted me to know on the same subject."

"That's quite a question, Ellie." Herb passed his mug of Russian tea back to Ruth in a gesture that meant he didn't care for it.

Ruth sighed and poured him a cup of leftover-from-breakfast coffee.

"John Bauman was what you would call a salt-of-the-earth kind of man," said Herb, scratching a spot atop his bald head. "He lived by the Book, and that's for sure. Everything he put his hand to had to line up with what he believed was right. Now, about his little girl taking up with a husband... well, he would have made sure he was a true-blue Christian. I can't imagine any feller going after his daughter would get very far if he weren't a God-fearing man."

The three of them exchanged glances and nodded. There was no disputing John Bauman's reputation for expecting the high road from people. He would expect those contemplating marriage to be equally yoked.

"After that, he would have wanted to know if the feller would be a good provider for his wife and future family," continued Herb. "I s'pose that's another way of saying he'd have to be a hard worker. Your dad could not abide laziness, and it was hard to keep up with him if you were working together. He would have insisted the man taking up with his daughter do likewise."

"In that case, I've scored two for two," said Ellie happily. "My Hugh is a new believer and takes his newfound faith seriously. He reads the Bible regularly and we often do it together. I believe he has a good work ethic and is conscientious about doing his work well."

Herb smiled again. "Then I'm sure you would have his blessing."

"At least one of the things your mother would have said to you is that when you marry someone, you marry the whole family," said Ruth. "It's like a package deal. It would be a recipe for strife if you cared for your fiancé but not the rest of his family."

Ellie became thoughtful. "Hmmm. It's not that I don't care for Hugh's two sisters. It's just that we aren't on the same page on a lot of things. That would be true for Hugh as well."

"Then the broader point is this: you go into the marriage with your eyes wide open. If tensions show up, you can't claim you didn't know beforehand," said Ruth firmly.

Ellie got the point and nodded.

"Another thing your mother would say, and I would totally agree, is that you have to accept your man the way he is, warts and all," her aunt added. "Because you can't change him. Many a woman has tried, without success. What you get is what you get. So make sure you know your man well. That way you can tell if you can live with his, shall we say, oddities."

Herb glanced at his wife with a look of surprise. "Now, now, Mother. Are you suggesting I have some oddities?"

"Wouldn't dream of it!" Ruth winked at Ellie. "I got most of them trained outta him a while back."

"Like what?" pressed Herb, taking another swig of his coffee.

"Never mind. We're supposed to be talking about John and Elizabeth's philosophy of marriage."

"I'm curious, too." Ellie stopped just short of laughing. "Unless it's too personal to share."

"Well then…" Ruth's eyes flashed brightly. "What about that time when you wanted to come to bed with your dirty socks on? I wasn't having any of that."

Herb didn't deny it. "I just don't like my feet to be cold."

"Another would be how you would wear the same pair of overalls day after day until they could stand up by themselves and stink to high heaven."

"That was so you wouldn't have so much laundry to do on account of me. I was just being thoughtful of you, milady. Besides, what's the point of changing clothes every day just to get them dirty same as the day before?"

Herb looked over to Ellie in search of her support.

"The point is that clean isn't just for Sunday," Ruth remarked. "It's for every day of the week."

"You used to do other funny and strange things… like add ketch-up to a bowl of chicken noodle soup. Oy vey!"

"You should try that sometime, Mother, it tastes pretty good."

Ruth sighed and looked at Ellie as if to say, *See what I've had to put up with all these years!*

"Well, if that's the worst of it, I didn't fare too bad," acknowledged Herb with a wink.

Ellie looked from her aunt to her uncle and back again. "I've heard that the hardest part of marriage is at the beginning, when couples sort out their preferences. When they figure out the 'oddities' until their relationship works like a well-oiled machine. Would you agree?"

"Sounds about right," Ruth said. "My mother—that would be your grandmother—said that you never really know what a person is like until you live with them. That's true, too. Eventually a person's true colours come out. It's a serious business, the making of a new home. But we made it, right, Herb?"

"Looks like. We're still here." He turned to face Ellie directly. "When our time comes to be with the Lord, I hope that I go first. I wouldn't last very long without my Ruthie. Truth is, she's the best thing that ever happened to me. And I'm a lucky man. I weren't the only one whose head she turned."

Ellie grinned. "Aww. That's so sweet."

"All in all, you've been a good husband to me, Herbert Wagner. If I had to do it all over again, I'd still choose you." Ruth turned to Ellie. "Let me give you another bead for your necklace. Love doesn't mean anything unless it comes with commitment."

"I think my mom would have said that, too," agreed Ellie solemnly.

"There will be days in the years ahead when you'll wonder at whatever possessed you to marry your man. You'll think you must have temporarily misplaced your brain."

"Now, now, Mother," interjected Herb. "That goes both ways."

"Right. Now what I was going to say?" Ruth shot her husband a dirty look. "Those days will pass. Commitment and perseverance is what gets you through. Hard times, whatever they are, test the depth and genuineness of love. I believe they're a good exercise to show what you're made of, and what you personally need to work on in your character."

"Have we thoroughly scared you away from getting married now?" asked Herb. "It's a big job. Not for the faint of heart. But there are some wonderful times, too. Don't get us wrong."

"Not at all," Ellie assured him. "I love hearing your take on the subject. I'm thinking you two should write a book. You have lots of experience to pass along."

Ruth threw her hands in the air. "Write a book! Gosh no. I'd rather bake wedding cakes."

Twenty-Six

ON DECEMBER 23, a special Christmas dinner was held between Hugh and Ellie and the rest of the Bauman clan. Hugh dressed in his best clothes, which were still his black jeans and a black western shirt. To look more Christmassy, he tied a red handkerchief around his neck.

When he came by to pick up Ellie, she looked him over. "Good. But I'd like to take you shopping for more clothing after we're married."

"Is this an example of what it's like for a man to be henpecked by his wife?"

Ellie merely shook her head. "Of course not."

Her Christmas outfit was a red dressy jumpsuit that featured a gold belt and scooped neckline. A gold necklace and gold dangly earrings completed her ensemble. Hugh didn't use words to express his admiration for her appearance; his eyes and crooked half-smile did it for him.

They entered Rob and Sarah's home bearing a shopping bag full of gifts. The house smelled wonderful with the aromas of the upcoming meal. Christmas carols played softly in the background. The dining table was set with Sarah's bone china. This dinner was indeed being treated as a special occasion.

It wasn't long until they were all called to the table. Rob took his traditional seat at the head, bringing his Bible with him.

"Hugh, since it's your first Christmas with the Bauman family, I'll explain to you that our dad, John Bauman, began an annual tradition that I've continued with my own family. Before we partake of the feast, we read some of the scriptures that record the reason we celebrate Christmas in the first place. It's our persuasion that without reviewing this bit of history, the Christmas season doesn't make sense. You'll likely hear the story from Matthew and Luke read to you at our church's Christmas Eve service, so tonight I'm going to read from Isaiah, who prophesied Jesus's coming and what He would be like."

All eyes around the table were trained on Rob as he opened his Bible to the ninth chapter of Isaiah and read the sixth verse.

"'For to us a child is born, to us a son is given; and the government will be upon his shoulder, and his name will be called "Wonderful Counsellor, Mighty God, Everlasting Father, Prince of Peace.' [18] What I want you all to think about, kids and adults alike, is this: how have you experienced our Lord as Wonderful? As Counsellor? As your Mighty God? As your Everlasting Father? And as your Prince of Peace?" Rob paused to gaze into the faces of everyone around the table. "Let's thank God for our food and all our blessings. Then we can dig in!"

Somehow the food seemed especially delicious.

"You've outdone yourself this time, dearly beloved," said Rob across the table to Sarah. "Best roast turkey ever! Nice and moist."

"Ditto," chimed in Trevor. "You're the best, Mom!"

"Well, thank you, kind sirs!" Sarah received the compliments graciously. "But I think it's the candlelight that does it. Everything tastes better in dim light when you can't really see what you're eating."

Hugh saw it again, and his heart ached with the joy of it—that special connection between Rob and his wife. It seemed so rare, so enviable. From his heart, he silently prayed that the Lord would bless the love he shared with Ellie, to make it as heartfelt and constant as what he saw in this family.

He reached across his lap to clasp Ellie's left hand under the table. He squeezed it firmly. Ellie seemed to understand and squeezed back.

---

[18] Isaiah 9:6, RSV.

"Can we do presents before dessert?" pleaded Charlotte. "I'm too stuffed right now anyway."

Beanie and Trevor strongly supported this idea.

"I'll agree to dessert later," said Sarah, "but I want the table and kitchen tidied before we exchange our gifts with Ellie and Hugh."

No one needed to be urged twice. Everyone helped bring plates and bowls to the kitchen and the leftover food was speedily put away, the dishes in the dishwasher.

"You go first, Aunty Ellie," said Charlotte. "And we want to give you and Uncle Hugh our presents last."

"All right then, here goes." Ellie passed out the parcels she and Hugh had brought.

Rob's gift was small in size, but he was pleased to receive a funny pair of colourful psychedelic-patterned socks and a pen which cleverly included a ruler, level, stylus, and two screwdrivers.

Sarah unwrapped a beautiful country scene jigsaw puzzle of a whopping 1,500 pieces. She liked it and said it would help her get through the winter doldrums.

Trevor received a thin book loaded with various photos called auto-stereograms. At first he didn't understand and appeared disappointed.

"You have to alter your visual perception so you can see a three-dimensional image on top of the two-dimensional background," explained Ellie. She took the book from him and turned to the first photo. In a moment she declared that the photo contained an elephant. "Think of it as looking *into* the picture."

Trevor tried but couldn't seem to get it. Rob took a turn. Within a few moments he saw the elephant, too. Trevor tried again and this time found success. After that he was keen to work out the images in the rest of the book.

Charlotte received a pair of books by George MacDonald titled *The Princess* and *The Princess and Curdie.* Ellie said these classics were among her all-time favourites.

"If you come to love them as I do, you'll be reading them once a year," said Ellie.

With that recommendation, Charlotte held them to her breast.

Beanie's parcel revealed an Etch-a-Sketch. She squealed with delight but then promptly set it aside. "Can we give our presents now?" she implored her mother.

Sarah nodded.

Immediately Charlotte and Beanie reached under the tree and retrieved two parcels. Charlotte handed one to Ellie while Beanie placed hers in Hugh's hands and then hopped up and down with excitement.

Ellie, with a puzzled expression, held up a book that was about training dogs to be obedient. Along the same theme, Hugh opened a shoebox that contained a pair of dog collars and leashes, a coarse brush, and a drawing of a double doghouse. He, too, looked into the faces around the room with a confused expression.

Sarah explained. "At the shower, you told the girls that you and Hugh were discussing getting a dog. That gave them some ideas."

"Can we get the rest now, Mommy?" begged Beanie, beside herself with anticipation.

"Yes, of course," Sarah replied. "Be careful not to slip."

This time, both girls ran out of the house followed by Trevor, who went as far as the back door. A moment later he held it open for them to come back inside. Each girl carried a fluffy, squirming little puppy.

Charlotte put hers in Ellie's arms and declared that it was a little girl, and that she had already named it Ruby. She hoped Ellie didn't mind.

Beanie thrust the puppy she carried onto Hugh's lap and explained that she had named the puppy Ruff because she liked that name for a boy dog.

"Oh my goodness!" cried Ellie. "She's the cutest thing ever!"

"Oho! What have we here?" Hugh was mighty surprised, but like Ellie he grinned from ear to ear.

"The puppies were actually free," said Trevor. "They came from the Moores' farm. Although they are tricoloured, like collies, they're actually mongrels. Ladd says they probably represent a little of every dog in the Swan Valley. These two are the cutest. Anyways, I built an extra big doghouse for your Christmas present so you would have everything you need to keep them."

"They seem pretty young," observed Ellie. "Are you sure they're old enough to be away from their mother?"

Trevor nodded. "They were eight weeks as of Monday, so the answer is yes."

"What do you think, Ell-ternative?" asked Hugh, thoroughly enjoying his face being licked by Ruff. "Are we ready for a pair of puppies?"

"If I hadn't seen them, I'd have said no. But…"

"Oh, Aunty Ellie, please say you'll keep them," pleaded Charlotte and Beanie together. "We'll help you take care of them."

Ellie searched Hugh's face. He was transformed into the likeness of a little kid, cradling the puppy as though it were a living teddy bear.

"I admit they're adorable," said Ellie, signalling that she was giving in. "Although after the wedding might have been better timing to bring them on the scene."

Hugh just smiled. "We'll manage."

With that bit of business happily settled, the kids now clamoured for dessert. It was back to the dining table while Sarah brought out a large, fancily decorated cake with *Happy Birthday Jesus* sprawled across the top. Charlotte followed behind toting a pail of vanilla ice cream.

After everyone had been served, Rob said, "Remember how the wise men brought Jesus wonderful gifts? Let's talk about the gifts we're each going to give Jesus for His birthday. Who's going to go first?"

At first, no one spoke. The only sound was the Christmas music playing on the stereo in the background.

"I guess I'll go first," began Trevor hesitantly. "I will give Jesus my future, because I don't know what I should do with it. We were supposed to choose an academic or general high school program, depending on whether we planned on continuing our education at a university or not. I chose the academic, but I honestly don't know what I want to do with myself after graduation… and that's only a year and a half away."

"That's a good gift," said Rob. "I'm sure Jesus will do the right thing with it."

"I'm going to give Jesus my love life," announced Charlotte shyly.

Rob gave her a sharp look. "What love life?"

"I'm fourteen now." Charlotte raised her eyebrows defensively. "I notice boys, you know."

"The only boys you can notice are your brother and me." After a few seconds' thought, Rob added, "And I suppose your uncles."

"Daddy, I just mean that when the time comes, I want Jesus to bring the perfect boy into my life to be my husband so I'll be happily married like you and Mom. I'd rather not waste time on a guy who's no good for me."

"That's mature thinking and therefore a wise gift," Sarah said quickly. "And when I was your age, I noticed boys, too."

"Humph!" And that was Rob's last word on the subject.

Sarah turned to their youngest. "Do you have a gift for Jesus, Bernadette?"

"I can't think of anything," said Beanie sadly.

"How about a song?"

Beanie brightened at once. "Okay. Right now?"

Sarah nodded.

In a clear, sweet voice, Beanie sang the lyrics of "This Little Light of Mine." And when she had concluded, everyone around the table clapped.

"I'm sure Jesus enjoyed that very much," said Rob. "As for me, I'm going to give Jesus our farm."

"You gave Him the farm last year," protested Trevor.

"Well, somewhere along the line I took it back. I know it because I began to worry about the weather and the crops and the harvest. So

I need to give it up again to help me remember that the Lord can do whatever He wants with it, because it is all His."

"I'm going to give Jesus 1981," said Sarah. "He can fill it with all kinds of interesting things that He would like me to experience, and whatever He would like me to do for Him."

The only persons left to offer Jesus a birthday gift were Hugh and Ellie, and the entire family looked their way expectantly.

"Ahh…" Hugh pursed his lips in uncertainty. "I think if I'm going to be wise like the rest of you, I should give Jesus myself. I want to be a good husband to your Aunt Ellie, so I need Jesus to make me into a good man."

"In that case," said Ellie, "I should match that and give Jesus my whole self, too, so He can make me into a good wife for you."

They gazed into each other's eyes until Trevor piped up: "Do people in love always have to be so syrupy?"

"Yes!" said the women and girls at the same time.

$$\sim$$

On Christmas Eve, the dealership closed its doors earlier than usual. The staff got to enjoy a bit of a party, beginning with pizza for lunch. By midafternoon, the boss sent everyone home with a poinsettia and sealed envelope.

Having just been recently hired, Hugh expected it would merely contain a Christmas card. He was therefore deeply surprised to find a bonus cheque for one hundred dollars. To a lot of people, that wouldn't have seemed a lot, but to Hugh it felt like more than he deserved for the few weeks he had been on staff.

He raced home so he could change into clean clothes. The plan was to enjoy a special Christmas supper prepared by Ellie just for the two of them. Then they would head over to the First Baptist Church for the candlelight service. Afterward they would return to Ellie's place, exchange gifts, and spend some time together. The new puppies might very well encroach on that, he realized, but that would only sweeten the evening, he figured, not detract from it.

Ellie had gone overboard setting a beautiful candlelit table for two using her mother's company dishes. Since Sarah had served turkey the evening before, Ellie chose to roast a strip of sirloin with all the traditional side dishes.

"You're every bit as good a cook as Sarah," said Hugh. "Thank you for an amazing meal."

"You're so welcome, and I'm glad to hear it."

The candlelight, poinsettias, and Christmas tree lights in the church contributed to making the Christmas Eve service feel special. But it was the singing of the hymns and reading of scripture concerning the birth of the Saviour that made it particularly meaningful.

For Hugh, it was the confirmation that he could, in reality, be in a father-son relationship with the God of the universe. Jesus's arrival signalled that his sins would be paid for, and that he was not consigned to a life of perpetual brokenness and estrangement from his Creator.

For Ellie, celebrating Jesus's birth reminded her of what He said of Himself—that He didn't come to condemn but to seek and save those who were lost.

They both left the sanctuary with grateful hearts and filled with the Christmas spirit.

Back at Ellie's home, they played with the puppies, delighted by their antics. Neither of them could recall a time when they'd had a puppy. Hugh remembered an old dog on the yard when he was a kid, but certainly not as a puppy. And the dog had simply been part of the landscape. It hadn't been a special pet.

It was similar for Ellie. The family had kept a dog when she was little, and of course they had raised farm animals for food or breeding. But when the animals were phased out, the need for a dog had gone, too. Eventually it had died, not to be replaced.

Snuggling and cuddling with the puppies now made them feel like they were catching up on something they had missed in their childhood. And it continued in that vein—that is, until Ruby piddled on Ellie. Then they were abruptly returned to their temporary housing in a big cardboard box.

After changing and putting on some Christmas carols on the stereo, leaving only the tree lights on for illumination, Ellie reached under the tree and handed Hugh her first gift. A few moments later, he was looking at a large picture book, a companion to the *History of Cars* book he had received on his birthday. Only this time the subject was trucks, large and small, old and current. Delighted, Hugh looked forward to studying it on the evenings when Ellie was away at work.

He then reached under the tree and brought out a rather large parcel to give to her. Soon she was holding up a bright pink velour bathrobe.

"I thought the day we start a new life together warranted a new housecoat. The one you usually wear begs for retirement, I think," said Hugh with a crooked smile.

"Point taken." Ellie brought the thick plush to her face. "But I'll miss my old chenille. It's put on a lot of miles with me."

Next, she reached under the tree and placed the last present on Hugh's lap. He unwrapped it slowly, as if wanting the suspense to last as long as possible.

It contained a new outfit of clothes. Ellie called them semi-casual, a step up from his usual western wear. It included a tweed-like sports-coat which Hugh put on at once.

"Nice threads," said Ellie admiringly, pleased that it fit him well.

"Makes me feel like a grown-up."

"Makes you look extra handsome! Maybe don't wear it too often. I don't want you turning anyone else's head."

She began to tidy up the wrapping paper strewn all over the floor.

"Wait," said Hugh, fishing a tiny box out of his pocket. "I have one more thing." He handed her the petite, silver-wrapped gift, noting the question in her eyes. "Open it."

Unwrapped, the tiny velvet box revealed a dainty necklace. The fine chain was fashioned of gold, while the pendant, a gold cross, intersected with a sparkling diamond. Two small diamond stud earrings completed the set. They sparkled like snow in the moonlight.

"Oh Hugh," said Ellie, breathless. "I hardly know what to say. They're so beautiful!"

"You said you didn't need diamonds, but I wanted you to have some. Not as proof of my love for you, but because they represent who you are to me." His voice was husky. "I hoped they would be suitable for you to wear on our wedding day."

"They'll be perfect with my wedding dress."

Her eyes filling with tears, she turned so Hugh could place the jewellery around her neck. Then they kissed, long and sweetly.

Later, in the moments before she drifted off to sleep, she thought about the adage that diamonds were a girl's best friend. She heartily doubted that, but she could possibly be convinced that diamonds represented devoted love and sacrifice.

Twenty-Seven

FOR ALL THE time and effort Gertrude Johnson had put into preparing her Christmas feast, one would have thought she was planning for a lot more than eight adults and two kids. Ed looked at the size of the ham and asked, "Will it even fit in the oven?"

Gertie glared at him above her glasses. "Of course it will."

"Who else is coming to dinner?"

"You know very well who's coming for Christmas. You needn't try to be funny about it."

"I'm not trying to be funny at all. I like ham, but it makes me ill to think we'll be eating ham leftovers until the end of January. One can only eat so many ham sandwiches with ham and pea soup, after all."

"If you're going to be an idiot, you should find something else to do—away from the kitchen."

Ed quickly replied in kind. "If you want me to go, I'll go. But judging from the heap of groceries on the counter—and everything that is in want of peeling, dicing, and slicing—there's no way on God's green earth... correction: God's white earth... that you're going to have Christmas dinner ready on Saturday. Not if you try doing it all yourself."

Without another word, Gertie got out her Dutch oven and set it on the counter. Then she pushed Ed up to the kitchen sink, placed a peeler in his hand, and brought the bag of potatoes to within his reach.

Ed sighed. "How many potatoes ought I to peel?"

"All of them."

It was a ten-pound bag.

The first to arrive was Diane and Bill with their little ones. Diane entered the house laden with packages and Amanda hanging on to her coat. Bill carried Sean and the diaper bag. There was momentary chaos while the arms were emptied and coats taken away.

Being the active toddler he was, as soon as he shed his winter gear Sean fled from his parents to the coffee table in the living room. Gertie had it laden with an open box of chocolates, a bowl full of nuts, a platter with assorted Christmas candy, and a basket of Japanese oranges still wrapped in green paper. Sean grabbed a handful of candy before Diane wrenched them from his sticky fingers.

Uncle Ed came into the living room jauntily carrying a large punch bowl filled with eggnog. He set it on the one bit of space available on the coffee table.

It was Bill's first time at the Johnson residence, so formal introductions were in order. And no sooner were the names exchanged than Margo and Larry pulled up. The temporary chaos began all over again with packages and coats and introductions, since it was also Larry's first time meeting Margo's relatives.

When everyone had found a seat, Ed passed out glasses of eggnog.

"Has a nice nip to it," said Bill.

Larry hadn't been expecting the nip. His rather large sip resulted in a startling cough that made his eyes water. "Excuse me," he said, trying to catch his breath. "Tastiest egg-flip I've ever had. I bet you have a secret ingredient in there."

"It's more fun to keep you guessing," said Ed good-naturedly. "I will admit, however, that it's an old family recipe."

While Ed continued to distribute eggnog to the ladies, Gertie tried to keep the conversation going with all the usual pleasantries. In sum, everyone said they were doing fine and no one had anything new to tell about themselves.

The light discussion soon turned to wondering where Hugh was and why he and Ellie hadn't shown up yet.

"What time did you tell him he should be here?" Ed asked his wife.

"Any time after lunch."

"That's vague enough to be any time before supper."

Uneasy with that possibility, Gertie got up and made a phone call to Hugh's house. There was no answer, and therefore she assumed he must be on his way.

In the meantime, the main activity seemed to be keeping young Sean from getting into the many treats tempting him, or plunging his little fists into the punch bowl. Amanda sat shyly next to her mother, bewildered by all the strangers. The menfolk exchanged stories regarding what they did for a living while the women mostly listened politely, uncertain where to begin with each other.

"Perhaps he's gotten himself into an accident," wailed Gertie anxiously after another half-hour had passed.

"I'm sure there's a good explanation," said Ed. "Let's not borrow trouble. In the meantime, perhaps we could play a game. Does anyone know of one?"

"I'd rather sip eggnog." Margo reached over to the bowl and refilled her glass. It was her third serving of the milky beverage, while the others were still sipping their first.

A few furtive glances were exchanged around the room, but no one said anything.

"We could turn on the TV and watch something," suggested Bill. "If we're lucky, we'll find a hockey game going on somewhere."

"Not hockey," Diane said. "But maybe a nice Christmas movie."

Seeing that the conversation had ground to a standstill, Gertie nodded weakly at Ed, who reached over and turned on the television. There weren't many channels to choose from, but one of them was showing *It's a Wonderful Life*. The group seemed satisfied enough to leave it on.

Pretty soon the men and Gertie were jerking their heads in an effort to stave off sleep. Margo and Diane concentrated on the storyline while nursing their eggnog.

By midafternoon, Gertie looked out the front window and squealed in glee. "Hugh's here! Thank goodness he's come at last."

She met him at the door, throwing it open wide so he could enter with his bags of presents.

"Merry Christmas, Aunty!" said Hugh when he crossed the entrance. "Merry Christmas, everybody!"

"You're late!" complained Margo, swirling the eggnog in her glass.

"I am?" Hugh turned to Gertie. "I didn't realize I was supposed to be here at a certain time. I thought you said any time after lunch."

"I did. I assumed you would understand about one o'clock from that."

"So what kept you?" pressed Margo. "It's Christmas, not a work-day."

Hugh continued to stand in the open doorway. "I was busy building an outdoor pen around the doghouse we got for Christmas."

"Can I take your coat?" asked Gertie.

"Not yet. The doghouse came with a pair of puppies and I brought them along. I thought the kids would enjoy them."

He went back to his half-ton and, upon opening the door, the puppies tumbled out. He had attached leashes to their collars and quickly grabbed them before they went exploring after new smells and objects.

"Aww! Look, Mandy." Diane lifted her daughter so she could see Hugh drag them up the walk. "Aren't they cute?"

Once inside, Hugh gave up his jacket to Gertie. He wore the new outfit Ellie had given him the evening before. Except for his high school graduation, he had never worn anything that resembled a suit. In fact, no one had ever seen him in anything other than jeans. Now he stood before them wearing navy slacks, a pale blue dress shirt open at the collar, and the grey and blue tweedy sport jacket.

"My, aren't you the dashing one," said Gertie admiringly.

Margo nodded in approval. "Pretty preppy for a country boy."

"Trying to make the rest of us guys feel bad?" asked Larry with a smirk. He, Bill, and Uncle Ed wore casual pants and pullover sweaters.

"I got these new duds last night," said Hugh. "I thought I'd try them out. They make me feel like an adult."

"You look very handsome," Diane assured him. "I bet Ellie gave them to you."

"You're right. She chose these."

Ed smiled. "Well, her taste is impeccable. Perhaps I should have her input when I buy suits and shirts to wear to work at the bank."

"What's wrong with my input?" Gertie demanded, offended.

"Nothing, dear. Just my way of granting Ellie a compliment."

Meanwhile, Amanda and Sean were taking turns cradling a squirming puppy in their arms. They giggled with delight as the pups licked their faces.

Hugh squatted down to their level and showed them how to hold a puppy so they would be comfortable and less fidgety.

Gertie was still looking around anxiously. "Speaking of Ellie, when will she be joining us?"

"Her shift isn't over until seven," answered Hugh.

"Seven!" yelped Margo. Everyone turned to look in her direction. In a calmer voice, she added, "I wanted to head back to Dauphin around then. Please say you're not going to make us wait for her."

"Oh, come on, Margo." Larry sounded annoyed. "Maybe just once think of someone else besides yourself."

"That's easy for you to say," she shot back. "You have tomorrow off. I have to get the shop ready for the Boxing Day sale."

Hugh looked from Margo to Diane.

"I don't mean to be a party pooper, but I was hoping to leave not long after supper so my kids could be in their own beds at a reasonable hour," said Diane.

Hugh nodded as he looked away from her and turned to Gertie.

"I did hope her shift would be over sooner than that," the older woman said. "I had planned to serve supper about six. What would you like to do?"

Hugh couldn't hide his disappointment. "I know what she would say: start without her. She wouldn't want to cause any unreasonable delays on her account."

"What about the gift exchange? Can we do that without her, too?" asked Gertie. "I was thinking of doing that before we feast."

"Sure," said Hugh after a second of hesitation. "Except for Ellie's gifts to you three ladies, of course. I know she would like to give you those herself and watch you open them."

Gertie nodded. "That seems fair."

"I guess so..." Margo exhaled. "But I want to be on the road by eight at the latest."

On that note, Ed turned off the TV and the puppies were confined to the back porch—after Gertie had first spread newspaper all over the floor, of course.

To make the gift exchange more fun for Amanda, Gertie pronounced her the elf who would hand out the presents as she called out the names on the packages. It helped the little girl get over some of her shyness and learn the names of her aunties and uncles.

When all the applicable presents were distributed, everyone began to open their gifts. For the men, the results were hilarious. The three younger men had all given socks to the other gents in the party. In Hugh's case, he'd added a multi-functional pen like the one he had given Rob a couple of days earlier. The guys seemed quite pleased with their gizmo pens.

"Perhaps the women are right," said Bill dryly. "We men don't have much for imagination."

Ed shook his head. "Never mind. Socks are necessary and frequently need replacing. I, for one, am grateful."

Margo had given her aunt and sister tops that came from her shop.

"You flatter me, Margo, if you truly thought I would fit into this." Gertie held up a blouse that was clearly marked M for medium. "I need a large at least, and sometimes an extra-large."

"Sorry, Aunt Gertie," said Margo. "I can try and exchange it for you."

"That goes for me, too." Diane showed them her shirt, also medium. "I've gained a few since you saw me in July."

Margo raised her eyebrow. "I see that. Fine. I'll take the tops back with me and see what else I can come up with."

Diane had given each of the ladies a jigsaw puzzle, which produced gushing thanks that were probably insincere.

The children received T-shirts from Margo and Larry, and a record album from Ellie and Hugh titled *The Music Machine*. But it was the toys from Gertie and Ed that produced the most excitement: a gorgeous doll for Amanda and a ride-on truck for Sean. As luck would have it, they were sufficiently entertained for the remainder of the afternoon.

The parcels from Ed and Gertie to the three separate households were alike in size. Unwrapped, they revealed identical electric coffee makers. Thank yous were said, but questioning looks were nevertheless aimed at Gertie.

"Well, I didn't know what to get you all," said Gertie apologetically. "Our coffee maker quit working not long ago, and it made me think that the ones you have might be on their last legs, too. Besides, I worried that if I gave you each something different, there might be jealousy. I didn't want to be responsible for that. So… coffee makers."

"It's great," said Hugh. "Truly. Everyone should have a spare coffee maker. Isn't that right?"

Diane and Margo mumbled their gratitude.

"I thought you had something else you wanted to give the three siblings," piped up Ed.

Gertie gasped, brightening. "That's right! I did."

She jumped up and went down the hall, returning quickly with three rolled-up bundles made of fabric and tied with a broad ribbon. Diane, Hugh, and Margo each received one as per the nametag and were encouraged to open them right away.

Unrolled, they revealed small quilts, suitable to cover a lap or perhaps an infant in a crib. The pattern for Diane's quilt was called a nine-patch in predominantly pastel-coloured prints. Margo's quilt featured a star-like pattern and was the most modern of the three. Hugh's quilt was chiefly made from light and dark blue prints sewn in the configuration called log cabin. The blocks were arranged in furrows.

"This is lovely," said Diane with instant admiration. "Did you make these?"

Gertie smiled broadly. "I did… except for Hugh's quilt. I had help with that one. They were done at the local quilting club for you to have as mementos of your parents."

That last revelation caused all three Fischers to turn to stone for about three seconds.

"So the cloth that went into making these quilts came from Mom and Dad's clothing?" asked Margo in a strange tone of voice.

"Yes, along with some of the linens they left behind," declared Gertie proudly.

Hugh had mixed feelings. "It's very nice. I'm sure Ellie will like it a lot."

"I'm positive she will," agreed Gertie. "After all, it was her idea and I thought it was wonderful."

"In other words, the plaid sewn into the border are from Pa's shirts," Hugh murmured.

"Most likely."

Hugh folded up the small blanket. "I liked it better when I didn't know that."

"So this is made from old stuff, not new fabric?" asked Margo sharply.

"It's meant to be a keepsake, something to remember your mother by." It was beginning to dawn on Gertie that these blankets weren't having the pleasing effect she had intended.

"Well, I think they're beautiful," said Diane stoutly. "I'm very happy to have something to remember Mama by. Pa's shirts just made it a bit more colourful. And look, his contribution is small. The quilt isn't about him. It's about Mama." She hesitated for a moment, grappling with her own emotions. "Whether we like it or not, Pa was our pa. He's part of our story and it can't be reversed, however much we might wish it."

Gertie nodded in gratitude. "Thank you. And it's okay to stow it out of sight in the closet if it's too painful. I dare to believe that someday you'll be glad to have a little something that represents your history. Something from which you can tell stories to your children..."

Her voice trailed quietly ending in awkward silence.

"Thank you very much for all your trouble," said Margo without feeling. "If I happen to forget it when I leave tonight, you can stow it in your own closet for posterity. I won't mind if you keep it as a souvenir to remember your sister by."

She leaned over the coffee table and topped up her glass with eggnog for the sixth time.

"Cut it out, Margo," said Larry, fully irritated. "It's amazing you haven't keeled over yet—"

"Are you counting?" she shot back. "Mind your own business—"

"Tell you what," broke in Ed. "How about I take the young men out for a tour of the district?"

Larry jumped up. "Sounds great! I haven't seen the lay of Swan River in years."

"I'll go," said Bill. "Are you coming, Hugh?"

"Nah. I've seen everything there is to see around these parts. But you go ahead. No doubt the fresh air will do you good."

The three men were out of the house in three minutes.

The time had come to boil the potatoes and cook the vegetables. As Gertie retreated into the kitchen, Diane followed.

Hugh selected one of the empty boxes that had previously contained a gift and began stuffing the torn Christmas wrap inside. Soon the room was tidy again.

He took the box to the back porch and checked on his puppies. On his return to the living room, he saw Margo top off her eggnog again. The bowl was nearly empty by now and Hugh brought it to the kitchen. Gertie received it with a smile and silent understanding.

Back in the living room, Hugh took his seat in the armchair. He watched Margo on the couch, pulling at her glass like a bee at nectar. He made himself comfortable. Setting his feet on the hassock, he interlaced his fingers and began to drum his thumbs together.

Margo stared back at him as if daring him to challenge her.

"I'm seeing the likes of Pa sitting in front of me," said Hugh evenly.

She breathed heavily. "I'm not like Pa. Not even close."

"You're glaring at me in the same way he did, and you have enough liquor in you so that you're not talking sense... just like he used to. You're belligerent... just like he was. If I sat next to you, I'm pretty sure I would smell the spirits on you... just like him..."

"Shut up," she hissed. "And leave me alone."

"Okay, I will. But before I do, I want you to hear this. I'm done with all things that remind me of Pa. If you continue to follow in his foot-steps, sister or not, we can't be friends."

He rose and departed the room abruptly.

Left to her own devices, as requested, a pair of tears coursed down Margo's face, but she continued to sit alone... and continued to sip from the glass in her hand.

Hugh sought out Gertie in the kitchen. "How long until dinner?"

"I'll be ready to serve in about a half-hour," she said. "Maybe forty minutes."

"I'd like to run my pups home. I can still be back in time for the feast, if that's okay with you."

"Do what you need to do," permitted Gertie cheerily.

Collecting his gifts, and then his little pups, Hugh got into his truck and aimed for home. At last, he felt he could breathe freely. Some-thing had been off with the family gathering but he dared not try to analyze it yet.

He turned on the radio and crooned along to the music, a mix of Christmas songs and country and western tunes.

The relief he felt when he turned into his own driveway was palpable. Even the dogs seemed much happier once unleashed and free to run around their new pen. He dreaded going back to the place where the air was somehow tetchy, where the Christmas spirit wasn't exactly in attendance.

That thought produced an idea for where the problem lay. If only Ellie was free to join them for the grand feast, he felt he could face the rest of the evening. At least the two of them were on the same page. He didn't know about the others.

Sighing deeply, Hugh got back into his truck and retraced the route to the Johnsons' place.

He arrived on the heels of Ed and his brothers-in-law. And as soon as they were unclad of winter wear, Gertie called them all to the dining table.

The overhead lights had been shut off and a dozen red and gold tapers glowed romantically from their crystal holders. Three small red and white poinsettias adorned the lace-covered table. Gertie's best china and silverware were laid out along with white cloth napkins. In the background, the stereo played "Deck the Halls."

Each took their seat and exchanged sincere smiles. The earlier disagreeableness and apprehension seemed to have disappeared, much to everyone's relief.

Gertie cleared her throat. "Ed, will you please ask the blessing?"

Ed nodded and recited one from his youth: "Bless us, O Lord, and these Thy gifts which we have received from Thy bounty through Christ our Lord. Amen."

"Merry Christmas, everyone!" said Gertie cheerily. "Dig in!"

When everyone's plate was full, Gertie tried again to make interesting conversation. "The last time we ate at this same table, I sent you home with an inheritance. It would be nice to hear what you've done with it."

She turned to Hugh, seated at her right, to begin the table talk.

"Nothing yet, Aunty," said Hugh when he cleared his mouthful. "It's sitting in a savings account until spring. But I intend to put it into the farm by building a large mechanics shop so I have space for long-term projects as well as short-term. And I want to make it long enough to include an autobody paint bay. If I can make the budget work, I'd also like to put up a Quonset for sheltering my equipment and the antique vehicles I found in the back bush."

This sparked immediate interest in the old relics. He quickly described each vehicle and the family wished him well in restoring them.

"Sounds like an excellent investment," said Gertie.

Ed nodded his agreement.

"A budget," Larry mumbled loudly enough for all to hear. "Now there's a novel idea."

"Don't start," said Margo tersely.

Gertie ignored the jabs from the far side of the table. "How about you, Diane?"

"Bill and I made a five-year term deposit with our bank with the intention of it being the start of our retirement fund."

"Very good," said Ed approvingly. "One can't start preparing for that stage in life too soon."

"What about you, Margo?" asked Gertie gently and encouragingly.

Margo swallowed her food. "I invested it in a very fine house in Dauphin's most prestigious neighbourhood. It will increase its value and build equity for me."

Larry choked on his food.

"Oh dear, are you all right?" asked Gertie, suddenly concerned.

"I'm fine," he croaked. He took a prolonged gulp of water from the glass by his plate.

Hugh's eyes briefly connected with Larry's across the table and understood. Larry didn't say another word, but his facial expression spoke volumes.

Curiously, Hugh seemed to be the only one who noticed the undercurrent of loathing between Margo and her husband. Diane and

Bill were too busy with their children to notice. And if Gertie and Ed were wise to the situation, they were playing dumb.

"There's plenty more food," Gertie said. "Please help yourself to seconds."

The bowls and platters were sent around the table once again, with a few takers along the way.

"Next week at this time we'll be celebrating the new year," said Ed. "What are you looking forward to in 1981? Anyone? How about you, Hugh? Will you and Ellie be taking a honeymoon vacation after your wedding?"

"Not immediately. We're talking about going to Niagara Falls in the spring, when the magnolias are in bloom. Ellie is keen to see something of eastern Canada. We haven't yet decided whether to fly or make it a road trip."

"I hope our business grows," Bill remarked. "Otherwise it's just the same old, same old, I suppose."

Larry spoke in a quiet, dissatisfied voice. "I can't say what the new year will hold. Guess we'll know when it happens."

Again, Hugh and Larry's eyes locked on each other. Hugh quickly realized that the man's innocuous statement held layers of meaning.

"What are you looking forward to, Uncle Ed?" asked Hugh, willing the conversation to stay light and pleasant.

"Well… since you asked." Ed looked across the table to Gertie. He had a twinkle in his eyes. "Come February, I'm going to take my bride on a vacation to Mexico. I think it's time we did a little exploring to see what other parts of the world are like."

Gertie gasped. "Why, Ed, that sounds wonderful!"

In her joy, she rose from the table, went over to him, and planted a big kiss on top of his bald head. The others added their congratulations as the plates were collected and the remains of dinner set aside.

Finally, a large platter of assorted Christmas baking was passed around as dessert, followed by a fresh pot of coffee. By some miracle, the chatter remained friendly and neutral.

Then, at 7:06, the doorbell rang. Ellie had come. There was a collective sigh of relief.

"Merry Christmas, everybody!" called Ellie as she came inside.

"Are you hungry, dear?" Gertie asked like a clucking hen. "Have you had anything to eat?"

Ellie smiled broadly. "I would love a plate of Christmas dinner."

"Would it be all right if we exchanged gifts first?" asked Margo bluntly. "I need to head back to Dauphin before long."

"Sure." Ellie seemed somewhat confused.

"Cripes, Margo." Larry rolled his eyes. "She hasn't even taken off her coat yet!"

Gertie took Ellie's coat away and Hugh immediately embraced her, adding a tight squeeze. "So glad you're finally with us," he said.

"Me too," said Ellie.

The party rearranged themselves around the living room. Space was tight. Hugh occupied the armchair as Ellie distributed her parcels to Diane, Margo, and Gertie in turn. The remaining two were set aside for Ellie to open.

While the ladies carefully unwrapped their gifts, Ellie tore open her parcels, revealing her jigsaw puzzle from Diane, as well as the top from Margo, sized medium.

"Very nice, Margo," said Ellie, holding up the garment. "Just my size. Thank you so much. And thanks for the puzzle, Diane. How did you know I enjoy doing them during the winter months?"

The sisters were visibly pleased that Ellie had acknowledged their gifts with sincere favour.

"Your gift is shared with Hugh, since you'll soon be cohabiting," said Gertie hurriedly. "I gave you a coffee maker for when the one you have conks out."

"How very thoughtful of you." Ellie grinned. "It's well-known how cranky people can get when their coffee habits are interrupted. Thank you for your forethought."

Gertie sighed with relief, grateful that at least one person understood her logic.

"You gave us our bridesmaids dresses as our Christmas gift?" said Margo with disbelief, looking down at the carefully folded gown.

"Partly. In the weddings I've been part of, we had to pay for our own dresses," said Ellie softly. "I wanted to spare you the expense. Besides, there's another package in the box. It's from both of us and I think you'll like it."

Somewhat chastened, Margo shifted through the tissue paper and soon produced a small, velvet-covered box. Diane did likewise. They each contained a fine-chained sterling silver necklace with sparkling cubic zirconia pendant. Matching stud earrings were included.

Diane gasped. "Diamonds?"

"No, not diamonds. I couldn't afford that, but it's a good quality substitute. I hope you like them. And please wear them with your bridesmaid outfit on our wedding day."

Ellie got up off the floor and crossed the room to give each of the girls a hug. This had the effect of making them feel a bit sheepish.

She turned to Gertie, who had just unwrapped a beautiful crystal vase.

"Did we get your gift right, Gertie?" asked Ellie playfully.

Gertie spoke with a catch in her throat. "A crystal vase! Oh my... How did you know I love crystal? This is exquisite! I don't know what to say..."

"With all the disappointment you're carrying this season, Hugh and I wanted to make sure we fit in a blessing for you."

"You mean David, don't you?" said Gertie, choking up even more.

"Yes," said Ellie. "Now that we're through sharing gifts, is it possible for me to nab a plate of leftovers? I'm famished."

Nonetheless, she had to set aside her plate several times over the next half-hour to give hugs and say goodbye to the other guests. And not much later, Hugh noticed that Ellie herself was looking pretty tired.

"I guess it's probably time to wind things down," Gertie said.

Ellie and Hugh couldn't help but agree, and soon they were on their way out the door toward their separate vehicles.

Before the evening ended, Ellie found herself sitting at home in her favourite armchair, with Hugh on the couch across from her, his feet propped up on the coffee table.

She turned off the lamp beside the armchair, the only illumination being the lights of the Christmas tree. The nostalgic ambience called for cuddles. Ellie got up and crossed the room so she could sit under Hugh's right arm where she fit perfectly, like a piece of jigsaw puzzle.

He didn't speak and she turned slightly, putting her arm across his chest to hold him. And waited. He still said nothing, but she felt she could almost hear the thoughts in his head bouncing around like a multitude of basketballs.

"Talk," said Ellie softly. "It will help sort things out."

Hugh sighed. "I don't even know where to begin."

"How was Christmas with your family?"

"In a single word... weird," he answered. "Kudos to Gertie and Ed for trying to create a happy occasion. It barely worked. We're all as different as the colours of the rainbow. We've gone our own ways and no longer know each other, despite being siblings. It was hard to find common ground..."

He trailed off, deep in thought and not sure how exactly to express himself.

"But that's not what bothers me so much. The whole occasion was like looking into a mirror. I saw myself in my sisters. They're messed up and don't seem to realize it. That was me... that is, until this summer. I saw shades of Pa coming out in Margo and it got to me. I addressed it with her, but a quiet voice inside was quick to remind me that I was no better. When pushed, I used to spew anger just as readily as Pa did. Today, I saw how lost my sisters are. It's very troubling. If you hadn't come along and shown me how broken I was and told me what I had to do to be mended..."

Hugh's voiced cracked and it took a moment to regain his composure. Ellie squeezed him tight across the chest to assure him that he was being heard.

"Well, I'd still be the miserable, defensive, angry, senseless rebel I see in Margo especially," he finished.

Hugh brought his other arm across Ellie to link with his right hand, locking her in his embrace.

"It scares me to think where I'd be if you hadn't come into my life," he continued. "I guess what I'm trying to say is that today I really saw the difference it makes to have God's Spirit living within me. I can see for myself how real He is, and how He is changing me."

"I can't tell you how much it thrills me to hear you say that," said Ellie, becoming misty-eyed. "And I sincerely hope your sisters will someday want what you and I have."

Stifling a yawn, she broke out of his arms.

"But you know what?" she added. "I'm getting sleepy. I think you need to go now."

"Have you any idea how much I hate going home to an empty house?" But he rose obediently.

"Only six more days, love. Only six more days."

Twenty-Eight

CHRISTMAS WAS OVER. The rest of the country would celebrate Yuletide all week, but on Boxing Day Ellie put aside all things Christmas and began the countdown to her wedding day. She had also promised the hospital three shifts before December 31, meaning it would be a busy six days.

In the morning, she took a half-hour to read her Bible and talk to Jesus-on-the-couch, but as soon as her coffee was consumed she switched gears and began to take apart the Christmas tree. Her other two brothers, Gus and Harold, were expected to arrive with their families in three days or so, and it behooved her to ready the house.

Hugh called from Swan River midmorning and asked her to meet him at the furniture store during the lunch hour. They were staging a great Boxing Day sale and he wanted her input on what seemed like a sweet deal for a new television, video cassette recorder, and stereo system. They had originally agreed to wait until after the wedding and use gift money, but Hugh wanted to take advantage of the reduced pricing.

Ellie hurried through the task of dismantling the tree, returning the decorations to their storage places, and even dragged the tree outside and away from the house.

A short time later, she and Hugh purchased their electronics. This was rather exciting. It meant that their first home together was almost completely outfitted. The salesman had wanted to sell them a personal computer as well, which was tempting, but there was nowhere in the tiny house to set it up. That would have to wait.

After dropping off the boxes, Ellie blitzed through the housework at her place. It was evening before all the laundry, towels, and linens were washed, dried, and beds remade.

She had just finished those chores when Hugh called again. He wanted her to come over to see the new electronics, by now all set up in the entertainment unit. Despite her exhaustion, she donned her boots and parka and made the six-minute walk over to his place.

Just as she let herself in, Hugh was in the process of saying goodbye to someone on the phone, his face lit up like the proverbial lightbulb.

"Good news, honey," said Hugh, practically skipping around the kitchen. "The Turners are coming up on Tuesday so they can hang out with us on Wednesday and help out with whatever needs doing."

"But that's going to be a crazy busy day. I won't have time to entertain her…"

"No, not entertain. Marcie wants to be your assistant, helping you get through your busy to-do list. And Brian has volunteered to be my slave for the day."

The look on Ellie's face conveyed her doubt.

"I've already accepted her offer on your behalf," said Hugh, his gladness reducing very quickly to a perplexed uncertainty.

Ellie felt uneasy. "This seems important to you, so I guess so. But I already feel awkward about having an assistant I don't even know."

"That will last five minutes, tops. These are wonderful people, honey. Fifteen years ago, they saved my life. You know this. You're going to love them, I promise."

~

After church Sunday morning, they both attended the funeral of Otto Hoffman. A luncheon followed in the church basement. Ellie made a point of greeting the man's wife and expressing her condolences. The widow seemed surprised to see her, and then very pleased.

"How kind of Elizabeth Bauman's daughter to honour Otto and myself by your being here," said Agnes. "Your mother was a good friend to me. I sorely miss her, as I'm sure you do."

Agnes patted the chair seat beside her, indicating that Ellie should sit down.

"Otto mentioned that you looked after him while he was recovering from his bypass surgery," continued Agnes. "He was very pleased with your services."

"I'm sure I didn't do anything out of the ordinary for him."

"Perhaps not in your estimation, but he was highly impressed. And thank you for the invitation to your wedding. I intend to be there."

"Oh!" said Ellie surprised. In fact, she didn't know who Sarah had all sent invitations to, only that many of her parents' friends had been included. "I'll understand if you feel it's too soon to socialize again. Don't feel obligated."

Agnes leaned over and spoke to Ellie in a low voice only she could hear. "Between you and me and the garden post, I'm not overmuch grieved by Otto's passing. More like liberated. Your mother would have understood."

~

Between Sunday and Tuesday, Ellie worked two more shifts. On Monday, her out-of-town brothers arrived with their families, and although much of the daily action was carried out at Rob's place, the Bauman farmhouse was in full pre-wedding party mode. The place was abuzz with nieces and nephews playing together and their parents catching up.

Somehow, between work and engaging with her brothers' families, Ellie managed to organize and pack her things so that on Tuesday evening, with a little help from some of her kin, her car was packed to the hilt with everything she meant to move over to Hugh's house. She kept behind only a small suitcase of the items she would personally need until her wedding day.

Hugh agreed to call Ellie on Wednesday morning when he was through sleeping so she could bring her things over. That call came a little before nine o'clock.

When Ellie arrived, he was still having breakfast, looking as excited as a little kid for what lay ahead. He jumped up and greeted her affectionately.

Before he let go of her, a royal blue sedan pulled up and parked behind Ellie's car. The Turners had come.

While Ellie hung back in the kitchen, Hugh opened the door and greeted first Marcie with exuberance and then Brian in a fervid bear-hug. Immediately he turned and pulled Ellie to his side.

"Meet my almost-wife, Ellie Bauman," said Hugh, beaming.

"So very glad to meet the girl who stole Hugh's heart." Marcie stepped forward to hug her. "He claims he's the luckiest guy alive."

Marcie removed her jacket. Seeing no place to hang it, she draped it over a kitchen chair.

"I'm very glad to finally meet you," said Ellie. "You've played a very significant part in his life, for which I've come to be as thankful as he. You'll be important to both of us now."

Ellie looked up at the tall, salt-and-pepper-haired woman in front of her. The hair was coiffed in a stylish wedge. She wore close-fitting jeans topped with a plaid shirt in white, blue, and pink, tucked in and belted. Ellie estimated her to be in her late fifties, yet she was lean, attractive, and had a confident air about her. A pair of reading glasses hung from her neck.

"I didn't imagine you as tall as you are," Ellie remarked.

Marcie smiled. "And I pictured you dark-haired."

Brian also stepped forward to hug Ellie and murmur his congratulations to the happy couple. She noted that while his head was fully grey, it was styled in a youthful crewcut. His physique was similar to Hugh's—almost as slim despite a slight paunch at the beltline.

"My grey hair is the evidence of just how experienced and wise I am for my age," quipped Brian, noticing her appraising look.

"Have you had breakfast?" asked Hugh. "I make a mean omelette."

"We ate at the café across from our hotel," Marcie told him. "But I wouldn't mind having a cup of coffee if we have time. It's up to Ellie. Apparently she has an extraordinarily busy day ahead."

"I do," confirmed Ellie. "I hope to be finished here by the noon hour. After that, I've got to help decorate the church and banquet hall. The wedding rehearsal is happening this evening."

Marcie snapped into efficiency mode. "Right then. That's a pass on the coffee. What's first?"

"Before I bring in my clothing, I'd like to take out the single bed and set up the queen."

"Let's get the guys to do the heavy lifting."

In short order, the linens were removed and the narrow bed carried to the storage shed. Ellie and Marcie adjusted the side tables so the headboard could stand between them and linked the bedrails with the footboard. The men then set in place both box spring and mattress.

Marcie had next in mind to send them on an errand in Swan River but felt she should compare notes with Ellie first.

"Wait a moment. I need to ask Ellie something," she said, turning to the bride-to-be. "We didn't bring a wedding gift, because we wanted to know what you needed first. Now that I see your place, I'm wondering about getting a larger mat in front of the door, as well as a coat tree."

"Great ideas, both of them," agreed Ellie. "They would be very helpful additions!"

After Brian and Hugh left on this errand, the women began to retrieve Ellie's clothing from her vehicle. Marcie hung items in the closet while Ellie filled the drawers.

Next, Ellie brought in the new queen-sized linens and together they made up the bed with white sheets and pillowcases. This was followed by adding the tartan-covered duvet and extra pillows with tartan shams against the sleeping pillows. A couple of throw cushions were exchanged with the dark plaid ones in the living room for a mix-and-match effect.

"Absolutely smashing!" raved Marcie. "It's classic, quaint, and stunning in one fell swoop."

The older woman stood in the middle of the kitchen and pivoted while she read the border along the ceiling.

"Hugh doesn't like feminine pastels or florals," Ellie explained. "The house was originally meant to be his living quarters alone."

"But you must have done the decorating in here. The Hugh I know would never have put such a tasteful room together on his own. I doubt he would know the difference between silk and denim... or polka dots and flower prints!"

"Yes, ma'am. The sofa set, the steamer trunk, and that corner lamp table are pieces I salvaged and refinished from his original family home. The kitchen table and chairs are rescues, too. He didn't like the idea at first, but I changed them enough that they barely resemble anything from his former life."

"I can well believe that," said Marcie soberly. "When he told us about the abuse he suffered at the hands of his father, I just cried my eyes out. And Brian's heart was cut to the quick. He must have told you about that."

"He did. But I have a question to ask of you."

At that moment, Darcey Unger drove into the yard and backed her van up to the front steps.

"I guess it'll have to wait until my friend leaves," said Ellie going to the door.

They both stepped outside just as Darcey got out of her vehicle. "Glad I found you here. I've brought you your wedding present."

"Wonderful! What is it?" asked Ellie.

Darcey swung the rear doors open. All Ellie could see was a blanket covering a large object.

"Wanna take a guess before I uncover it?" asked Darcey coyly.

"What do you think, Marcie?"

The elder woman narrowed her eyes in thought. "Must be a piece of furniture of some sort."

"Hmmm, doubtful," said Ellie. "My friend knows this place hasn't room for more furniture."

"Shall I unveil?" asked Darcey.

Ellie nodded and the blanket was yanked free.

"It's a butcher-block island for your country kitchen. I had Hugh bring extra barnwood, and of a heavier sort than we used to make your cabinet doors. Tony and I built this. It has an extra shelf below."

"It's fantastic!" cooed Ellie.

"It's also pretty heavy," said Darcey. "It may take all three of us to get it inside."

It did. Darcey took one end while Ellie and Marcie held up the other. The three women had to take it slow, but they soon succeeded at manoeuvring it into the centre of the kitchen.

Darcey took her opportunity to point out the island's special features, which included three hooks on one end and a towel bar on the other. The unit was large enough to be useful and small enough to tie up minimal space.

"It's perfect!" declared Ellie, completely delighted. "Thank you so much! I'm moving my things into Hugh's house today, and tomorrow I'll finally be able to call it our house. But I can spare a few minutes if you'd like to have a cup of coffee with us."

"Are you sure?" Darcey said. "You've got company and I wouldn't like to interfere."

Marcie shrugged. "Don't feel that way on my account. Unless you're seeking a private moment. In which case I'll go for a walk and leave you two alone."

"No, that's fine," said Darcey quickly.

After formal introductions were made, Ellie prepared a fresh pot and then showed Darcey the newly furnished bedroom.

Darcey seemed truly impressed. "Beautiful! Absolutely timeless. As good a place to make babies as I've ever seen."

Marcie laughed outright and Ellie turned crimson along with smiling shyly.

"That *is* the plan, isn't it?" asked Darcey, the corners of her mouth curled up.

Ellie looked abashed. "Yes, but you make it sound so crude."

"Me? Never. According to Genesis 9, it's our sacred duty. And I appreciate that the good Lord did not condemn all parts of the process to pain."

Ellie cast a glance at Marcie, trying to read the older woman's response to Darcey's bluntness. She was relieved to see her enjoying the remarks.

Once the coffee was brewed, Ellie poured three mugs and set them on the table along with some store-bought cookies she found in the cupboard. They each took a seat.

"I like your style, Darcey," said Marcie with a smile. "Straightforward. Unconventional. Grounded in common sense."

"I do my best," answered Darcey glibly.

"What do you do with yourself? Are you trained in a particular career?"

"Absolutely. I hold a master's degree in domestic engineering. Towards my doctorate, I'm working on a thesis in parenting daughters… and I have three experimental subjects on which to practice my theories. Besides that, I offer household support to one Tony Unger, amongst other things." Darcey winked at Ellie. "It's a highly demanding job, but I get to be the one to do it."

Marcie clapped her hands. "Bravo! Well spoken. Good for you."

"Thank you." Darcey turned to Ellie. "Are you excited about tomorrow? Nervous? Comme ci, Comme ça?"

"Definitely not the latter. Perhaps both excited and a little nervous."

"Excited, I get. But why nervous? What could possibly go wrong?" asked Darcey with feigned naivety.

Ellie laughed. "We'll have to wait until tomorrow to find out."

~

Working with Marcie was easy. From the outset, she anticipated what Ellie wanted done and then gave herself to the task. Ellie unpacked the boxes meant for the kitchen and rest of the household while Marcie cleared the cupboards of all the old items Gertie had given Hugh earlier in the summer. When an empty box became available, she repacked those things to be stored in the former cabin.

"You were going to ask me something just before Darcey arrived," Marcie reminded her.

"Right. Hugh has told me all about his mostly miserable life on this farm. I'm curious. From your point of view, what was he like when you met him? And while he lived with you in Winnipeg?"

"I had an idea you'd be interested in that." Marcie paused to consider this. "Hugh has already assured me it's okay to answer any questions you might have. He wants his life to be an open book to you."

"Thank you. The sentiment is mutual."

"I may never forget that day as long as I live," began Marcie. "I had no advance notice, you understand. I was expecting Brian, of course, but when he walked in with a strange, shy, forlorn-looking teenager in tow, I was mighty surprised. But since Brian isn't the type to bring home every stray puppy he comes across, I also knew he must have had a good reason for bringing this particular boy home. My part was to trust his good judgment and listen with all my ears."

"All your ears?" asked Ellie, somewhat confused.

"The ears on my head, as well as those of my heart," clarified Marcie. "Brian took me aside and told me he had managed to get the gist of the boy's story—that he was running away from an abusive situation he could no longer cope with. Brian felt sure he was not of a bad sort and that we should try to help him out, at least until he was oriented to city life and could manage on his own. We had an extra bedroom, and suddenly I had a clear understanding that we were supposed to make it available to one of God's lambs."

Ellie stopped to stare at Marcie. "Your reference to lambs... do you mean in the biblical sense? I'm curious about your faith."

"Yes," admitted Marcie freely. "Brian and I take the Bible seriously when it tells us how to live and how to treat others."

"I remember Hugh telling me that he went to church with you, but also that he was bored to death with the services," said Ellie delicately.

Marcie chuckled. "I'm well aware of that. Our church, compared to most Protestant communities, is rather formal and liturgical. I could see that Hugh wasn't getting much out of it, but we weren't about to change the church we'd been part of all our lives just for his sake. For the unfamiliar, it might seem stiff and stuffy, but we believe that God is real, that Jesus is His Son who was sent to die for the sins of the world, and that every word of scripture is true and meant to be obeyed. And there you have it!"

"I'm very happy to find we're on the same page," said Ellie. "I suppose Hugh has told you that he submitted his life to the lordship of Jesus Christ this past summer."

"He did. And he has sounded different ever since." With this, she returned to the story of how Hugh came into their lives.

"Brian and I sat down with Hugh and asked him to be completely truthful and straightforward concerning his circumstances. In return, we promised to help him pick up the pieces of his life and begin anew on solid footing. The look of relief on his face was palpable. The first thing was to make sure he finished his high school education. I took care of getting him transferred to a local school. We agreed to a three-month trial period to determine whether we could live together compatibly. Well, that trial period stretched out to three years—until he graduated from both high school and trade school. It took a while for him to relax. For the longest time, he lived in fear that his father would find out where he was. So he kept minimal contact with the rest of his family. I think that bothered me more than him."

"When I worked with him this summer, he had bitter anger issues."

"Right. That showed up later, after he left our place to live on his own," said Marcie. "I believe it was a result of not really dealing with his family problems, only suppressing and avoiding them."

"That was my insight as well."

"Do you think he has satisfactorily dealt with them now? If not, they'll likely loom large in your marriage, cropping up at a most inconvenient time. That seems to be the way dysfunction plays out."

"I think so… I hope so…" Ellie drew a deep breath. "We've both endured deep hurt and helped each other come to grips with it. It's one of the reasons we believe God brought us together."

Marcie nodded with conviction. "In that case, to borrow the words of Jesus: *'What therefore God has joined together, let not man put asunder.'*"[19]

Ellie stopped and stared at the woman thoughtfully. Marcie returned her gaze, a question in her eyes.

"You remind me very much of my mother," said Ellie after a few seconds. "Not in appearance, but in your wisdom and candour."

"I'll take that as a compliment."

It didn't take long for these two women to organize the cupboards and drawers with the new kitchen wares, nor for them to tidy the front room of empty boxes and packing materials. It gave Ellie a sense of great satisfaction to know everything was ready for her to begin a new chapter of her life.

They had probably sat for no more than fifteen minutes when Brian and Hugh returned, having brought in the Turners' wedding gifts as well as still-warm pizza for lunch.

They laid out the new entrance rug, replacing the almost useless one that had sat in front of the door. Brian and Hugh proceeded to assemble a sturdy and handsome coat tree, which was immediately put to use.

~

---

[19] Mark 10:9, RSV.

The next item on Ellie's to-do list was to decorate the church—and after that, the community hall. Because Sarah and Ellie had worked out in advance what they would do and had all the materials on hand, the task could be completed forthwith, in large measure because there was no lack of skilled hands available to carry out the bride's vision. Soon the wintery theme of frost, snow, and ice had been reproduced in flowers, crystals, mirrors, and tiny white lights. Aunt Ruth brought over the three-tiered wedding cake, now beautifully and perfectly smoothly iced with fondant. All the women and girls watched as Ellie and Ruth wound a spiral of white and pale blue flowers around the cake.

At the end of the afternoon, the women pronounced all the decorating efforts "gorgeous." The men just sighed with relief that they were no longer required to help.

The wedding rehearsal supper was held in the church basement. Ellie's sisters-in-law had prepared large pans of lasagne and bowls of Caesar salad. Many introductions were made between the two clans, and the Turners as well. Afterward Pastor Leland kept the gathering on schedule, with everyone who played a part in the ceremony practicing their entrances and exits. The Bauman side of the family went through their paces with complete familiarity, but Gertie, Diane, and Margo maintained the stunned looks of a deer in headlights.

Other than Hugh, no one seemed to notice that Ellie, despite the smile pasted on her face, had grown quieter and quieter as the day progressed.

At about 9:00 p.m., the rehearsal was over and everyone was sent home with a sincere wish to have a good night's sleep.

As everyone departed, Hugh cornered his fiancée in the church vestibule.

"I know you can catch a ride with Gus or Harold, but I'd like to take you home myself," he said.

"I believe we've reached that point where the bride and groom aren't supposed to see each other," objected Ellie. "We're certainly not supposed to be together until we meet at the altar. Besides, I'm bushed. I can't get into my bed soon enough."

"Understood. Now get into my truck."

Neither spoke until they had cleared Minitonas and crossed Highway 10.

"Are you going to tell me what's bothering you?" asked Hugh, reaching for Ellie's hand.

"I'm fine. Just super tired."

Hugh slowed down to make the ride last longer. "Sure. But I don't think that's the whole story."

Ellie sighed deeply. "Maybe planning a January 1 wedding wasn't such a good idea after all. It's been busy, busy, busy since the middle of December. I've hardly had a moment to myself to think, pray, and simply be. As a result, I've got an unanticipated case of the jitters."

"The jitters," repeated Hugh dully. "You mean, like, you're having doubts? You're second-guessing marrying me?"

"I'm out of sorts and so tired that I can't think straight." She sounded irritable. "I just want to go to my bed and fall asleep instantly… and stay that way for eight hours or more."

When they reached the Bauman farmhouse, Hugh leaned over to kiss her goodnight, as much to reassure himself as to affirm his loving feelings toward her. She responded with a limp peck on the lips and quickly hopped out of his truck.

He watched as she entered the house without so much as looking back with a wave. It did not sit well.

Hugh entered his house feeling weary and irritable himself. One look around the room proclaimed its readiness to share life with his bride. Everything screamed Ellie's touch. He had read her jitters to mean she was having doubts about going through with the marriage.

He recalled his own doubts from some months before. He'd felt deeply unworthy of a girl like Ellie—and similar thoughts assailed him now. What if she was thinking of backing out? What if she thought he wasn't good enough for her? What if she thought their relationship was one big mistake? What if...

The only thing that had freed Hugh from that circular line of thinking was talking things out with Pastor Leland. And prayer. It was too late to seek out the pastor, but prayer was available anytime and anywhere.

Sitting on the plaid couch with only the low light of the lamp for illumination, Hugh poured out his fears and anxieties to the Lord until the much-desired peace entered his heart.

A little before midnight, he felt ready to retire for the night. When he walked into the bedroom, he stopped short upon seeing the new queen-sized bed in place all made up in beautiful linens.

In a snap decision, he turned on his heel and left the house, locking the door behind him. He would take a room at the Minitonas hotel tonight. No way was he going to inaugurate that bed until his wife shared it with him. A vow was a vow.

⁓

Not everyone was in bed when Ellie entered her family home. Gus and Helen were still setting up sleeping bags on the living room floor for their kids. In Ellie's bed, still awake and waiting for her, was niece Lillian, one of Gus's daughters.

Ellie had forgotten she had promised this sleepover-with-aunty. The girl's eyes glowed with supreme happiness for having this special one-on-one time with her rarely seen aunt.

Sighing, Ellie changed into her pyjamas, crawled into bed next to Lily, and submitted to a few minutes of girl talk. To the girl's credit, it did have the effect of relaxing Ellie so that she fell asleep while Lily was still talking about her dream wedding and the kind of bridal gown she envisioned wearing when she grew up...

Twenty-Nine

STILL WANTING TO be as involved as much as possible, the Turners offered to be Hugh and Ellie's taxi service on their wedding day. Originally it was agreed that they would take Ellie from her Bauman home over to Cynthia's around 10:00 a.m. so she could help with styling the bride's hair and dress her in the bridal gown they had designed together.

But as soon as the sun was up, the household woke and the hustle and bustle began. As much as Ellie loved and enjoyed her family, she also felt desperate for a few minutes to herself.

She called Marcie and asked if it would be possible to be brought into Minitonas sooner. A few minutes later, Ellie climbed into the Turners' car, lugging her suitcase along with her.

"Where do you want to go, ma'am?" asked Brian in the guise of a cabbie.

"To the First Baptist Church in Minitonas, please," said Ellie.

Marcie, in the front passenger seat, turned and looked at Ellie questioningly. "We met Hugh in the lobby of the hotel this morning. Seems he slept there last night."

"In the hotel? Whatever for?" Insight flashed across her mind and she shook her head as though tired. "Wait. He refused to sleep in the new bed without his wife, right?"

"That's what he said," Marcie confirmed. "Is everything all right between you two? He seemed a trifle upset... but tried to brush it off."

Ellie sighed. "He thinks I'm having second thoughts because I admitted to having pre-wedding jitters yesterday."

"I see. Well, you certainly aren't the first bride to be nervous on her wedding day. You know... if you need to talk, I am right here."

"Thank you. I do need to talk. To Jesus. I need an hour with just Him and me and no one else. Then I'll be right as rain. I'm sure of it."

"Understandable," said Marcie, nodding. "Then we'll pick you up and take you to...?"

"To Cynthia's place," Ellie replied. "That's my friend and the seamstress who created my wedding dress. She's going to help me with my hair and dress so that when Hugh sees me, hopefully he'll be completely bedazzled!"

Brian and Marcie exchanged relieved glances.

An hour and ten minutes later, Ellie exited the church. The Turners were waiting for her, already dressed up in their finery. She flashed them her best, most sincere and grateful smile.

"All better?" asked Marcie.

"Completely back on keel." Ellie happily climbed into the back seat. "I hope I never forget that the secret to maintaining balance in life is to spend personal time with the Lord daily. I let that slide over the last couple of weeks and it just about undid me. I have no idea how I managed to live through my carnal youth."

"Sounds like there's an interesting story to tell," said Marcie as they drove out of the parking lot.

Ellie glanced away, evasive. "Perhaps another day."

A minute later, they stopped in front of Cynthia's house.

Marcie turned to her with a hopeful expression on her face. "I'm available to help you dress in your bridal gown."

"Many thanks." Ellie offered a smile. "But I'm guessing Hugh has more need of you than me right now."

"You're probably right. We'll make sure he knows how to put on a suit and tie."

Brian laughed. "I've got the ball and chain ready for him in the trunk!"

~

Hugh was glad for Marcie and Brian's company for the remainder of the morning. He had been invited to dress at Rob's place, but ultimately he decided it would be a lot simpler just to meet everyone at the church fully attired.

"What a beautiful suit," Marcie remarked when he came out of the bedroom.

"Thanks. Makes me feel like a different man. I don't know who that is when I look in the mirror." He wasn't entirely joking, either. Hugh held up the pale blue tie. "One of you will have to show me what to do with this. I've never learned how to make the knot."

While Brian demonstrated the art of putting together a man's necktie, Marcie went to their car and retrieved a narrow box containing a dozen red roses and baby's breath with fern. She arranged them in a pitcher and set it on the kitchen table. She also laid a large bar of dark chocolate beside it.

"You think of everything," said Hugh gratefully.

"I would like to see your special day end as beautifully as it begins. Just remember, it's probably not possible to romance a woman too much." Marcie gestured for him to follow her into the bedroom. "One more thing. Let's turn down the covers in preparation for later..."

~

At the church, Hugh, Rob, and Trevor waited in Pastor Leland's office until it was time for the ceremony to begin. The candlelighter and maids waited in the nursery, unseen by the arriving guests, at the rear of the sanctuary just off the vestibule.

The ceremony was meant to begin at 2:00 p.m., and at precisely five minutes past the hour Brent Clifford opened the door to the church and held it open as Ellie came inside, careful not to trip on her gown. Cynthia held up the train behind her.

The ushers, Gus and Harold, stood stock still as they gazed upon their transformed sister.

"Is that really you, Ellie?" asked Harold, staring rather stupidly, as though this was the first time he had ever seen a bride.

Gus gawked wordlessly yet smiled from ear to ear.

For Ellie, their reactions were enough. If she passed the wow factor with her brothers, she figured her appearance was sure to have the same effect on her groom.

When Gus and Harold recovered from their shock, they cued the maids to join the bride. Sarah returned from pinning boutonnieres on the men and entered the foyer at the same time as the rest of the bridesmaids. Every single one of them gasped when they looked upon Ellie.

That Ellie was a beautiful bride was somehow an understatement. Her makeup had been applied with special care, lending her eyes a subtle yet sultry appearance. Her lips were full and alluring. Knowing Hugh favoured her hair down, Cynthia curled Ellie's hair into loose ringlets bringing some of the tresses to the back of her head to be held in place by sparkling combs, yet leaving wispy tendrils spiralling down the sides of her face. As for the dress, the closely fitted bodice created the illusion that the heavily sculpted lace had grown out of her skin, just covering her breasts. It barely capped the shoulders. From the waist, the lace flowed like lava onto the wide skirt. The hem and train were further embellished with lacy detail.

"I've never seen a more beautiful wedding dress in all my days," murmured Gertie in astonishment. "Or bride, for that matter! Ellie, you look like a goddess... or one of them Royal Doulton figurines."

Margo looked on with wide eyes. "I have to admit, the gown is very impressive."

"Thank you," said Ellie simply.

"Aunt Ellie, when I get married, can I wear your gown?" asked Charlotte, completely awed.

Beanie reached out to touch the gown with the greatest respect. "Me too."

"I won't be surprised if Hugh can't take his eyes off of you," said Diane. "You're so beautiful, I think I'm going to cry."

"She's right," added Sarah in a low voice. She handed Ellie her bridal bouquet. "You've outdone us all. But we can't stand here gawking, ladies. As soon as I take my seat, Gertie can get this show on the road by lighting the candelabras."

A minute later, Gertie made the slow walk down the aisle to the music of Pachebel's *Canon in D Major*. She lit the candles one by one, ending with the tapers on each side of the unity candle.

After that, Pastor Leland led Hugh and Trevor to take their places at the front of the sanctuary. Rob took a seat with Sarah in the first pew to play his next part before joining the groom on stage as the best man.

The organist shifted to playing Beethoven's classic *Ode to Joy*. Thus began the procession of bridesmaids, featuring Margo and Diane, followed by Charlotte as the junior bridesmaid. All the maids were lovely, their frosty blue gowns swishing delicately on the way up the aisle.

As soon as Ellie prompted Beanie to begin scattering white rose petals down the aisle before her dramatic entrance, the church door opened. A youngish man dapperly dressed in suit and tie and an open camel-coloured trench coat topped with a dark grey fedora on his head entered the foyer.

Upon seeing Ellie standing in the entrance to the sanctuary, he leapt up the steps. "Do I have the right wedding? I'm looking for..." He paused to withdraw a paper from his breast pocket and read, "Ella Rose Bauman and Hugh Richard Fischer."

"Yes, I'm Ella Rose Bauman," replied Ellie clearly puzzled. "Who might you be?"

"Master David Johnson, Esq.," The gentleman spoke in polished English before adding, with a friendly smile and slight bow, "At your service."

Meanwhile, the organist noticed that Beanie had arrived and taken her place next to Charlotte. That was her cue to switch to the traditional entrance march, Wagner's *Bridal Chorus*. Once she adjusted the knobs to unleash the sound of a full-throated organ, she hit the opening trumpet-like chords.

In one motion, the audience stood, heads turned in the direction of the sanctuary's entrance. As the music shifted into the familiar refrain of "Here comes the bride..." there were looks of confusion.

No bride was to be seen.

Hugh stood on the platform close to Pastor Leland, his back to the audience. He hadn't yet had a glimpse of Ellie, and the look in the pastor's eyes had gone from normal expectancy to strange puzzlement.

"What is it?" whispered Hugh.

The pastor seemed uncertain. "I'm not sure. Ellie was there, and now she's not."

In an instant, Hugh's heart fell. Fighting the urge to panic, he took a deep breath... and then another.

"Don't worry," said Pastor Leland. "I'm sure there's a good explanation."

Hugh wanted desperately to believe him, but all he could think of was Ellie's admission of pre-wedding jitters. To him, it portended that she was backing out. He felt sick.

The congregation was looking around uneasily, whispering to each other. Rob turned around to look directly down the aisle to see what had become of the bride. The space where she had stood was completely vacant.

Rob covertly sent Harold, at the end of the pew, to learn what had become of Ellie.

Not knowing what else to do, the organist kept playing. Already it was more of the chorus than she had ever played for a single procession. Along the way, she lowered the volume, uncertain about the state of the ceremony.

~

"David!" shrieked Ellie in a hoarse whisper. She left her post in an instant, flying towards the young man who'd just entered the church, and hugged him with her arms around his neck. "You came! You actually came. I can't believe it!"

"Yes... well, you did get through to this arrogant, self-centred, supercilious jerk. At least I think that's what you called me." David smiled, his eyes twinkling.

"I would say I'm sorry, but I really believed you deserved it," said Ellie ruefully. "You're too late to see your mother light the candles, though. She was first on the program."

"I came as quickly as I could. I flew into Winnipeg this morning and rented a car to get here. I'm amazed not to have earned myself some speeding tickets."

"Well, you're here now and Aunt Gertie is going to go nuts when she sees you."

"Right." David peered into the sanctuary. "Where are the folks sitting?"

"Near the front on the right side of the auditorium. But I don't think you should alert her to your presence yet."

David immediately comprehended. "She'll create a scene, won't she?"

"Must likely, and that will steal my thunder!"

"We can't have that now, can we." David took a step back from her. "Very beautiful, by the way. I'm sure my cuz feels most fortunate to have you for his bride."

"Ellie!" cried Harold in a stern, loud whisper upon reaching the foyer. "What the heck? You've got the whole church thinking you've jilted the bridegroom!"

Ellie felt suddenly worried. "Oh dear. Sorry. I'm truly ready now."

"It's my fault," said David quickly. "I interrupted the proceedings at a most inconvenient time."

"I'll say," said Harold, clearly annoyed.

When the bride's brother saw David slip into the rearmost pew, and Ellie standing at the ready at the top of the aisle, he returned to his seat and cued the organist to begin the *Bridal Chorus* all over again.

This time Ellie made the slow walk towards the platform to the oohs and aahs of all who craned their necks to see her. She watched Hugh's expression change, going from worry to relief... and finally to breathtaking wonder. Ellie felt so happy that she thought her heart might burst.

When she reached the first pew, she stopped.

"Who gives this woman to be married?" the pastor asked.

In a clear voice, Rob answered, "I do, on behalf of her parents, John and Elizabeth Bauman, who are with the Lord."

Hugh then approached Ellie and together they completed the few steps needed to stand in front of Pastor Leland and a church full of caring family and friends.

"You had me going, Ell-elujah," Hugh whispered on the way. "I thought for sure you had changed your mind."

"Never," vowed the radiant bride.

~

After forty minutes of poignant, endearing, and sentimental ceremony, the organist pulled out all the stops. The new Mr. and Mrs. Fischer walked out of the sanctuary to Mendelssohn's *Wedding March*. Immediately the wedding party formed a receiving line to greet, and be greeted by, the guests.

Five minutes into this process, they heard a piercing shriek.

"That will be Aunt Gertie," said Ellie with a chuckle to Hugh. "Your cousin David has shown up, and apparently they've just met. He's the reason I was late walking down the aisle."

"No kidding! That's great. But I still have little appreciation for his timing."

"Were you really so worried I was going to stand you up?" Ellie's tone conveyed a trace of hurt.

Before Hugh could form a reply, a strange woman took his hand and shook it warmly. She looked straight into his eyes.

"I'm wondering if you remember me," the woman said, casting a warning glance for Ellie not to spill the beans just yet.

Hugh took a few seconds to look her over. He shook his head. "Sorry. It's not coming to me."

"We went to school together back in the day. I sat behind you so the teacher couldn't easily tell if I skipped class."

Hugh shook his head again.

"I'm Teresa Westcott," she said. "And Ellie is right. You do kinda sorta look like Tom Selleck without the moustache. Not like the skinny, acne-faced beanpole who once sat in front of me."

"Thanks," Hugh said with an uncertain smile. "I think." He couldn't tell whether she was teasing him or not.

Teresa turned to Ellie. "That was the most beautiful wedding I've ever seen, and you're among the most beautiful of beautiful brides. Glad I stuck around to see it."

"Thanks, Tee," said Ellie sincerely. "Are you feeling better? Will we see you at the banquet?"

"Nope. I'm heading to Winnipeg from here to resume my life. The ribs are still pretty tender, but I'm healing nicely." Teresa paused as if she intended to move along, but then she turned back. "I'm happy for you guys. Glad you found each other. You make a good-looking pair. Heck, I can picture your kids! And I might be a little jealous…"

With that, Teresa ended the conversation abruptly and made a beeline for the church exit.

⁓

Immediately following the receiving line, the Baumans and Fischers went over to Brent and Cynthia Clifford's place for photos. Because Hugh felt he was an unofficial son to the Turners, they were invited to come along, too.

Brent had converted the garage into a photography studio and a great many pictures were taken in groups both large and small, some with the bride and groom, and others with the various nuclear families. Gertie made sure that a set of pictures included David, who humoured her by fulfilling her every wish. Every time he did so, he made sure Ellie noticed, earnestly trying to improve her impression of him.

Diane and Margo were mostly reserved, neither having taken part in an occasion quite like this one before. They, too, were invited to have nuclear family pictures taken. Gertie was game for this and organized them. Larry strongly objected to any arrangement that included him, and only after considerable coaxing and substantial pressure did he relent. Later, when he noticed Hugh off to the side, he sidled up to the groom and slipped his business card into Hugh's hand.

"Hang on to it," Larry said. "Just in case you should one day have reason to call."

With that, he crept away with Hugh looking after him.

At the end of the photo sessions, Brent and Cynthia whisked Hugh and Ellie away to snap some shots down by the river and at a nearby park. By the time darkness fell, it was time for the banquet to begin.

Gus and Harold had been conscripted as co-masters of ceremonies. They introduced the wedding party as they took their seats at the head table. A core group of FBC ladies had taken on the catering, serving up a delicious traditional Christmas meal—roast turkey with all the trimmings. Everyone ate to a parade of love songs put together by Trevor and Charlotte at Ellie's behest. The crowd occasionally sang along, and many men were seen slipping an arm around their wives.

Following the meal came a series of stories meant to gently and humorously roast the bride and groom. There were also the traditional toasts to the couple and a kind of talent show. And when the glasses clinked, the couple were under pressure to kiss. All in fun, of course.

The bridesmaids, including Charlotte and Beanie, opened the wedding gifts and made a display of them for guests to look over.

Ellie and Hugh made a point of briefly visiting with each guest as they passed out slices of cake following the cake-cutting ceremony. And when they reached the table including the sum total of Hugh's known relatives, they lingered a bit to speak with cousin David.

"So you're my nearest-in-age cousin," David greeted, smiling from ear to ear as he shook Hugh's hand. "And this beautiful lady is your beloved? I daresay you're a lucky man."

"And I know it. Thanks for making the trip out here for the occasion. It means a lot."

"I've been unequivocally reminded of the importance of family ties," said David glancing at Ellie. "I'll be in the area two more days before heading back. Will you two be taking a honeymoon right away? If not, perhaps we can get together. I'd like to become better acquainted."

"I'm fairly sure we can make that work." Ellie looked to Hugh for assent; her new husband nodded. "We're planning a honeymoon in May when the tulip trees are in blossom. We'd like to see the Niagara Falls."

"That's close to my neighbourhood," said David. "Perhaps I can guide you to a few interesting sites."

Ellie smiled. "That's thoughtful and kind. We'll certainly keep that in mind. And as for a visit before you leave, why don't you come to our place on Saturday? For lunch."

"That sounds perfect." David glanced around to make sure Gertie and Ed were busy chatting elsewhere. "In the meantime, what is there to do around here? I fear that I'll have seen all there is to see by 2:00 p.m. tomorrow."

Ellie gave him a hard look. "What you should do is get to know your parents again. Ask them to share their personal histories, what they like and don't like, their triumphs and failures, their joys and fears. That sort of thing."

"Ouch! Put in my place again," said David grimly. He turned to Hugh. "You've won yourself quite the fox there. Do you think you can handle her?"

"So long as we're on the same side, we'll do fine." With this, Hugh nudged Ellie to carry on with other guests.

Once they had finished personally serving the wedding cake, only one item remained on the evening's agenda. Brian Turner slipped out to bring round his car while some of the tables were pushed to the side to prepare for the couple's send-off.

The guests formed a large circle around Hugh and Ellie. Trevor, who had been put in charge of the music, played Anne Murray's "Could I Have This Dance for the Rest of My Life," a track which had been released that past August. Hugh and Ellie slow-danced while the guests swayed along in rhythm.

At the song's conclusion, the couple waved goodbye amidst clapping, cheers, and whistles and rushed out to the waiting car.

⌒‿

As soon as the Turners parked in front of Hugh and Ellie's little house, Marcie jumped out, ready to take a photo of Hugh carrying Ellie over the threshold. Hugh didn't know if he could manage it given the bulk of Ellie's gown, but he succeeded to everyone's delight.

Stepping inside, Marcie thrust a plastic bag into Ellie's hands. "Wedding cards. Sarah wanted you to take them so they wouldn't be lost. She suspects many of them include gift money."

Ellie took the bag and set it on the table. Hugs were exchanged all around as they said their thanks and goodbyes.

"Enjoy each other," said Marcie with a twinkle in her eyes as she closed the door behind her.

Suddenly, the house was quiet. Hugh and Ellie stood facing each other. They were home together at last. And alone.

Thirty

FOR A MINUTE, it was a bit awkward between them. They had saved themselves for this moment of perfectly legitimate intimacy. Had ached for it... hungered for it. Yet now that the privilege was truly theirs, they suddenly felt shy.

Ellie broke the moment by reaching up to her hair, intending to begin removing the sparkling combs.

Hugh reached out and stopped her.

"Not yet," he said softly, taking her hand in his and bringing it to his face. "I want to look at you a bit longer this way. You've always been beautiful to me, but today was... something else. Something over the top." The words caught in his throat and his eyes were misty.

"That goes for you, too," she returned gently. "I'm sure I've never laid eyes on a more handsome man... and now you're mine. All mine."

Hugh pulled her close, kissed her on the forehead, and then released her.

"I want you, and rather badly, but I also want to take my time, you know?" Hugh led her to the little table next to the kitchen. "There's some dark chocolate here. How about a little snack while I look at my gorgeous wife?"

Ellie gasped, only now noticing the extravagant bouquet of roses, baby's breath, and fern.

"Oh my! How absolutely beautiful," she cried. "As for the chocolate... perhaps later... or tomorrow. Help yourself, though, if you like."

Hugh shook his head.

"Marcie brought it. She wanted everything to be arranged as romantically as possible."

"Well then, she's right. It is all very beautiful. Thank you."

Curiosity caused Hugh to look inside the plastic bag on the table and subsequently spill out the mess of cards. More curiosity led to the couple opening them to read the greetings and best wishes. Many included cash as well and the amount added up to more than enough to cover the cost of the electronics they had purchased on Boxing Day.

The contents of one envelope, however, made Ellie gasp. The card was signed by Agnes Hoffman, who wished them every happiness. The woman also included a note that said the late Otto had instructed her to give a wedding gift of...

Shocked, Ellie looked at the enclosed cheque, filled out in the amount of $1,200! She showed it to Hugh, whose eyes also went wide.

"But I don't believe this is exactly a wedding gift," said Ellie dryly. "I'd say it's more guilt money, and an opportunity to save face. This cheque will go into the farm account. I'm grateful, though. The Hoffmans were under no obligation to give us anything."

Hugh rose to his feet. "Agreed."

He drew her up and into his arms, placing a gentle, searching kiss on her lips. She closed her eyes and leaned into it.

When their lips parted, neither could stop panting. Desire. All desire.

Hugh removed his suit jacket and hung it on the back of a chair.

"Wait. Let me help you," said Ellie a little breathlessly. She reached up and unfastened the tie at his neck.

Hugh turned her around and removed the sparkling combs from her hair. She shook out the curls so the tresses fell in loose waves over her shoulders. Facing Hugh, Ellie undid the buttons of his shirt, which he then quickly removed, exposing a well-developed, muscular chest amply covered with soft dark hair.

He reached behind her, searching for the tab that would unzip the gown while Ellie unbuckled his belt and pulled down the zipper of his trousers. Almost in synchronization, they stepped out of their wedding clothes. Another quick movement removed what remained of their clothing.

That was it. They stood before each other completely naked and unashamed, tingling with excitement. Ellie traced the muscles of his right arm with her left forefinger, the sensual look in her eyes expressing great appreciation for his attractive and sinewy male form.

Her touch electrified him. In one smooth motion, Hugh gathered her in his arms, carried her to their new bed on which he laid her, and slid in after her.

⁓

Somewhere near one o'clock in the morning, give or take, Hugh and Ellie were still awake, holding each other in their arms and talking softly in the afterglow of intimacy.

Suddenly, a loud, discordant ring of the telephone jarred them, invading the sweet ambience of their marriage bed.

After two rings, Ellie ventured to ask, "Wrong number, do you think?"

"I can hope, but my gut thinks otherwise."

After two more rings, Ellie changed her tune. "Late-night phone calls often represent emergencies. Deaths or terrible accidents... things like that. Maybe we should take the call."

"I guess," said Hugh, reluctantly pulling away from his bride. He crossed the room to get to the phone and barked into it. "Yeah?"

"Well, finally!" responded Margo with a sneer. "What took you so long?"

"Do I have to remind you that this is my wedding night? What's so important it couldn't wait until tomorrow?"

"A wedding night doesn't compare to what just happened to me!"

Hugh could hear the panic in her voice. "I'm listening, but make it quick," he grumbled.

"Larry just left a few minutes ago. What I mean is, he's moved out. He said he's moving in with his girlfriend. Personally, I don't care about that. But he said he would no longer put anything into our—that is, *my* house. I could either buy him out or we'll have to sell to get his name off the mortgage."

"That's rough, Margo," said Hugh tiredly. "But look, nothing can be solved tonight. Go to sleep and we'll see what can be done tomorrow."

"I know what has to be done, you idiot!" shouted Margo. Hugh held the phone away from his ears. "You have to give the farm back to me!"

"The farm was never yours."

"Well, part of it is! You owe me. You owe me everything!"

"Margo, stop this. Go to bed. I'll call you tomorrow."

He hung up the phone and was halfway to bed when he turned around and took the receiver out of its cradle. They couldn't hear the dial tone when the bedroom door was closed.

The sombre intrusion of Margo's late-night call had successfully shattered the couple's desirous feelings and nothing seemed to revive the passion. At last they stopped trying, laid next to each other like spoons nesting in a drawer, and eventually fell asleep.

Ellie woke first. It took a few seconds to realize where she was.

Then she remembered. Along with a cat-like stretch, she looked at her left hand, admiring the double bands.

Hugh was no longer right behind her but had turned on his side to face the other wall. He was fast asleep and looked as vulnerable as any baby.

Ellie's heart flooded with love and joy as she contemplated reaching over to take his beautiful masculine shape into her arms and kissing him awake. But the ill-timed phone call from Margo came to mind and she thought it would be kinder to let him sleep as long as he needed. He would need wisdom and discernment to take on his sister's latest demands. Poor girl. She really did seem to be lacking in common sense and wisdom. What would it take to get her back on solid ground?

Jesus.

Ellie was pretty sure Margo had no ears for that message.

Ah well, she thought. *A solution will eventually present itself. Six months ago I was something of a basket case myself.*

A random memory from her past surfaced. She had once met someone who wore a large round pin attached to their jacket, one that displayed a confusing message: PBPGINFWMY. What was it supposed to mean?

With a smile, the answer came back: "Please be patient. God is not finished with me yet." It was a good answer and she had never forgotten it.

Careful not to disturb her husband, Ellie slipped out of bed and left the room, taking the new pink velour housecoat with her.

The first thing she saw were the wedding clothes strewn all over the floor and furniture. It brought a pleased, contented smile to her face.

Even so, the right thing to do was tidy up. Very quietly, she carried Hugh's wedding clothes into the bedroom and hung them in the closet. Then she fetched the large box Cynthia had provided, to store her wedding dress. It would be stowed, for the time being, in the Bauman farmhouse across the road.

The thought of the place where she had grown up suddenly felt different. Her association with it was severed; it was no longer home.

Funny thing, that. Home is here… home is wherever Hugh is.

With the front room mostly tidy, Ellie set the receiver back on the telephone cradle and set aside the cards and money to clear the table for breakfast. She intended to fix a special first meal of French toast with whipped cream and strawberry preserves with crispy bacon on the side. And, of course, coffee.

Her hair felt awful, sticky from the abundance of hairspray that had been used to set her curls the day before. A peek in the bedroom informed her that Hugh still slept soundly. Time enough for a shower then.

Not many minutes later, Ellie was back in the kitchen putting on a pot of coffee.

The bedroom door opened and Hugh came out wearing his own bright blue velour housecoat. He leaned against the refrigerator and watched as Ellie whisked eggs, milk, and cinnamon together in a bowl.

Aware of his presence, Ellie glanced at him sideways with a warm smile.

"Good morning, Mrs. Fischer," said Hugh with a happy grin.

"Has a nice ring to it, doesn't it?"

He walked up behind Ellie and hugged her from her backside, resting his chin atop her damp head.

"I'm sorry," he said with a note of sadness.

"Whatever for?"

"I'm sorry that our first day together as husband and wife is weighed down with a big family problem. It's not what I wanted for us."

"It's not the way I pictured our first day together either," admitted Ellie, turning around to face him. "But it's not your fault. We'll work it out together."

Hugh looked directly into his new wife's eyes. "I have no idea what tomorrow, or the days ahead, are going to throw at us, but I do know one thing for sure."

"Which is…?"

"I love you."

To be continued in...
The Minitonas Diaries, Book Three:
Winding Trails

About the Author

SANDRA VIVIAN KONECHNY is mother to two sons and two daughters, and grandmother to nine grandchildren. She and her husband Michael of close to fifty years live as retirees on an acreage northwest of Saskatoon, Saskatchewan. During the period when her nuclear family lived in Swan River, Manitoba, she accepted Jesus into her heart as Saviour and Lord. She was baptized two summers later at Wellman Lake in Duck Mountain Provincial Park off the shores of the Bible camp established there.

Her passion for story and dialogue began as a youngster playing with paper dolls. She would give the dolls a scenario to act out and lines for them to say. Apart from writing short stories, she has also done much in the area of crafting: sewing, quilting, cross-stitching, baking, and gardening. She enjoys word games and jigsaw puzzles. Some of her favourite blessings call her Grandma.

Rock Bottom is her first novel. She published one previous book in 2007, *When God Asks You…*, which examines thirteen questions in the Bible that God asked of various individuals.

She also has a children's book coming soon, titled *An Improbable Adventure at Grandma's House*. This tale was born out of playing a game with her grandchildren regarding a picture that hangs on the living room wall.

ISBN: 978-1-4866-2429-4

It is June 1980 ...

WHEN HUGH FISCHER comes to a crisis point in his life, he seeks to make a big change: move back home to the abandoned family farm and start over again, living alone out in the countryside where he can't trouble anyone—and where no one can bother him.

Ella Bauman was living carefree in the big city when everything turned on a dime. After a bad breakup and the unexpected passing of her mother, she must face depression and dysfunction by returning to the home of her youth to do some serious soul-searching and recentre herself.

A tentative friendship forms between these two neighbours as they slowly dare to open their lives to one another. Will this friendship be part of their healing process or will it serve to further entrench the great pain and brokenness each they've already endured?